STEFANIE LOZINSKI

Manifest

Storm and Spire Book 5

"Happiness is not only a hope, but also in some strange manner a memory ... we are all kings in exile."

G.K. Chesterton

Contents

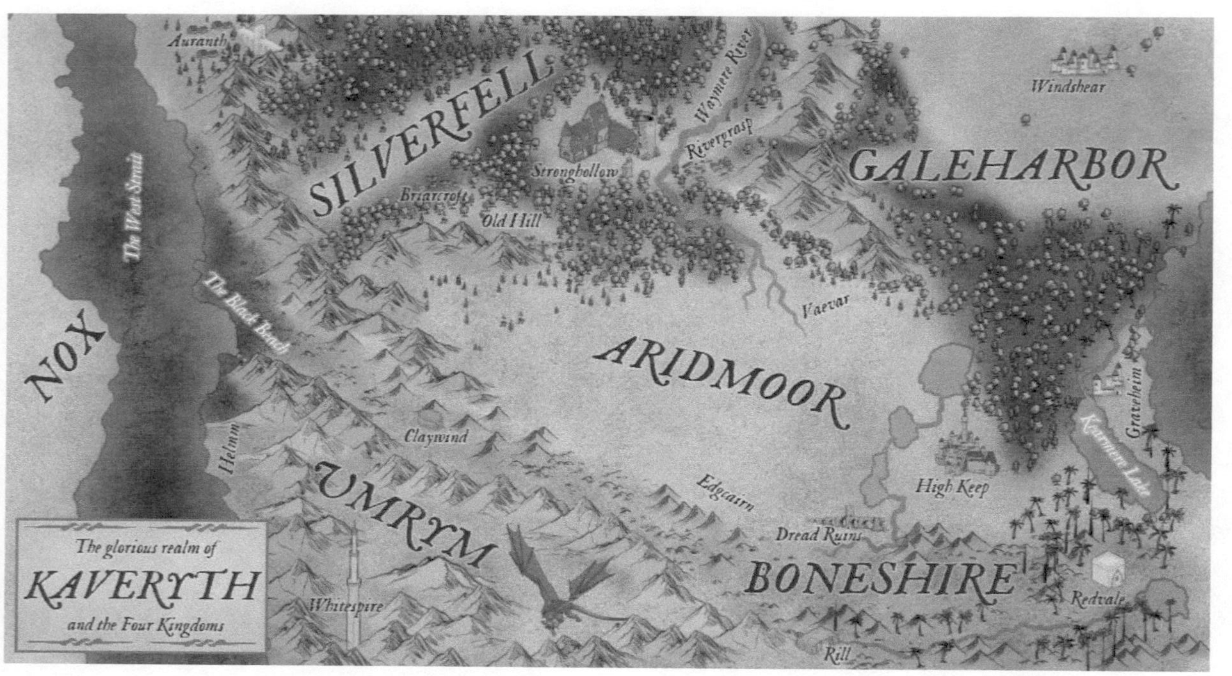

SILVERFELL
GALEHARBOR
ARIDMOOR
NOX
UMRYM
BONESHIRE
Auranth
Windshear
Waymere River
Rivergrasp
Stronghollow
Briarcroft
Old Hill
Vaevar
Gravebeirn
Kearmere Lake
High Keep
The West Strait
The Black Beach
Helmm
Claywind
Edgcairn
Dread Ruins
Whitespire
Redvale
Rill
The glorious realm of
KAVERYTH
and the Four Kingdoms

1

Prologue

ORIA
BEFORE

Oria felt herself waking up, but she pressed her eyes shut, not ready to accept the loss of sleep.

Her dream had been a pleasant one, all green grass and summer flowers. A time before her world fell apart, where things made sense. She breathed slowly, feeling the cool air rushing through her nostrils, trying to settle herself, to go back. It felt so close, the corner of a memory that she could reach out and touch–

The pain hit her all at once.

Her eyes were open now, and she could feel her jaw clamping shut against the agony as she shifted her wounded leg. Her neck ached after hours of laying still against the ground, but she forced herself to lift her head, ignoring the thrumming feeling of her blood pulsing through to her head.

The wounds were still there, of course. Three of them, red and angry, but no longer bleeding. The belt was in place, fastened tight near the top of her thigh.

I should be dead. High One, I–

"Shh," came a voice, just loud enough to be heard over the breeze. "Don't move. Keep still."

She ignored him and forced herself into an awkward sitting position, ignoring the way that the leather belt bit into the edge of one of the knife wounds.

There was no real sunshine, but it was dawn. The forest was soft and gray with mist, and she could hear the happy sounds of morning as birds flitted from tree to tree overhead.

She did not see the man, but she knew the voice.

"I told you to run, Kamil," she choked out, pressing her eyes shut again as she shifted her weight and sent a fresh wave of pain up her leg.

"And I told you to keep still," he scolded. She felt a hand on her shoulder and turned to look at it. It was a huge hand, dark and worn, with bits of dirt under the edges of the man's fingernails.

"I should be dead."

"You may die, still."

He sounded so troubled that she found herself chuckling, the sound of it lonely amid the trees. It made her head hurt, but she didn't care.

"The High One performed a miracle," she said, thinking of the other bandit who had nearly finished her off but instead ran away. "At least one. Probably two or three."

For a long moment, Kamil said nothing.

She brushed a few stray leaves off of the front of her tunic, a shiver rushing up her back. The trees were thick, but she hoped some sunlight would still peek through when it was high enough in the sky. It would be pleasant to feel the warmth of light on her skin again.

"So you don't mind if you die?" the man asked, tightening his grip on her shoulder ever so slightly, as if she might get up and run off into the fog.

She turned, careful this time not to let the belt shift against her wounds. Kamil's face was close to hers, his brown eyes narrowed in concern, his forehead wrinkled. He looked older and younger than she expected, all at once.

"Last night—I guess it was last night—I made my peace with the High One. I got to see the stars. I got to say goodbye to this world," she said carefully, hoping that the words came out right.

Kamil raised an eyebrow, saying nothing, so she continued on.

"The High One asked me to trust Him, and I did," she said quietly. "I tried to, anyway, the best I could. And I'm still here."

She felt a smile tugging at her lips again, and she didn't try to stop it, even as her companion stared at her in bewilderment.

"We need to find a healer. That tourniquet has been on for hours. The flesh will die."

"It should have already," she pointed out, gesturing to the wound nearest to the ends of her fingertips. "But look. Pink. Alive."

"Hmm," the man said, glancing over her knee.

"I don't want to die, Kamil," she said firmly. "Accepting death and desiring it are different things. Perhaps I should want to die, to be closer to Him whom I love, but I am not there yet. I want to live. And I am *alive*."

Tears were spilling from the corners of her eyes now, her

words caught in her throat as she swallowed a sob.

"The High One wanted me to live, and I will keep on living until He chooses otherwise."

"I understand," Kamil said, giving her shoulder a gentle pat, the weight of his hand comforting and warm. "I almost didn't come back."

He paused, and for several seconds, she debated whether or not to speak.

"Did you kill them?" she asked, unable to let the words remain unsaid.

The memories of the night before flooded into her mind, all darkness and fear, so different from the pleasant dream that had followed.

I should never have drawn my own knife.

Kamil shook his head. "I ran from the others, leading them south for a while, and then I hid in some brush. Eventually, they gave up."

She breathed out in a rush, relief washing over her. Kamil did not get blood on his hands on her account.

"Once they had passed, I waited. It was cold, and the darkness was thick. I've never feared the forest before, not until that moment. I realized just how powerless I was, all by myself. But I knew I could never go back to what I knew before. Back to robbing, to hurting, to..."

He let the words fade away, and Oria bent her head down, looking at the crushed leaves as a frog made his warbling call somewhere in the distance.

"You could have still kept going," she said.

Kamil shook his head. "I wanted to."

He paused again, looking around the small clearing, as though wondering how he had ended up there at all.

"But?"

"But I knew, somehow, that you were still alive. And that you had no one else who could help you. Sitting here now, though, I see it's foolishness either way. You can't even walk. I have nothing left. Everything I owned in the world is with the others, and I'm sure they're thrilled to add to their coffers. One less mouth to share the meat."

He let out a sigh, drawing his hand back from her shoulder and rubbing at his temples.

"Thank you," she said.

"It's okay."

"I know you're probably tired of my preaching," she continued. "But indulge me. Let me say one thing."

She thought she could hear the hint of a sigh under his breath, but he nodded.

"You didn't lose everything. We have more treasure now than we ever have before, I promise that to you. We just need to reach out and to take it."

"The miracles?"

"Yes," she said, feeling a smile breaking across her face once more. He understood. "When we are at our weakest, the High One has room to act. He fills the space. I know it's hard to believe, but you will see. I know you will."

She caught his eye, and for a moment, she feared that he would tell her it was all nonsense, or worse, that he'd walk away. If he did that, she would die. Of that, she was certain.

But instead, he smiled. A small smile, perhaps a little forced, but it was beautiful.

"Stronghollow can't be far," he said, glancing off into the distance. "They'll have a healer. And from there, we can figure out what's next. Now, if you lean on me on your good leg, you might be able to walk a little. After that, I suppose you're not too heavy. I will carry you."

She did not tell him that Stronghollow was where she had been heading in the first place. Until that very moment when he confirmed it, she had not wanted to believe how close she was to Elder Bram. It seemed impossible, even now, but he had no reason to deceive her.

"Thank you, Kamil," she said, ignoring the screaming in her leg as the Vilzanian man helped her to her feet.

"You're welcome. Please, be careful. Put your weight on your good leg, as much as you can."

She did as he instructed, using his thick arm to support herself as she took one step forward, and then another. It hurt, but at that moment, she didn't care.

She'd survive.

She'd make it home.

"The High One will reward you," she said as they moved over the uneven ground, the words choked out between gritted teeth. "I promise you that."

She let the words hang there in the silence as they walked on.

As each minute passed, the sun drew higher in the sky, the mist fading ever so slightly where it touched the first branches of the trees.

It was going to be a beautiful day.

2

Chapter 1

KESSARA

"That's the last of them," Kessara said, watching as a caravan of men on horseback headed north. Within a few minutes, they were gone, the final horses swallowed up into the starry horizon of the desert. The air felt cool as she stood there in the open, with no trees or buildings to protect her from the late autumn breeze.

"I hope they'll get help with more supplies in Edgecairn," Alder said, putting an arm over her shoulder and pulling her toward his chest. She didn't pull away. Being near him was like basking in the light of her own personal sun. He always felt warm, no matter the weather.

She drew a breath, inhaling the smell of him, thinking about how thankful she was.

It's impossible, but we're both here.

She never wanted to forget the joy and wonder of it. Ever since she'd met the Aridmoorian, she'd known that some-thing was different about him. For whatever reason, whatever plan of the High One, the two of them had been drawn to one another from the start, a fierce sea rushing toward a rocky shore.

But only recently had they learned that their love was possible, that the dreams they had hidden away in their hearts could actually come to pass.

She shook her head, her blonde braids falling into her face and probably tickling Alder's nose. The future was coming one way or another, but there was more to it than just their love story. A lot more.

"They made it this far. The High One will continue to provide," she said quickly, hoping that he could not hear the worry in her voice. The past few weeks had passed quickly, with fall rushing toward winter. The company of men had wanted to leave before now, hoping to outrun any early snowfall that may come once they left the deserts of Boneshire, but it had taken longer than they had hoped to prepare.

The freed slaves who had escorted her here had not wanted to go home once their task was completed, but to Auranth, where they could aid in the war effort.

After their arrival–which had been quite a to-do in the small village of Rill–they had all gone to the inn in search of food, drink, and rest. Alder had befriended a pleasant barkeeper there called Fira, and to Kessara's surprise, the women had immediately begun to convince her patrons that it would do no good for them to sit around waiting for King Ursa's soldiers to come and conscript them into his Red Army. She urged them instead to choose to fight this impending war on their own terms, and many had agreed to join the slaves in heading north to join the Envoy's small force.

It had taken some time to procure the necessary donations of supplies and coin, but finally, they were on their way, a much larger group than Kessara could have ever hoped for.

"I'm glad they're going," Alder said, absentmindedly stroking the end of her hair. "I just wish I knew what they were walking into."

"It's been quiet," Kessara agreed. There had been few travelers and little news in the last couple of weeks, which wasn't exactly surprising in such a small and unimportant village, but it still made her nervous. "But they'll be all right. Bargren and Mella will welcome them. Perhaps Wes, Celesyria, and Aelrie are there already."

Alder made a noncommittal noise in his throat, and she resisted the urge to clench her jaw.

She knew what he was about to say before he said it, but it did not lessen her frustration when he spoke.

"We should be with them."

He kept stroking her hair, his fingers gentle, but she could sense the heat of his anger, no matter how well he tried to hide it.

"We will," she said. "Soon enough, okay?"

She closed her eyes, listening to the sound of his breathing and the steady thumping of his heart. She hoped that this detour wouldn't prove to be a mistake. Alder had questioned her from the start, but after over a week of arguing, he had finally decided to trust her judgment.

This time, anyway. Might be the first and last.

"I miss them," she added, filling the silence. "They're always on my mind. Anyway, Nazzan will be happy to be leaving. He's not been in the best mood lately."

Alder gave a half-smile. "He hates camping alone, you

know that. Especially out here."

Kessara's shoulders relaxed as she released a breath. For the moment, at least, Alder was going to let the idea of returning immediately to Auranth go, and she was thankful.

"Everything is packed. All that's left is to say goodbye to Holga and Gohr," he continued, pulling back from her and glancing off into the night. She followed his line of sight, but nothing seemed to disturb the peacefulness of the desert night. "I'll head over there at first light."

"They'll probably be happy to get a little freedom from their strict new dad," she joked, grinning at him.

"Ha-ha," Alder said, pretending to flick her right shoulder. "They'll miss me terribly. Especially Gohr, I think. He's been kind of caught up in... everything."

Kessara nodded. Finding out that your older sister was actually adopted would be difficult enough, but in Gohr's case, his not-sister also happened to be the lost queen of Boneshire. Holga adored her little brother, and Kessara knew that she wouldn't push him aside, but it had to be challenging for him, anyway.

"You're good at it," she added as the two of them began to walk back toward town, a comfortable silence having fallen between them.

"What?"

"Being a father."

"Sure," he said, looking over at her and rolling his eyes.

"I mean it. When all of this ends—"

"Don't, Kessara," Alder snapped.

For a second, she didn't respond, so hurt that she couldn't form words.

"I didn't mean—" he started, reaching out for her hand

before she snapped it away.

"I thought you wanted children. Little redheads with blue eyes, roaming the plains."

"I do," he said. "More than anything."

"So what's the problem?" she asked, crossing her arms over her chest as she continued to walk toward the dots of lamplight in the distance.

"I want to think of the future when things are a little more clear," he said firmly, taking her chin in one of his strong hands and turning her face until she was gazing straight into his green eyes. "That's all. I'm sorry."

The strength of his touch made her feel like she wanted to dive into his arms, but she reminded herself of her annoyance and stood firm.

"We thought we couldn't be together, but the High One made it happen. I don't think it is foolish to believe He will carry us through our hopes the rest of the way," she said.

"I never said it was foolish."

"But you acted like a –"

Before she could argue further, his lips were on hers, his fingertips knotting into the back of her hair. She forgot the chill. She didn't notice the twinkling of the stars. For several seconds she kissed him back, struggling to remember why she had been mad at him at all.

Without warning, he pulled away, the spell broken.

"What's wrong now?" she asked, her annoyance flooding back as a chilly breeze rustled across them, sending her hair into her face.

"I want children," he said, the corner of his mouth turned up in one of his usual teasing smiles. "I want *this*."

He looked at her, and she knew what he meant.

"But it does neither of us any good to get ahead of our-selves," he continued, leaning over and planting a kiss on her forehead before grasping her hand and pulling her toward the village once more. "We need to think about the here and now."

"Such as?"

"Holga," Alder answered easily. "She's made a lot of progress, even in just a couple of weeks. Don't you think so?"

Kessara knotted her free hand in the fabric of her dark blue skirt, pushing aside a thousand competing emotions. He was right. They had to be careful.

"Yes," she said quickly. "I had my doubts about her plans to stay here instead of trying to go to Auranth and rule from afar, but her judgment has impressed me so far. It's hard to believe she's so young."

"Do you know if they got their keys today?" Alder asked, nudging a small lizard off of the dirt path with the toe of his boot. The little gray creature slithered off without protest, and Kessara resisted the urge to shudder.

"One of her guards told me that they planned to move them in a few days, just as soon as the promised coins from their *mysterious benefactor* made it to the seller."

Alder rolled his eyes. "Look, if Mr. Braddock doesn't want anyone to know that he bought the new queen a house of her own, we should respect that."

"And I do," she said quickly. It was true.

She knew that Alder and Holga had met the man back in Vaevar when he had helped them to free Gohr from imprisonment, and that at first, Alder had had doubts about his intentions. Now that the secret of Holga's lineage was slowly beginning to seep out of the seams of Rill, however, they could think of few other people who might have been willing or able to donate such a sum to her cause.

"I'm still scared for her, though," she added.

"Me too," Alder agreed, giving her hand a gentle squeeze as they stepped carefully down a hill of red stone and loose sand. "She still has a lot to learn about the administration of Rill itself, let alone the whole Kingdom. And once word really gets out, she will be surrounded with friends and foes in abundance."

"At least she should be wise enough to tell them apart," she ventured.

"So we hope," Alder said. "Corruption has snuck under the nose of more than one King or Queen in history, and none of them were literal children."

She opened her mouth to say more, but Alder continued before she could.

"I'm confident in her, you know," he said fiercely. "Despite everything. She's careful. It's not like she's marching up to the ruins of Redvale palace and demanding that she be put in charge. By the time she has prepared herself, the people will trust her. I really believe that they will."

Kessara didn't want to argue, but there was a niggling aspect of the whole issue that bothered her.

"Do you trust Malka to care for her? And for Gohr? They're still children. They still need guidance."

She swallowed, always feeling out of sorts whenever she said Malka's name. The herbwoman and midwife was the closest thing the children had to a mother now, but Kessara did not find it so easy to forget the evils of the woman's past.

"I've gotten to know her well enough," Alder ventured. "I

keep wanting to ask about the children. About what she has done. It's never quite come up."

"But it's over?"

Alder nodded. "Holga confirmed as much. She sticks strictly to births now. But how Malka actually feels about her past is a mystery."

The village was closer now, and Kessara took a couple of steps away from Alder, allowing more open space between them. Rill was a rough village, not overly concerned with propriety, but she figured that they had best set as good of an example as they could while they were here.

"She's all they have," Alder continued. "So I guess I don't have much choice but to trust her. To answer your question."

There was another silence then, and this time, Kessara noticed every sweeping breeze, every chill that rushed through her blonde hair and touched the back of her neck.

She walked a little faster, trying to keep her legs warm beneath her dress, but before long, Alder was several paces ahead. This was unlike him, especially out here, where all sorts of dangers could be waiting.

Finally, after what felt like a very long time, he turned his head and looked over his shoulder at her.

"Is something wrong?" she asked, trepidation twisting in her gut.

"You know what's wrong, Kessara," Alder said, his voice dangerously quiet.

She did know, but she wanted to hear him say it.

"I don't want you to go to Ursa. The more I think about it, the more I'm convinced it's a stupid idea."

She felt herself flinch, but she hoped he couldn't see her expression clearly in the dark. She understood his concern.

She really did. Alder had been a member of King Kylan Ursa's personal Protectorate army until he defected for the sake of joining Wes Cervos and his cause. To make matters worse, Alder's former captain, Drohma, hated him even more than the King did. If Kessara was going to have any chance at meeting with the King, she would have to go on her own. Giving them any chance to spot Alder was not worth the risk.

"We can't keep going on like this, and you know it," Kessara said, trying to keep the frustration from her voice. "We're already on the same side. In Auranth, our men fought with his Red Army. Without them—"

"I know," Alder said softly, rubbing his forehead with his fingertips. He looked as though he was about to yawn. It was late, and tomorrow, they would be traveling, in one direction or another. "The Gorok was only part of it. The elves might have—Kessara, you have to believe me that this isn't about pride. King Ursa is power hungry, and giving him a chance at more control is dangerous."

He paused.

"But?"

"I'm not blind. I see that we don't have much of a choice. Unity of command is essential to battle strategy. Right now, we're two totally different forces, trying not to step on each other's toes. The elves are disciplined. Once they really start pushing, we're going to be in trouble. I just wish it didn't have to be you."

"You know it does, Alder."

He didn't respond, and she could see that he was clenching his jaw tight, trying to calm himself before he lost his temper even more.

"And even if we can expel the elves," he continued. "I

don't want to end up in a second war, fighting for control of Kaveryth."

"Which is a real risk," she conceded. "But it's our best option. Arguing with me doesn't change that."

"I'm trying to keep you safe. How do you even know that he'll be willing to see you? As far as everyone—including his guards—knows right now, you've been stripped of your crown. Why should they let a commoner begging for the King's ear into the palace?"

She shook her head. He was right. Though they had learned that they were permitted by the High One to marry, no one else knew about it yet. She hadn't exactly had a chance to ask her father to reconsider the punishment he had ordered when she had refused to marry Wes.

"I still have hope," she said after a long moment. "I still believe that he can do the right thing now, even after all of his evils. I've known him longer than I've known how to walk. I'm not going to pretend that means nothing."

"But to him, it might. He could have you imprisoned."

He didn't say the other option out loud, but she could see the fear in his eyes.

"I'll be safe," she said firmly. "Look, if this appeal has any chance of succeeding, it's going to have to come from someone he cares about. I'm the only candidate. He might say no, but he'll listen. I know he will."

Alder stopped walking and turned to her, taking both of her hands within his own and looking into her eyes, his gaze so intense that it was almost frightening.

"I'm scared for you, but—" he paused, giving her a gentle kiss "—I trust you. It—it will be all right."

They continued to walk, the quiet night stretching out

between them, both lost in their own thoughts.

The lights of Rill were close now, hundreds of soft yellow stars dancing on the horizon. She felt safer here than she had in a long time, despite the poverty and the crime.

He was here.

She was safe.

3

Chapter 2

WES

"The air smells strange," Wes said, pressing his hand to his forehead, watching the trees.

Aelrie nodded, but Luna and the others said nothing, glancing between each other and looking over their shoulders. It was midday, but the sun was half-hidden by clouds, and few rays reached the forest floor, giving the whole place an eerie feeling.

"He's just talking about the water," the elf said quickly, pointing toward the mountains that lay ahead. "The West Strait is near. We're close to Auranth."

"And to Nox," one of the freed slaves, a woman whose name Wes could never quite remember, chimed in.

She was correct—the homeland of the elves was just beyond the Strait, a channel of water that joined the North and South Seas—but he wished she would be quiet all the same.

"We're safe here," Aelrie insisted, giving a quick glance at the thick trees that surrounded them in all directions. "You trust me, don't you?"

You helped to free them from enslavement. I'd hope that they do.

Luna, the apparent leader of the Remnant, nodded, and the others joined her.

"Good," Aelrie said, brushing a lock of black hair behind a silvery ear. "The mountain pass that will lead us into the city should be nearby, and if we can keep walking all night, we should make it there by dawn."

Wes could hear a collective groan rising from the crowd. They were exhausted, he knew, but their grumbling still made him grit his teeth.

"Wait," he said, raising a hand and silencing the group momentarily.

He stopped for a moment and stood on a nearby rock, trying to get a look at the sky through the trees. Jaconial and Celesyria were somewhere up above them, carrying several people who had sustained minor injuries on the journey. They had found deer easily enough in the thick forests of Silverfell, but still, the heavy load of riders must have been tiring to carry.

"How close is the pass?" he called out to Celesyria in his mind.

"We can see it just ahead. It's clear, as of now."

Relief swelled in his chest. Even here, there was always the risk of running into bandits, or worse.

He relayed the information to the others, and to his annoyance, their grumbling started up again just as soon as he'd spoken. Aelrie caught his eye, and gave him a small smile, which he couldn't help but to return.

She was standing several feet away from him, trying to

stay near the edge of the crowd, her elf-senses attuned to the sounds of the nearby forest. All he wanted to do was to rush over and kiss her, and never stop. Every morning when he woke up, he was amazed to remember that he *could* kiss her. Hold her hand. Love her. It was a miracle that hadn't stopped amazing him.

His thoughts were interrupted by the appearance of Luna, only inches away from where he stood. A strand of her coily black hair bounced into his cheek as she addressed the crowd.

"Be quiet," she called out, her voice hard.

He found himself sucking in a breath, though she had not been talking to him. Even though she was the leader of this group of freed captives, most of them having begun their journey as part of the Remnant in the east, she had always deferred to his leadership when necessary.

Still, he had no interest in interrupting her, and when he glanced over at Aelrie, he could see that she was watching the woman with the same rapt attention.

"Many of you came to Kaveryth to be enslaved," she said, her voice carrying over the group as she shook her head in disapproval. Wes stole a glance at the sky again, wondering if Celesyria and Jaconial were close enough for their keen hearing to pick up snatches of her words. "Even those of you who didn't choose such a fate still ended up in that tent, waiting for death, or worse."

Wes watched the crowd, noticing a few flushed faces. He couldn't blame them. Luna, apparently, was quite skilled at chastening her friends when necessary.

"For weeks now, the vast majority of you have traveled on foot," she continued, gesturing toward the canopy of trees over their heads, indicating the dragons above. "We've had only a little water, and even less food. These lands are swarming with evil men, and even I wondered if we would come to a quick end, but we didn't."

"The High One brought us through," came a small voice. Wes saw that it was a brown-haired little girl, who couldn't have been more than eleven or twelve.

"Yes, Grazia. Exactly. The High One brought us through," she continued, beaming at the child, her broad white smile seeming to soften her entire face. "He has sustained us through impossible days. And now you complain because we must spend one more night on foot? One more night hungry?"

Her voice rose with each word, and within seconds, she was joined by the crowd in a triumphant cheer, her smile reflected in dozens of faces. Wes shouted right along with them, raising a fist to the sky. It felt good to smile. Victory was so near, and tomorrow, he would see Auranth. It was the closest thing he had to a home now, and he missed it terribly.

With a final nod to Luna, who was still offering encouragement to the crowd, he stepped down from the stone, glancing around the dark trees.

"We're still alone, I think," Aelrie said, striding toward him with her usual quick elven steps. "I haven't heard anything. Not in two days. I think our enemies are finally afraid of our little fortress."

Wes smiled, but a twinge of doubt still rested in the depths of his gut. As far as they knew, Auranth still stood, stronger than ever, with more allies from every corner of Kaveryth pouring in as time went on. But he wouldn't feel sure, not until he smelled Mella's cooking and sat with Bargren around a cheerful fire.

"I'm glad she's encouraging them," he said, gesturing to Luna. "They've been through a lot. I know what it's like to reach the limit of your strength. It's hard to keep going, even if it's only a few steps."

Aelrie shook her head. "I still don't understand how we made it this far."

"Me either," he agreed.

Every time that the food had nearly run out, they had managed to find or to hunt just enough to keep everyone going, and the meat they had always stretched much further than it should. More than once, they had been certain that they were about to be robbed by bandits, only to find a small group of helpful peasants, willing to give them a night of shelter in an old barn and some bread to take with them on the road.

Their own water stores had run out within only a few days, and even the most fearful among them had been forced to drink wild, possibly cursed, water. Somehow, the small remaining bottle of the herbal remedy that he, Alder, and Kessara had been given so long ago remained at least a quarter full even as they used it.

They never had enough to feel satisfied, but their needs were met. They had been able to keep putting one foot in front of the other, and that was enough.

They stood side by side in silence for a few seconds before Wes got up the nerve to reach out and take Aelrie's hand. The elf smiled, her pale blue eyes gleaming even in the shadow of the thick trees.

Foolish. She wants me to be near her. She wants to feel my touch.

"Well," he said, clearing his throat. "We're in the High

One's world. I suppose we should get used to miracles."

Aelrie leaned over then, planting a soft kiss on his scarred cheek. He resisted the urge to reach up and feel his skin, imagining that her warm lips had left some kind of mark that he could look at in a mirror later. He shook his head at himself. He did not need such silly thoughts, not any more. He loved her, and she loved him. He did not need to be afraid that she would run away at any moment, leaving only the shadow of a kiss behind.

"Speaking of the High One," he added. "Are you ready?"

Aelrie gripped his hand more tightly, drawing in a slow breath.

"I'm still nervous," she admitted, allowing Wes to tug her gently forward as the rest of the group finally began to move toward the pass again. "But I think–I think it feels right. Auranth is the place."

"Are you sure? The High One just wants you to accept Him. The location isn't what counts."

"It's not that," she said, her words accompanied by a soft sigh. "It's just... I want the others to be there. Especially Kessara. I watched her jump into that river near the Dread Ruins, even when she was terrified. She didn't pretend that her fears didn't exist. She acknowledged her weakness, and she moved forward, anyway. She inspires me. I want her to be here."

Wes hurried his pace, noticing that Luna and the others were getting ahead of them. He didn't want them to run into trouble without him and Aelrie nearby.

"She might be there already," he pointed out, giving the elf's hand a squeeze as they strode around a small, mosquito-swarmed pond, following dozens of muddy footprints. "With

Alder, and Nazzan. Safe and sound."

"Right," Aelrie said, her voice sounding a little too bright.

They fell into silence again.

There was a chance that his words were true, he knew. Alder had separated from the group a long while back, and they had no way of knowing if he was still alive at all, let alone if Kessara had succeeded in finding him.

They had asked after their friends all across Aridmoor and Silverfell as they made their way to Auranth, but heard only whispers that could not be trusted.

"There's always hope," he said, his words sounding sudden and loud after so many minutes had passed.

"I know. I believe we'll be together again," Aelrie said, not quite meeting his eyes. "I just hope it's soon. I hope it's *here.*"

He had nothing to add, so instead he kept walking.

The pass was close.

They would have their answers soon enough.

CELESYRIA

"It's okay! Everything's okay," Celesyria called out to Wes in her mind, flapping her wings against the air as she took a final turn over the outskirts of the city of Auranth.

She was glad that they would be landing in a couple of minutes. Between the iron manacles that still clung to her ankles, and the extra weight of her passengers, travel had been exhausting. All she wanted was to curl up in a warm nest of blankets and take a nap.

"Thank the High One," Wes replied.

She watched as Jaconial pulled out ahead of her, angling

her body downward as she took the now-familiar route to the old forge that now served as what she could only describe as her home. It looked just like it had when they left it, only busier. Crowds of people swarmed around the thick stone outer walls, still small from her altitude.

Things had changed in the main city, too. All around the outskirts, she could see tents that had not been there before–hundreds, perhaps even thousands of them.

How quickly change comes.

Auranth had once been an isolated city, famed for their weaponmaking, but rarely visited. Ever since she, Wes, and their other friends had taken refuge on the outskirts several months back, it had blossomed into something else entirely. Something new, and shining, and full of hope.

She could almost feel the presence of the High One as she basked in the gleaming sunlight.

It was here where the people of Kaveryth came to seek answers, to turn away from the illusion of the Dracodei in hope of finding the truth. It was here where a truth sought became a love fought for.

She was so thankful to be a part of it. All her life she'd felt out of place, and when she'd first met Wes Cervos, she had become more hated by the general public than she ever had been among her fellow dragons back in Umrym.

Now, when she flew overhead, she could hear the cheers from the streets below.

Here, she was loved. She was home.

She let out a roar of happiness, and immediately she felt the weight on her back shift as the three injured women she carried lurched in surprise.

"Apologies," she called back at them, unable to hear their

response over the rushing breeze.

As soon as Jaconial was out of her way, she followed the same route downward, toward the blown-out hole in the stone ceiling of the forge that they had never bothered to fix. It was the perfect entrance for dragons, and she fit through the space easily, folding up the ends of her wings slightly in order to avoid scraping her claws against the rock on her way down.

"Bring the others," she said to Wes as she landed gently on the floor. The broken stone had been fully repaired in their absence, the patches of grass covered with gleaming new tile. All around her, things looked the same, but improved. The doors hung on freshly oiled hinges. Their makeshift bonfire pit was now at home in a massive bowl of hewed marble. Thick fabric tapestries hung on the walls, most of them looking as though they had come from right here in Silverfell, though a few were woven in the Boneshire style. The whole place was beautiful.

"Celesyria!" came a delighted female voice, and she turned to see Mella, standing near the end of her tail.

"We're so glad you made it back," Bargren said as he rested a hand on his wife's shoulder, beaming through the perpetual mask of soot that always seemed to cover his face. The man had been head of the Armory Guild, before being dragged into managing a small army, and she doubted that he would ever give up working with his hands in a sweaty, dangerous forge.

"Where are the others?" Mella asked.

"We have quite a few unexpected guests," she said, noticing the woman's open-mouthed expression. "They'll be in shortly, I'm sure. It's been a long journey. They're weary."

"I'll see to them," Bargren said, giving his wife a kiss on

the cheek before rushing off toward the rapidly expanding crowd.

"Kessara and Alder?" Mella asked, not quite meeting the dragon's eyes.

"Long story, but last we saw them, they were both alive and well," she said quickly, not wanting to tell the whole long story at the moment.

"Right," Mella said, shaking her head. "Now, Celesyria—there's something you need to know. I think it would be best to go out to the courtyard so I can hear myself think."

Celesyria found it difficult to argue. The great hall was filled to capacity, and she was struggling to avoid knocking people over with the ends of her wings.

As soon as she emerged into the dim daylight, before she could get her bearings, she heard a familiar voice.

Dread pooled in her gut.

No. Not that. Anything else, please.

"Mother," Celesyria said, her heart aching as she watched Sharsi hobbling her way out into the center of the courtyard. What had been an injured back leg, damaged in the Whitespire collapse, was now nothing but a scaly orange stump, cut off at the knee.

Sharsi did not smile.

Celesyria watched as Mella took a couple of tentative steps back, her mouth a grim line. A few other women who had been standing nearby began shuffling toward the back entrance of the building, glancing back over their shoulders at the dragons as they went.

Celesyria opened her mouth to speak, but before she could, Sharsi cut her off.

"It's your father, darling. He's—he's gone. He's dead."

4

Chapter 3

ALDER

The walk to Malka's house had become familiar, but Alder did not let his guard down. He doubted that he would run into any trouble so early, but still, he was not a believer in taking foolish chances. Only a week before, he had narrowly avoided being robbed of the remainder of his coin by a traveling peddler who had come through Rill, claiming to offer boot repair.

He shivered as he made his way past the shabby huts, the windows still dark. Dawn had not yet come, and it was very cold. He hoped that the people here had enough firewood to last through the brisk desert winter. Trees were not exactly easy to come by here.

The children will be warm at Malka's, at least.

He was glad that he'd been able to convince Kessara to stay behind in her warm bed at the inn. Nazzan was still camping out past the edge of town where he wouldn't be seen, but he and Kessara had found themselves fitting into the small town better than he'd expected. As much as he hated to leave the Princess alone at all, he trusted the barkeeper, Fira, to keep his beloved under close watch. At least she could get another hour of rest before they departed for Aridmoor.

Aridmoor.

It was his home, but at the moment, the very thought of the place made him feel sick. He knew that Kessara was right, but that didn't mean he was going to be happy about going along with her plan. He could trust her all he wanted, but that didn't mean he would ever trust King Kylan Ursa.

He let out a sigh, his breath rolling out in a thick white cloud as he tramped along the dirt road, his steps making a shush-shush sound in the quiet.

So much could go wrong. Kessara was smart and strong, but he was under no illusions about her physical limitations, especially after...

He kicked at an old broken pot someone had left in the road, listening as it clattered against the side of a nearby stone shed. He didn't want to think about that night, and neither did the woman he loved.

She's been through enough. I will never let her feel that fear again. Never.

"Oy, soldier," came a voice, startling him so much that he nearly drew his sword.

"Malka," he said instead, his heart continuing to pound as he stared at the woman standing on her porch, a leather bag slung over her shoulder. "You scared me."

The herbwoman chuckled, looking him up and down. "I doubt that."

"It's true," he said, giving her a half-smile. "You're quite menacing."

Malka made a tutting sound with her lips and stepped onto the dirt, grasping a glass jar from her windowsill as she went. "There's a birth begun this morning. East, toward the dunes."

"Will you make it?" he asked, looking over in the general direction. Rill was the only settlement for many miles, and often Malka was the only midwife or healer available to help those who lived on more isolated properties.

"No idea. But I'd better go."

"Right," Alder said, stepping past her, toward the blue front door of her little hut. "Be safe."

The woman nodded, whistling a tune as she continued along the street, her wispy brown-and-gray hair fluttering in the breeze.

Suddenly, a few steps later, she stopped short.

"Wait," she said, turning to where Alder still stood, examining a crow's skull that she had left to dry in the sun. "You and the Galeharbor girl are leaving today, ain't you?"

Of course she knows. Half the town knows now, after Fira helped us to send so many of their men to Auranth.

"Yes ma'am."

Malka closed the distance between them, moving surprisingly fast despite her short frame. Before Alder could even work out that he was surprised, the woman had her arms around his belly, wrapping him in a gentle embrace.

She pulled away before too long, smoothing her permanently-wrinkled linen skirt. "Well, then, I wish both of you the best."

"Thank you," Alder said, finding himself rather touched, even though he still felt wary around the woman. The dark business of her past was not so easy for him to forget, but perhaps Holga was right. Perhaps she had not only stopped the killing she had been engaged in, but had come to see just how evil it was.

"I have to be getting on–"

"Malka," Alder said quickly, placing his hand on her arm as she turned to leave. The sun was nearly rising now, casting a soft glow over the shabby street. "Watch over the children. Please. Even when they're all settled in the merchant's district."

"Of course."

Without another word, she began to walk away, and within a few seconds she was gone, leaving the street silent and empty.

Alder stepped up to the door and rapped on the wood with his fingers. As he waited for Holga to awaken and let him in, he cast a final glance up and down the street, trying to see if there was any movement in the shadows.

He saw nothing, but still, he could not shake his nerves. He was glad that the two children would soon be living in a much safer part of Rill, though even the wealthiest areas were dangerous compared to the careful order of his childhood home in High Keep.

Holga had hired security–how she'd convinced them to take on the sort of wage she could offer, he had no idea–and he hoped that they would keep watch at her door when she slept. He knew from the experience of his friends that royal blood was a dangerous possession.

The door was yanked open from within, and he stepped into the dimness without a word.

Holga gave him a quick hug, putting a finger to her lips and gesturing toward the small bedroom where Gohr must have still been asleep.

He took a seat in one of the small wooden chairs that Malka

owned, trying in vain to get comfortable in front of the gentle fire. Holga stood near the flames, prodding at the embers with a poker as she tried to get two fresh logs to light.

Finally, they caught, and she sank into her own chair across from his, pulling her robe more tightly around her body as a hiss of wind made the thin window panes clatter.

"So," the child said, looking up at him, her expression unreadable. "You're leaving today."

"We are."

"Thanks for coming to say goodbye."

"You're welcome."

They sat in silence for a moment as Alder warmed his hands by the fire. "Should I wake Gohr?" he asked.

Holga shook her head, braids bouncing. "He struggles a lot with goodbyes. I think it would be better if you just let him sleep on."

"Okay," Alder agreed. A moment later, he got to his feet, gesturing toward the shadowed depths of the little house. "I won't wake him, promise," he added.

Holga got up from her own chair and walked with him to the back bedroom, where Gohr slept peacefully, the yellow light of a single candle emanating from the stand on the night table. Alder glanced up at the hanging herbs and various bits of animal bone, wondering where Malka possibly slept, if she'd given up her bedroom to the little ones.

"Goodbye, my friend," Alder whispered to the child's sleeping form, leaning down and planting a kiss on his smooth forehead. Gohr did not stir, and for a moment Alder waited, watching the gentle rising and falling of his chest beneath his tunic. "May the High One continue to protect you from the darkness."

Holga cleared her throat, and he followed her back out to the living area. It was warmer now, the logs finally having caught the flame. "I think we'll like it in our new house," the girl said, sinking back into her chair. "Malka's will always be home, but it will be safer there. I want Gohr to be able to play outdoors without me having to worry about him. This street is safer than it used to be, did you know that? When I was little, really little, I remember that there were fires in this part of town. Later, my father told me that they'd caught an arsonist–you know, someone who lights fires on purpose–can you imagine such a thing?"

Alder certainly could imagine it, and worse, but he didn't want Holga going too far astray on one of her tangents.

"You'll still have to worry a little, I'm afraid," he said, giving her a pinched smile. "Probably not about arsonists, though," he added.

Holga pulled up her knees to her chest, looking suddenly pensive. "I know that, okay? I'm not a fool. Don't treat me like one."

The child was intelligent beyond her years, true, but he still felt compelled to remind her of the dangers. For now, she and her brother were safe. He made sure of that. But in an hour, he'd be gone, off on the desert road out of this town, and he'd have to rely on others to protect them. Others who he struggled to trust at all.

"I didn't mean to insult you," he said carefully, running his fingers through his red curls, which had finally begun to grow back properly, despite the terrible trim that Kessara had attempted to give him a few days before. "I have total faith in you. You will make a wonderful queen. But this? This calm? It's not going to last. Power attracts wickedness. I've seen it time and time again. You're placing a target on your back by bearing this crown, or even preparing to bear it. I just want you to be ready."

Holga seized the fire poker from where it rested and prodded the wood, sending a small pile of sparks cascading onto the stone hearth. "I know," she repeated. "I'm amazed by the good people in my life who have been willing to help us, but I know that the bad will come. I'll handle it. I'm ready."

For a moment, neither of them spoke. Alder glanced up at the small window near his head, where he could see the dawn light growing slowly brighter. He had to fetch Kessara soon. As cold as he was now, he knew that it would be wise to cover as much ground as they could before midday.

Soon, we'll be in Aridmoor, where the seasons don't play tricks.

Despite the risks he would take just by being there—there were plenty of soldiers who would be happy to capture a man they saw as nothing more than a traitor—he felt a pulse of excitement in his veins. The plains Kingdom was home, and it was always wonderful to go home.

"Alder," Holga said, interrupting his daydreams. "Did you ever consider..."

She didn't finish, instead letting the words trail away as a blush rose to her cheeks. He gave her a sad smile. He knew.

"Did I ever consider throwing Raela's letter away, and letting you live out the future that you expected?"

"Yes."

"For a moment, I did," Alder admitted, thinking back to the day when his beloved childhood caregiver, Raela, passed away, leaving him to bear her darkest secrets. "I have two people close to me who are greater House nobles. It makes it a little difficult to be naive about the reality."

"Not to mention the fact that you're going to be one yourself, when you marry Princess Kessara," Holga pointed out, smirking at him.

Alder did not want to think about that fact, but Holga babbled on before he could stop her.

"It's quite interesting, really, how our Four Kingdoms chose to handle such matters. I've read histories that tell of ancient peoples, far beyond Kaveryth's shores, where only the women change their names. Imagine, if Kessara Manta became Kessara Cadogen!"

He quite liked the thought, but he wasn't about to argue with thousands of years of tradition. There was no noble blood within him, so his title–King Alder Manta–came by way of his future wife.

Holga opened her mouth to say more, probably to go off on some brilliant tangent that he really did not have the time for, but instead, when she spoke, her voice sounded almost sad.

"I still can't get over it," she said, glancing down at her feet.

"What?"

"My name."

"Holga Noctua?"

Holga shook her head. "I suppose that will be strange, and feel a bit insulting to my dear departed parents, but... what bothers me more is that Gohr will not share it. Finding out that he is not truly my brother was painful enough, but to have my name changed feels like another bit of forced division between us."

"Holga," Alder said, getting up from his chair. It took him only two steps to stand at the child's side, extending a hand

and pulling her gently to her feet. "He is your true brother. Never doubt that. The bond of blood is real, and it matters, but the High One can create families however He wills."

He drew Holga toward him then, hugging her tightly against his chest. She felt so small, so vulnerable. He didn't want to leave her, not here. But he knew that there was no other way.

"I need to go to Kessara," he said finally, drawing himself away after several seconds. "We need to leave as soon as we can."

Holga straightened, her chin held a little higher than usual. The hollow sadness in her eyes nearly broke his heart in two.

"I'm sorry," he said, not knowing what else to say. "I'm sorry I have to leave. And I'm sorry for placing this burden on your shoulders."

"Don't say that."

"It's a lot to carry, even for someone as brave as you are. I wish things were different."

"I don't," Holga said, her green eyes fierce. "It is my duty, and it will be an honor to fulfill it for the sake of my people. Even if I am afraid."

With one final kiss on the child's forehead, Alder retreated out the front door and made his way toward the Inn.

Kessara would be waiting, and if he didn't walk away now, he'd always find a reason that he had to stay.

5

Chapter 4

FALLOREN

The capital city of Nox did not have a name, and as far as General Falloren knew, it never had. Then again, he'd only been alive for four hundred years, so perhaps there was history that he was missing.

No matter. It's hardly the most important question of the morning.

The elf hurried down the streets of the unnamed city, passing by only a few other people as he went. Most of the citizens of the city had already been conscripted, and were either in Kaveryth already, or on duty near the borders. Not that it was likely that the humans and Guardian dragons would attempt to invade, but Falloren was a believer in being prepared.

"General," came a voice at his right. There was a man sitting there who he had not noticed, pressed up against the side of a huge stone housing block, giving him a salute. He looked old–eight or nine hundred, easily–and Falloren wondered briefly why he was still alive at all. There was no place for such men. The darkness could grant them years, but no one was immortal, not any more, and after a time their bodies simply wore out.

"As you were," Falloren responded, giving the slightest tip of his head. No matter. If the administrators had not seen fit to send this burden of a man off, he wasn't going to step in and demand it himself.

He had more important things to do.

He had spent that morning tidying his comfortable apartment, high up in the nicest tower, reserved for the most important and powerful people in Nox.

Before the war, he had always enjoyed looking down at the city below, watching as thousands of elves moved through the streets, going about their lives in perfect order.

Every so often, someone would break the rules, and those were his favorite days. He'd drink some smuggled dwarven liquor and stand by his window, looking straight down at the nearest square, where the gallows, the stretching machine, and the whipping post were featured prominently, and wait for the poor fool to be brought in.

It never took long.

He knew that in Kaveryth, the humans took their time with their verdicts, and especially their punishments. They wanted to know with certainty that their criminals were guilty. He found the whole idea quite silly. Guilty or not, there was always a need for culling, for trimming off the edges, for keeping things straight and tidy. Those who broke the law only made it easier to decide who should live and who should die, but the system wasn't perfect. Not for the individuals strapped to the stretching machine, at any rate. For the rest of the population, everything worked out quite well.

He walked past one such square now, smiling placidly as he observed the empty manacles, the unguarded judge-box. He did not want to leave, but at least he would not be missing much entertainment while he was away. He was not looking forward to living in the General's quarters near the port, but he supposed it couldn't be helped. In any case, after Kaveryth was taken, he and his friends would have their pick of places to live.

Still smiling, he made his way toward the main road, waving at a few especially beautiful elf-maidens who had inexplicably been exempted from fighting. Perhaps Meira Daeleth would allow him to take one of the noble-owned mansion houses in Galeharbor, or perhaps Aridmoor. He deserved it. Despite the whole messy business with that blasted dragon, it seemed that the Regent was impressed with his work.

***

A few hours later, he finally arrived in the port city.

To his good fortune, he had managed to catch an early transport that was moving a large group of-low level soldiers south, to join their brothers and sisters in Umrym. The land of the dragons was already more or less under elven control, thanks to their settlements, but he was glad to see that they were taking no chances when it came to providing reinforcements.

He felt his mouth curl up in a smile at the thought as he pressed his way past a group of three young men who were walking in the middle of the main road, their long hair hanging tidily at their backs.

Let the humans see endless boats on their horizon. Let them see that we will crush them completely. Let them fear.

It was much busier here, near the sea. The tiny village had swelled to several times its normal population, thanks to the recent influx of soldiers from across Nox. Most elves did not want to live near the sea, so close to Kaveryth, but now they had no choice.

He made his way toward the docks, the road dipping downward at an increasingly steep angle as the West Strait came into view. He took a moment to appreciate the blueness, and the smell of salty air. There were boats bobbing in the water in all directions, all of them elven. The humans were gone now, scared away toward the North Sea. He could see the edge of the Black Beach in the distance, abandoned, waiting only for their boats to land. The humans had retreated. They were winning, and in Falloren's view, the score was not close.

After taking a few refreshing breaths, shaking the final hints of exhaustion from his limbs, he made his way toward the pier.

It was abandoned, and he sank down to the worn gray wood, seething. Jishon was late once again.

Fortunately, he had been wise enough to pack some food, and he took it out and ate, watching as yet another boat was loaded with male and female soldiers and sent off toward Kaveryth. The sun was shining, and despite the winter chill, he found himself feeling quite comfortable. There had been a slight break in the cold the last few days and, fortunately, it had not yet gotten cold enough for the strait to be impeded by ice.

"General Falloren!"

He turned, staring blankly as the younger man rushed toward him, his boots clattering on the boards of the pier. He turned to put away the remains of his early lunch before glancing back up at his companion.

You're lucky that I am not as cruel as Meira.

He said nothing, instead waiting for the soldier to give the customary salute and bow to his superior.

"What's going on, General?" Jishon asked, placing a hand to his forehead to block the sun as he stared out over the Strait.

"I don't know much more than you do. Apparently, the humans are supposed to be sending a message, and we're supposed to collect it."

"Which humans?"

Falloren pressed his thin fingertips to his forehead, staring at Jishon. "King Kylan Ursa, you ignoramus."

Jishon took a step back, hands raised, as though worried that Falloren might strike him for his insolence. At the moment, he was considering it.

"He's King of Aridmoor and Steward of Silverfell. He's obviously the only person in Kaveryth worth making a deal with."

Jishon looked up at him, his handsome brow knitted with confusion. "But what of the Envoy?"

Falloren ignored him. The boy was not King and never could be, and his so-called army consisted of a few peasant boys hiding in the mountains and playing with wooden swords. He was not worthy of their concern.

"I was the one to broker our end of the agreement," Falloren said instead. "The Regent sent me to High Keep palace to deliver a message to the King personally. She's giving him a better deal than I ever thought she would, but I suppose we'll see what comes of it."

Jishon stared at him, surprised enough that he kept his mouth shut and listened, for once.

"Anyway, the King promised to send back his messengers with his reply, so long as I agreed they would not be harmed upon reaching our borders."

He paused for dramatic effect. Before three seconds had passed, Jishon was stepping toward him, as eager as a baby kelpie seeking rotten fish.

"And you—we—agreed?"

"Yes," Falloren said smoothly. "The Regent gave me full authority to act, and I accepted the King's proposal."

What he did not say was that despite Meira's assurances that she trusted him to act, he had been terrified of giving the King an answer that she would later disapprove. The woman was not known for her forgiving spirit.

"So where are these messengers?" Jishon asked, staring out at the chilly water again as another boat full of soldiers floated by the pier.

"The boat was spotted just north of us. It should be here any minute. Hence why you shouldn't have been late," Falloren couldn't help but to add.

"Apologies, sir," Jishon said, but he barely heard him.

"Well," the elder elf said "it seems you were lucky this day."

He gestured with one finger toward the Strait, where a simple fishing boat of obvious human design was approaching.

They waited, but when the boat reached the end of the pier, it did not stop.

Falloren felt a clenching in his gut as he examined the boat more closely, alarmed by the slow way that it was bobbing along in the current.

"It's going right past us," Jishon said, the words several moments too late, as he stared.

Falloren shouted at the vessel, demanding that they dock immediately, but his words were half-obscured by the sound of the winter breeze rushing against the water.

Could Ursa's men have fallen ill? Is anyone even on board?

"This might be an easier mission than we thought," Jishon joked.

Falloren turned to stare at him, resisting the urge to let his mouth fall open. Instead, he grabbed the man by the top of his collar, his silvery fingers wrapped tightly in the leather fabric.

"If the King thinks we harmed his men, any chance of a deal is off," he snapped, holding his face barely an inch away from Jishon's. "Now, I may not care, and you may not care, but for whatever reason, Meira Daeleth does. And she will kill us if we do not carry out her orders."

He let Jishon go, turning to head down the pier without waiting for the blundering fool to follow him.

"You!" he shouted to one of the men working nearby, who was holding a large coil of partially frozen rope. "Seize that human vessel immediately, or it's your head!"

Jishon appeared a moment later, and the two men watched as the dockman sprung into action, calling on two of his associates to help him. Within seconds, they had managed to dig their metal hooks into the boat's wooden side, no doubt sending freezing water belowdecks.

"We can't pull it in, General," one of the men called to him, gesturing to a chunk of ice that lay directly in front of the vessel, blocking its path.

That, King Ursa, is why one should generally send manned ships.

He gave a sigh and motioned to Jishon to follow him, pushing past the men, who stood there shouting apologies. No matter. He'd handle this himself.

"Ah," he said after looking at the edge of the water for a couple of moments. "Get in."

He waited as Jishon boarded a small rowing dinghy, eyeing the twin oars with suspicion.

"There's no magic in this kind," Falloren said, rolling his eyes and taking hold of one of the oars. "We have to provide the power. Let's go."

Jishon grabbed hold of the other oar, and the two of them managed to pull up beside the fishing boat. Falloren took hold of the rope ladder that hung off of the side of the human vessel and pulled himself up on it, and motioned to Jishon to follow.

There was no sound as the men made their way up to the deck. Falloren could feel the gentle motions of the water below, and he placed his free hand against the siderail to steady himself as he took hold of his sword.

Jishon did the same, and they began to walk toward the wooden hatch, keeping their footsteps light. If this was a trap, Falloren was not about to make it easy for them to spring it on him.

As his feet hit the floor of the lower deck, he struggled to blink away the sudden darkness.

"Show yourselves!" Jishon shouted, holding his sword straight in front of him.

Falloren was about to chastise him for being a coward

and a fool besides, but before he could say anything, he felt something hit the end of his toe.

He blinked again, the room slowly coming into focus.

He could see the streaks of sunlight that were pouring in through the holes in the hatch door, casting a pattern of prison bar stripes against the ground.

He could see the barrels of provisions stacked up near the steep stairs, and smell the hint of ale and dried fish.

And laying on the floor in front of them, he could see a dozen elven men in full armor, with flowers clasped against their chests in folded hands.

The two elves stood there in shock for a moment, but finally, Jishon broke the silence.

"Look," he choked out, a hand to his mouth as though he might be sick.

Falloren saw the note right away, a piece of parchment rolled neatly and held instead of flowers by one of the men.

He plucked it free, suddenly uninterested by the horrible tableau that lay in front of him, and began to read the short missive.

I'm sure that the meaning of my "message" is obvious, but allow me to spell it out for the Regent:

No deal.
Never.

Yours,

Kylan Ursa,
King of Aridmoor

Steward of Silverfell
Leader of the Red Army

6

Chapter 5

WES

As soon as Wes stepped into the great hall, he knew that something was wrong, but he struggled to see what was going on. People pressed in on all sides, far more than the building could comfortably fit, and he gripped Aelrie's hand more firmly within his own as he walked.

Struggling to concentrate as dozens of people greeted him, some bowing, some with tears of joy on their faces, he reached out to Celesyria within his mind.

"Celesyria? What's going on?"

There was no answer, but he doubted that he would have been able to hear her even if there was. He watched as Jaconial flew back out through the hole in the roof, probably to collect a few of the other captives who had been lagging behind on their way into the city. They had pushed hard today, and many were close to collapsing from exhaustion, but at least they had finally made it to safety.

Jaconial's voice sounded in his mind, startling him. *"Get to the back courtyard, Wes. Quickly. It's Celesyria."*

He couldn't find the words to reply. Terrible possibilities swirled in his mind as he tried to push through the crowd, the chattering din making his headache even worse than it had been all morning.

"Wes?" Aelrie asked as she kept pace with him, people stepping out of her way as she went.

"It's Celesyria," he said, stopping for a moment and turning to look at her. There was no use in panicking. "Something is wrong. I have to go to her. Can you stay here?"

Aelrie's brow furrowed with concern, but she nodded, giving his hand a squeeze.

Just then, Wes spotted a familiar face. Moorn, a Silverfell soldier who he had known since he was a child. He called to him, and the man embraced him in a hug, no doubt hoping for a pleasant reunion.

"I'll talk to you later, okay?" he said brusquely, disentangling himself from his old friend. "Can you take care of Aelrie?"

Moorn glanced at the elf and extended a hand for her to shake, his face filled with more than a little trepidation. Wes hated to leave Aelrie in any uncomfortable situation, but she would trust Moorn easily enough.

If Celesyria needed him, he would be there, no questions asked.

Not so long ago, she had been the only one who believed in him, the only one who believed that the Envoy was destined to be more than a delivery boy for an ancient protection racket. Without her, it was unlikely that Aelrie would be here now, preparing to profess her allegiance to the High One.

With a final parting glance at the elf woman, he made his

way to the back door and raced through it, nearly knocking over a group of women who were making their way back into the fray.

"Sorry," he said flatly, spotting Celesyria and her mother, Sharsi, walking together near the far side of the expanse. The rest of the courtyard was deserted, save for a few teenage boys hanging around near the sparring grounds. The training area had been expanded since he left, and he couldn't help but to notice the tidy new weapon racks and bow targets as he hurried past.

"Celesyria?" he asked aloud, feeling suddenly embarrassed to be intruding on an important moment between mother and daughter.

"I'll be in my new quarters," Sharsi said, taking a couple of stilted steps and jumping into the air. He watched for a moment as she flew, noticing that she still moved strangely thanks to her half-missing limb.

Celesyria said nothing, but her expression spoke volumes.

"It's my father," she choked out, bowing her head so low that her chin almost brushed against the dirt.

Wes was at her side at once, placing his hand gently against her flank, the feeling of her orange scales familiar against his palm.

"I'm so sorry," he said, knowing that the words were entirely inadequate.

"We might have been able to save him," she said, raising her head to look at him, her yellow eyes filled with an anger that he had never seen in them before. "But there was never a chance."

He opened his mouth to speak, but she continued, standing up to her full height. Without quite meaning too, he took a couple of steps back, drawing his hand away.

"There was always something more important, someone who needed me more. Now my own flesh and blood, the creature who raised me ever since I escaped my egg, is gone."

Guilt poured through him, as harsh and bracing as ice water.

She was right. He couldn't imagine how he would feel if he had refused even a small chance to save his family. He'd never forgive himself.

"Celesyria, I'm—"

"Stop!" she said aloud, her words escaping in a roar that sent him tripping backward to get away. Until that very moment, he had never quite realized just how powerful the dragon was. He had never seen her angry like this, not at him.

For a long moment, they stood there, the teenagers watching open-mouthed from across the courtyard as they faced off.

Wes forced himself to meet her gaze, hoping that she understood what he felt he could not quite say.

I love you, Celesyria.

I'm sorry.

I wish we had chosen differently, or had found another way to help him. I hope you'll forgive me.

He waited, and after a while, the dragon was the one to break the silence, the rage fading from her eyes just as quickly as it had come.

"Don't apologize," she finished, her usual girlish tone returning with an undercurrent of bitterness. "It's not you I'm angry at. This is the fault of the High One."

KESSARA

Kessara sat upright in bed as she heard the knock at her door, trying to blink the sleep from her eyes.

"Hold on, my love," she said, forcing her tired limbs to move. She stepped onto the floor, wincing as the cold wooden boards hit her bare feet, and unhitched the lock.

Within a moment, Alder was inside the room, and they were kissing. She felt awake at once, enjoying the feeling of his lips on hers, the current of energy passing between them. Soon enough, the other travelers at the Inn would be heading down for a taste of Fira's cooking, but for the moment, the place was quiet and still.

She placed a hand on Alder's chest, savoring the feel of his taut muscles beneath her fingertips as he continued to press his lips against hers.

They didn't have to stop.

No one would ever know.

"Wait," Alder said at once, as if reading her thoughts as he pulled away, wiping his lips with the back of his hand.

The High One would know. He would know that after He made a way for us, we spit in his face in order to chase our desires.

"I'm sorry," she said.

Alder shook his head.

"No. I'm the one who needs to be more careful. Forgive me, my Princess."

She reached over and gave his hand a squeeze, taking a moment to examine his features, committing every inch of him to memory. His red curls were messy, and his green eyes were searching hers. He had been awake for several hours already, but he did not look the least bit tired.

"I know I'm lovely to stare at, but we need to leave," he said, pointing toward the leather bags that rested near the edge of her bed. She stuck out her tongue at him, but did as he asked, picking up her few belongings and shoving them into pockets.

"I can't believe that I used to have servants to do this," she said, not turning to look at him. "And servants to carry my bags on the road, too."

"I'd do it, but you'd say I packed wrong," Alder retorted, sitting down on her mattress while he waited. She couldn't resist a smile. He wasn't wrong. She'd yet to meet a man who knew how to pack for a journey properly.

"I miss it," she said, stuffing two simple blue dresses into the last bag and forcing the drawstring closed.

"Having servants?"

She shook her head, though she supposed she did miss that, just a little.

"I miss knowing who I am, and knowing exactly what I'm supposed to do with my life. Knowing who I'm meant to be."

"Freedom is a gift," Alder said.

She nodded.

"I know it is, and I'm thankful for it," she assured him, leaning over to give him an innocent peck on his stubbled cheek. "But that doesn't mean it isn't frightening. I used to have it all together. I had a destiny. And now, I'm lost."

"I guess I can't relate," Alder said, picking up two of her bags and slinging them over his shoulder. "I grew up with a prostitute for a mother and a father in jail. I was never meant to be anything. I pushed myself to get everything that I have."

"So humble," she said, pretending to punch him on the arm as she grabbed her final, smaller bag. She was only half joking. Alder tended toward pride and arrogance, but then again, she understood why he did. His life had been difficult from the start, and he'd been forced to rely on himself even as a young child.

To her surprise, he did not joke back. Instead he rested against the door frame, looking off into nothing.

"You're right, you know," he said finally, adjusting the weight on his shoulders. "It wasn't all me. The High One led me, even before I knew who He was. Left to my own devices, I would have found the bottom of a barrel and the inside of a cell, just like my father."

"You still had to obey Him," she insisted. "You fought to be free."

"That's true, I suppose," he said, pushing the door open and ushering her through.

"In any case, you still have your purpose, Kessara. Your father will understand. He'll take you back, and you'll be Princess of Galeharbor again, just as soon as you explain what's going on."

"And then time will pass, my parents will die, and we will be King and Queen."

"Maybe we'll have a difficult, stubborn, unreasonable daughter of our very own," Alder said.

She laughed at the serious look on his face.

Despite everything that was happening in her life and in the world, she was happier than she had been in so many years.

Thank you, High One. For him. For us. For all of this.

They made their way down the stairs and into the bar, where Fira was already hard at work. Her cat, Nibbler, stood atop a shelf filled with beer mugs, yowling at the ceiling.

"Good morning, my loves," the barkeeper said, handing them each a metal flask painted with geometric patterns in every color. "A gift. So you won't forget to come back and visit us in Rill one day."

"I promise that we will," Alder said, reaching out to shake the woman's hand. Kessara leaned forward to give the woman a hug over the countertop, passing her flask to Alder.

"Thank you for all of your kindness," she said.

She had enjoyed her time in the village very much, despite the poverty and the crime that had surrounded her. Only the wealthy, highly educated folks knew her face, and Rill had relatively few such people. It had been pleasant, not having to hide, and more than that, she'd enjoyed seeing the kindness in people when she had nothing to offer them. There was good here, even in the wild depths of Boneshire, and she was sad to leave the place behind.

With a final goodbye to Fira, and a couple of local men who had stumbled downstairs while they talked, they made their way out into the streets of Rill.

Alder clasped her hand as they walked silently in the dawn light, and even though they had to pass by several of the roughest streets in town to reach their destination, she felt at peace.

When they reached their camp, Nazzan was already awake, pacing around the remains of the prior night's fire as he waited. Within a few minutes, their bags secured to his saddle, they were climbing onto his back.

"Are you sure about going to High Keep, Princess?" Nazzan asked, stretching out his long green neck to look back at them. "We could go to Auranth now, as we had once planned. Or even to Galeharbor, to see your parents. We don't have to go to Ursa."

"Did Alder put you up to this?" she asked, raising her

eyebrows in the dragon's direction.

"Yes," he admitted. "But I agree with him. You're taking a real risk."

"I understand the risks," she said firmly, turning to look at Alder. "But you both need to trust me a little. I think I've earned it, after all this time."

"I do trust you," Alder said, rubbing at his temples with his fingertips as though she'd given him a sudden headache.

"Me too," the dragon chimed in as he faced forward again. Kessara watched as he lifted a wing, feeling the direction of the wind.

She took hold of the saddle straps.

"Alder," she said, forcing herself to keep her voice gentle. "I understand why you feel this way. I do. But you can't let your personal feelings for me and concern for my safety override what's best for Kaveryth. If there's even a small chance to change the course of history, we need to take it. We cannot lose this war."

Alder said nothing for a moment, gathering his own saddle straps in his hands.

"Okay," he said finally, letting out a slow breath. "High Keep it is."

She held on tight as Nazzan leapt into the sky, his powerful wings pumping against the current of air.

She'd talk to Kylan, and all would be well. She knew it.

7

Chapter 6

CELESYRIA

The next few days passed in a blur, and Celesyria was thankful to find that she was able to go through the motions of life despite her sorrow. Wes, Aelrie, and her mother tried to comfort her, but their words did not help, and she felt guilty for causing them more pain. For the most part, she sought to avoid people entirely, which was not so easy in the newly-bustling forge. Even Auranth itself was busy now, with few places where she could find solitude.

But there was always the sky.

She was flying now, beneath the moon and the stars, thankful for the silence. She glanced down at the forest below, wondering if any bandits or elves waited there, hidden in the trees. Even now that the leaves had fallen, there were still plenty of shadows to spare. She knew that she should stay over the skies of Auranth, where it was safe, but she couldn't help but be drawn to the vastness beyond.

She could see the West Strait, black and rippling, probably

filled with elven boats. To the east were the mountains, and beyond them lay the greater forests of Silverfell, so large that the race of men had not come close to mapping them all. Here, she was free.

Almost free, at any rate.

She felt the tightness of the manacles on her ankles, a reminder that the past wasn't always easy to ignore.

Not that I want to forget everything. There are so many things I want to remember, even if the memories break my heart.

She glanced at the sky, spotting constellations, a habit that had been instilled in her by her father ever since her hatchling days. The stars were beautiful here, away from the bright lights of Auranth below. The humans would be awake for several hours yet, and she doubted that she would return before most of them retired to their beds, putting out candles and torches and lanterns as they went.

"*Hello, father,*" she called out in her mind, noticing Vavoren, the Shield, her father's favorite constellation. "*I hope that wherever you are, you're happy.*"

She waited, remembering.

She and her father had shared so many happy nights. Her mother would scold them for venturing so far out of the caverns of Whitespire, but she always relented eventually. Clear nights in Umrym were frequent, and with the dwarves and dragons living in caves, there was little light to sully the blackness.

She wondered if her mother regretted not coming with them, now that her husband of hundreds of years was dead and gone.

She turned in the sky, tilting her wings so that she banked gently to the left. The thoughts in her mind were so troubling that she struggled to keep her altitude steady.

"High One, did he suffer?" she asked aloud, her voice echoing through the mountains as she approached. "If he did, will anyone ever tell me? Will I ever know how his life ended?"

She had not expected an answer, but still she was surprised by the anger that took hold of her heart.

All she knew was that father had died in retaliation for the deaths of a group of elves that King Ursa's men had killed. The King had delivered their bodies by boat to Nox, intending to send a gruesome message.

Gossip about the surrounding events had been swirling for a couple of weeks, before Celesyria and her friends arrived. Apparently, the Regent of the elves had sought to make a deal with the King, securing the surrender of the Red Army and the citizens of Aridmoor and Silverfell in exchange for some sort of joint rule. King Ursa knew better than to trust such an offer, and even if Meira Daeleth's words were somehow genuine, Celesyria doubted he ever would have surrendered, anyway.

The whole thing made her feel numb. She admired her father's courage in standing up to the elves in the first place, back when even her mother was unwilling to openly question the status quo. But in the end, his death seemed pointless.

She wasn't angry at Wes, or Aelrie, or even King Ursa. She knew that they had other loyalties and factors to consider in deciding what to do.

But for her, it was different. It was her father. Was her duty to Kaveryth as a whole really more important than her duty to her family?

Had the High One wanted her to go to Nox, to try and save

him, even if she went alone?

She slowed her pace as she reached the foothills of the mountains, watching below for any movement. Depressed as she was, she harbored no desire to be struck with enemy arrows.

"You could talk to me any time, High One," she said aloud again, looking over at the city in the distance, where her friends were probably worrying about her as usual. "Perhaps if You told me what You want from me now and then, I'd find it easier to please You."

She heard only the sound of the breeze as she flew, the cold air burning her nostrils as she picked up speed, taking another loop near the mountains. She was not quite ready to go home, if she could even call Auranth that.

She thought of the body of her friend, Gramnok, laying somewhere beneath the ruins of Whitespire, the home that she and her mother had left behind. The place was probably swarming with elves by now.

Jaconial would be leaving in a few days, just as soon as she'd gotten enough rest. As a Guardian, her oath bound her to fight the elves directly, and she wouldn't risk much delay.

She thought of Nazzan, wondering if he was still with Kessara and Alder, or if he had heard the same call by now. Assuming he was alive at all.

Concern for her friends pierced the dryness of her heart.

She didn't want to imagine Jaconial and Nazzan on the battlefield, hopelessly outnumbered. But even worse was the thought of the Guardians not being there, of the entire defense of Kaveryth being left to the race of men and a few dwarves.

"Will we fight them, too?" she called out to the sky, her

voice thick with bitterness. "Will we come to our end on the battlefield, cut down, nothing but blood and flesh? Do we matter to You at all, after all we've sacrificed?"

Her throat felt raw as her words rose into a shout, but she welcomed the pain. It was better than feeling numb.

Before she could say anything else, she noticed movement out of the corner of her eye on the mountain pass below.

She dove, pulling her wings toward her body in hope of making herself a slightly smaller target. She had to get a closer look. As far as she knew, no messengers had been sent heralding new soldiers coming to fight. If enemies were marching on their gates, she had to warn everyone, and fast.

The moon cast shadows amid the stones, bathing much of the path in darkness, but she could see no flash of steel to indicate weapons. She squinted against the darkness, flapping her wings as she drew as near as she dared.

Slowly, the strange scene began to come into focus as the mysterious figures strode into the pale moonlight. And all at once, she knew.

They were not soldiers, but dwarf women, pulling carts laden with dragon eggs.

ALDER

The fog clung to the plains of Aridmoor, a stubborn veil that made it almost impossible to navigate the open, nearly featureless terrain. Alder leaned down against Nazzan's green neck, clinging carefully to the ridge of thick scales along his spine as he tried to get a decent view of the ground.

Every so often, the mist would part for a few moments, but it usually revealed nothing more than open grassland, the sunlight piercing the haze and sweeping away the shadows below.

"See anything?" Kessara called from where she sat, perched more securely on the saddle behind him. He glanced over his shoulder at her, shaking his head. Though the late afternoon sun was warm, the air itself was cold, and every time he spoke, the harsh breeze irritated his lungs. Kessara wore her woolen cloak pulled tightly over her blonde hair, with a scarf to cover the bottom of her face. Still, he knew that she couldn't be very comfortable with the cold wind buffeting her body at every moment.

The past several days of travel had been unpleasant for all three of them, and tempers had run high more often than he would have liked. Winter had come to the plains, and though the snow had not yet begun to fall, the air was vicious.

"We'll have to fly low soon," Nazzan said aloud, for Kessara's benefit. Alder could feel the rumbling of the dragon's chest as he spoke, and he settled himself back into the saddle in front of Kessara. "It's going to get dark, and I need to know where I'm landing. High Keep has to be close. The constellations last night cannot deceive as the mists do. "

"*I see no better option,*" Alder said, glad that he had improved his mindspeaking skills enough to speak with Nazzan when necessary. It was certainly preferable to shouting over the icy wind. "*Just try not to land in a Red Army camp.*"

"*Knowing my luck, I'll stick my foot straight into a tent full of elves,*" Nazzan quipped.

Satisfied, Alder rested as Kessara wrapped her arms around his shoulders, trying to borrow some scrap of his nonexistent body heat. Annoyance and guilt coursed through him in equal measure. She was the one who had forced them to take this road, in the most open part of Aridmoor, to get to High Keep. Elves aside, he would have still preferred to fly nearer to the western coast, where the seasons were a little more forgiving.

On the other hand, she was the woman that he loved, and it made his heart ache to see her in any sort of pain. He hated that he couldn't do anything to make it better. Their stores of food were running thin, but they could not risk stopping here to purchase more supplies. He wouldn't allow Kessara to venture into one of the small villages alone, but he was far too infamous in these lands to attempt it himself, especially without the means to construct a proper disguise.

No. They would simply have to push through.

He leaned into Kessara's embrace, thankful that she was near. No matter what they'd been through together, her presence had a way of making everything better.

Nazzan continued to fly for what felt like a long time, flapping his wings against the currents of wind, tilting and shifting his position to keep them as steady as possible.

Finally, the sun dipped below the fog, and within minutes it became nearly impossible to see.

"I'm heading down," Nazzan said, banking to the left as a particularly nasty gust of wind hit him full in the face. Alder could hear Kessara murmuring some kind of response, her head buried in his back, trying to avoid the cold.

"Sounds good. We won't be able to see until the stars are out, and I don't want to miss it," Alder replied, lowering his own body until he was almost level with Nazzan's neck. At this point, he didn't care if they made it or not. He just wanted to land, and hopefully find a place to hide from the wind.

Alder grasped the saddle straps tightly as Nazzan dove

beneath him, making his stomach lurch. Despite his misery, he felt like letting out a whoop of happiness. He loved to fly.

Just as soon as they'd broken through the thick cover of mist, he realized that they had made the right call.

Up ahead, not two miles away, he could see the towering stone buildings of his home city, the capital of Aridmoor.

My sisters and mother are safe in Graveheim, Raela is dead, and half of my old friends have probably joined Wes's army in Auranth by now. There's nothing waiting for me in High Keep.

He felt a pang in his heart at the sight of it, all the same.

"I don't see many trees," Nazzan said as he circled over the grassland below. "Where am I supposed to wait around this time?"

"You won't be alone this time," Kessara called out. "Alder will be keeping you company."

"Come on, Kessara. I agreed about you going to High Keep, but you need to allow me to escort you, at least."

He considered reminding her of what had almost happened the last time she was alone in this city, but decided against it. That night had traumatized her enough already, and besides, Kessara wasn't stupid. She could hardly have forgotten.

Before the Princess could answer, Nazzan spotted a large rock, with a few scraggly trees growing next to it. The dragon circled a final time, his keen eyes searching for hidden foes within the sparse shadows, and after a few more seconds they were safely on the ground.

"By the Wrathlands!" Kessara swore, yanking her packs off of Nazzan's saddle and rushing toward the far side of the rock, pulling her cloak tight against the screaming wind. Alder followed her, relieved that the huge stone served as a decent windbreak. He doubted a fire would be possible until the weather calmed down, but at least they could catch their breath.

The wind howled through the trees, a lonely sound that reminded Alder of a woman crying. He sat next to Kessara, their backs against the stone, as Nazzan tried to fit as much of his massive form as he could in the shelter of the rock. Alder wondered if being coldblooded made such temperatures more or less unbearable, but for the moment, he had more important questions to ask.

"Anyway," he said, turning to meet Kessara's eyes. "As I was saying, you need to let me escort you to the palace."

"Just because King Ursa's men have looked the other way the last couple of times they've seen you doesn't mean you should wander onto his home turf," Kessara said.

She wasn't wrong. When it came to their external enemies, he had found himself allied with the Red Army out of necessity, but he knew that such courtesy was limited.

"You'll be recognized," the Princess continued, undoing her blonde braids as she spoke and letting her hair fall loose. "It was bad enough before, but now all of the citizens will be waiting for elves to appear on their doorstep, not to mention the soldiers. You won't be able to sneak in this time."

"And you will? You're the Princess of Galeharbor, for Dracodei's sake!"

"I haven't been restored to the monarchy yet."

"Doesn't mean the people have forgotten your face," Alder snapped. "Don't be foolish."

"I'll find a way," she said coolly, pulling her hood back, the residual breeze taking hold of her hair and sending it flying into her face. "You need to trust me, Alder, or—"

"Or what?"

"If you'd let me finish a sentence, maybe you'd know."

"I want to know. What were you going to say, Kessara?"

"You can guess, you brute—"

Suddenly, there was a sound like thunder.

"Enough!" Nazzan shouted, his voice so loud that Alder could feel the rock shaking slightly behind him. For once, he was happy for the storm. Had the evening been clear, the dragon would've been heard all the way in High Keep.

Kessara caught his eye, her cheeks pink, and he wondered if there was more to her blushing than simply the cold.

He didn't speak. Instead, he extended his hand, and to his relief, she knit her small fingers with his large ones. He breathed out, trying to let go of the knot of frustration that rested deep within his chest. He hated fighting with the woman he loved, but he doubted that their arguments would disappear any time soon. He'd just have to find a way to keep himself on a more even keel, whatever the Princess said.

"Now," Nazzan said, lowering his head, his huge eyes searching their faces. "Have you both settled down?"

Chastened beneath the dragon's almost fatherly gaze, he nodded, and gave Kessara's hand a gentle squeeze, which she returned.

The Princess nodded as well.

"I should really be the offended one here," Nazzan said, raising a single scaly brow. "No one thought to ask me what *I* think should be done."

Resisting the urge to sigh, Alder asked, "What's on your mind, Nazzan?"

The dragon gave them a sharp-toothed grin, pausing for a little longer than necessary before answering.

"Kessara won't need a disguise at all."

"What do you mean?" the Princess asked, pulling her knees to her chest and looking up at the dragon. Alder nodded in agreement.

"Everyone knows her face. A disguise would be pointless," the dragon reminded him. "I think a more direct route is called for. I think that the Princess should march right up to the city gates and demand a meeting with the King."

8

Chapter 7

ALDER

Alder opened his mouth to argue with Nazzan, but as he thought about the idea more, he remained quiet.

It was a gutsy plan, but he had to admit that the dragon had a point.

He knew from personal experience that many of the men in the King's Protectorate were a bunch of pigs, but he doubted that even they would dare to cause any sort of bodily harm to a member of the House of Manta. And if she wasn't hiding from the soldiers in the first place, she wouldn't have to worry about running into unsavory characters on the streets.

"That...actually makes sense," Kessara said finally, catching Alder's eye. "If King Ursa is going to refuse to talk to me, what does it matter if I'm at the gate or in the palace?"

"True enough," Alder said. "It's the best option. But I'd feel a lot better if I brought you near the city walls, so I can make sure that you make it safely into the custody of the soldiers."

He kept his words soft, expecting her to argue, but to his surprise, she readily agreed.

"You just need to avoid being seen," she added.

Alder scoffed. "Do you forget who you've fallen in love with, my dear? I know how to hide in the shadows."

Kessara rolled her eyes, but when he leaned over to offer her a gentle kiss on the lips, she didn't pull away.

"The way you humans show affection is quite repulsive," Nazzan said, curling a lip in disgust. "So undignified."

Alder chuckled. "I hope you'll give Jaconial whatever sort of dragon hug you prefer when you finally see her. I'm sure she misses you terribly."

Nazzan glanced overhead, though there was nothing to look at but the mist that continued to hang stubbornly in the sky, unbothered by the rushing wind.

"I miss her, too," he said, not meeting Alder's eyes. "She's strong, I know that, but I still have worries. Just like you do with Kessara."

"Admittedly, your betrothed is a dragon," he pointed out, planting a mock-punch on Nazzan's shoulder. "Kessara is a tad more breakable."

"Hey," the Princess warned, picking up a small stone that rested near her feet and throwing it at him. "Just because I don't breathe fire doesn't mean I'm weak."

"Fair enough," he said, shaking his head. Kessara *was* strong, and that fact tended to get her into trouble.

"Well," Nazzan said, stretching out his front leg, his front claws making a terrible grinding sound against the tall stone. "I think that now is as good a time as any to head out. The faster you get this done, the faster we can find somewhere decent to really rest."

Alder looked up in surprise. He'd expected that they'd wait until dawn, but he didn't blame Nazzan for wanting to hurry. The dragon would be forced to sleep out in the elements, and he doubted he'd even be able to pitch their tents in this wind.

"Fine by me," Kessara said, getting to her feet and brushing bits of dead gray grass from the back of her blue skirt.

"I agree," Alder added. "Besides, there will be fewer guards to charm at night."

It took nearly an hour for the two of them to reach the outskirts of the city, the weather remaining stubbornly terrible for the entire walk.

Still, Alder was thankful for the fog and the darkness. Now that they were on the ground, he knew the area well, and he only needed a small circle of lamplight to guide their way. He doubted that anyone would see the light through the mist, but still, he kept a fair distance behind Kessara as they got closer, though never so far that he wouldn't be able to take up his sword and defend her at a moment's notice.

He saw no guards on the dirt road that led to the main gate, and he assumed most of them would stay against the well-lit wall tonight. When he was a soldier, he would have done the same. It was foolish to try and guard a road separately in the dark.

Finally, he could see the heavy wood-and-metal gate up ahead. Kessara looked over her shoulder at him, and he waved her on, waiting behind one of the decorative oak trees that had been planted alongside the wide path.

He watched as she approached, and as soon as he saw the gate guard, his hackles rose.

It was an older man, named Broma or Groma or something of the sort, and he was known for his unpleasantness. He closed his eyes for a moment and said a brief prayer to the High One, hoping that their stroke of bad timing did not jeopardize the plan.

Of course, even if she had snuck in, she would have had to pass some kind of guard, but the smaller gates to the east and west of the city were not so heavily watched, nor so heavily armored.

He cupped a hand to his ear, straining to listen as Kessara pulled back her hood, revealing her identity. As if by a miracle—and, considering his prayer, perhaps it was—the biting wind settled a little, and he could just make out what was being said.

"I'm Lady Kessara Manta, and I wish to request an urgent audience with the King."

He could hear Brom or Grom chuckling, his own hood obscuring his face in shadow, though Alder recognized his tall, slender form all the same. "Princess Manta may have been able to make such a request, but I'm afraid Lady Manta may not have the same sway."

Alder could see only Kessara's back, but he could picture her face now, smiling sweetly at the man and taking a few steps closer to him as she spoke.

"I think only of you when I say this, my good man, but you would be wise to let Kylan Ursa be the judge of that. I've known him since we were children, and he's not the type to take kindly to insubordination."

The man shook his head.

"Nothing appealing about an uppity woman," he muttered, and Alder flinched, waiting for Kessara to lose her temper. To his relief, she remained quiet as the man continued to talk.

"You can't see him anyhow. He's off to Galeharbor, to see

the King. Perhaps you might have known that, if you had not shirked your duty to your people to marry that filth Cadogen."

Alder was amazed at just how detailed the gossip was, even after it spread halfway across the continent.

Still, Kessara did not move.

"May I ask the reason for this meeting?" she said, altogether too politely.

To his surprise, the man stammered a little as he responded, sounding almost contrite.

"Rumor is that the Red Army wants those boats back in the West Strait. I'm not surprised, considering."

Kessara shifted her position, and Alder could just see her face through the mist as she stared at the man, as though daring him to mention her part in pulling the navy back to Kingsvier Landing in the first place, but he said nothing.

Good. The Strait may be weakened, but at least Galeharbor has something to bargain with.

"Anyway," the guard continued, sounding almost pleasant. As usual, Alder was amazed what a little regal charm could accomplish. It was not a talent he expected to master. "Some Red Army men have defected to Auranth. Especially the Galeharborian conscripts, I hear."

He paused, and he could imagine Kessara weighing her words, wondering whether or not to take the bait the man offered. Instead, the Princess said nothing, offering the man a half-bow of thanks before turning to face the road out of the city once again.

Alder waited, grasping the leafless branches of the oak tree between his fingertips as the surly gate guard returned to the shelter of his little hut.

The Princess did not give him even a glance as she passed,

instead walking at a steady but relaxed pace, a ghost retreating into the Aridmoor darkness as the man she loved kept watch.

WES

Wes gazed down into the crackling fire, watching as orange sparks danced against the patch of night sky that he could see through the hole in the ceiling. His head had been aching ever since he stepped out of his comfortable bed—which had, to his great surprise, been reserved for him all this time—but sitting here now, he could almost forget the pain.

Aelrie was resting gently against him on the bench, her small frame engulfed by a huge quilt that Mella had covered her with.

At first, he'd been so shy to be so near to her in front of everyone, but in the end, he decided it was probably far safer than getting close to her while they were alone.

Despite the black cloud of Celesyria's mood, he and Aelrie had spent a pleasant evening together, sitting around telling tales over the flames with friends new and old. Finally, as the moon rose high over the old forge and the stubborn winds began to seep in through the cracks in the walls, the others had finally left the two of them by the fire.

He glanced over his shoulder, careful not to jostle Aelrie. Bargren's youngest son, Vade, had not moved in the last half hour. Supposedly, he was fixing one of the stone walls leading toward the sleeping quarters, but Wes was sure his real purpose was to keep an eye on the two of them, by orders of Mella or perhaps Bargren himself.

Still, they had been granted enough privacy to speak without need of whispering, and Wes had spent the last while carefully avoiding the topics that they most needed to talk about. Not that he didn't want to discuss her accepting the High One publicly, or their future marriage, but it was nice just to be with her for once, when they weren't fearing for their lives.

"I'm happy here," Aelrie was saying, her breath tickling his ear as she rested her head against his shoulder. "It feels more like home than anywhere else has in a very long time. Perhaps ever."

"I know the feeling," Wes said, clearing his throat, wishing that his heart would stop hammering in his chest every time he felt her fingers brushing his own. "I mean, Stronghollow palace was home, but..."

He didn't need to finish his sentence. She had seen with her own eyes what had become of it.

For a moment, she said nothing else, and Wes worried that he had soured the conversation. Even though the elf had given every indication in the world that she not only tolerated him, but loved him, he found it difficult to shake his general feeling of inadequacy.

She pulled back for a moment and stretched her hands over her head, letting out a yawn, and he took the opportunity to memorize her face once again. Her bone structure was beautiful, like that of any elf, but unlike the others, she did not feign her beauty with magic. Her soft silver skin, her ice blue eyes, all of it was just who she was.

He looked down at his lap before she could catch him staring again, remembering that before he had met her, he was not only plain looking, but pudgy, as well. Would she have cared about that, or would she have felt the same about him as she apparently did now?

Their love was so fresh that it felt almost delicate, as if he might shatter it with the simplest of mistakes.

He couldn't decide if his worries had merit or not, but sitting there now, the fire warming his knees and the woman he loved resting on his shoulder, he decided that it didn't matter.

The High One had given him a miracle, and he was not about to let his own self-doubt ruin it.

"How many soldiers do we have now?" she asked, silencing his racing thoughts.

He shook his head. "Even Bargren doesn't seem to know exactly. Men have been showing up faster than he can document them. But it's more than I ever imagined, that's for sure."

"Not to mention the small Auranthian force that was already here, and the aid that the civilians have been providing," Aelrie added. "One of the women working in the kitchen told me that even the Magistrate is with us, and most of his staff besides."

Wes hadn't heard much about the loyalties of the Auranthian administrators, but he didn't doubt her words. Bargren had been well-respected from the beginning, and their toleration was the only reason that they'd been able to put down roots of resistance here at all.

"Even King Ursa seems to be leaving us alone," Wes said, pausing to plant a kiss on Aelrie's cheek before he lost his nerve. Even though he'd kissed her on the lips more than once, he knew that every touch they shared was important, significant. He wanted to savor them all, and to please the High One besides.

"Despite the population increase, this place seems almost more isolated than before," Aelrie mused, leaning into his lips with her cheek. He could feel her smiling, and it set the butterflies in his stomach dancing once more. "There were no sacrifices demanded for the autumn feast, apparently."

"To be fair, that may be because the Septemvirate is gone," Wes pointed out, dredging up another memory that the two of them did not often speak of. Elder Bram was the Septemvirate's leader, and they had seen him die back in Stronghollow.

"Unless Elder Jate still lives," Aelrie said. "He'd be head elder by default, wouldn't he?"

Wes nodded. "He would, but that doesn't mean he'd be able to do much. Even collecting the treasures and taking them to the base of the great spire without me requires a good deal of manpower."

"True enough," Aelrie said. He could feel her shivering beneath her blanket, and he jumped up from the log that they were sitting on and threw a couple more thick sticks on the fire. They would need to sleep eventually, but he was in no hurry to send her away, and in the meantime, he'd keep her as comfortable as he could.

"Jaconial saw something interesting when she flew past the mountains the other day," Aelrie said after a pause.

"Oh?"

"Apparently she was escorting a couple of the new soldiers back, but as she rushed over a village a little to the southeast of the pass, she saw a group of three women on a wagon. The back of it was stuffed full of coins and jewels. She saw diamonds glistening in the corners of the wagon bed."

Wes let out a breath.

He'd heard rumors that people were still heading to the temples, trying to bring treasures to appease the Dracodei, even without an Envoy or access to the great spire. Even though the truth of the High One was spreading quickly across the continent, that didn't make it easy to accept.

Even now, as Kaveryth burned, the people still awaited the false salvation of the Dracodei. It was all that they knew.

"I suppose I shouldn't be surprised," he said. "It's not so easy to turn to the truth when you've been fed lies from the cradle."

Aelrie let out a wry chuckle. "I can certainly sympathize with how difficult it is."

Wes placed an arm around her shoulder, pulling her in, as though his nearness might be able to chase away the dark memories that plagued her.

"In any case," the elf said, a strand of her black hair tickling at his nose as she leaned into his embrace. "Aside from that troubling development, it's been almost too quiet around here. The calm makes me nervous."

"Me too," Wes agreed. "The elves know exactly where we are. Even if we didn't have new recruits walking through the city gates every few days and showing them the way. In any case, I doubt we've managed to avoid spies entirely."

"That's a pleasant thought," Aelrie joked, a gentle smile resting on her lips. He wanted to kiss her again, but a quick glance over in Vade's direction made it clear that they were still very much being watched. Not that the boy would have minded, but Wes could only bear so much embarrassment in one night.

"I know what you mean," he said. "Bargren has been handling things incredibly well, considering that he was thrown into leading this place while I was gone, but I still wish Kessara and Alder were here."

Aelrie nodded her agreement. "They're a good team, when they're not arguing. Kessara has the diplomacy down, and having a fighting man's insight is always helpful when one is talking about war."

"Speaking of fighting, has Bargren roped you into helping with the trainees again?"

"Of course he did. About five minutes after we got here. Actually, I promised to help the archers out at dawn, so I really do need to head to bed in a minute."

Wes gave her hand a squeeze and muttered something incoherent in response. He wanted her to stay forever, but figured it may be a tad pathetic to admit as much.

A moment of silence passed.

"Well," Aelrie said, pulling the quilt over her shoulders and revealing her simple black tunic and skirt beneath, "Aren't you going to give me a kiss goodnight?"

"Oh—yes," Wes stammered, blood rushing to his cheeks. *Will you ever stop making a fool of yourself in her presence?*

She turned to him, a teasing smile on her lips, but before he could work up the nerve, he heard the sound of flapping wings from overhead. He glanced over at the hole in the ceiling just as Celesyria's head and neck burst through, her eyes wide and filled with worry.

He got to his feet as she landed, and Aelrie did the same, not letting go of his hand. His chest clenched. Celesyria hadn't said anything to him, but it was clear by her expression that something had to be wrong.

"Wes," she said, bowing her head so that she could catch his gaze. "There are guests approaching that you will want to consult with urgently. Aelrie, too."

Unspoken words passed between them, the dragon apologizing to him and begging him for help all at once. He disentangled his hand from Aelrie's and pressed it against Celesyria's flank, her orange scales cool beneath his palm.

I'm here for you, Celesyria. Whenever you need me, and whenever you don't.

"What guests?" Aelrie was saying. Over near the stone wall next to the sleeping quarters, Vade was pretending not to eavesdrop.

"Eggs," Celesyria said, turning to look at the elf. "Brought by dwarf women."

Wes didn't know what he had been expecting her to say, but it was certainly not that.

He took Aelrie's hand again as she leaned against his chest, her expression filled with sudden pain as the memories of what she had seen flooded back. He knew what she had told him–eggs being destroyed, on purpose, by order of the elves and with the permission of their own mothers–but the burden of having seen such vicious destruction firsthand was something he could not imagine.

"I need to tell Bagren and Mella," Celesyria continued. "Luna, too. She can probably help. I need them to prepare some hatching space."

"Okay," Wes said, nodding quickly. "You tell them. Aelrie and I will meet them."

"They'll be nearing the city gate by now, on the main road," Celesyria said, stepping from foot to foot, as though she couldn't bear to stand still a single moment longer.

"Let's go," Aelrie said, tugging on his hand and nearly dragging him toward the front door of the great hall. He quickened his pace as the two of them burst into the night, the cold air as welcoming as a bucket of water being dumped on his head. He swore under his breath as they began to run, the long path into the city proper stretching before them.

As they passed the first residential streets, they saw a few women peering out of their windows, no doubt curious about what had sent the Envoy and an elf racing off into the night. They passed a few guards, Wes slowing just enough to glance at them apologetically as he struggled to keep up with Aelrie.

He didn't blame her for hurrying. The dwarves would be safe once they made it inside the city walls, but they wanted to be the first to welcome them and their fragile cargo.

Finally, they reached the main gate, and Aelrie came to a stop in front of the two guards. Wes sucked in air as quickly as he could, struggling to catch his breath, but the elf woman did not seem even slightly strained from the run.

"There are important guests arriving at any moment," she said, plastering a smile on her face. The two men looked over at Wes for confirmation, and he resisted the urge to roll his eyes. Even though the people here knew Aelrie, and she was finally free to come and go as she pleased, he knew it would take time for them to trust an elf completely.

"Aelrie is correct," he said pointedly, holding the nearer man's gaze. "Dwarf women, and dragon eggs. Please send for a few more men, in case they require transport assistance up to the old forge. And give us your lanterns."

The man scurried off immediately, giving Aelrie an exaggerated bow as he shoved his lantern into her hands. After giving Wes an extra lantern from the gatehouse, the other guard hauled on the pulley, and they stepped through as soon as the huge metal gate had lifted high enough to fit them.

A few seconds later, they were on the outside of the city walls, the dark of the forest pressing in as though preparing to consume the cheerful yellow lights of Auranth. There were guards watching from the top of the wall above, but on the ground, they saw no one as they walked tentatively along the path toward the dark woods.

"I wonder if Cingra is here, somehow," Aelrie whispered. "She was in prison, last I heard, but it's possible she escaped. I know that most of Umrym's prisons are farther east. Perhaps the elves haven't made it there yet."

"I hope she did, too," Wes agreed. "Stealing dragon eggs in order to protect them from murder is hardly a crime."

Wes shivered as he pressed in beside the elf, wishing that they'd taken a couple of seconds to grab their cloaks on the way out. As they trudged through the dark, Aelrie's keen eyes watching the shadows, he thought of Gramnok.

At the time, they hadn't understood why the dwarf had been willing to plant a bomb beneath the caverns to free Celesyria, risking the life of everyone who lived above, but once they had learned of the woman he fancied being thrown in prison, his rage made much more sense.

High One, have mercy on him.

A moment later, Aelrie held out an arm, gesturing for him to wait.

Four dwarf women appeared out of the darkness, the glow of their lanterns scarcely bright enough to light their faces. They came to a stop, letting the handles of their wagons fall to the ground behind them.

"Are you Wes Cervos?" one of them called out in a deep, rumbling voice.

"Yes."

"I'm told the little ones will be safe here."

"You're correct. Please," Wes said, gesturing for them to come forward. The women glanced at one another, but complied, dragging the wagons along behind them.

"There's an elf with me," he added. "She's a friend."

To his relief, the women kept walking.

Introductions were made, though Wes forgot the names immediately, save for the woman who had first spoken, who called herself Ramlia.

"Our friend made us promise that if anything happened to her, we would get them out," Ramlia said, gesturing to the eggs in the wagon behind her. So far as Wes could count, there were at least three in each wagon.

"Is your friend's name Cingra?" Aelrie asked, standing behind Wes, as though she might accidentally scare the women back into the forest.

The dwarf women nodded in unison.

Aelrie glanced at Wes, and he could tell what she was thinking by the sad look in her eyes. At best, Cingra was still in prison. At worst...

Before he had to say the words, Ramlia spoke again, glancing over at her friends.

"Cingra was brave. She got several out, with the help of other dwarves and human allies who sent the eggs away to be hatched in secret. Of course, it wasn't long before she was caught."

She paused, and Wes watched as she drew a breath.

"Once the elves took over Umrym, they decided they needed more space in the prisons. They liquidated all of the dragons that were being held, and most of the dwarves as well."

Ramlia did not need to say more. She glanced at her friends, letting the meaning of her words linger in the cold night air.

Cingra had been executed. There was nothing that anyone could do for her now.

9

Chapter 8

ELDER JATE

Elder Jate looked straight ahead as he passed one guard, and then another, refusing to cower away from their gaze.

"Almost there," he muttered under his breath, glancing over his shoulder at the lump of grey cloth that lay in the wagon box behind him. "Just one more man, and we'll be out."

He clucked to the horse, flicking his rump gently with the end of his whip, urging the large mare forward. He didn't want her to move too quickly–that would be suspicious–but neither did he want to linger.

The moon was high now, half-obscured by wisps of clouds, and he was thankful that the early winter night was mild.

Perhaps the High One had a hand in this, just as the young man and the girl from Boneshire said. Perhaps He is aiding me, now that I have finally chosen to do right.

He passed the gate guard, the tension in his chest releasing as he realized it was a man he recognized. The guard wouldn't even think to ask where he was going.

Elder Jate had been respected at the Academy ever since he had arrived, but now, he supposed, all of that would change.

The man waved him through with a friendly smile, and he forced himself to keep his eyes trained on the road ahead, listening to the rhythmic sound of the horse's hooves on cobblestone and the clattering of wagon wheels. He carried on like that for a while, pressing down the urge to look back, even though he knew that he had not been followed.

It had been so quiet in the strange city already–the place did not even have a pub–but here, staring off into the silent wilderlands, he realized just how alone he would soon be.

"Not alone," he said, chuckling to himself. It was safe now.

He signaled for the horse to stop, and climbed down from the wagon, giving the animal a few pats on the shoulder as he eyed the emptiness. Even in the daylight, he knew, there would be little to see but open space for miles and miles. The horse had been born and bred in Aridmoor, but he couldn't blame the creature for feeling unsettled by the vastness surrounding him.

He made his way to the back of the wagon and pulled a latch, sending the back flying open with a sound so loud that he was sure the horse would bolt.

Biting back a curse, he looked over at the creature, who was tasting the air, but otherwise remaining quite still.

Another stroke of luck, perhaps.

But the words of the child–Holga, he recalled– echoed in his mind as he climbed into the wagon bed. Talk of the High One, and of offering even the greatest sufferings to Him.

She'd told him that her God could turn pain into joy. Was it possible?

At that moment, he wasn't sure, but he hoped it was, and that hope was enough to have gotten him this far. It was something.

He pulled back the gray blankets, finding his nephew sleeping just as he had left him, his face resting near the wooden edge of the wagon where he could breathe. The boy looked more like his uncle than his own mother, a fact that Elder Jate had known since the child's birth. There was something about the way the child's nose quirked when he laughed that reminded the old man of seeing his own young face in the mirror, so very long ago.

He reached out and touched the boy's arm, testing his responses. With the help of an unwitting nurse, he had given the boy a sedative—he couldn't risk the child making some unthinking noise while they were still within earshot of the Academy—but he hoped it would be wearing off by now.

To his relief, the child's eyes began to flutter, and he stroked his brow, waiting, enjoying the silence. It was just the two of them now. The choice had been made, and he would have to live with the consequences.

The child opened his gray eyes, blinking up at the cloudy sky, his face nearly blue in the moonlight. He shivered, and Elder Jate grabbed the nearest blanket, tucking it around his thin body.

"Uncle?" the boy asked, as if noticing for the first time that his old uncle was crouching next to him. "Wh—where are we?"

"I can explain all of this better once we reach our first rest stop," Elder Jate said softly, glancing over at his horse once again. "You should sleep. I just wanted to check that you were well."

The boy stared up at the sky, not moving his head, and Elder Jate wondered if he was at that moment being assaulted by one of his horrific headaches.

Was it foolish to have brought such a sick boy out here, to travel across the world in a wagon as war breached their borders?

He pushed the thought away. The little girl was right. He had to do the right thing, no matter what the cost was. He couldn't allow his courage to falter now.

"I don't understand," his nephew said, not shifting his gaze away from the moon. "Are you taking me somewhere else where I can be cured?"

Elder Jate's tongue felt dry and heavy in his throat. His nephew knew that the scientists at the Academy had been working on a treatment for the water sickness, but he had no idea that his own uncle and Elder Dorold had stolen another little boy in order to do it.

"No, son," he said, gripping the side of the wagon with his fingertips, not wanting to meet the child's eyes. "We're not giving up hope, but it's become clear that human means are not going to be enough to heal you."

For a long time, no one spoke. He could hear the slightly wheezy sound as his nephew breathed, his chest rising and falling as he looked off into the vast night sky. Elder Jate glanced around in all directions, feeling suddenly very vulnerable out here in the open, but he saw nothing but endless dead grass.

"Are we going home, then?" the boy asked finally, his expression stoic.

"We can't. If we do, they'll bring you back to Vaevar. I can't explain right now why that would be a bad idea, but I hope you'll trust me."

"I trust you, Uncle," the boy said almost immediately. "But I want to understand."

The old man's heart softened in his chest. Despite what he had just told this dear child, he still trusted him. He still believed that his uncle would do the right thing, and make the right decisions.

If he knew all of the things I have done...

He swallowed, trying to push down the guilt that gripped him. There would be time to confess later. Right now, at least, he was doing what the High One wanted, and considering that he could not change the past, it was the best that he could hope for.

"You will. I promise," the Elder said, leaning over the boy and meeting his tired eyes. "But for now, you should sleep. We have a long journey ahead, though there will be time to rest on the way."

"Where are we going?" the boy asked, his eyes already beginning to flutter closed. Elder Jate took hold of another one of the blankets and tucked it in around him as a cold breeze swept over the plains.

"Somewhere quiet, where you can rest. Somewhere where no one will come for us."

The boy looked puzzled, but his exhaustion was too much for him to resist. A few seconds later, his eyes were closed, and Elder Jate let out a slow breath of relief. He had expected the conversation to be more difficult, underestimated the wonderful trust of a child, even a child who had just been told that he was being condemned to death.

As he stepped off of the wagon and closed the back latch, he felt hot tears welling in his eyes. With a final glance at the child he loved, he rubbed them away with the edge of his robe and climbed onto the wagon seat, taking the long leather reins in his fingers.

I hope the Cenobites in Graveheim still owe me a favor.

He had no backup plan, no other place he could think of where he—and more importantly, his nephew—would be safe. They wouldn't be able to stay forever, but for the moment, it was the best option. He was too old to be of use to the war effort, and so far as he could tell, the rest of the Septemvirate was gone.

For now, he had only one responsibility, one concern.

He would care for his nephew, pray to the High One for a miracle, and bide his time.

KESSARA

Kessara continued to walk into the mist, not daring to turn back.

Not yet.

Alder was following her, she knew, though she could not hear even the slightest sound of his boots on the dirt. The old guard at the High Keep gate wouldn't be following them—the ease of sitting in his gatehouse was far too tempting—but still, she wanted to be sure.

Finally, she came to a stop, glancing around at the mist that shrouded the landscape in all directions. She could see nothing, hear nothing, and for one frightening moment, she almost forgot the direction she had been walking in, all sense of place swallowed up by the fog.

"Kessara," came Alder's voice behind her.

A second later, he was there, wrapping her in his arms,

his chest so comfortable that for a moment she managed to forget the wind and the cold. He pulled away a couple of seconds later, a disapproving look on his handsome face as he pulled her hood back up over her hair.

"I heard it all," he said, warming her ears with his fingers. "I suppose it's good news, despite the detour."

Kessara nodded. She was not pleased that they had ventured into this frozen Wrathland for nothing, but it couldn't have been helped. "We can go to Galeharbor and I can speak to him on familiar ground."

"We'll get a chance to talk to your father about recent developments," Alder said.

She looked at her feet. The idea filled her with an unexpected sense of dread. Her father had practically disowned her for refusing to marry Wes Cervos, and even though the High One had given her a way out, she feared that it might not make a difference to King Errol Manta.

"Hey," Alder said, reaching up and taking her chin gently within his fingers. "It'll be okay. He''ll understand. I know he will."

"I know," she said, forcing herself to smile as he planted a kiss gently on her cheek.

She took his hand, and the two of them walked back toward where Nazzan was waiting, lost in their own thoughts.

She shivered beneath her cloak, the cold and the worry refusing to grant her peace.

She was free to love Alder, and he was free to love her back, but there were still so many obstacles that they had to overcome.

She pressed her eyes shut, letting Alder lead her along, remembering.

The Gorok screaming.

Celesyria's wings pounding against the sky.

Alder, sword drawn, jumping from her back.

Falling.

She gripped Alder's hand more tightly, pressing herself against him.

I thought you died. For that terrible second, I experienced a world without you in it.

The words continued to run through her mind, fears that she couldn't bring herself to give voice to. She could hear his steady breathing as he walked beside her, the only sound on the desolate road. She could see his muscled form, the only thing she could see at all in the mist.

The pain was bad enough when she wasn't allowed to love him.

Now, he was hers, she was his, and they were going to get married. They would be together forever, lashed together like twin boats cast out into a raging sea.

If something happens to you, after everything we've fought through to be together, I'm not sure I'll be able to keep on living.

The words sent a shiver up her back that had nothing to do with the cold. Surely, they weren't true. She had the High One. She had her family—well, hopefully she would again, once she got a chance to speak with her father. She had her friends.

And yet, the thought remained.

The memories of standing on the beach at Kingsvier Landing, watching the sea, her toes sinking into the sand, the forbidden longing to walk forward until the pain and the fears faded away.

She had more now to lose than she ever had before, and she

was afraid.

10

Chapter 9

CELESYRIA

There were thirteen eggs, and all of them had survived the journey from Umrym to Auranth without incident.

Celesyria touched one of them—blue with a slight hint of green—with the tip of a claw and waited. To her delight, the occupant of the egg moved within, making the egg rock just slightly on its bed of old quilts in the corner of the great hall.

She heard the loud slam of a door and looked up, preparing to growl at the offender if necessary, but no one was there. It was warm outside, despite the setting sun, and the others had for the most part concentrated their evening activities outdoors so as not to disturb the hatchlings.

Celesyria had tried to convince Mella to have some of the men drag the long rows of dining tables out into the courtyard as well, but so far, the woman had resisted. Mealtimes were cheerful affairs, all too loud for the growing ears of the hatchling dragons, but she supposed they would have to endure it.

When the dwarves had first brought them, Bargren and Wes wanted to set up the hatchery in an empty dressmaker's shop on the eastern end of Auranth, but Celesyria had not been able to fit, and, so far, had refused to leave their side at all.

It had been Aelrie who had defended her, and insisted that the little ones should be kept in the great hall, where the dragons could care for them. There had been much debate on all sides, but in the end, they had agreed that having a more natural incubation was probably the best thing for them.

Still, the others grumbled as they spent their days out in the increasingly chilly courtyard practicing their sword fighting, organizing weapons, making clothing, mending saddles, and all of the other tasks of a force preparing for battle. When they did come in, with the exception of mealtimes, Celesyria insisted that only whispers be heard.

She heard the complaints the soldiers made when they thought she wasn't listening, but she was content to ignore them. Luna had come around to the idea almost at once, and was often heard reminding the others that these were big fellows already, and within a week, it was likely that they would be ready to hatch.

The dwarf women stopped by now and then to check on the eggs, but it was clear that they had no experience with such matters. They had been friends of Cingra, but so far as they told Celesyria, they had never actually set foot in the hatchery.

"My little dear," Celesyria said to the blue egg as it settled back into place, "I hope you get some rest and dream the most lovely dreams."

She examined each of the other eggs in turn, marveling at

their bright colors and the smooth firmness of their shells. They were beautiful, like large jewels that contained an even more beautiful treasure within.

"How could anyone throw you away?" she asked a dark yellow egg, wondering when the little ones would be able to understand mindspeak. For the moment, she hoped her gentle voice was comforting to them, even if they had never heard the songs of their mothers before.

The egg didn't answer, of course, and Celesyria had no explanation of her own to give.

Few dragons were born as it was. The older ones—and some not so old—were dying off. The High One had permitted her race to uphold the illusion of the Dracodei for a thousand years, but finally, his promised punishments were coming to pass.

If the dragons did not turn to the true God, they would perish. Even so, they continued to choose their own greed, snuffing out the gift of life that the High One continued to give them despite all that they had done.

At least, that was the story that the Codex Veritatis had told, and the story that she had believed.

Now, there were new doubts needling at her heart, painful and difficult to shake.

"Be that as it may," she continued, talking to the egg as though the hatchling had heard the rest of her thoughts, "You were brought here, to Auranth, and you will be safe. You will be free, and you will learn the truth before you even learn to fly. No one will harm you here. I promise."

As she spoke the words, she heard the sudden clashing of swords and clanking of armor through the thick wall of the old forge. She let out a sigh. It couldn't be helped.

War was near, and she doubted that she would escape it. Whatever happened to her, she could only trust that the others would take care of these precious little ones.

And if the battlefield was her fate, she was sure that Wes and Aelrie would be there with her.

She hadn't spoken to either of them much as of late. She wasn't angry at them, but they reminded her of the High One, and at the moment, her feelings about Him remained complicated.

Her mother, to her credit, did not pry. She had kept to herself, settling into the simplicity of her new life, leaving Celesyria to heal from her father's death in her own time.

Jaconial, however, was much more persistent.

"How are the little monsters today?" the dragon asked as she flew through the hole in the ceiling, interrupting Celesyria's melancholy. *"Any cracks yet?"*

"None yet," Celesyria replied, not bothering to hide her annoyance. She had told Jaconial that she needed time, but her friend had appeared at least once a day to try and drag a discussion out of her.

Missing her tone, or perhaps ignoring it, Jaconial made her way toward the makeshift hatchery, lowering her huge head to examine an orange egg.

"This one is totally going to look like you," she said, closing one eye and pressing the other as close to the shell as she could. *"Or like me, I suppose. But it would probably be better if it had your loving personality."*

Celesyria gritted her sharp teeth. Usually, she would thank her friend for any sort of compliment, but that would involve continuing their conversation.

"Jaconial, I'm not upset with you, but I–"

Before she could finish her sentence, her friend had drawn herself back from the egg, staring at Celesyria with searching eyes.

They stood like that for a moment, silent as the sounds of swords clashed around them. Jaconial drew a slow breath, her gaze never wavering.

"I'm leaving, Celesyria. It's time. I just wanted you to know."

For a moment, Celesyria felt as though she couldn't remember how to form words. She'd known since they had arrived that Jaconial would have to leave for Umrym in order to fulfill her oath as a Guardian, but the reality of the situation had yet to sink in.

She stared down at the rainbow of eggs, blowing warm air out of her nostrils, trying to keep her emotions hidden, but it was no use.

Jaconial, someone who had been her enemy not so long ago, knew her far too well.

The other orange dragon took a few tentative steps toward her and rested her head on her shoulder. Outside, the sounds of battle training continued, but Celesyria hardly heard them.

She felt as though she was being torn apart from the inside, the weight of all that she had gone through finally enough to shatter what was left of her strength.

She rested in her friend's embrace, listening to Jaconial's steady breathing as the eggs stood guard in silence.

Several moments passed, but the pain remained, as jagged and fierce as it had begun.

"Celesyria, I know you don't want me to keep bothering you, and soon I won't be able to."

"No, I'm sorry–"

"Just listen."

Celesyria pulled away, looking up at the eggs, which were sitting exactly as they had been a few moments ago.

"Okay," she agreed.

"The High One has asked a lot from you. No one can doubt that," Jaconial said, her words tumbling out in a rush. *"And to be honest, he's probably going to continue to do so. I know I could remind you that He allows you this suffering because He has given you more strength than most to bear it, but you know that already, and I imagine it won't help very much right now to be reminded."*

She paused, eyebrows raised, and Celesyria nodded.

"But all of that aside, I do want you to know one more thing. I want you to know that you are the reason that I'm following the High One, and I will be thankful for that as long as I live."

Celesyria wanted to argue—after all, it was the High One who had been merciful to all of them—but Jaconial pressed on before she could say more.

"You're the best of us, Celesyria. Even though you might not feel like it right now, it's true. Your father would be proud. Your light shines on so many people."

Jaconial paused for a moment, and Celesyria found herself looking down at her feet, joy and guilt mingling within her chest.

Jaconial had been through a lot, too. She had been separated from her betrothed, and didn't even know if he was alive or dead. And yet, instead of pointing out that fact and telling her to get a grip, as Celesyria had expected her to do, Jaconial had chosen kindness.

"Anyway," Jaconial continued. *"I need to leave, but I just wanted you to know that."*

Celesyria lifted her head and looked at her friend, wanting to thank her, but the words would not seem to come.

Finally, Jaconial turned to leave.

I can't leave things like this. She's going to war. I may never see her again.

The thought made her feel sick, but that didn't make it any less true.

"Wait!" Celesyria cried aloud.

Jaconial stopped short, the hint of a grin on her scaly lips.

Celesyria glanced around the mostly-empty grand hall. She spotted Moorn heading in from the front door, and called over to him.

"Is everything alright, my lady?" Moorn asked, and Celesyria nodded quickly, amused as usual by his insistence on treating her with the deference that was usually reserved for humans.

"Can you watch the eggs?" she asked, ignoring the way Jaconial was staring at her open-mouthed. "Just for a short while. They could hatch any time now. I don't want to leave them alone."

She hoped that her trust in the young Silverfell soldier was not misplaced.

"Of course," Moorn said quickly, glancing over at the jewel-toned eggs. "I won't let them leave my sight."

Jaconial snorted.

"I'm serious," Celesyria warned. "These eggs had better be in perfect condition when I return."

With a final glance at the hatchlings, she followed Jaconial as she leapt into the air, her strong orange wings propelling her through the hole in the ceiling. As soon as she broke free of the stone ceiling, she realized that the first snowfall of the year had come to Auranth.

Celesyria glanced up at the expanse of white overhead as they began to fly higher, circling over the forge a few times before heading out over the city. Her keen eyesight picked up the thousands of individual snowflakes dancing through the air, making their way slowly toward the ground.

Suddenly, she heard Jaconial laughing, diving low toward the practical stone roofs of Auranth before soaring upward again on outstretched wings. Her scales were dotted with thousands of the tiny white flakes.

"Come on! One last race," Jaconial said, flying so close to Celesyria that their wingtips could have touched. *"And there will be no time for do-overs when you lose."*

Celesyria let out a happy roar of her own, flying as fast as she could, the two dragons neck and neck as they sped back toward the barrack tents.

And as the cold snow pricked at her eyes and the city buzzed with life beneath them, she found the strength to keep on believing, even if only for a moment.

ALDER

Alder brushed the snow from his red curls for what felt like the thousandth time, trying to keep a decent grip on the saddle as Nazzan flew toward Windshear.

"I'm ready for spring," he said, trying to rub his hands together to warm them without letting go of the leather straps entirely.

"Winter has only just started!" Kessara protested. "We had enough rain back in the autumn, and you want spring? Besides, the snow is pretty. It makes everything look magical, especially near the sea."

He turned to look at her, and, to his great irritation, she did not seem bothered by the snow in the least. In fact, she looked even more stunning than usual, her tanned skin and bright blue eyes contrasted by the expanse of white sky that surrounded them.

Despite the snow and the clouds, everything looked bright, and for the first time in days, there was almost no wind.

He grinned at her. "Unfortunately, my love, I do not control the weather, so I can assure you that your beloved winter and horrible snow will continue for several more months."

Kessara smiled back, rolling her eyes, and he turned to face forward before she could manage to gather enough snowflakes to chuck a snowball at his head mid-flight.

"I don't much like snow, either," Nazzan chimed in before flapping his wings a few times, sending them several feet higher in the sky. "We coldbloods much prefer the summer sun."

"My own reasons aren't entirely selfish, either," Alder added. "Snow makes battle difficult."

"Fair enough," Kessara chimed in behind him. "Though I guess the dragons and dwarves in Umrym will be fighting off the elves from their caves right now, anyway."

Alder heard Nazzan blowing out a slow breath, certain that the dragon was thinking exactly what he was: living underground had its advantages, but it also meant that they had ceded the high ground to the elves before the war had even begun.

"*Are we going to tell her?*" the dragon asked in his mind.

"*Not right now,*" Alder said firmly. "*There's enough to worry her as it is.*"

Two nights before, as Kessara had slept mid-flight, Alder and Nazzan had spotted an elf camp somewhere on the border of Aridmoor and Galeharbor. There were more than a dozen of them, and in the end, they had decided not to engage. The forested area would have made it difficult for Nazzan to fight, and it would have meant putting Kessara at risk.

The two friends had been troubled since, keeping a careful watch for more signs of elven incursion beyond Umrym, but so far, the ground below had been deserted.

"If you say so," Nazzan said, not sounding particularly convinced.

Alder gripped the leather straps more tightly in his hands until his knuckles went white.

"If you could spare Jaconial pain or fear, wouldn't you?"

His words came out more harshly than he'd meant them, and for a moment Nazzan said nothing, catching a pocket of air and gliding to the left in a gentle curve.

"I don't know the answer to that, Alder," Nazzan said finally. *"But she's going to realize what we're facing soon enough, whether you tell her or not. You can't protect her forever."*

The dragon was right. He could only do so much to keep her safe, but that didn't mean it wasn't worth trying. And for the moment, despite his own discomfort, he was glad to see her happy, flying through the glittering snow.

"Are you glad to be almost home, Kessara?" Nazzan said aloud after a few moments had passed, ending their silent conversation.

"Yes. I miss it, but I'm still nervous to see my parents again. Especially my father."

"I don't think you need to worry," Nazzan said as gently as he could, his voice so deep that Alder could always feel his chest rumbling.

"It's going to be difficult to explain," she said. Alder didn't disagree. He could only imagine the look on King Manta's face when his daughter told them that they had freed the leader of the remnant from captivity in Boneshire, only to have the woman tell them that, actually, the High One did not want the Envoy to marry a human at all. The story sounded completely mad.

"Still," Nazzan said. "It's the truth."

Kessara chuckled, and Alder turned to face her, letting go of the saddle with one hand so he could brush her snowy hair out of her face.

"It's going to be okay, my darling," he said, hoping that Nazzan did not notice as he leaned in to give her a soft kiss. The dragon did not always appreciate their romance unfolding on his back. "He's your father. He'll listen."

"What if he doesn't? What if he won't take me back?"

"He will," Nazzan said firmly as he dipped lower in the sky, making Alder's stomach lurch.

"Besides," the dragon continued, "from what you've told me of Queen Manta, she's not going to let him send you away again even if he wanted to."

Alder grinned. Nazzan had a point. Though Queen Manta usually obeyed her husband's wishes, when it came to their daughter, she had a fierce streak. He doubted that she would continue to permit her only child to be stripped of her House titles and cast out of their family.

For the next hour or so, they flew in silence, Alder continuing his battle with the falling snow with little success. Kessara seemed content to watch the wintry landscape below, but Alder knew her well enough to sense the worry behind her blue eyes.

The sun was beginning to set behind the clouds, and Alder hoped that they would be able to find a better place to camp than they had last night. They were well into Galeharbor territory now, and though most of the Kingdom was not so thickly forested as the neighboring Silverfell, it was much easier to find shelter than it was on the plains of Aridmoor.

"I'm not angry with him anymore," Kessara said after a long while, interrupting Alder's daydreams of warm fires and bedrolls. "I understand why he did what he did. He was trying to protect me, and he had nothing else to bargain with."

Alder had understood King Manta's actions from the beginning. After all, he had done worse himself to ensure that Kessara would marry Wes for the sake of herself and her Kingdom. Still, he hated that the two men she loved most had hurt her, even if the intentions were good.

"I'm sorry," he said, looking down at his hands, not wanting to turn and face her.

"For what?"

"For pushing you away. For making you think that I no longer loved you, no longer wanted you. I hurt you, and I'm sorry. I should have found another way."

He felt her fingertips on his arm, and forced himself to glance back at her as she rested her chin on the wet shoulder of his cloak. Her eyes searched his face, but she did not speak, and he wondered what she was thinking.

Had she believed him?

A part of him wanted to ask her, to know the full extent of the pain that he had caused, but another part of him couldn't bear it.

The moment passed.

"How about you?" she asked. "Are you nervous to see my parents again?"

"A little," he said, turning his head and planting a kiss on her cheek, glad to be on safer ground. "They've suddenly become my future in-laws, after all."

Kessara let out a breath. "It's going to be interesting, that's for sure."

"I'm not really worried," Alder said. "They'll obviously love me."

Kessara muttered something under her breath about his incredible humility, and he chuckled, but his thoughts were elsewhere.

Try as he might to deny it, the truth was, he was afraid. He was a peasant, nothing more, and it had been altogether stupid of him to manage to fall in love with a Princess. He'd become a member of the House of Manta, but he'd forever lack the blood for it, not to mention the upbringing. Taking permanent vows for a woman was frightening enough, but he'd also be making his promises to a Kingdom.

"They really will love you," Kessara added. "But the news is going to shock them. They've been preparing for years for me to be Queen of Silverfell. They were counting on having more men to rule, and on being able to challenge King Ursa's tyranny. Now it's going to be up to Aelrie."

Assuming that she and Wes are still alive.

A chill seeped into his bones at the thought.

"An elf queen is not going to be popular," Nazzan chimed in. "No matter how much good she's done for Kaveryth."

"I'm sure the entire continent knows that she defeated the Gorok by now," Alder said. "But that means they'll also be gossiping about how exactly she pulled it off."

"It is the High One who wishes for her to be queen and to reverse the oath," Kessara reminded them. "If it is His will, He will make a way. We just have to trust that."

Alder didn't argue, and for another hour they rode in silence. The sun was almost gone, and he knew that they would have to land soon.

"Do you see any good places to stop, Nazzan?" he asked.

The dragon would have probably been content to keep on flying for a while longer, but Alder's entire body ached, and though the snow hadn't abated, he was looking forward to at least being able to hide from it in his tent.

"Oh, I'd say so," the dragon said, and Alder could imagine the twinkle in his eye.

He leaned over and gave his friend a playful smack on the shoulder, the green scales so cold that they stung his palm.

"What do you see?"

"The towers of Windshear Palace," Nazzan said, a chuckle rumbling in his throat. "I figured that we may as well go the rest of the way."

Alder rested in the saddle, his stomach twisting.

Now that they were actually here, he realized that all he really wanted was to fly off back to Auranth.

"We can do this, okay?" Kessara said, pressing into his back, the closest she could come to giving him a real hug.

His heart was racing, and for a moment, he knew exactly how sick Wes must feel when he flew. He glanced over Nazzan's side, seeing nothing but blowing snow and endless trees below.

"I'm right here," Kessara added. "I'll always be right here."

He gave her offered hand a squeeze, and continued to stare

off into the sky.

He could just see the towers that were beckoning them, their spires jutting out of the white snow that blanketed the ground in every direction.

His future home was waiting.

11

Chapter 10

WES

Wes felt the headache before the cold.

As soon as he attempted to open his eyes, he was met with blinding pain. He laid against the pillow, pressing his eyelids shut as he massaged his temples. The headaches had been this bad before, but they didn't usually start up before he'd even had a chance to get out of bed.

High One, help me.

Even the thought was enough to send fresh waves of pain radiating through his skull and behind his eyes, but there was nothing to do but fight through it. The curse was not going away, and his mission was far from completed. The High One would give him the strength.

As he sat up, he found the pain had dulled enough for him to stand on unsteady legs.

It was dark still—dawn would not arrive for another half hour—and he wanted to get outside for a walk before everyone began to wake. He needed quiet and time to think, and since they'd arrived in Auranth, he'd found himself pressed on all sides, everyone always seeming to need him at once for one thing or another.

He bore the moonscar. He had been born to serve, and even though the role of the Envoy had changed a fair bit in recent months, his responsibility to the people had not gone away. It was exhausting.

He shivered as he pulled on a pair of woolen underpants, brown trousers, and two tunics. Winter had come to Auranth last night with the first snow, and despite the cold, he was eager to see the beauty of the land that lay outside the old forge.

The hallway was quiet as he stole out of his room, glad to find that his pain had faded to a nagging ache. He could bear that much.

As he stepped into the great hall, he glanced up at the hole in the ceiling. Jaconial would be well on her way to Umrym by now, and though his friend had revealed nothing but courage, he wondered how she was really feeling, flying across Kaveryth alone. Had Nazzan heard the same call about what was happening in Umrym? Was he there fighting already?

He didn't allow himself to think of the other possibility.

The two dragons had been separated for far too long, and it seemed now that their only reunion would come on the battlefield. At least they'd be able to fight side by side.

"Do you want some company?"

Wes nearly shot out of his boots at the sound of Celesyria's voice in his mind. He turned and headed back toward the corner that housed the makeshift hatchery, where the orange dragon still appeared to be asleep, save for one open eye.

When she spotted him, she raised her head and gave a stifled yawn that was still loud enough to wake half of the forge, but he didn't mind.

There was something different in her eyes this morning. Something that had been missing ever since she'd heard about the loss of her father.

"I'd love some company," he said, glancing down at the eggs. *"But who will watch the babies?"*

Celesyria followed his gaze, her yellow eyes alighting on each egg in turn, the slightest hint of a smile poking through her lips.

"My father probably would have died no matter what I did," she said after a while.

He did not know what to say to that, and he was thankful when the dragon continued to speak.

"These hatchlings are safer here than anywhere else in Kaveryth. Even if we have spies in our midst, they wouldn't be among those sleeping in the main building. I can leave them here alone. Moorn was right. It's not like they can get up and roll away."

He was glad to see that she was finally willing to relinquish control of the hatchlings a little, but he didn't understand what her father—or Moorn, for that matter—had to do with it.

"I'm not sure I follow," he said, reaching down to place a hand on one of the eggs, a green one that was a little smaller than the others.

"The High One is the author of life and death," Celesyria explained, poking one of the other eggs gently with the tip of her nose. *"I can make the best choices I can, but in the end, His plan will come to pass."*

"Celesyria—"

"I'm not saying that we don't try," the dragon continued. *"Or*

that I know for certain I couldn't have saved him. But I'm so tired of being afraid."

Her final few words came out with surprising force, and she glanced over toward the hall door, as though worried that the people could somehow hear her mindspeaking.

"I guess what I'm trying to say," she added, more gently, *"is that I want to learn to trust. I want to leave these hatchlings alone when I need to, and to spend some time with my best friend. I want to make my choices each day and rest easy. Because it's not all on my shoulders, not really. In the end, it is the High One who holds us all in His hand."*

Wes smiled at her, and she smiled back for the first time since they had arrived in Auranth.

"Now, all of that aside, I'd like to see the dawn."

With a final glance at the eggs, safe in their little nests, she and Wes headed out the front, toward the wide road that led into Auranth, which was big enough for him and Celesyria to walk side by side.

"We're a strange sight," Wes pointed out. *"Would you prefer to fly?"*

"Yes, but I know you wouldn't."

"I'm getting better," Wes argued.

It was true. His stomach had settled down in the last month or so, and much of the terror he felt at great heights had finally dissipated. Still, with his headache as bad as it was, he was thankful not to have to add any dizziness or vertigo.

They fell into a comfortable silence, watching as the endless flakes of snow made their way from the clouds and through the sky. The sun had risen, though they could not see it, bathing the entire landscape in a surreal, white glow. The city wall was visible ahead, and he could imagine the children of Auranth peering out of their windows, marveling at the way their world had changed overnight.

He was glad that there were more children here than in most of the Four Kingdoms, but still, there were not enough. He hoped that once this war was won and the High One was worshiped once more, things would change. The people of Kaveryth had been lost for so long that it was difficult to imagine that they could change, but he knew that nothing was impossible. Even if he doubted that he would live to see it for himself.

As the sun rose higher, the brightness became difficult to bear, and he looked at his feet, blinking away the light as his head pounded. He wasn't sure he would live to complete his own mission, let alone live to see the outcome of what the High One had planned.

The thought had paralyzed him when the headaches had first begun, but slowly he had started to come to terms with it. Going to the Eternal Lands before he was ready was frightening to consider, but what he really feared was the pain of those he would leave behind, especially the elf he was planning to marry.

"The winter Feast will be upon us soon," Celesyria said, breaking the silence. He glanced over his shoulder at the distant forge, amused by the strange shape of their trail in the snow. Celesyria's tail had dragged most of the way, making it look as though a massive snake had crawled up the road.

"I know," he said. *"It's been on my mind, when I wasn't worrying about you."*

"Or thinking about Aelrie?"

"Or thinking about Aelrie," he said, daring a glance up at her and ignoring the fresh wave of pain the blinding whiteness

sent through his head.

He wanted to tell her what he was thinking, tell her that he was afraid he wouldn't even be able to crawl to Umrym, but he couldn't bring himself to do so. This had been the first time that he'd had a chance to just be with her in a long while, and he didn't feel like wasting it with his own complaints.

Before either of them could change the subject, however, he caught a flash of movement ahead, near the city wall. Celesyria saw it too, her head raised, eyes alert.

"A guard?" she asked.

The pain in his skull intensified, so strong that for a moment he thought he would fall to the ground. He sucked in the cold winter air, leaning against Celesyria's flank.

"No," he choked out. "Elf."

Celesyria straightened to her full height and began to march forward along the path, with Wes trailing cautiously behind her.

"Be careful," he said, pressing a hand to his forehead.

"He's no match for me out in the open," she said in his mind.

Celesyria shouted at the creature as they got closer, her voice echoing off of the stone wall that stretched out in both directions. The creature turned slowly, and Wes realized at once that it was not a man, as he had assumed, but a woman.

Her hair was black like Aelrie's, and she shared her pale blue eyes, but that was where the similarities ended. The elf-woman looked over at them with a sneer, her hands raised over her head as though she wouldn't be able to reach for the sword at her belt in seconds.

His head continued to ache, distracting him. He was thankful that Celesyria was out in front, her knife-sharp teeth bared at the intruder.

"I don't want any trouble," the elf said, her voice reminding Wes of tinkling water. He knew that the sound was an illusion like the rest of her beauty—every elf he'd met aside from Aelrie used glamors to conceal the true decay of their flesh—but still, it unsettled him. Even though he knew better, he couldn't help but to wonder how something so lovely could be so filled with darkness.

Wes did not know what elves looked like in their natural state, but Celesyria had seen it, once, in a secret meeting of a traitorous council in the depths of Whitespire. A magical obelisk had prevented the dragons from mindspeaking and the elves from concealing their true appearance. By her account, the elves were so hideously ugly that she struggled to describe it.

Still, glamor or no glamor, the curse did not lie. He could sense the evil emanating off of her like a cloud of poison, pushing him back.

High One, help me to stand before this darkness and bring light.

With the simple prayer, he felt his headache abating slightly. He kept one hand against Celesyria's flank for balance, and waited.

"Why are you here?" Celesyria asked aloud, teeth still bared. She kept her body slightly in front of Wes, shielding him from any sudden attack that the elf may attempt.

"I've been given a message for the Envoy," the woman said, a smile on her lips that did nothing to soften the harshness of her face.

"You're alone?" Celesyria asked.

"I am. But if I do not return to Nox, the Regent may send others."

A shudder went through Wes's spine. No message that

Meira Daeleth had for him could possibly be a good sign. The war felt closer and more real than it ever had.

"Again," Celesyria said, her gentle voice marred with a growl. "What do you want?"

"Nothing," the woman said, lowering her hands gently to her sides and leaning back against the wall. "I come with no demands, just a notice. We gave the same warning to King Ursa, and figured that your little crew might appreciate the respect. Though I suppose you're already well aware of the consequences of the King's actions."

Wes felt the heat of rage rising within him. This elf knew that they had killed Celesyria's father, and here she was, ready to rub the dragon's face in it.

"Don't take the bait," he warned his friend. The elf was right. They could kill her easily, but it wouldn't be worth it. They would only be trading one guilty life for the death of many innocents.

Celesyria snorted with disgust. "Thank you for your concern. Spit out what you have to say, and leave this place before I burn you alive."

The elf gave a mocking bow.

"Very well."

Wes took a couple of steps closer, knowing that the message would not be repeated.

"It's nothing you haven't guessed," the elf said, her voice sounding almost apologetic. "War is here. Umrym is about to fall, and once it does, we're coming for the rest of Kaveryth. The whole continent will be ours. Sea to strait."

12

Chapter 11

KESSARA

Nazzan came to an abrupt landing in the courtyard of Windshear palace, his claws dragging furrows into the white snow as Kessara clung to Alder's back. When she finally looked up, she expected to see a group of Red Army soldiers as they had the last time, but instead, the stone square looked to be deserted.

The city of Windshear was almost unrecognizable, even to Kessara. The already white buildings had seemed to blend together into one when they flew overhead, and the detailed carvings that topped most of them were covered with thick clouds of white.

Night had nearly fallen at last, and the sky overhead was an oppressive gray, giving everything a strangely claustrophobic feeling. Perhaps everyone was simply inside to stay out of the weather, but still, it was strange to see the place so empty.

Her heart pounded faster as she climbed out of the saddle, landing softly in the deep snow. Alder followed, and Nazzan shook the snow from his wings, sending white powder flying into the air.

"Well, at least I didn't damage any walls," Nazzan said, glancing around the space.

Kessara glanced around the stone walls, and had to admit it was a reasonable concern. The palace itself was large, but this part of the courtyard was small, no doubt an intentional defensive design that was nonetheless inconvenient for dragon allies.

Just then, she heard the sound of the front gate being heaved open.

She shrunk back behind Alder, waiting as those inside pushed aside the heavy snow that blocked the path of the door. Finally, to her great relief, she saw four Galeharbor soldiers walking out onto the front steps.

"Princess—Lady Kessara," one of the men said, stammering as he tried to remember which of her titles was the correct one. The other three men came to stand next to their companion and bowed to her, their eyes shifting as they took in Nazzan and Alder.

"Where is everyone?" she asked, waving a hand and urging the men to get to their feet. She recognized two of the four palace guards, though their names escaped her at the moment. "Are my parents—King and Queen Manta—are they all right?"

The men nodded in unison, and she was thankful to have Alder's hand in hers, keeping her upright. Though she had not had any reason to suspect that her parents were at risk, in these days, it seemed that all manner of dark things could happen at any time.

"Thank the High One," Alder said, resting a hand on the

small of her back. "But if there has been no attack, where are the rest of the guards? We flew over all of Windshear and saw no one."

"Every man that could be spared has already been sent west, sir," one of the soldiers whom Kessara did not recognize said. "The elves sent a messenger here, straight to these very steps."

Kessara sucked in a breath and wrapped her arms around herself, shivering against the blowing snow. She felt violated, somehow, as though the elves had left a miasma of darkness in their wake that she could still feel now.

"In any case," the man continued, "their Regent wanted the King to know that their invasion of Umrym was well underway, and that they would be pushing toward Galeharbor as soon as they could. We saw no reason to doubt their threats. The civilians are terrified after the incident with the Gorok, and especially considering the passing of the Autumn feast. They worry that these troubles have come because the Dracodei no longer favor us."

Alder swore, and Kessara didn't blame him. No matter how much the truth of the High One had spread, there were tens of thousands of citizens committed to their own course. Years of offering their treasure to the dragon gods had become a habit that would now be difficult to get them to shake.

"We were warned of this," she said, shaking her head, thinking of Luna and the others. "The elves had been building their settlements for months, probably years. It was only a matter of time before they acted. The cessation of the Feasts of Offering at the same time has created a perfect storm."

"Shall we head inside?" one of the soldiers suggested, gesturing to the open door where snow was quickly beginning to blow in.

"Right, my apologies," Kessara muttered. "Of course. But our friend, Nazzan–"

"Don't worry about me," Nazzan said firmly, taking a couple of steps closer to the stone steps, his claws buried deep in the white snow. "I have to leave anyway, as soon as possible."

Kessara stared at him, her brow furrowing. "Whatever for? It's freezing, and dark, and you're in desperate need of rest."

She felt Alder slinging his arm over her shoulder, pulling her close.

"He has no choice, my darling," he said softly into her ear, the touch of his breath sending a thrill through her despite the circumstances. "Nazzan is a Guardian. He must fight to uphold his oath. Now that he is sure of an elven attack, it's his duty to stand against them at the earliest possible opportunity."

Kessara had heard all of this before, but her other worries had driven the thought far from her mind until that moment. "Can't you stay until morning?" she pleaded, gesturing to the guards, who had already begun to step through the door and out of the blowing snow. "Our guards will find you food, and shelter–"

"Princess," Nazzan said, glaring at the guards as though daring someone to correct him. "If Jaconial made it to Auranth, she almost certainly would have heard of what's going on in Umrym. I need to go to her, and I won't waste any more time."

She paused.

Even when Alder had abandoned her, all she had wanted to do was to run after him, even if it would have meant watching from afar and making sure that he was all right. She wouldn't attempt to dissuade her friend from doing the same.

"We'll miss you," Alder said, leaning against Nazzan's green flank and giving him a hearty pat on the shoulder. Kessara joined him, attempting to throw her arms around the dragon's thick neck. She lingered there as long as she could before pulling away.

"Until we meet once more," Nazzan said, bowing his head.

Alder took Kessara's hand and pulled her gently back as Nazzan balanced on his hind legs, flapping his wings a few times before taking a few steps and rushing off into the air.

The guards were shuffling from foot to foot impatiently, but Kessara ignored them, watching the sky until Nazzan finally disappeared behind blowing snow. An even deeper silence had fallen on her home city, suffocating her. She swallowed a lump in her throat, hoping that no tears would slip out of her eyes. The dragon had his duty, and she had hers. What was done was done.

She turned to the men and gestured toward the opening of the door, where a veritable drift of snow had since accumulated. She stepped over it, Alder at her heels, and as soon as they had passed the threshold, all four of the guards struggled to heave the door closed.

I guess we won't be leaving in a hurry. Not by this route, at any rate.

As soon as the wooden door had slipped shut, Kessara heard the sound of arguing, and a second later, the door to one of the hallways burst open.

Her mother rushed through it, not bothering to hold the door for her husband behind her, and rushed over to Kessara. She was wearing only a nightgown, far too thin to withstand the cold foyer, but she did not seem to notice the chill. She threw her arms around her daughter, sobs escaping as she held Kessara to her chest.

"Mother," Kessara managed to choke out, the Queen's arms surprisingly strong around her.

"Oh, my dear," she said, not breaking her hold. "I thought you were dead, you hear me? Dead! You're going to worry me into an early grave."

Kessara wondered what Alder's expression would have revealed just then—after all, it had been the King who had sent her away in the first place—but he was wisely standing closer to the guards.

After what felt like a very long while, her mother let her go, stepping back to look her over, as though checking for suspicious bruises or bloody wounds that would require tending.

Kessara could see her father then, standing a few feet away, his arms crossed over his chest as he observed the scene, missing fingers pressed into the front of his tunic. His face was dark from the sun, despite the winter weather, and she could see that new lines had formed across his forehead. She couldn't help but to think he looked old, at least, far older than when she had left him.

He also looked furious.

"Jinna," he said, his tone revealing nothing. "I know you miss her, but your emotions cannot rule you."

He turned to face Kessara, his blue eyes burning into her own with all the fury of a storm on the North Sea. "You're not supposed to be here, Kessara. You've been banished from this palace."

Kessara broke their gaze as Alder stepped in beside her,

taking hold of her hand within his own, firm and certain. She could almost feel his anger, the warmth of it radiating off of his body in the cold room.

"Your Highness–" Alder started, his voice deathly calm.

Before he could say more, her father stepped toward them, covering the distance in two steps.

"Do you two fools not see what you have done?" he yelled, the sound echoing through the space as her mother clutched at his arm and looked up at him with pleading eyes.

Kessara had felt Alder flinch, but she'd been ready. She stood still, staring at him, trying to keep any emotion from her face as her father paced back and forth, waving a hand like an insane composer.

"King Ursa has demanded that nearly every able-bodied man in Galeharbor push for the borders of Umrym," he spat. Kessara had learned as much from the guards, but figured that it would be less than wise to point that out.

"He *conscripted* those who refused to volunteer. *Conscripted!* My men, in my Kingdom!"

She caught her mother's eye, but the Queen only shook her head, looking at Kessara with eyebrows raised, as though to say, "You knew this would happen. Just get through it, and it'll be fine."

"And what could I do? I couldn't exactly tell him off, after most of my men had already fled to his Red Army. Now Windshear is defenseless, just waiting for elves or bandits to come and take us over."

Kessara dared a glance at Alder. She was sure that a fair number of those fleeing soldiers had ended up in Auranth.

"You should have been in Silverfell by now, wearing a crown," he said, pointing at her head with his good hand.

"We could have worked together, found more men to fight. We could have stood up to him."

"Things have changed, father," she ventured, trying to keep her voice from shaking. To her surprise, her father did not immediately begin yelling again, so she took a few slow breaths, trying to think of a way to gather her thoughts. There was so much to explain, and all she really wanted was her warm bed.

"You've changed your mind?" her father asked, stopping short where he stood and peering at her from beneath his gray brows.

"No," she said.

Her father's face fell, but she spoke again before he could say anything.

"We've had everything wrong from the beginning," she said quickly, glancing first at her father, and then her mother. Alder squeezed her hand, and she took a deep breath, happy that he was there with her. "I never was supposed to marry Wes. There's someone else who is meant for him."

"And I'm meant for Kessara," Alder added. "I plan to make her my wife."

He sounded so strong, so certain. It made her want to lean over and kiss him right then and there.

"What do you mean?" the King asked, eyes narrowing. "This had better not have something to do with this High One business. We need Silverfell as our ally. That hasn't changed."

"We should hear her out, Errol," her mother suggested, gesturing toward one of the hall doors. "Besides, I'd like tea. It's freezing."

***

Kessara gave her mother an appreciative smile as they filed into the hall, walking deeper into the palace in silence. King Manta took up the lead, and aside from a few mutterings that may or may not have been curse words, he said nothing. Alder fell in beside her, his hand pressed to the small of her back, guiding her gently down the long passageway.

The throne room looked exactly as it always had, an open expanse overlooked by a huge loft, her father's study door tucked away at the far end. Ever since she was a child, the room had inspired awe. Now, as they settled into the comfortable chairs that rested along the wall, she couldn't help but to feel a ripple of apprehension.

The silence was heavy as they waited for her mother to fetch tea from the study. Out in the hall, Kessara could hear the guards whispering to one another, and she could only guess at the gossip that would flood into the streets of her home city in the morning.

She'd been in this very room a few months back when the city had been attacked, and she couldn't help but to imagine the chaos that had taken place outside, the bodies cut down by swords, the desperation of their men to protect their women and children. They had survived that attack, but many of their citizens had been taken as slaves. Now, something even worse was coming for them, and she feared that they wouldn't be able to stop the elves in time.

Queen Manta reemerged from the study, carrying a tray of tea and biscuits. Kessara took a mug of tea and several of the biscuits, hoping that they would calm her growling stomach until this conversation ended. Alder did the same, tossing an obscene number of sugarcubes into the dark brown liquid, no doubt seeking a much needed jolt of energy.

"Now," the King said, declining tea and leaning back in his chair, his fingers steepled in front of his chin. "I expect you have an absolutely marvelous explanation for this madness."

Kessara caught Alder's eye, and he nodded toward her, gripping his mug with his callused hands. It would be better if she did the talking.

She launched into an explanation of everything that had happened since they had last seen each other, trying her best to downplay the danger involved in freeing the captives. In fact, she omitted their river escape from the Dread Ruins entirely, figuring that her mother would be having enough of a heart attack at the thought of her daughter being chased by slaving bandits.

She had expected her father to ask for more details as she recounted her exploits, but instead, he remained silent, his expression blank. Alder said little, chiming in every so often with a clarification or a reminder.

"Anyway, once we got the slaves free, we realized that there were some interesting folks among them," Kessara said finally, unsure of how exactly to broach the meat of the conversation. It was getting late, however, and she was exhausted. She would have to push her way through the discomfort soon enough if she wanted the reward of rest.

"Interesting how?" her father spoke at last, raising a single brow.

She nodded, glancing over at Alder for reassurance, but he was already gripping the sides of his chair with white-knuckled fingers, as though preparing for an explosion.

Wise.

"I'm sure you've heard the stories of the people that went east, to where the map ends, hundreds of years ago," she ventured, avoiding her father's eye.

"Of course," Queen Manta said, giving a tinkling laugh. "Quite a story. I always wanted my mother to tell it to me when I was a girl."

"It is a story, mother," Kessara said, fighting to keep her expression neutral. "But that doesn't mean it isn't true."

The King placed his forehead in his hands.

"We met one of their leaders, Luna," Kessara said quickly. "She had been given knowledge that has been lost to history here in Kaveryth, passed on for generations. The prophecy that Wes had been counting on–"

"I am not concerned with some fortune teller's ramblings," King Manta said, his voice dangerously low. "Wes Cervos was to marry you because Roven Cervos could not."

"Things changed, father, as I can explain if you'd let me," Kessara snapped, unable to contain her frustration. "He had changed his mind, too, a long while back. In the end, he was willing to marry me because he thought that I, as Queen of Silverfell, would be able to reverse the oath the elves have taken with the dragons."

Her parents stared at her, likely wondering why they would want to reverse the oath at all, but she hoped that they would allow her to explain that part later.

"Luna has made it clear that that was an error on his part," she continued. "His marriage must be with an elf, which rules me out."

She cringed as the words came out. Even her mother was looking at her like she had just tried to use sugarcubes as kindling in the fireplace.

"I know that you have your doubts about the High One. I understand that. But if marrying Wes is against the will of the High One, I must continue to refuse."

She took a breath and glanced down into her lap, certain that she would wither away to nothing if she met her father's gaze.

"And, aside from that fact, it has become clear to me that Alder Cadogen is the one I am supposed to spend the rest of my life with. And I am going to do so."

As Alder had anticipated, the tension in the room boiled over in a moment, the King rising from his chair so quickly that the wooden legs of the heavy furniture clattered against the stone floor.

"Errol," her mother warned, but he was beyond hearing her.

"So you came here to tell me that you're going to change the entire future of Galeharbor because of what some bedtime-tale-come-to-life told you?" he snapped, his blue eyes so filled with disappointment that Kessara might have felt like crying, if she hadn't been so furious.

She forced herself to take a breath, and then another, twisting her fingers in the fabric of her still-damp dress, waiting for her anger to fade for several long seconds.

High One, give me the words. Help him to understand.

Her mother had gotten to her feet and placed a restraining hand on her husband's arm, managing to get him back into his chair with some urging.

"Errol, please," the Queen said, her voice honey-sweet as she poured a mug of tea and forced it into his hands. "Just listen. Kessara has disappointed us both, but she's not stupid. Her ideas are worth hearing."

"I know it's a lot to take in, Your Highness," Alder ventured, clearing his throat.

The King glared at him as he took a generous gulp of his still-hot tea.

"You're telling me that you plan to marry an Aridmoorian peasant while our Kingdom faces annihilation at the hand of an elven army," the King said, setting his tea on the end table with a clatter and turning to Kessara. "A lot to take in, indeed."

Kessara clutched the edges of her chair with her fingertips, tendons bulging as she tried to avoid losing the remaining shreds of her patience. She glanced over at Alder, half-hoping that he would find some way to defend her honor.

But Alder said nothing, sitting back in his chair and crossing his arms over his chest, not taking his eyes off of the King. Her mother got up from her chair and placed a delicate hand on her husband's shoulder.

"Need I remind you, my love, that you were not thought to be the best match for me, either?"

The King grumbled, but Kessara felt a half smile slipping out. Her mother had been born to the King and Queen, while her father was a lower member of the House of Manta. He hadn't been a peasant, it was true, but plenty had looked down on him nonetheless.

"And you turned out to be a great king," Kessara said firmly, reaching over and touching the top of her father's grizzled hand. There was no need to lie. She and her father butted heads, but she never doubted his deep desire to do the right things for the people of Galeharbor. His reign had proven his skill and devotion without a doubt.

"I was not a commoner," King Manta said. He no longer

sounded angry, only tired. "I had been educated by the best tutors, went into the navy as a teenager—"

"Alder joined the Aridmoor army under King Radagar Ursa at age fourteen," Kessara chimed in. "And became a war hero not long after. You're not so different."

The King closed his eyes for a moment, as though seeing his argument defeated was simply too much to watch.

Finally, Alder spoke.

"My King—" he nodded to her father "—my Queen. There is a lot to discuss, but I confess my body is growing weary. Our travels across Kaveryth were long, the weather was punishing, and our supplies ran low."

Kessara wrinkled her nose. While it was no doubt true, Alder was not typically one to admit to physical weakness of any kind. He'd rather stay awake for two days than lose face.

Her mother got to her feet at once, her eyes wide as she stared at Kessara. "You're hungry? By the Dracodei, child, you should have said! These biscuits will not be enough!"

Kessara smiled weakly at her, and without another word, she strode off across the vast throne room, no doubt on her way to the kitchen. The space fell silent, and for a moment, no one sought to break the calm.

Alder looked slightly alarmed, and Kessara shook her head, wishing very much that she could laugh aloud. Clearly, he had not intended for his complaints to send their only ally racing off to make them sandwiches.

"King Manta," he said at last, meeting her father's eyes once more, his jaw set. "The matter of our marriage can indeed wait, at least for now. But Kessara's titles are more urgent."

King Manta's brow furrowed in confusion, and finally,

Kessara understood what Alder had been getting at.

"King Ursa will be here any day now," Kessara said quickly, stealing a glance at Alder, who nodded. "Even with us on dragonback, he had a good start–"

"Wait," her father said. "King Ursa? What are you talking about?"

"He's coming to Windshear to meet with you," Alder said, confusion written on his handsome features. "I apologize. I–we–had assumed that you knew already."

King Manta gripped the edge of his chair so tightly that Kessara feared the old wood might snap.

"Excellent. Not even a messenger to warn me. He'll have more demands, no doubt. Demands I cannot meet. Did you find out anything else?"

Kessara nodded. "He seeks to return our navy ships to the Strait."

King Manta looked down at his lap and swore, the veins in his thick neck bulging as he tried to get his temper under control. Finally, he glanced up at Alder.

"Fine. What does my daughter's title have to do with this?"

"You know the answer," Alder said carefully. "King Ursa has always fancied her. We've witnessed him going easy on her when he could have chosen otherwise. She's in the best position in your House to negotiate, and you know it."

Kessara watched as her father leaned back, releasing a slow breath.

"That can remain true, whatever happens with her choice of husband," Alder added quickly. "But however blinded he may be by her beauty and charm, he's beholden to tradition like the rest of us."

Kessara looked at her father expectantly. Alder was right,

and she could see by the faraway look in her father's eyes that he knew it, too.

"Fine," the King said at last, getting to his feet. He took a few steps toward the marble thrones that stood near the middle of the room, his heavy steps echoing through the air. Alder turned to her.

"What is he—"

She silenced him with a soft kiss, watching to be sure that her father had not yet turned to face them. As his lips met hers, she felt the stress and fear that her body held beginning to ease away, falling against him, a moment of rest that had felt very long in coming.

All too quickly, however, the moment was over, and she stepped back.

"You did well," she said in a whisper. "Brilliant, actually."

Before he could come up with some sort of cocky response, however, the King was striding toward them, a dull ceremonial sword in his hand.

She opened her mouth to speak, but he silenced her, holding the weapon at chest level.

"Kneel. I'm ready for bed."

She obeyed, and Alder moved to do the same. The King rolled his eyes, no doubt thinking that Alder the peasant had a great deal to learn, but did not correct him. He placed the sword on each of Kessara's shoulders in turn as he began to speak.

"By my House, I proclaim. By my duty to kin and Kingdom, I declare. By my blood, I command."

Several seconds of silence passed.

"May it be," Kessara said.

"Kessara Manta, you are hereby reinstated as Princess of

Galeharbor and heir presumptive. May you reign in good health."

13

Chapter 12

CELESYRIA

The next several days passed in a blur.

Celesyria had already been struggling to sleep, and the problem had only worsened now that the dragon eggs had hatched. Finally, her anxiety over their safety had eased, and she'd allowed Luna and some of the other women to take over the majority of their care, but she still found herself checking on them at least a couple of times each night.

Even if she hadn't, their little cries for their feeding would have woken her, even though Luna was always at their side in a heartbeat. In the daytime, she found herself spending time with them whenever she got a free moment, happy to simply watch them as they played and grew. Among so much death, she was thankful to be a witness to the persistence of life. The hatchlings renewed her hope in a way that little else could.

Most of her time was spent in discussion after discussion, as Wes, Aelrie, Bargren, Mella, and the others tried to figure out their next move. They had tried to keep the elf's visit and the Regent's threat a secret, but, of course, the word had spread through the whole forge and into the city within mere hours.

Nox had always been close—only the narrow channel of the West Strait separated Auranth from the land of the elves—but now, the threat felt much more immediate. The people wanted answers, and she and her friends struggled to find them.

They could see only two options. Either everyone had to flee, leaving the fortress that they had done so much to build behind, or they would send most of the women, the children, and the elders away, while leaving men behind to protect their home.

To Celesyria's surprise, it was Bargren and Mella who favored the first option, preferring to leave their lifelong home rather than to risk standing in it as it fell. Still, it did not take long for them to see the flaws in their plan.

Auranth was nearer to the elves than most places in Kav- eryth, but at least the city and the forge had strong walls and a largely self-sufficient infrastructure. Their population had been decent before the Envoy's army began, and it had swelled massively since. They could think of nowhere in the whole continent that could take so many people in, even if they wanted to.

In the end, Wes had argued for a third option, and the others agreed that it was the best of several risky ideas. The young and old would be asked to stay, if they could, and the others—most of the able-bodied men and even some of the women—would head for the battlefield in Umrym at once. If they could manage to stop the elves from encroaching further, the city would not need to be defended.

Their soldiers were far from ready for war, but their time to train had come to an end, and to Celesyria's relief, they had readily agreed that they would fight for Kaveryth at once. The whole city had been abuzz with activity, taking the next several days after the decision had been made to churn out new weapons and armor and to prepare their supplies as best as they could.

Still, no matter how much they prepared, she knew the fighting was going to be exceptionally difficult. Sharing trenches with one's allies was hard enough, but they would be fighting on the same side with King Ursa's Red Army. The best that they could hope for would be to be left alone, but Celesyria doubted it would be so simple.

She had tried to talk to Wes about what was coming, but found that he was strangely absent, often retreating to his room for hours in the middle of the day. When she'd asked him about his behavior, he'd shrugged it off, insisting that they had to put all of their energy into their preparations. She had even tried to see if Aelrie knew what was going on, but the elf was even more difficult to read. In the end, she'd given up, spending every second that she wasn't offering her size and strength to the soldiers with the baby dragons.

They seemed to grow visibly each day, and she was sad to think that by the time she returned, they would be full-sized hatchlings. But waiting around was what she hated most.

She wasn't eager for war. Unlike most of the weapon makers and shop owners who made up a significant portion of their army—and even some of the seasoned soldiers in their ranks—she had fought elves, and she knew what they were capable of. And yet, not going to battle was worse. The fear and anticipation hung over her like a layer of dust she could never quite brush away.

Finally, on a fine winter morning, the sky a crystal-clear blue, Wes had given the order that their troops would make for the Severed Summits the very next day.

She had no idea what she would be flying into. Either the elves remained stalled in Umrym, which did not bode particularly well for Jaconial, or they had been able to fight their way east.

If it was the latter, she would have more open space to fight, but even so, she couldn't shake her apprehension. The question of whether or not to use her fire still plagued her. Luna had not given her any direct answers when she'd asked, only telling her to pray to the High One for guidance. Celesyria had her doubts that the remnant leader knew the answer at all.

The details of the ancient oath remained murky, likely lost for good, but in the end, she decided that she would not take the chance. The elves were smart. She doubted that they would fight without human allies to serve as shields.

In any case, despite her attempts to strengthen her faith for the battles to come, she couldn't help but to feel weary of the High One's silence. She would have given anything for someone to have a prophetic dream like Alder used to, or for a mysterious fragment of the Codex Veritatis to appear in Auranth's library, but there were no such wonders at hand.

The dragon pushed her worries aside as she made her way down the path into the city, the sun stinging her eyes every time she looked up. It was already mid-afternoon, and if she wanted to say goodbye to her mother before dinner, she did not have much time to spare.

Her morning had been spent with one leg at a time stuck into the back door of the working forge, where two of Bargren's sons had attempted to remove her ankle manacles once and for all.

She'd been carrying them for months, and had hoped to face the elves without them, but once again, their attempts to get the cuffs off had failed. Whatever strange iron the dwarves had used to craft them was beyond the knowledge of even Auranthian smiths to dismantle. The boys had apologized profusely, and, disappointed as she was, she tried to reassure them as best she could that she would be fine.

She could hear the metal clanking against her scales as she walked, her feet leaving prints in the thin layer of snow that had not yet melted away in the gleaming sunlight.

All at once, as she stared up at the looming city wall ahead, hoping that the guards would not be in the mood for too much small talk, she was struck by words.

These chains are not what you think they are.

She stopped short, her claws jutting into the slush at the edge of the road.

It wasn't a voice, not exactly, but it wasn't just a thought, either.

You have asked Me to take them from you.

She stood still, hardly breathing, closing her eyes, with a fleeting thought that she hoped no one would walk by and see her.

So much silence. So much waiting. And yet...

I always answer Your prayers, dragon. Have I not proven that?

A part of her wanted to defend herself, to let her own thoughts mingle with the words pouring into her head, but she could not form a sentence. Somehow, she knew that she had no defense. None at all, let alone one that would be adequate.

I do not seek to sadden you, dear one, only to remind you of this truth.

I give only good gifts.

That is my promise.

She waited for more words to come, but she could hear only the sound of winter birds chirping as a breeze rippled across the snow. She opened her eyes. The path was exactly as she'd left it. The city lay ahead, quiet and waiting for all that was to come.

She glanced at the position of the sun in the sky and continued to walk. She felt numb, like everything was the same, but with a little of the color washed out of it. She couldn't deny what—who—had spoken to her, and yet, she was afraid to admit it could be true.

She was a dragon.

Dragons were made for the Farplace.

She did not have a soul.

The High One promised that He answers my prayers. He promised.

She didn't know what it meant about her manacles, her soul, her eternal fate, or anything else, but she knew in her marrow that it was really, truly Him.

He was not silent at all. She had just been too stubborn to listen.

***

It was the first time that Celesyria had set foot in Sharsi's new home, and it was not at all what she had expected. When

Mella had told her that her injured mother would be living in a new dragon dormitory housed within an old ship factory, she'd expected to find some old, empty-looking building with dragon nests dotted about.

Instead, she found herself walking into the closest above-ground replica of their traditional caverns that she had ever seen. Her mother raised a wing in greeting from across the room, but Celesyria stood where she was, unsure where to glance first.

Somehow, despite the usual demands of keeping a remote northern city going, not to mention the challenges of preparing for an upcoming war, the citizens of Auranth had pulled together something wonderful.

The walls were not the plain cement block that the exterior of the building would suggest. Instead, they were lined with stacks of stone, just messy enough that they could almost pass for natural formations. The windows had been covered over with thick quilts, blankets, and tapestries—likely donated by the local inhabitants—and their light had been replaced by the gentle glow of hundreds of candles.

"*Mother,*" she said at last, stepping deeper into the space, the huge metal door swinging shut behind her and casting out the last of the intrusive sunlight. For a moment she was transported home to the depths of Whitespire, memories coursing through her mind as she stepped carefully across the black-painted floors. "*This is...*"

Words failed her. She accepted her mother's embrace, thankful for the solid, secure weight of the older dragon's orange neck resting against her own.

"*If only there were more of us to fill it,*" Sharsi said, gesturing toward the far end, where comfortable nests had been set up on the floor, giant versions of the hatchery that Celesyria had helped to create within the great hall of the old forge. They were empty. They had not gathered many dragons to their cause as it was, and the handful that had apparently been here before had all been Guardians. Like Jaconial, they had already been sent away to join the battle in Umrym.

"There will be more of us," Celesyria said, pulling back and giving her mother what felt like her most genuine smile in days. *"I don't know if you heard, but the hatchlings have made it out of their eggs. All of them, safe and perfect and wonderful. There is nowhere better for them than here, where you can look after them. If you're up to it, anyway. I'm sure the others will agree."*

"I would be honored," her mother said. She smiled, but Celesyria could sense a shadow behind her eyes that she couldn't ignore.

For a couple of moments, they walked in silence, coming to rest in a far corner of the room where the candles had been set on hundreds of tall stands, leaving a huge circular space in the middle that was perfect for sitting down to talk. Celesyria collapsed onto what she could only describe as a dragon-sized version of a human pillow, and her mother did the same.

"I'm leaving tomorrow," Celesyria said quickly, not wanting to keep the sad words inside any longer than she had to.

"I know. Most of you will be," her mother said, her voice soft. She sounded so different from the dragon she had once been, a tough Guardian who did not suffer fools lightly, even when her own daughter was the fool in question. The physical and mental pain of the last several months had clearly had an impact on her. *"I'm glad I got to see you before you left. I wish I*

was fighting with you."

She gave a half smile and looked at the ground, drawing back her destroyed leg a little, as if she could hide it away.

"I'm sorry that I didn't come sooner," Celesyria said, struggling to keep her voice cheerful. Her mother had enough pain to carry as it was.

"You were going through a lot. We both were. I don't blame you for needing some time inside your own head."

"I'm not sure it helped in the long run."

"Maybe not, but that doesn't mean it wasn't what you needed for a little while," her mother said, curling her tail around her body and letting out a sigh. *"I miss him every day, but I'm starting to realize that I know how to keep living, after all."*

Celesyria lowered her head until it rested on the pillow beneath her. She was tired. When she'd first learned of her father's passing, Wes and her other friends had urged her to try to get some rest, to eat well, and to take care of herself. Instead, she had tried to outrun the sorrow, throwing herself into taking care of the hatchlings. Unlike everyone else around her, they couldn't pry.

"Do you know what I mean?" her mother prompted.

"Yes. Everything was so dark and heavy at first that I thought for sure I would drown in it. But it has gotten a little better. And yet, that makes me feel even worse."

Her mother looked alarmed.

"Because of the guilt," Celesyria said quickly, not meeting her mother's eyes. *"I don't want to get over his death. It's my fault he's gone, and I don't feel right forgetting that."*

Suddenly, her mother was on her feet, yellow eyes flashing with unmistakable anger.

"Don't you dare say that this is your fault, Celesyria," she

snapped, lowering her head until her face was inches from her daughter's. *"This was the fault of the elves, first and foremost. They have free will, just like the rest of us, and they choose evil, time and time again."*

Celesyria opened her mouth to speak, but her mother pressed on. She had no need to stop for breath.

"We treat the elves like they're a natural disaster, a storm that can't help but to tear villages to the ground. It's madness."

"Sometimes it feels that way," Celesyria ventured.

"I know," her mother said, candlelight dancing on her scales as she lay back down, breathing more slowly. *"But it's not true. This darkness is not inevitable. I just wish I knew how we could change it."*

Celesyria had considered the same questions many times before. She knew that the elves were, as individuals, capable of turning back to the High One. Aelrie had, not to mention the fallen elf whom Alder and Wes had aided on his deathbed. Still, it was difficult to imagine them taking a different path as a whole.

"We can't," Celesyria said. *"Only the High One can, and He's not often in the business of telling us His plans."*

Silence stretched between them. To Celesyria's surprise, her mother had not dismissed mention of the High One as she would have not so long ago. She did not yet believe, but at least she could bear the sound of His name. It was a start.

Celesyria could not see outside, but she was sure that the sun had to be near to the horizon now. She still had to get back to the forge and to eat before turning in for an early night. It would be her last comfortable sleep for who knew how long, and despite the worries that threatened to keep her awake until dawn, she knew that her body desperately needed the rest.

"*It's not only the fault of the elves,*" her mother said finally, her voice only just above a whisper. "*I bear responsibility as well, and far more than you do. When they came for him, back in Whitespire, I knew that what he was saying was true. We all did. We knew that the elves were encroaching on our land, corrupting our administrators, and all the rest. But I was too afraid to stand up for what was right.*"

The pain and regret in her mother's eyes was almost enough to shatter Celesyria's heart, but she said nothing. Just as she had needed silence, her mother finally needed to speak.

"*He was my husband, so of course they questioned me. I lied about all of it, pretended to be the perfect citizen, and in the end, they bought it and let me go. I justified it to myself, told myself that it's what your father would have wanted. In a way, I'm sure it was.*"

Celesyria nodded.

It was true. Her father would have done anything he could to protect his wife. Had she been captured, Celesyria was sure that he would have been screaming about her innocence until they shut him up. But that didn't make it right for her to deny the truth.

"*I was a coward, and a liar, and my freedom is not worth the guilt that I live with,*" her mother continued, her jaw set firm. "*My own husband died alone because I was too afraid, and now many more in our homeland will share his fate. All of the Guardians let this happen. Had we stood firm right away, the settlements would have never gotten such a foothold.*"

"*You can't let this guilt eat away at you anymore, mother,*" Celesyria said, shaking her head. "*The High One will forgive you. He has given you this chance to live. Do not waste it."*

To her surprise, her mother gave a chuckle, tilting back her head as the sound echoed off of the stone.

"So wise, ever since you were a hatchling," she said, a few of her sharp teeth peering out at the edge of her lips. *"And yet, you don't take your own advice. You don't need to feel guilty, Celesyria. You've always been brave. Your father knew it, and so does everyone else. If there were more like you, Kaveryth would be a different place."*

Celesyria closed her eyes, letting her mother's gentle words pour over her, as warm and comforting as the candles that filled the room. She wanted to believe them, but the doubt and fear remained like a cold shadow that she could never fully shake.

"You need to get back to the forge," her mother said at last, getting to her feet and stretching, thousands of pinpricks of light glimmering on her scales. *"I'll be awake for the sendoff, but I probably won't be able to find you to say goodbye."*

Celesyria strode toward her mother and rested her head gently on the larger dragon's shoulder, not sure how it was possible that joy and sadness could take up so much of the same space within her heart.

"I promise that I will do everything I can to get home," Celesyria said firmly. *"But I need you to promise me that you will speak to Luna, and let her teach you about the High One. I won't ask you to promise to believe, but I hope you'll be willing to listen."*

Despite her own fears, and her own doubts, she was thankful that she still had Him to hold on to. Even when she was faithless, He waited, immovable and secure. She only had to remember, and to trust.

"*Everything will be fine, my darling,*" her mother said. She was trying to smile, but Celesyria could hear the wavering in her voice. "*Soldiers have poured in from all across Kaveryth. We'll have enough men. We must.*"

Celesyria wanted to agree, to provide her mother with a final shred of assurance, but something stopped her from saying anything more.

With a final embrace, she headed for the door, eyes closed against the burning of the sun.

14

Chapter 13

FALLOREN

The tree was unexpectedly comfortable.

Falloren rested against the trunk, his black clothes ensuring that he remained completely hidden in the shadows, despite the barrenness of the branches and the blue moonlight overhead.

He was quite high up–this was an old tree, some sort of gnarled desert variety–and he could see for several miles. The narrow strip of Boneshire land stretched to the distance, and he wondered if he would be able to see the very edge of Aridmoor once the sun rose. For now, it was the best he could do, and the Regent would simply have to accept the limits of surveillance.

Ever since King Ursa had defied her, Meira had been even more mercurial than usual. She had also sent her own messages of defiance across Kaveryth. As far as he knew, residents of Stronghollow, High Keep, Windshear, Redvale, and even Auranth had all been put on notice, but it was not enough for her.

She had insisted that Falloren head off into Kaveryth himself, to be her eyes and ears, and he had accepted, although refusal would have likely resulted in his execution. It had been an intriguing journey, in its way. He'd had a chance to pass through Umrym first, where the elves were near victory, despite the remaining Guardians and even some of the dwarves putting up all sorts of fuss.

Now that Umrym was nearly under their control, they'd been able to spare more warriors to push toward the interior. The small strip of sand that constituted the western half of Boneshire was their first stop on the way to Aridmoor, where he suspected the real resistance from the humans would begin.

Falloren yanked a watersack off of his belt and took several long drags of his favorite dwarven liquor, a parting gift from one of the captains in what was formerly the city of Helmm.

He stayed like that for what felt like a very long while, the rising moon casting cactus shadows all around him, as he struggled to keep his eyes open.

What is taking them so long?

He was traveling ahead of the army with a small party of a dozen or so. Since leaving the mountains, they'd had more and more trouble with the locals. Twice now, their supplies had been sabotaged or stolen by men from local villages so small and irrelevant that they had never been noted on the maps the elves carried.

Tonight, that would change.

Falloren took another long drink, thankful, in a way, that only their meat and wolf-feed had been tampered with the night before. He was hungry, but he'd survive. He wondered if these desert barbarians even knew how long his race could live without need of food or drink if necessary.

Chuckling to himself, he sat up as straight as he could, determined to keep his eyes open. After all of this waiting, he wasn't about to miss the show.

Finally, as he reached the bottom of his waterskin, he heard the first screams filling the sky. At first, they were sharp and disparate, cries of surprise interrupting the lazy silence of the desert, but then they became more numerous. The screams turned into wails, hundreds of voices joining together in one keening cry.

Finally, he smelled the smoke.

He tossed the empty sack onto the ground, watching as it sent a cloud of the horrible red dust into the sky, and settled in to enjoy the sights.

One by one, orange flames leapt up in the distance, searing the sky. As the flames spread from hut to hut, they reached the larger buildings, where the fire combined and grew so tall that Falloren imagined it might touch the moon.

He watched for a long while until he grew bored, leaning back against the trunk of the tree again and contemplating if he would wait for the others to return before retreating to his tent for a well-deserved rest. No one would dare come near their tent tonight, nor would they come tomorrow.

And it had only taken a few men, and even fewer torches.

ALDER

To Alder's great relief, breakfast was much more substantial than last night's tea and sandwiches had been.

He had risen early, awoken by Kessara knocking at the door

of the guest bedroom where the King and Queen had put him up for the night, and the two of them had headed downstairs through the winding halls without haste.

He had expected to eat in the dining room, but instead, after a brief and unreadable greeting, Queen Manta had urged them to take up their seats from the night before in the throne room.

King Manta had hardly said a word, focusing most of his attention on devouring his toast and drinking his thick-looking coffee. The food was plentiful, but the presentation was far more simple than Alder would have expected. Kessara seemed to have been thinking the same thing, staring at the table with her brow furrowed in confusion as her mother set down the large breakfast tray herself.

"I hope the food is acceptable," the Queen said as they ate, brushing away the nonexistent wrinkles from the left sleeve of her dress. "We still have servants, of course, in such a big place as this, but I've taken on more of the work where I can."

"It's delicious, my love," King Manta said, pausing to smile at his wife before returning his coffee mug to his mouth. "Our people were paying enough tax as it was, and with this war, we've had to milk them for even more. The least we can do is suffer a little austerity ourselves. Of course, we're still paying the staff, but the principle stands."

"The food is wonderful, Your Highness," Alder agreed, wiping crumbs from his lips with the edge of a neatly-pressed napkin. He had already devoured three pieces of toast, several slices of bacon, and two sausages, and there was still more to sample. All of it, so far, had been cooked to perfection.

He thought back to camping on the Aridmoor plains with Kessara a long while back, when she had surprised him by making some of the best rabbit stew he'd ever tasted. It was refreshing to see that the House of Manta was not afraid of a little hard work, even work normally reserved for the peasant class.

Kessara nodded, and Queen Manta beamed at all three of them, finally picking up her own fork and stabbing at a piece of steaming fried egg.

No one else spoke as they continued to eat, and after a few moments, the silence that had seemed almost companionable quickly became awkward. They had not left things on a particularly peaceful note the night before, and Alder did not want to be the first one to bring conversation around to the issues at hand, so he focused instead on making up for his recent traveler's diet.

As he downed the final dregs of his second cup of coffee, he heard a loud knock at the door. Kessara's father looked up, setting his own mug—Alder had long since lost track of how many refills the King had poured—down on the table with a thunk that rattled the cutlery.

"Come in!" he called, his deep voice echoing through the big room.

Two soldiers pushed through the doors and strode toward them, bowing as quickly as could still be considered polite.

"Your Highnesses," one of them said, glancing over at Alder with what seemed very much like recognition, "King Ursa and a small company of Protectorate men have arrived. We have them waiting in the courtyard, but they insist that they need to meet with you urgently."

Alder was not surprised by the news, of course, but it did seem rather providential that he and Kessara had made it here just in time.

"We were recently made aware that they were coming. You may let them in," the King said, running his hand with the missing fingers through his hair, which seemed to have gone even more gray overnight.

"I have one favor to ask first," the Queen said, gesturing to the remains of their breakfast. "I have already sent most of the domestic staff home before our visitors arrived yesterday. If one of you could be rid of this in a hurry, I would appreciate it."

"Of—of course, my Queen," the soldier who had not yet spoken said, staring at the table a little too long before he began to corral the scraps of food onto the tray.

"I'll escort the King in," the first soldier said, heading out of the room with a final bow. A few seconds later, his companion followed, the heavy tray held aloft on slightly unsteady hands.

"I'm not sure he will know where the kitchen is, mother," Kessara noted, shaking her head as the young man narrowly avoided crashing into the doorframe.

She looked very much the part of a Princess this morning, if not a Princess preparing her country for war. Somehow, despite their exhausting night and early morning, she had found the time to do her hair in a more regal style, with at least a half-dozen blonde braids framing her face. She wore a blue dress like her mother, nicer than her traveling clothes, but still plain, with a few beads along the neck and wrists and little other decoration.

Alder felt a rush of affection as he gazed at the woman he loved. Like her parents, she had been raised as a greater House noble, never wanting for anything. But when difficult times had befallen her people, she was willing to go without in order to empathize with them, even when she didn't need to. The gesture was small, but as someone who had grown up watching the nearby politics of High Keep society, he knew how far even a small act of humility went in the eyes of everyday folk.

"I suppose I should hide," Alder said, forcing himself to look away from Kessara and focus on the meeting at hand. "The Red Army soldiers have ignored my presence when they've been forced into a corner, but I am sure that the King would still be happy to see me locked up."

"You'll still be able to hear from Father's study," Kessara chimed in with an apologetic smile.

He glanced over his shoulder toward the small door that lay in the shadows at the far end of the room. He had hidden in the King's study–actually, the closet–with Wes once before, and he wasn't eager to repeat the experience, but it was probably for the best.

To Alder's surprise, however, King Manta was shaking his head.

"No. You'll stay right here," he said firmly, pointing at the chair that Alder already occupied. "I'd like to see that overgrown teenager arrest one of my guests in front of me."

"Errol," Queen Manta warned, an amused smile tugging at the corner of her lips.

"Are you sure about this?" Kessara whispered as the sound of boots began to sound down the hall.

There was no time to change his mind. Alder stayed where he was, reaching over to take Kessara's hand, but she pushed it aside.

"Trust me," she said, her pretty blue eyes pleading.

The door swung open again a few seconds later, and King

Kylan Ursa stepped through with Captain Drohma at his side, the two mens' boots clacking firmly against the floor as they strode toward the little alcove where the others waited.

Alder relished the looks on their faces when they caught sight of him, especially Captain Drohma, but they masked their surprise almost immediately. The two men sank to their knees in unison, bowing low to the King and Queen of Galeharbor. Alder thought he caught a flash of annoyance in the King's eyes, but the Queen's face revealed nothing as she offered a tanned hand for them to kiss.

"I take it my guards escorted you here as I asked them to?" King Manta asked, glancing back at the door.

"Yes, Your Highness, but I asked them to remain in the foyer. I knew the way, and I wanted to speak with you alone," King Ursa replied.

Alder noticed the slimy smile on Captain Drohma's face as his superior spoke, and he wondered how much diplomatic chaos it would cause if he got up and punched the man square in the jaw. He had not forgotten the disgusting things that the Captain and his men had said about both Kessara and Queen Manta when they didn't know they were being watched, and that was the least of the Captain's vile acts.

He settled back into his chair and forced himself to loosen his fists. Men like Captain Drohma did not evade justice forever, but now was not the time.

"Very well," Queen Manta said cheerily, gesturing toward two empty chairs that sat along the far wall. "I apologize that we were not better prepared for your visit, but I'm sure Alder would be happy to fetch you both a seat."

"No need, Your Highness," King Ursa said, walking toward them. Captain Drohma followed, saying nothing, and each man took hold of a chair and carried it back to the table. "It wasn't as though we were expected. I have no desire to impose."

"I do have tea," the Queen said, smiling at the men and proffering two mugs, which they both accepted.

"Well," King Ursa said after the first few sips of not-quite-hot tea had been drunk, "this is interesting. I must say, I did not expect a reunion with my dear childhood friend as well as the most notorious deserter in all of Aridmoor."

Alder tensed in his seat, his knuckles going white as he gripped the arms of the chair, the veneer of pleasantry in the room falling away at once.

King Ursa smiled and took another sip of his tea, and for the first time, Alder noticed just how much older he looked than he remembered. Despite his youth, he could see gray hairs mingling with the King's red curls, and there were new wrinkles along the edges of his sharp green eyes.

Just like the rest of Kaveryth. Battered and worn before the war even began.

"I suppose you need my navy in the West Strait," King Manta said, ignoring Ursa's remark.

The King of Aridmoor nodded, a couple of red curls falling against his forehead. "The elven boats haven't stopped coming in weeks, Errol. We've been trying to stop them once they hit the shore, but so far, we've failed. Thanks to their associates in Boneshire, the Black Beach is overrun, and the coast of Umrym is barely passable even when we're not worried about a storm of arrow fire. We're bleeding men, and we keep having to pull back. So far, they haven't moved much further north, but that doesn't mean they won't. I think they're just trying to make sure their hold on Umrym is firm before they make for Aridmoor."

"They have a lot of men, but even the armies of Nox are not infinite," the Queen put in mildly, filling the silence as King Ursa paused for air.

"True enough, Your Highness, but it's hard to predict just how many more they have waiting across the Strait."

Alder glanced over at Kessara. They had known from the start that basing their army in Auranth had its risk, considering the proximity of the Strait, but if what the King said was true, they still had a little bit of time. He just hoped that it would be enough.

"Well, it shouldn't take a great intellect to figure out how many men we have left, *Kylan*," King Manta said, drawing out the young King's first name a little longer than necessary. "You can see it for yourself. This palace is nearly empty of servants, let alone guards. Windshear is defenseless, and our people are starting to realize it. The temples are busier than they've been in years, filled with desperate grandmothers and their prayers to the Dracodei for a miracle."

Alder watched as Kessara flinched. The news didn't surprise him, but it was troubling all the same. These people needed the aid of the High One more than ever, and yet here they were, turning back to what they had been urged to leave behind as the truth spread across the continent.

"I understand that," King Ursa said calmly, looking over at Captain Drohma, who had so far managed to avoid ogling the Queen or her daughter as he sipped his tea in silence. Drohma gave the slightest tilt of his head, a nearly invisible signal that Alder could not hope to decode.

"You can't ask me for more men," the King said, leaning forward in his chair. "I will not command suicide."

"Is that what you think of us?" Captain Drohma cut in at last, meeting the King's eye with what Alder could only describe as a sneer. "That we care only for our own people, and want to see Galeharbor burn?"

"Of course not," Queen Manta said, her voice pleading. "But whether you intend it or not, what you ask is unreasonable."

Kessara nodded in agreement, and Alder wondered when she was going to offer her own proposal. He caught her eye, hoping that she could understand his questioning glance. As soon as the others looked away from her, she turned to him and put a finger quickly to her lips. She knew what she was doing, but the whole thing still made him nervous. They hadn't even gotten the chance to consult with Wes about their plan, but that couldn't be helped.

"Your Highnesses," King Ursa said, raising a hand to call for quiet and giving his Captain a warning glance. "You are entitled to make your choice, but–"

"I have a choice, do I?" King Manta said, raising his voice. "Is that what you tell yourself in order to sleep at night?"

"You always have a choice," King Ursa said, an edge of anger breaking through his usual icy calm.

"Surely, my King, you do not think that *any* of our choices can be made without consequences?" Captain Drohma asked.

Kessara glared at him, clutching her tea mug between shaking hands. "Every choice has a cost, big or small."

There was a lull in the arguing for a moment.

Alder watched the scene with some confusion, but it was clear that everyone could sense a threat from the Aridmoorian.

"I want my wife, daughter, and guest to hear the consequences," King Manta said at last, his voice booming across the large space. "I want you to say it, Kylan Ursa."

The King shrugged, but there was a hollow, haunted look in his eyes that he could not pretend away.

"You need Aridmoor's grain more than ever. Winter is here, the seas are empty," he said.

"This is not the time for histrionics, Manta. It's only politics," Captain Drohma added, his tone light.

Ah, I see. This is the choice you've come to offer. Let Galeharbor's people be slaughtered, or let them starve to death.

Alder felt sick to his stomach, and suddenly very much aware of the heavy sword that hung faithfully at his side. Kessara had continued to hope that Kylan Ursa could change, that there was a good man somewhere inside of him, but at that moment, Alder wished that he could bring him to his end once and for all. Cutting down the sadistic Captain Drohma would be even more satisfying.

High One, help me. Help us.

"Enough of this!" Kessara snapped before anyone else could say more, slamming her mug down hard enough to send a puddle of tea sloshing across the table. The brown liquid reached the far edge and began to drip onto the floor, forcing Captain Drohma to move his feet to avoid soiling his shoes. Alder suppressed a smirk. Kessara was not one for outbursts, and everyone knew it. The others stared at her, startled into obedience, as the Princess continued to speak.

"I can offer you more men, Kylan," she said quickly, before the others had a chance to come to their senses. "Thousands more."

King Ursa scoffed.

"I'm not sure you're in the position to offer me anything,

Lady Manta."

"Her title has been restored, and I would appreciate it if you used it," Queen Manta said primly, picking up a napkin and dabbing absentmindedly at the spilled tea. Alder caught her glancing at her husband, who was sitting back in his chair and watching the drama unfold in silence.

"Is that so?" King Ursa said, glancing over at Drohma. "How interesting."

Alder once again thought of his sword.

You imagine that if she's not going to marry Wes, you'll be able to continue as Steward of Silverfell for as long as you like. Power hungry snake.

"Princess or peasant, it matters little," Captain Drohma chimed in, shaking his head. "I assume you refer to your little band of peasants in Auranth? Those fools have gotten in our way enough already. If you think—"

"Shut up, Drohma," King Ursa said mildly. He leaned forward in his chair and looked over at Kessara. For a long second, the two of them looked at each other. As usual when she was deep in the role of politician, Alder could not read the expression on Kessara's tanned face, but for a moment, he wondered if perhaps Kylan Ursa could. Perhaps there was something he could see, some connection between them, formed long ago, that made him want to listen to her now.

Kessara lifted her chin, not taking her eyes off of the young King before her.

"Captain Drohma and his men fought heroically in Kingsvier Landing," she said gently. "Without their aid, I believe that hundreds of innocent men, women, and children would have perished."

She paused and turned to Drohma, giving him a slight bow,

her blonde braids tumbling over her shoulders. "Thank you, Captain. I'm sorry that I hadn't had the chance to offer my gratitude properly until now."

Alder watched as King and Queen Manta glanced at each other for a half second before bowing their heads along with her. Captain Drohma, of course, looked absolutely murderous.

"Thank you, Princess," he choked out after the silence finally became unbearable.

Kessara smiled sweetly at him and sat at her full height once more.

"As for my offer," she continued, her gaze falling on King Ursa, "Our force in Auranth has grown significantly in recent weeks. Moreover, the city itself has given us full support. As you well know, my King, a war is not won only with soldiers, of which we have many. Supporting infrastructure must also be in place, and we have it."

Alder sucked in a breath. News of Auranth's growth had spread across Kaveryth, and he didn't doubt that everything Kessara had said was broadly true. But they hadn't seen the city for themselves in a long while. She was going out on a limb, and he could only hope that everything she'd said would be proven accurate.

"What are you getting at?" King Ursa asked.

"If we could fight together, truly unified, under the more experienced leadership of your army, we would be able to take down the elves. We would be able to free our continent."

King Manta looked alarmed, but his wife rested a gentle hand on his arm, and to Alder's surprise, he remained quiet.

No one spoke.

"That is my offer, Kylan," Kessara said softly. "The

Auranthians will join the Red Army, and they will fight under the command of your men. The strategy will remain yours. You will also provide the Kingdom of Galeharbor with the food products we need at a fair price, as previously agreed."

Drohma opened his mouth to protest, but Kylan silenced him with a raised hand, not taking his eyes off of the Princess.

"And in return? Surely that is not all you want."

Kessara gave a half-smile.

"True enough. What I desire most is for you to help us to bring an end to the worship of the Dracodei. It's already happening. The autumn feast failed, and the winter feast draws near. Elder Jate on his own cannot manage the gathering of the sacrifices."

Kylan Ursa stroked his jaw. "He's missing, anyway. I received word nearly a fortnight ago that he left Vaevar Academy. No one knows where he is. The Septemvirate is finished."

Kessara didn't respond. Kylan Ursa looked up at the ceiling, lost in thought, as his Captain glared at the Princess from behind another mug of lukewarm tea.

"You have no interest in the Dracodei, Kylan," Kessara reminded him. "You supported the regime because it provided you with money and power. Now all of that is gone. You have nothing to lose."

"There must be more. Some catch."

Alder felt his breath catching in his chest. This was the difficult part, the one aspect of the plan that he, Nazzan, and Kessara had spent hours discussing over various campfires on their journey from Rill. He had worried that they were asking too much, that they should try and walk away with a compromise, but Kessara had been insistent.

He remembered her words as she looked up at the stars, curled up beside him in a blanket, sparks dancing.

Kaveryth will bow to lies, or it will bow to the Truth. There is no half-victory. We will win this land for the High One, even if it takes another hundred years. No compromises.

"You're clever, Kylan," Kessara said at last, her nerves hidden away beneath a practiced, diplomatic smile. "Always have been, ever since we were children. I offer the victory you seek, and you realize that victory is always costly."

Captain Drohma rolled his eyes, and Alder noticed that he was fiddling with the hilt of his own sword, no doubt dreaming of some violence against his own King that he was far too cowardly to carry out.

"Just tell me your exact terms, Kessara."

Kessara drew a breath.

"You must give your word that, after this battle is won, you will dissolve the Red Army and relinquish your Stewardship of Silverfell."

"To Whom?" King Ursa asked, incredulous.

"To the elf woman who is to be their queen."

15

Chapter 14

WES

Wes felt his stomach lurch as Celesyria took a hard turn to the left, narrowly avoiding hitting a large pine tree with the end of her wing. Aelrie clung to his back, shifting her weight easily with each new motion, and in that moment, Wes very much envied her for being an elf.

His head had been bothering him almost constantly since they'd left Auranth—sleeping on a thin bedroll likely had something to do with it—but it was bearable at present, and he was thankful for that small mercy. His usual flying sickness had improved over the last several months, but he doubted he would ever be as much of a natural as Aelrie was.

Maybe I'll get there, if I live long enough to keep practicing.

Despite his rather morbid thoughts, it was a pretty morning, the sun shining in a clear blue sky as they continued to pass over the forests of Silverfell. They flew low, in front of the troops, where they could patrol the area for any dangers. Every few minutes, however, they were forced to circle back,

162

not wanting to get too far ahead. The humans were making good time on their march below, but they were no match for a dragon's speed. Wes hated the twists and turns, and part of him thought even a long ground march was preferable to the constant pain and nausea, but at least here, he could be with Aelrie.

At first, the three of them had been alert at every moment, waiting for an ambush that they were certain was imminent. Over the last several days, however, they had been able to settle in and attempt to enjoy the picturesque journey as best they could, despite the anxiety that loomed like a constant cloud in the pretty winter sky.

A couple of days into their journey, once they had set up their large camp for the night, a small contingent of their soldiers had ventured into a nearby village in search of news. Apparently, they learned, the elves were still working their way through Umrym and pushing up from the southwest into Aridmoor, which meant that they still might have a chance to meet them before they reached the more populous areas of the continent.

The rural people of Silverfell were angry and terrified, fearing that the elven invasion was punishment by the Dracodei for missing the autumn Feast of Offering, and though the soldiers had returned from the village unharmed, Wes feared that their army could face sabotage from the very people that they were trying to protect.

Aside from that minor unrest, however, the north had remained astonishingly quiet. No matter how carefully he, Celesyria, and Aelrie combed the forest for threats, they saw no one. Either the bandits and slavers had gone into hiding, or they were already with the elves.

Whatever they were up to, Wes had not forgotten Meira Daeleth's latest threat. For the time being, the best thing that they could do was to reach the battlefield before the elves conquered any more territory.

And then hope that by the grace of the High One, the Red Army is content to ignore us.

For not the first time in recent days, he wished that Alder and Kessara were here. It was strange to be separated from them so long, and even though he was confident that the Aridmoorian soldier could protect them both, Wes knew better than anybody how unpredictable the situation in Kaveryth had become.

"Are you okay, my love?" Aelrie said, jolting him out of his thoughts. He glanced back over his shoulder at her, trying to avoid looking at the reeling trees below, and accepted her kiss on his cheek.

He should know better than to think that the woman who knew him best would fail to notice his pensive silence. If anything, he was surprised that Celesyria hadn't asked him if he was alive back there before now.

"It feels like the end of the world," he said honestly. "Everything is coming to a head, and our friends aren't even here. I feel lost."

Unconcerned with balancing in the saddle, Aelrie let go and swiped her dark hair behind her ears with her slim silver fingers.

"They aren't here, but that doesn't mean we're not to-gether," she reminded him, her voice a sweet song on the winter wind. "The High One is with us, no matter how far we go. He brought us all together for His purpose. We're always going to be a family, no matter what happens in the space between us."

Wes considered her words, tightening his grip as he continued to face backward. Celesyria was flying at a slow enough pace, but she continued to circle every so often, honing in on shadowy glens and secluded meadows in search of bandits.

"Your faith is deeper than mine already, even though you never ended up accepting the High One back in Auranth like you'd planned."

He said the words gently, trying to keep any hint of judgment from his voice, but he could still see the slight fall of her face as she answered.

"I wanted to. I wanted a celebration, with everyone there, something special. But when we heard about Celesyria's father..."

She didn't need to finish the sentence. Wes knew exactly what she meant, and though Celesyria seemed to be enjoying the brisk, bright weather rather than listening to their quiet conversation, he was sure that the dragon would appreciate Aelrie's consideration.

"You don't need to feel guilty," he said, daring to take one hand off of the saddle strap and take hold of hers. "A lot happened."

He paused, meeting her eyes, which looked even more pale than in the crisp winter light, like pools of ice in a cold blue dawn.

"But that doesn't mean that you should wait," he said firmly. "Especially now."

As you make for the battle that could be your last.

The thought filled him with such a deep dread that he could almost taste it on his tongue, bitter and thick. There was a pause as he looked at her, still as amazed as he was every single day that a person so beautiful and so kind could actually have managed to stumble into loving him, of all people.

"You're right," she said, gazing up at the sky as Celesyria took another stomach-twisting dive. "You're right. Let's do it now. I'm ready."

"Aelrie wants to accept the High One," Wes called out, loud enough for Celesyria to hear despite the cold breeze rushing past her ears.

"Praise to the High One," Celesyria said. "Er, should I land first?"

"No," Aelrie said quickly. "I want to do it now, before I lose my nerve."

Wes knew what she was feeling. Though his own acceptance of the High One might have happened a little more quickly, he still didn't feel like he'd gotten to the place that Celesyria or even Alder and Kessara had. Years of self-loathing had taken a toll, and even now, there were days when he felt completely baffled that the High One had chosen to love him at all. After all of the dark things that Aelrie had seen in her much longer life, trying to accept the embrace of the High One couldn't have been easy.

"Celesyria, do you know a good prayer that I can say?" Aelrie asked, placing a hand on the dragon's scaly orange flank.

"Let me think," Celesyria said, silence falling over them as she circled back over the troops, inspecting the neat lines of men for anyone or anything that might be out of place. The sun was finally beginning to lower in the sky, and the promise of dinner seemed to be urging the soldiers to walk faster than they had been for most of the day.

"*Are you okay, Celesyria?*" he asked in the dragon's mind.

"I know that you've been struggling lately. I can pray for her, not that I know what I'm—"

"It is an honor to bring another soul to the High One," she said, her voice gentle but firm. *"Please. I need...I need the reminder."*

"Okay."

Wes gripped the saddle as Celesyria passed the final rows of men on the ground and headed south once again. Aelrie rested her head on his shoulder from behind, and he kissed her cheek, waiting.

"I know a prayer that I think would be right," Celesyria said at last. "I read it in a Codex fragment that was later lost in the fire at Helmm. I remember most of it, I think."

"Thank you, Celesyria," Aelrie said warmly, still leaning against Wes. He was in no hurry to push her aside. Despite the cold, despite his tiredness, it was wonderful to still be with her, flying over the sleeping forest below.

The dragon paused for a long moment. Wes dared a quick glance over her side, but saw nothing beneath but endless pines and barren maples.

"I'm still not sure how to do this. There's probably more to accepting the High One properly, but Luna isn't here to ask."

"Don't worry," Wes said, reaching down and patting the side of her neck. "Alder and I had to help someone on the verge of death. At least Aelrie will get a second chance if you mess up."

Wes could feel the dragon's chuckle beneath him as she continued to fly, and he felt warmth spreading within his chest. She would laugh properly again, in time. Even the deepest wounds could not ache forever.

Wes thought of his own mother, father, and brother. The hollow pang in his heart remained—it always would—but the memory of them no longer held him down. They stood beside him now, as strong and wonderful as they appeared in his memories, reminding him that suffering could be a gift, if you let it.

Celesyria finally began to speak, Aelrie repeating each line of the ancient prayer.

Wes sat in silent awe, listening to the melodic voices of the two women.

His beloved and his best friend, elf and dragon, soul and soulless, promising all that they had to a God that they could not even see.

But that's the most important kind of love.

Wes closed his eyes, the afternoon sun gleaming against the snow as Celesyria banked to the west.

The love that isn't blind, but blinding.

16

Chapter 15

KESSARA

Kessara waited for the words to sink in, not daring to take her eyes off of King Ursa.

Captain Drohma was the first to speak. He muttered something about how disgusting the whole thing was and got out of his chair, but to Kessara's surprise, Kylan did not follow.

"Go get some air," Kylan said, gesturing in the direction of the hall. Drohma stared at his King in surprise, but said nothing, offering him a quick half-bow before storming off across the throne room.

The door slammed behind him with an astounding noise, but Kessara did not flinch. With Drohma gone, the rest of their conversation should go more smoothly.

She was almost there, she was sure of it.

"To be clear," King Manta growled in King Ursa's direction. "This is the first I'm hearing of this elven marriage business."

Her mother nodded emphatically. "Such a thing is so

offensive I'm at a loss for words."

Kessara wished that she could sit closer to Alder, drawing courage from his strength, but of course, he could say nothing, offering only a near-imperceptible tilt of his head.

She drew a breath.

"We met members of the remnant, Kylan" she said gently. "It's a long tale that I do not have time for, but–"

"Fine," King Ursa cut her off, his expression unreadable as his green eyes searched her face. "What must I know?"

"There is a lot that I will tell, someday, hopefully to all of our people," Kessara said. "There is so much about the history of Kaveryth that is a lie, a lie that all of us have been fed. But what I can say for certain is that if Wes and I marry, the outcome will be disastrous. He has to marry an elf. There is no other way to achieve victory over Nox."

"Assuming we can trust the woman who told you this," King Manta added.

Kessara faltered for a moment, feeling suddenly warm beneath Kylan Ursa's gaze. If even her own father didn't believe her, why would he?

The room was silent for a long moment.

"You can trust your daughter, my King," Alder said finally. "That should be enough."

For a moment, Kessara was sure that her father was going to relapse back into his earlier temper, but for once, her mother's gentle hand on his arm was enough to keep him quiet.

"If Kessara can find her own happiness and help our Kingdom, we should be celebrating," the Queen said gently.

"As fascinating as the Princess's love life is, my immediate concern is this war," King Ursa said, steepling his fingertips against his chest. "Say that I believe you, and this remnant. Say that the Envoy marries this elf. Why would the people of Silverfell accept her as queen after everything her race has done?"

Kessara found her fingertips playing with the end of her braid before she could stop them. The King was right. Despite all of the good that Aelrie had done, she knew that many in Kaveryth would always look upon her with scorn. It was not so easy to leave Nox behind, no matter how far you managed to run from it.

Fortunately, the King's objection was not a surprise to her. Thanks to hours spent practicing this very negotiation with Alder, she had thought of a plan for every possible reaction. All she could do was to carry it out. The rest was in the hands of the High One.

"Kylan," she said at last, clearing her throat. "I would much prefer it if we could speak about this alone. I just want a few more minutes of your time."

The King's eyebrows rose, but Kessara's father objected before he could decide one way or another.

"Your mother and I rule this Kingdom, Kessara, and we will not be driven away from our own negotiation table."

"I'm not leaving you alone with him," Alder said, getting up from his chair. To Kessara's relief, his indignation sounded entirely authentic. In a way, she supposed, it was. "If there is more to say, say it out in the open."

High One, please.

As the men continued to bicker, Kessara glanced over at her mother and caught her eye, pleading without words. She had to understand.

To her relief, Queen Manta got to her feet and took her

husband's hand.

"Alder was right the first time," she said gently, looking between the men. "I trust my daughter."

Without another word, she walked across the throne room, her long blonde hair trailing down the back of her simple gown as it swayed across the ground.

Kessara suppressed a smile as King Ursa stared after her.

She did not pick up her pace, nor did she look back.

The room was silent, save for the gentle shushing of her blue slippers against the floor.

Before she had made it even halfway to the door, King Manta let out a sigh and followed his wife, just as Kessara knew that he would.

With a final warning glance at King Ursa, Alder got up from his seat and strode off after them as planned, steadying his sword against his belt. Kessara could only hope that Captain Drohma had sought fresh air of the outdoor variety by now.

She leaned back in her seat as Kylan did the same, waiting.

Finally, the door clicked shut.

This was it. If he would not listen to her now, he never would.

Seconds passed, and then a minute, the silence growing increasingly oppressive as the two of them looked at the door. *Good.*

The quiet was doing what it was supposed to do, tempting her to break it, but she would not speak first. No. He might have been the King of one entire Kingdom and Steward of another, not to mention the ruler of Kaveryth's largest army, but in this negotiation, he had to believe the power belonged entirely to her.

It was the only way to make him believe her when she let

the mask fall away.

It took longer than she'd thought it would, but finally, the young King broke.

"I thought you were only going to take a few more minutes of my time."

"I'm sorry, it—It's hard to know exactly what to say. Especially with everyone watching me, waiting for me to screw up and ruin this Kingdom."

"Kessara, just tell me what it is you want me to understand, because as it is now—"

"As it is now, you see no reason to accept my offer?" she asked, infusing her voice with sadness as best as she could.

"Correct," he said. His voice was blunt, no-nonsense, but she could see the slightest confusion in his eyes.

Perfect.

She sighed, and pulled her feet up beneath her on her chair, sitting more like a child than the Princess she was.

"Want a drink? A proper one? I'm sure my father's study is unlocked," she offered.

Kylan shook his head, but just as she hoped, he was already settling himself more comfortably in his chair, letting the practiced stiffness of his back soften just a little.

It was just as her mother had always taught her.

If you have true nobility, people will rise or fall to the bar you set. If you are regal, they will be regal. If you relax, they will relax. But this nobility does not merely reside in your blood, Kessara. It's a skill that you must learn for yourself.

"I've known you forever, Kylan," she said, tucking her knees beneath her chin, her long dress flowing off of the edge of her chair. "Ever since we were little kids. And now look at us. Isn't it strange? You used to make me mud pies decorated with dandelions, and now..."

She trailed off. She didn't need to pretend to get lost in her memories. They were real, the innocent and gentle memories that most children had, of grass stained knees and pretending to hit the boys she fancied.

Kylan Ursa had been one of them, long ago, before she really understood the feelings that rose in her heart at the sight of him.

"We've grown up, Kessara. That's the way it is. Our parents were the same. You fell in love with Roven Cervos, and I–" he paused for a moment, rubbing at his temples, as though the thought of his late rival had given him a headache. "Well, I grew up as Prince of Aridmoor."

"I grew up as Princess of Galeharbor," she said, giving him a soft smile. "But we took different paths, Kylan. I watched you, all that time. I watched you as you learned to crave power above everything else."

She paused, expecting for him to object, but he only looked down at his lap, as though it would be too painful to meet her eyes.

"I remember the rumors. They all said that you had something to do with Queen Ursa's death, but I doubted it. I didn't want to imagine that a boy that I had cared so much for could do such a thing."

He said nothing.

"And then your father died young, too, and by then, my faith in you had become so shaken that I thought you might have actually done it."

"We can all believe rumors, Princess," he said, not looking up. "We know for a fact that your dear friend Wes killed my brother."

Kessara felt an ache in her chest at the thought of Zanek Ursa, Queen Ursa's illegitimate son. It was true. Wes had killed him, but only to prevent his own death. It was not the same, and Kylan knew it.

She decided to let the matter pass.

"You've done a lot of good as King," she said instead, trying to keep her voice light. "Despite our differences of opinion, I'd be foolish to deny it. You and your Red Army have protected the innocent, and you've kept an admirable amount of order in this chaotic time. I commend you for that."

King Ursa looked pleased to hear it, but a moment later, the spell was broken. He set his jaw firmly and looked up at her, eyes narrowed.

"Is there a point to any of this flattery?"

"It's not flattery," she said, shaking her head. "I mean every word."

"Fine. But I still don't see why your opinion of me should mean anything."

For a moment, she didn't respond. She looked him up and down carefully, marveling at just how quickly that he had aged, the weight of Kaveryth on his shoulders. Though hardly a match for Alder, he was still handsome, but there was a haunted look in his eyes that he had no way to hide.

She was right about him, she knew it.

All that was left to do was to make him see who he really was.

"Because even after all you've done, and even if the worst of the rumors about you are true, I still have hope in you, Kylan," she said gently, reaching out and placing her hand on top of his own.

He did not pull away, so she pressed on.

"Beneath everything, however much you object to the path I've chosen and the friends I keep, you still care for me. I can see it. You wouldn't allow harm to come to me."

"Now you flatter yourself," he scoffed.

"You can deny it all that you wish," she said, drawing her hand away, "but everyone knows the truth. It could have been the two of us. We could have been King and Queen of Aridmoor, together. Many expected it, in both of our Kingdoms. But I chose Roven Cervos instead."

She watched as he gripped the arms of his chair, his knuckles going white, his face pale even for an Aridmoorian.

"Again," he said, his usually commanding voice so low that she could barely hear him. "What is the point of telling me all of this?"

He isn't even trying to deny it. His heart still longs for mine, even after all this time.

How easy it would be to deceive him. With a little convincing, she knew that she could make him think he had a chance.

Perhaps, once, she might have been willing to carry out such a deception, to betray and to cheat as so many nobles in every House did.

When she had lost Roven, the despair had been so complete that she had nearly lost herself. She was hollow, wasted. All that was left for her, all that she cared about, was Galeharbor and its people, and she had thrown those dark years of her life into making her Kingdom strong. She would do anything, even if it cost her her life, to be sure that her family would never suffer what the House of Cervos had.

But despite the longing for vengeance that breathed within her, the passing of years had had a way of scraping off her rough edges. She began to notice the sun rising again, the smell of rain on fresh grass, the feeling of contentment in her heart when she behaved as her parents had always taught her.

Even so, there were many nights that she mourned. She would close her eyes, alone in her chambers, thinking of Roven Cervos. A young future King, barely more than a child, a sapling severed before the roots could take.

There had been one such night that she remembered well.

A storm outside, branches clattering against the palace walls, wind screaming as it rushed over the city.

Laying on her bed, gasping for breath as she sobbed.

She couldn't remember his eyes. Not properly. Not as she used to know them, her memory tracing the curve of his irises, noticing every fleck of gold and fire within their brown depths.

She tried, and tried, but it was as though the knowledge had floated away somewhere just out of reach. He was on one side of a chasm, and she was on the other. She could still see his face, still imagine how he smiled at her, but the edges of the memory were blurred.

She wanted to scream and to throw things, to lash out at anything that she could hurt.

Her heart was pounding so hard that she was sure it was going to leap out of her throat.

But all at once, there was something else.

Not a voice, not a sign in the raging sky, but something else.

A singing on the wind, voiceless and screaming all at once, the knowledge as clear and piercing as the waters of the North Sea.

I may forget his face.

I may forget the way his lips felt against mine.

But I will never forget how good he was. And if I don't try to be good like him, all of this sorrow will be for nothing.

"Kessara," the King prompted after a while, tapping his fingertips on the edge of his chair. "I am losing patience. If you brought me aside to humiliate me, then I congratulate you, you have succeeded."

Kessara found the words.

They were the only words, the only way to tell him the truth, whether he wanted to listen or not, she had to try.

"You were my friend, Kylan," she said at last, tucking a braid behind her hair as she forced herself to face him. "Even if it was long ago, I don't give up on my friends without a fight."

The King crossed his arms over his chest, his green eyes burning into hers, but he allowed her to continue.

"You ordered wanted posters for Wes Cervos to be put up all over the Four Kingdoms. You threatened him. Threatened Celesyria. Threatened Alder. And yet, you left Auranth alone. All this time, you've allowed the Envoy's army to thrive."

"Fascinating."

"It was, actually. It's something I've been pondering for the last few months. You had every reason to crush us at the first opportunity, but you didn't. Even when it became clear that Wes could pose a real threat to your power, you ignored us, at least, when we didn't end up fighting side by side with your Red Army. Why?"

Finally, with an exasperated sigh, he spoke.

"I didn't want to split my forces, Kessara, and I knew I'd have time to deal with the Auranth problem later. This war just came about a little earlier than I'd expected."

She smiled at him.

"I don't believe you, but I suppose the elven invasion has become a rather convenient excuse."

King Ursa let out a sigh.

"Fine. If you won't listen to me, I'd love to know what your theory is."

Kessara paused, gathering her thoughts. She had given the matter a great deal of consideration, and she could think of only one explanation that made sense, but she supposed she could still be wrong. If she was, the fate of her people and all of Kaveryth was at stake.

I guess I have to be right.

"I think that deep down, you want something more than power. Sure, you still wanted control of Aridmoor and Silverfell, and it pleased you that your Red Army began to bring men from even further afield into your fold. But you were cautious. You waited. You let Auranth's army grow, made empty threats to my friends, but you never planned to destroy them."

The King's face was unreadable. She pressed on.

"Deep down, there's still a part of you that knows the truth. You know that even if you were to have dominion over the whole world, it would never be enough to fill the hollowness in your heart."

Kylan scoffed.

"Even if you had never chosen Roven Cervos, or that peasant deserter Cadogen, the love of a pretty girl is hardly more important to me than the legacy of the House of Ursa. This broken continent is in desperate need of competent rule, and that is what I have offered."

Kessara paused, trying to keep her own tangled emotions from revealing themselves on her face.

"You're right, Kylan. It was never about me. You had feelings for me when we were children—no one would deny that, least of all you— and even now, you still care for me. But that is not why you're sitting with me today, is it?"

She waited for him to protest.

He didn't.

"You wanted to hear me out because I remind you of another path that you could have taken, a fork in the road that you turned away from all those years ago. I remind you of a time when you weren't so bitter and jaded. I remind you of a time when you were a good man."

She paused then. The King did not speak, but when he looked up at her, there was no mistaking the vulnerability reflected within his eyes.

She got to her feet, moving slowly, as though the strong King before her had suddenly become delicate glass that she was terrified to shatter.

"There is someone out there that can fill the emptiness, Kylan. All I'm asking is that you give Him a chance. Help us. Help us to defeat the elves."

Kylan opened his mouth, and closed it again.

She waited for what felt like a very long time, straining to hear any sound from outside of the throne room and finding only silence.

"Even if we manage to win," he said at last, "you have no idea of the mess that will follow. The people are not going to accept an elf as queen. We will be creating a power vacuum in Silverfell. And if I formally endorse ceasing the sacrifices to the Dracodei–"

"The High One will handle what comes after. Please, Kylan. Please. Trust me, just for a little while."

Kessara watched as Kylan swallowed, the apple of his throat bobbing as he stared at his feet, the ceiling, everywhere but at her.

"Together, we can win this war," she continued, hearing the desperation in her own voice but finding herself unable to quell it. "And once we do, you will see that I told you the truth. I know it."

Finally, Kylan sat up from his own chair. She let out a breath as he closed the space between them with two long strides.

He lifted a hand to her face, tracing a gentle finger along the side of her cheek, and looked into her eyes.

He nodded.

17

Chapter 16

WES

The snow was blinding.

Wes narrowed his eyes, trying to figure out where the sun rested in the sky. It had to be after noon-day, but he couldn't be sure how many hours had passed. The storm was brutal, and most of his energy was focused on clinging to the saddle and hiding his face from the sharp pangs of blowing ice crystals.

Aelrie clung to him, trying her best to hide herself against his back as he lowered himself as tightly as he could against Celesyria's neck. Even with his hood pulled tight around his face, the wind managed to slither down his tunic and cloak, tearing away every bit of body heat he had left.

His headache had been growing steadily worse over the last few days, and though Celesyria struggled to know exactly how much progress they had made in the direction of Umrym, he knew that they had to be getting close. The darkness was near, taunting him with pain that he found increasingly difficult to conceal, and in case he did not have enough to worry about, the winter Feast of Offering loomed before him like a waiting shadow.

"I'm heading down," Celesyria called out in his mind, and he shouted the same warning to Aelrie. With the wind ripping so quickly past her passengers, even the carefree dragon was inclined to take precautions.

Wes closed his eyes, wishing that he had the lung capacity to swear as the shards of ice flew into his face. At least Aelrie was a little more protected sitting behind him, but at the moment, it was difficult to find much comfort in chivalry.

A few seconds after they lowered their altitude, Celesyria told them that she was going back up. He saw nothing, knew nothing of where they were or what lay ahead. He was totally reliant on the dragon's senses to keep them moving in something resembling the right direction. Even if he could have been able to see, the plains of Aridmoor held few landmarks.

"The troops are struggling," the dragon told him, flapping her wings hard and fast, trying to keep her body balanced as the wind buffeted them on all sides. *"The snow is deep, the wind is brutal, and they must be losing strength."*

Wes did not give voice to the more pressing concern. What was left of the safe water that they had brought from Auranth would likely be frozen solid, and the soldiers would be forced to drink from any source that continued to flow—assuming they could find any such water in the first place. There was nothing else that could be done. Either they would die of thirst, or, like many citizens of Kaveryth, they would be forced to gamble with a curse.

"We'll have to stop soon," he agreed, *"But it's safer to march*

as long as our men can bear it. We're getting closer to the elves now. We don't want our camp to be ambushed."

Celesyria agreed, and on she flew, the minutes falling away into yet more hours as the frail light grew dimmer and dimmer. Wes wrapped the leather saddle strap around his wrist, trying to make sure that he remained steady, but it was of little use.

Sometime later—he couldn't be sure of when—he felt himself sliding, falling, his eyes jolting open as he glared down at the whiteout below.

Aelrie took hold of him in a heartbeat, her slender limbs propelled by elven strength as she straightened him in the saddle.

"Are you all right back there?" Celesyria asked, no doubt having noticed the sudden unbalance.

"Yes," Wes said quickly, turning to look at Aelrie, suddenly very much alert. *"I just started to fall asleep. I'll be careful."*

"We need to—"

"Keep going a little longer, Celesyria," he demanded.

The dragon did not question him, and he felt fresh guilt mingling with his pounding headache. He had lied to her. It wasn't sleep. It was sheer and complete exhaustion, brought on by an illness that he had hidden from his best friend for far too long.

"Let me ride in front," Aelrie was saying, looking him over with concern in her pale blue eyes. "I'll bear some of the wind for you. You're sick."

He shook his head.

"I'm fine. I'm just tired."

Liar.

"Wes, you're suffering. It's plain on your face."

"I'm not going to allow you to be my shield," he snapped, just as a fresh gust of wind ripped the words away. "Not you, Aelrie. Not unless I have no other choice. I can keep going."

Wes faced forward again, leaning against Celesyria as the wind continued to howl, Aelrie following suit against his back. As soon as there was a lull in the noise, the elf spoke once more.

"You need to tell Celesyria that you've been poisoned by the cursed water. You cannot keep this from her."

"I will when the time comes," he said, forcing himself to glance up at the dragon whose neck was stretched out ahead of him, her orange scales bright against the white expanse. "I need you to trust me."

"I do trust you," the elf shouted to be heard, resting a delicate hand on his back as she continued to shield her face. "I always will."

Suddenly, there were new words on his lips, precise words that he had never quite managed to string together in a row. She knew, and he knew, and yet, he'd never told her, never quite been able to work up the courage. He had kept waiting for a perfect time that never seemed to come.

He closed his eyes, the snow and ice continuing to pelt at his face, his head pounding, his legs going numb.

But she was there, the High One was there, and that was all that he needed.

"I love you, Aelrie," he said quickly, raising his voice against the competing wind. For a terrifying second, he thought that perhaps she hadn't heard him. Or that she wasn't going to answer.

"I love you too," she said, laughing a little, the sound like tinkling bells. "I thought you knew."

Before he could attempt to turn and kiss her, there was a particularly wicked gust of wind, and he pressed himself almost flat into the saddle. She did the same, the side of her face pressing into his back.

After a few more seconds, he felt the wind ebb away, reduced to its usual whining cry. He sat up straight in the saddle, blinking away the snow. The sky did not look white anymore, but gray, as thick and ominous as a summer thundercloud over the plains of Aridmoor.

"As I was saying," he joked, turning to give her a small smile, "I wish that I had a ring to offer you, instead of this Wrath—"

He stopped short as he saw her expression, closing his mouth against the words.

She was staring past him, and he followed her gesturing hand.

Just ahead, somewhere out there in the sky, he could see color.

First blue, then green, then orange.

One by one, the dragons appeared out of the thick haze, like glittering fish poking their heads up out of a pond in search of food. There were three that Wes could see through his burning vision, flying toward Celesyria on pounding wings.

"Guardians," he said under his breath, trepidation rippling within his stomach.

Celesyria flew in a broad, slow circle, no doubt mindspeaking with the newcomers.

"Didn't they threaten to imprison her?" Aelrie asked, her silvery brow furrowed as she watched the silent exchange.

"They did, and not so long ago."

Like the humans, most of the dragons had chosen to see

Celesyria as a traitor, even as the elven threat gathered within the mountains of Umrym. But perhaps things had changed. If the situation in Umrym was as dire as they'd heard, he doubted that the Guardians could afford to lose a potential ally.

Wes rubbed a hand through his dark curls. In the face of such a huge threat, was it too much to hope that many of the old tensions and conflicts would simply fade away?

"They were scouts, trying to get a lay of the land. They seem content to take any help that is offered," Celesyria said at last. Wes let out a held breath, watching as the Guardians continued past them. *"But the battlefield is a few miles ahead, and the Guardians are struggling to keep the elves from advancing."*

"Tell them that help is coming," Wes said firmly. *"Tell them we will be there at first light, if they can hold the elves off that long. In the meantime, we make camp where we stand now. It will have to do."*

After relaying the information to Aelrie, he prepared himself for a rough landing, holding onto Celesyria's saddle with white-knuckled fingers. The dragon circled back, flapping her huge orange wings hard as she found herself on a current of air. Wes pressed his eyes shut as the blowing snow became a maelstrom of ice shards, flying into every inch of exposed flesh. Aelrie clung to his back, unable to say nor hear a word.

A few seconds later came the lurching in his belly as Celesyria dove, impossible weightless seconds, and finally, the jolt as her front legs slid against the ground. Wes opened his eyes just in time to watch her sending a torrent of thick snow through the air as she came to a stop.

Before he had a chance to catch his breath, Aelrie was

leaping from the dragon's back, landing delicately on her feet, and brushing snow from her black trousers and tunic.

As he followed her–more clumsily, on unsteady legs–he imagined what it would be like to see her dressed for something other than travel, training, or war. Still, despite the decidedly unfeminine attire, she was so striking that Wes often found it hurt to look at her.

The strangest part is that she looks at me in just the same way. Like I was placed here in this world just for her.

"My Lord!" one of the soldiers was shouting, the pain behind Wes' eyes yanking him firmly back into reality. Celesyria had gone off a short distance away, waiting as several soldiers helped her to remove her saddle and the load of packs she carried. "My Lord! Is there news?"

"Are we going to rest?" said another man, one of the dwarves. He had two companions standing beside him, and all three looked so similar that Wes wondered if they were a set of triplets. Auranth's army had grown so quickly that he'd long since given up on trying to keep track of who was who. "It's not the best place, I realize, but I figure if we work fast, we might be able to use the snow as a windblock. I mean, it won't be enough to protect the whole camp, but we can keep the injured a little warmer, at least."

Wes nodded, trying to focus on the man's words through the pain in his head. The darkness was near, the scent of it festering in his nostrils and making him want to retch.

How am I going to lead these men? How much closer can I come to this evil?

"That's a brilliant idea," Aelrie said, placing her hand in the crook of his arm and leaning gently against his side. "If anything, every man should be trying to create a small windbreak before his own tent. We can afford to spread out a little more than usual. If there are bandits here, they'll almost certainly be fighting alongside the elven army, anyway. I don't foresee trouble tonight."

The dwarves and men who had assembled looked at each other, and then at Aelrie.

Wes swallowed a sigh.

"Yes, gentlemen. Please do as Aelrie says. And that goes for whatever she says, is that clear?"

"Yes, my Lord," one of the men said quickly, the others nodding their agreement before scurrying off in search of the most agreeable spot to start piling his own wall of snow.

The sky was still dim and gray, but the snow was finally letting up, and Wes expected that they would have at least an hour or two of half-light to work by.

"Are you okay?" Aelrie asked as soon as the men were out of earshot, resting a hand against his chest and gazing up at him. "You seemed a little out of it for a moment there."

He pulled her close without warning, savoring the warmth of her breath against his tunic and the smell of her raven hair as it tickled his nose. Even the wind had abated somewhat, as though the weather was offering him a few moments' truce. It felt wonderful just to breathe without his lungs burning from the rushing cold.

"It's the elves," he admitted, running his fingers along her spine as she melted into his embrace. "They're close, and it's making it difficult for me. And then when the men started shouting... I'll be fine. I just needed a minute."

It was true, or at least, he hoped it was. The blinding pain had subsided to something nearer to his normal dull ache, and considering the circumstances, it was the best that he could hope for.

High One, You will have to lend me Your strength. Just for a little while. My people need me.

After a few more blissful seconds, Aelrie pulled away, brushing a few stray snowflakes from Wes's lips as she did so.

"Let me ready your tent, at least," she asked. "You need to rest for a little while before twenty other people demand your attention. I don't mind, I promise."

He wanted to argue with her, to insist that he should be the one getting her tent ready as well as his own, but something held him back. As long as he'd known her, she'd never sought to compare her strength or skill to his own, not to mention her profoundly superior looks. She'd always treated him like he was important, like he had something to offer her, even when he couldn't always see it for himself.

Now, he was weaker than he ever had been before, including when he was a fat teenager who struggled to swing a sword. There was no way to hide what he had become. No matter how badly he wanted to be invincible like Alder, protecting the woman he loved at every turn, the choice wasn't up to him. And if he was going to be humbled, he may as well start working on his pride now.

"I'd appreciate that," he said quietly, meeting her eyes with his own. *I hope you understand how difficult it is for me to accept your help, my dear. And I hope you know how much your help means to me, all the same.* "I need to speak to Celesyria, anyway."

Aelrie tilted her head up and accepted a peck on the cheek before heading off to gather their tents. Wes watched as the hundreds of soldiers milled about, talking to one another as they moved snow and unpacked their few belongings. The camp buzzed along, their pace practiced after many similar evenings, but as he glanced from face to face, he could see that something had changed.

For many of them, the war still hid beyond the edge of the map, an adventure that they were confident they could face as they daydreamed or swung practice swords.

Those were the uncertain faces now, their eyes glancing toward the horizon every few seconds, waiting for the menace that had suddenly become real.

And then there were the others, the soldiers borrowed from the armies of the Four Kingdoms, men who had gotten close enough to war that the battlefield had lost any sense of romance.

They walked with purpose, performing their tasks with unthinking efficiency, their mouths set in grim lines. A few of them still smiled at their friends, joking to one another, the promised rush of adrenaline enough to keep them from despair, but Wes was not among them.

He had taken life before, and though he still knew how to smile and to laugh, he knew that a part of him had been wounded beyond repair.

Tomorrow's promised battle held nothing but dread. It was the possibility of what came after that kept him moving.

After a while, Celesyria made her way over to him, trying not to knock anyone over with her tail as she left her craterous footprints in the deep snow.

She updated him on the state of the camp—she'd been able to make both him and Aelrie an excellent windbreak with only a few swipes of her front claws and she'd soon return to help some of the others—but he could tell by the look in her yellow eyes that there was something more important she wanted to tell him.

"What do you think about everything?" he asked her after a while, the two of them having found a nearby fire where they could borrow a hint of warmth. The light was almost gone now, and the camp was lit with hundreds of lanterns and torches, stretching far into the distance, their view no longer obscured by the storm.

"Our soldiers have amazed me," she said, bowing her head in the general direction of the tents. *"They've carried their packs, they've marched in all weather, and only a few have complained. The High One has blessed us."*

He nodded, and silence stretched between them as the fire flickered against the snow.

As far as he knew, not a single soldier had defected since they marched out of Auranth. Somehow, their army of misfits had come together when it counted, loyal and strong. But whether or not they would be able to withstand an elven army was another thing entirely.

"Aelrie keeps telling me I need rest, but I don't expect to sleep tonight," Wes said. *"I keep turning what we know over and over in my mind, but nothing seems to fit together. I have no idea how to command these people. I wish Alder was here."*

Celesyria lowered her head, using the tip of her snout to give him a gentle push against the chest.

"Alder is not the Envoy. These soldiers may respect him, and Kessara, and even me, but they are here because of you. They are part of this force because of you."

Wes knit his fingers together, staring into the fire as the smoke danced, rising into the sky in twisting tendrils until it faded out of sight.

"And anyway, you must command this army differently than Alder would," Celesyria continued, using a single claw to slide a loose stick back into the base of the fire.

"What do you mean?"

"You can't be foolish, Wes. You need to stay safe. You're not here to die."

"Isn't that a given?"

Celesyria shook her head. *"Alder would stay on the front lines. You can't. I need to keep you in the air as much as possible, and we'll just have to land now and then when you have to give new orders."*

Wes wanted to argue, but he knew that she was right. As much as it sickened him to admit it, he had a prophesied role in restoring worship to the High One, and he'd already taken enough risks. Not to mention the small fact that if he got much closer to the elves, he probably wouldn't be able to walk, anyway.

"I understand," he said finally, *"but Aelrie needs to be with me, too. However useful she'd be as a ground scout, we need her to reverse the oath. We can't lose her."*

"And she also happens to be the woman you're madly in love with, and you want to keep her safe," Celesyria teased.

He smiled.

"True enough."

The dragon gave a quick nod. *"So it's settled, then. I wish we had another mindspeaker on the ground so I could at least talk with them without having to land, but we'll just have to make do with what we have."*

"I think Moorn should be in charge, with the help of a few of the more experienced Aridmoorian soldiers," Wes said, gesturing in the direction of the Silverfell soldier, who was standing

beside a tent nearby. *"Viggo and Vard as well. They've never fought in a war, but I trust their judgment, and I'd rather they be near the front than their father."*

Celesyria nodded. *"Bargren is strong, but he's too old to be on the frontline. We need him to manage the camp, anyway."*

"I just wish we knew what the Red Army was going to do," Wes said, letting out a long sigh. *"I guess the best that we can hope for is that they stay out of our way."*

Celesyria paused for a moment, as though debating with herself, until finally she spoke.

"Once we know what we're facing firsthand, you know what happens next," she said softly.

"I hold on for dear life and try not to die?"

"You know what I mean."

Wes kicked at a chunk of snow with his foot, sending it a few feet through the air before it hit a rock with a wet thump. He did know, far too well.

"I'm terrified to marry her. I have no idea what I'm doing."

"It must be done, Wes," Celesyria said, lowering her head so that their eyes could meet. *"The High One will make you ready."*

"Do you still believe that?"

He let the question hang in the air as the camp bustled around them. Dozens of men and several women walked by, carrying supplies and looking up at the clear night sky, their boots shushing against the snow. Fires dotted the landscape before him, dozens of them, like little warm flowers budding in white soil.

He watched the cold air billowing in great plumes out of Celesyria's nostrils. On any other day, she would have answered at once, filled with certainty if not enthusiasm, but now, things were different.

If even Celesyria's unfailing faith was struggling, what chance did he have?

"I do," she said aloud at last, her voice dropping to a whisper. "I have to. He's all I have left."

18

Chapter 17

KESSARA

Kessara waited patiently as her mother wrote out the contract in her neat, practiced hand. There would be no one to enforce it—it was not as though her father and King Ursa had a higher court that they could appeal to—but at least the ink and paper felt more solid than mere words.

Her mother had asked her to stand close by, keeping watch for any mistakes, but she knew that the Queen would make none. The little black curves and loops seemed to slip from her pen like magic, detailing the finer points of grain provision, navy allotments, and other matters currently under advisement.

The curtains of her mother's library were open, but the dim sunlight had finally faded away, leaving her to work by candlelight. She hardly seemed to notice, lost in the repetitive and yet vital task that lay on the desk in front of her.

"Is this the last page?" Kessara asked after a while, blinking her tired eyes a few times as her mother lifted her pen.

"Yes," she said, pulling the candle stand closer to the sheet of paper. "After that, a walk through the gardens would be lovely. There's something I'd like to discuss with you."

"Can you not tell me now?" the Princess asked, glancing over at the window that framed the starless winter sky. It would be a pretty stroll, but not a warm one.

"Be patient," her mother scolded, picking up her pen again and continuing to write. Within seconds, she was completely absorbed in her task. Kessara wouldn't have been surprised if she forgot that her daughter was there.

She tried to keep her eyes on the perfect, error-less lines of text, but as usual, her thoughts made their way to Alder.

Ever since she had met with Kylan in private earlier that day, she'd scarcely had a moment with the man that she loved. To her surprise, her father had asked that Alder spend the day with him while he and Kylan hammered out the details of their plan. Alder, for his part, had been less than thrilled with the idea, but the King insisted, and Kessara found herself alone with her mother.

Both King Ursa and her father had wanted the contracts completed before messengers could be sent to Auranth, but at her mother's prodding, they had finally agreed to send three men straight away on stagback. Kessara suspected that the Envoy's army may have already moved toward the front, but it was worth trying to catch them, if they could. Captain Drohma had been sent ahead back to High Keep, which Kessara was glad about, but she hoped that Kylan would eventually see that the man was a snake and dump him entirely.

"Kessara? Kessara!" her mother was saying, waving a

hand in her direction. "I asked you if the wording looked all right. For the last two lines."

"Oh, right," the Princess said, blinking a few times. Suddenly, she was very tired. "It looks perfect, mother. In any case, Kylan might end up wanting to amend it, anyway, so there's no point in fussing too much."

"True enough," her mother said, closing the documents within their heavy wooden case and placing her pen on a tray. "Are you ready to go?"

"You're sure that they won't need us yet?"

Her mother rolled her eyes. "Darling, Alder lived without you for most of his life. I'm sure an evening won't kill him."

"That's not what I meant," Kessara protested, rushing to keep up as her mother strode toward the double doors, her dress trailing against the polished marble floor.

The halls leading toward the back door of the kitchen were deserted, lit only with a few haphazard torches that left most of the space in shadow. The Queen walked confidently, but Kessara found herself looking over her shoulder every few seconds, jumping at every little sound.

"It was strange for me at first," her mother said, not turning around. "When we sent the servants home and lost most of the guards, I mean. Our home has always been bustling and alive, but now..."

She didn't finish. They had reached the main kitchen, which was massive, intended for preparing food for the entire royal family as well as the guards and other staff. Ordinarily, the countertops would have been filled with dishware, recipes, cutlery, bags of flour, and all manner of odds and ends. Tonight, though, the smooth stone surfaces sat empty, save for a couple of small vases filled with long-forgotten dried flowers. The fireplace was dark and silent, and only a couple of candles lit the way.

Kessara and her mother strode across the room in silence, as though they might disturb some ghost. They took hold of two of the thick wool cloaks that hung by the door and pulled them over their dresses, and stepped through the gate.

Finally, she could breathe.

Despite the thick layer of white powder that obscured the shape of everything it touched, the Princess knew every inch of this place. Windshear palace had several gardens, including a particularly grand one that extended out from the east courtyard, but this one had always been her favorite.

She thought back to the beginnings of summer, where she had walked through this very gate and first laid eyes on the love of her life. It felt so far away, a life that another woman had lived, especially now as she considered the cold and the snow.

"I can't wait to see the flowers again," her mother said as they made their way past the carrot patches and the wooden trellises that would soon be crawling with beanstalks. "I've never cared much for winter, but this year things feel especially hollow. I hope that the locusts are kinder to us this growing season."

Kessara bit her lip. She remembered how awful they'd been last year, great swarms of the well-armored beasts washing across Galeharbor and devouring everything in their path. They had managed to preserve most of the palace garden thanks to the high walls, but most of Galeharbor's farmed crops had suffered, leaving their Kingdom with even less of a winter reserve than usual.

"I am hopeful that they will not come at all, mother," she

said, peering out with one eye from beneath her woolen hood. "If Wes can succeed in restoring worship to the High One, things will change all across Kaveryth. The world will not be so dark. Even when the ice and the snow come."

For a long while, her mother did not respond. The moon had risen enough that they could see without needing to keep their torches lit, and the Queen stepped through the archway that led into the garden maze, Kessara following closely at her heels.

As they made their way through the twisting passages, Kessara brushed snow from each statue and piece of topiary, revealing the shadowed faces of mermaids, kelpies, and other sea-beasts. She supposed the place might have been intimidating to strangers, but to her, it was peaceful, even in the dark.

"Our temples have been busy lately," her mother said at last, reaching over to help her clear the carved face of a water nymph. "I've thought of going. I've gone, really, straight to the doors. But I've hidden my face. I don't trust anything I've heard about the Dracodei anymore, even for the sake of keeping the peace. I've been losing everything I've been raised to believe. Everything I've raised you to believe. It's hard to bear."

Kessara nodded. "We had sought the Codex Veritatis, wanting certainty about what we were doing, but we found the remnant instead. I learned a great deal about the true history of Kaveryth, and it is beyond a doubt to me now that the Dracodei is nothing but a cruel lie. But that doesn't mean accepting the High One is any easier now than it ever was."

"Right," her mother said, tucking a stray blonde hair beneath her hood. "I want to accept Him. At least, I think I do.

But I still feel like I'm grieving. It's like I've lost the world."

Kessara glanced up at the sky overhead, watching as a cloud blew across the pale moon, obscuring the garden below in deepening shadow.

"I know that sounds foolish," her mother continued, shaking her head.

"No," Kessara said quickly. "It doesn't. I understand. It's not just the Dracodei, the temples, the treasures... it's like losing the entire lens that you see the world through. Everything feels blurry for a while. But it does get better."

The Queen paused again as they rounded a wall, stepping into a wide passage lined with a dozen stone fountains, long since drained of their babbling streams of water.

"There's something I need to say, Kessara."

The Princess waited, falling in step beside her mother and listening to the sound of the snow crunching against their boots.

"The news about Wes and Aelrie is a mixed blessing," her mother said. "I want you to see it with clear eyes."

Kessara felt her jaw clench.

"It's going to be fine, mother. When our people learn about all of the good Aelrie has done, not to mention when they come to understand the true history of Kaveryth, they will accept her as queen."

I hope I'm right. There is no other option.

Her mother shook her head.

"That's not what I meant."

"What is it, then? Is this about Alder? Because he's not of noble blood?"

Her mother smiled.

"It's nothing like that. Despite his attitude, even your

father likes him, though he would probably deny it."

Kessara knotted her fingertips in the fabric of her cloak, trying to stop her hands from shaking.

"Anyway, he has some rough edges, but far lesser men have become good rulers when called upon."

The Queen let her words hang there in the cool night air.

"Mother," Kessara said through gritted teeth. "Please just say what you mean."

"Every time you leave Windshear, I worry," her mother said. "I suppose that's an understatement. The fear consumes me. And it's the same with your father. How can I hand my most precious jewels to the world, expecting them to come back to me untouched?"

Kessara nodded.

"I know what it's like."

She didn't need to say his name aloud. Her mother and father had liked Roven very much, and his parents had been their close friends. Their deaths had been a tragedy for her entire family.

"Roven's death was tragic, but it was also a surprise attack. No one expected the elves to come to Stronghollow that day, or to do what they did."

"Why does that make any difference?"

"Alder is a soldier, Kessara," her mother said with a sigh. "He will remain one, even as King of Galeharbor. It's a part of who he is, and even loving you will not change that. I know that you hope the High One will restore this broken continent, but you have to accept that there may be other wars, even if he survives this one."

The Queen paused for breath, pulling her cloak more tightly across her chest as a gentle breeze began to blow.

"He will make decisions that infuriate you. He will be stubborn and stupid. You will watch him go, again and again, and it will hurt. I speak from experience."

Kessara felt a shiver coursing down her back. She'd seen Alder come near to death more than once. She couldn't bear to fathom how she would feel if it really happened, if the man she loved disappeared from her world once and for all.

"The pain of loving him terrifies me," she admitted, looking down at her feet as they continued to make boot prints in the snow. "He has disappointed me already, if I'm being honest with myself. He has a way of being stubbornly human."

"That feeling will never leave you," her mother said gently, tugging at her sleeve. Kessara stopped where she stood and met her mother's eyes. "I need you to know that before I tell you the rest."

"I do know it. And I still choose him. He's worth the pain."

Kessara leaned into her mother's embrace, soaking in the smell of her favorite lavender perfume, safe and warm.

"Despite our imperfections, loving your father is the same," the Queen said as she pulled back. "I'm glad I never chose to be anyone else. Being a wife, mother, and queen is my greatest pain, true, but it's also my greatest joy."

Kessara swiped at her cheek, surprised to find that a few stray tears had landed there.

"And," her mother continued, "Despite my worry about letting you and your father go out into the world, there is a part of me that always hopes. Maybe it's your High One, I don't know, but I've found ways to believe that you both will come back to me."

Kessara drew a deep breath, willing her mother to understand what she was about to say. She wouldn't like it, she knew, but she wasn't willing to hold back the truth.

"I won't be at home waiting for him," she said, forcing the words out before she could lose her nerve. "I will go to the battlefield, whether he wants me there or not."

Her mother said nothing. She continued to walk, moving past the fountains and toward the passage that would eventually take them back inside. Kessara followed, a silent shadow beneath the moon, waiting.

"I was hoping that you'd be smart about this."

"I'm sure Alder wishes for the same."

The Queen let out a long breath, pressing her hands to her head.

"Why was I given such an impossibly stubborn child?"

Kessara did not answer.

Silence spread between them as they walked on, the palace wall visible now between the topiaries once more. It was late, and she imagined that the two kings and Alder had likely finished up their cigars by now. Soon enough, she'd be able to retire to the comfort of her warm bed. Her mother was angry, but so long as she waited her out, eventually the queen would relent.

Finally, they reached the gate that led back into the darkened kitchen. Her mother placed her hand on the bolt, and turned to face Kessara once more.

"I spoke to your father," she said.

Kessara's heart thudded beneath her cloak.

"About what?"

Her mother fiddled with the metal lock, twisting the silver bar between her delicate fingertips and making it clink.

"It took some convincing, let me tell you. He's as stubborn

as you are."

Kessara stared at the gate, drawing in one breath after the next, trying to maintain her patience to no avail.

"Mother, please! I've heard enough riddles."

"Very well," the Queen said, sliding the bolt free and pushing the door inward, the gate groaning as it swung on ancient hinges. "War is near. Your father knows it, and as much as he can be tough, he has never been cruel."

Kessara stepped into the kitchen, blinking fast as her eyes adjusted to the darkness. As she moved to light her torch, she realized that her fingers were shaking.

Her mother placed a steadying hand over her own.

"The decision has been made, if you will accept it," she said, a smile teasing at the edge of her lips. Even in the shadow, Kessara was certain that she could see the glimmer of joy in her mother's eyes. "You both deserve a proper last kiss before the battle begins."

Kessara felt the air rush from her lungs.

High One, please, let it be true.

"If you wish to marry Alder Cadogen, you should do it now."

ALDER

Alder leaned toward the open window over his head, trying to take in some of the fresh night air that wasn't tainted by clouds of tobacco smoke. King Manta and King Ursa had been chewing on their cigars for a good while, and though Alder was accustomed to the habit thanks to his years in the Aridmoorian army, he could only bear the smell for so long.

Their discussion had gone on for several hours, and despite understanding only about half of what was being said, he was thankful that he'd been invited to sit in. If he was going to be King of Galeharbor one day, he would have to learn it all.

Finally, King Manta got to his feet, stretching out his thick arms over his head and snuffing out his final cigar in an overflowing ashtray. King Ursa followed suit, though even he had not been able to keep up with the elder King's smoking prowess. His own little mountain of ash was much smaller.

"Well, gentlemen, I suppose we've gotten everything sorted. The contracts will be ready to sign by now," the King said, gesturing toward the door that led back into the throne room.

Alder got to his feet and followed obediently, waiting for King Ursa to make his way first. Though Kylan had barely spoken to him since Kessara and the Queen had left them alone, he could no longer see the usual hatred on the young King's face. Whatever Kessara had said to him in private had clearly had an impact, and Alder was eager to find out just what their conversation had entailed.

Mostly, though, he was ready to find a guest room and fall asleep. It had been an incredibly long day, and every one of his limbs seemed to ache at once. The world would make more sense in the light of dawn.

As he stepped into the throne room, he nearly tripped over Kessara, who was standing right beside her father and King Ursa.

"Kessara?" he said stupidly, glancing around for any sign of Queen Manta or the contracts that she had been working on while the two Kings made their deals. He watched as King Manta pulled Kylan to the side, talking to him in a loud voice about the spring corn crop.

Kessara took hold of his hand, half-dragging him into the

breakfast alcove where they had sat earlier that day.

"Did your mother go to bed? I don't blame her. I'm exhausted. All that–"

Before he could finish his sentence, Kessara's lips were on his, her soft fingers touching his jaw as he fell into the kiss. For a beautiful moment, he could forget the fact that the two Kings were mere feet away, but it didn't take him long to return to reality.

"Darling," he said, pressing a fingertip to her lips. "Your father–King Ursa–"

Kessara was smiling, and he could see the soft gleam of tears in her eyes.

"Mother is getting everything ready," she said, her voice shaking slightly as she placed her hand in his own.

"Ready for what?" he asked, squeezing her hand, though he had no idea what had put her in such a state. He glanced over at King Manta and King Ursa, who had made their way to the far end of the room. Kessara's father was showing off the nautical mosaic tile that lined the edge of the floor, and neither seemed to be paying any attention whatsoever.

"Our wedding," the Princess announced, her cheeks flushed as she nearly jumped off of the ground with excitement.

Alder's knees felt like they were going to collapse under him.

"Wedding? Now?" he hissed under his breath, pulling her closer to the wall as her father and Kylan strode by.

Kessara nodded, her smile never faltering.

"Does your father know?"

"Yes," she said quickly, casting a brief glance in King Manta's direction. "I couldn't believe it, either, but my mother talked to him. She convinced him that if we really were serious about this, it would be best to commit to our course of action now, before we face the elves."

Alder held both of her hands in his own as he pulled her behind one of the thick pillars that held the vaulted ceiling. His fingers were shaking.

"And you're sure about this?" he asked, holding her gaze with his own.

Kessara stood on her toes and leaned in to kiss him on the cheek.

"I love you, Alder. Difficult times will come, and I'd rather have you as my husband when they do."

He paused for a moment, trying to slow his breathing.

"If you're not ready, I can wait," Kessara added, her blue eyes filled with concern as she searched his face. "I know your mother and sisters are away in Graveheim, not to mention Wes and our other friends–"

"I've been ready to marry you for a long time, Kessara Manta," he said in a whisper. "And your mother is right. We're about to walk into a war. It would be a great gift to face it knowing that we are right, together, before the High One."

She smiled at him, and he couldn't help but to consider the shape of her curves hidden beneath her pretty blue dress.

She had been stunning from the first moment he'd laid eyes on her–any man would have to be blind to deny it–but he had never felt more blessed to know the workings of her heart than he did right at that moment. The Four Kingdoms were filled with women that were pleasing to the eye, but a woman as good, smart, and kind as Kessara was a treasure that he would give anything to keep.

"So it's settled," she said, trying and failing to pull her face into a serious expression. "Wait here, and I will ask a guard to collect you when it's time. I need to get dressed."

His brow furrowed as he glanced down at his own worn traveling clothes.

"Don't I get to get dressed?"

She looked him up and down for what felt like a long time. Her father and King Ursa had wandered closer to where he and Kessara stood, and Alder wondered how much longer that King Manta would be able to keep distracting him.

"I'd rather you like this," she said firmly. "This is how I want to marry you. A soldier. A traveler. Always handsome, and always my protector."

"I'd marry you in my nightclothes if it made you happy," he said truthfully.

"So it's settled," she said once more.

Without another word, she strode toward the other two men, gave her father a quick kiss on the cheek, and headed for the door that led out into the hall.

Alder stood where he was, trying to stop his mouth from hanging open as he watched her go. She held her head high, and her steps were confident, as though she'd had her whole life to prepare for this moment rather than an hour or two.

Before he could think what to do with himself, King Manta sidled up beside him, with King Ursa a couple of steps behind.

"There's been a bit of a change of plans tonight, Kylan," Kessara's father said, placing his wounded hand on the younger King's arm. "But we will be ready to sign at dawn, and move out shortly after, if that suits you."

Kylan's eyes narrowed into slits as he crossed his arms over his chest.

"What plans could have changed at this hour? I was hoping

for some sleep, myself."

"And you'll have it, in the nicest chamber I can find," King Manta said quickly.

King Ursa turned to Alder.

"And what will you be up to, Cadogen?"

He froze, trying desperately to catch King Manta's eye, but the man's face was unreadable.

Well, he will know soon enough, I suppose.

"Princess Kessara and I are getting married tonight," Alder said, forcing himself to meet Kylan's eyes.

For a long moment, he did not speak, and Alder could almost see the tempest of anger that swirled within the King's green eyes.

He could call off the deal. This could ruin everything.

He struggled to suppress the panicked tightness that filled his chest.

Stupid, stupid, stupid idea.

Before he could wonder whether or not he should chase after Kessara and call the whole thing off, King Manta spoke.

"A surprise to all of us, I assure you," King Manta said, looking more cheery than Alder had ever seen him. In fact, he looked absolutely bursting with happiness.

The entire situation was so absurd that he could have nearly laughed aloud, had he not been so terrified.

Finally, with a slow sigh of breath, the lines on Kylan's face began to soften. He extended a hand to Alder, who shook it at once, scarcely believing that this night was anything but a bizarre and very realistic dream.

"Kessara is a good person, Cadogen," he said quietly. "Treat her well."

Alder gave him a stiff nod.

"I must go and see to my men before I retire," Kylan said, turning to King Manta. "I appreciate any lodgings you can give us."

King Manta waved a hand, and as always, Alder couldn't help but to gaze a few seconds too long at his severed fingers.

"As I said, you will rest well within the walls of Windshear Palace. Your men as well. Goodnight."

A few moments later, the door of the throne room slammed shut behind King Ursa, leaving Alder and Kessara's father alone in the cavernous space.

Alder said nothing, staring at the closed door for as long as he could, until King Manta rested a hand on his shoulder.

"I'm still not sure about this High One business," he said, clearing his throat. "But something about this mad plan feels right. Come now. We have a wedding to get to."

As he strode off after the man who was about to become his father in law, Alder was more certain of the High One's power than ever.

19

Chapter 18

CELESYRIA

Celesyria could not feel her tail.

She flicked it back and forth as she flew, trying to restore some sensation to the frozen appendage, but it was of little use. The snow was falling again, thousands of tiny flakes filtering across the soft pink sky, but she struggled to appreciate its beauty at the moment.

She could feel Wes and Aelrie shifting their weight on her back yet again as she turned to the right, her wings pushing against the cold morning air. They were just as nervous as she was, struggling not to fidget as the battlefield ahead drew closer and closer.

She could see the lines already, hundreds of human men, most in Red Army uniforms, stretching as far as she could see. There were dragons, too, further ahead, but she had not yet attempted to speak with them. She had so much to say, so much to ask, and yet she and the others had spent most of their early morning journey in silence.

Their own army was coming behind her, following along the path through the snow that she scouted, with Moorn in the lead. They would be silent, too, clutching at their weapons as they waited, each trudging step bringing them closer to the enemy that had haunted them from afar for so many centuries.

She pressed forward, riding on a current of frigid air as thick snowflakes landed in her eyes.

She blinked them away, eyes narrowed as she tried to see across the expanse. Up ahead, she could see the silhouette of the Severed Summits, their jagged peaks half-hidden by the blowing snow.

Umrym.

Celesyria pushed herself faster, surging ahead over the Red Army lines. She would have to circle back to their own soldiers, but at the moment, she didn't care. She had to see for herself.

The elves stood out against the snow like a deep shadow, their black clothing stark even against the haze. They were moving forward, their disciplined steps bringing them closer to King Ursa's army with each passing moment.

There were thousands of them.

They marched in silence, but Celesyria could hear the sound of their heavy armor clanking as they moved. Unlike the humans, who wore red scarves over their mouths, the elves left their otherworldly faces exposed, unconcerned with the cold.

Wes said something to her, but she didn't hear the words. She couldn't look away. They were mesmerizing, like beautiful ants building a colony, each part working together to form a perfect whole. Celesyria remembered Luna's words.

Long ago, these elves were chosen to counsel men, to help them to rule Kaveryth justly. And instead of obeying the High One, they threw Him away.

She circled overhead, drawing a deep breath as she lifted them higher. The Red Army was moving closer now, shouting at the sky as they marched, trampling the perfect blanket of white snow beneath thousands of heavy boots.

For a second, the elves remained quiet. Celesyria circled back around, watching as the battlefield seemed to draw a long breath. The Red Army men stopped short, their spears sticking straight toward the snowy sky, their swords held aloft. Their war cries ceased.

"What's going on?" Wes said in her mind.

"I have no idea," she said, furrowing her orange brow. *"The elves are just... standing there."*

She watched the male and female elves at the front of the line. She was close enough now to see their faces, but their expressions revealed nothing.

She flapped her wings and headed upward, circling around once again. The Envoy's army had to be getting closer to the back of the Red Army lines, but the snow was falling faster now, and she couldn't make anything out in the fog of white.

"Look!" Aelrie cried out.

She banked tighter, but before she could get herself entirely turned around, she could see a hail of arrows below, flying toward the Red Army soldiers. There had been no warning. One moment, the elves were standing casually in the snow, the next they had nocked a thousand arrows and let fly.

The men raised their round red shields, and she could hear the sound of the sharp elven arrows plinking against the sturdy wood as she turned to face the enemy once more.

"Hold on!" she said aloud, flapping her wings as hard as she could as another volley of arrows from both sides met in the air. She twisted and turned in the air, narrowly avoiding several of the sharp projectiles that had been sent in her direction.

The other Guardians must still be in Umrym.

She was too cold to feel the shiver that coursed through her spine.

If they were behind the elven lines, they were most likely dead by now, but she couldn't allow herself to think such thoughts. Jaconial and perhaps Nazzan were there, and they were too strong for the elves to push aside so easily. She would hope until she was given a reason not to.

The two armies met below, and the sound of clashing swords and battle cries filled the air as the Red Army tried to hold their ground against the onslaught.

"What in the Wrathlands are those things?" she heard Wes shout.

She did not need to ask what he meant.

Along the edges of the lines below, she saw at least a dozen strange beasts, rushing toward the Red Army soldiers with a female elf on each of their backs. They looked like wolves, but they were massive, easily twice the size of the largest Ironwolf. Their paws left tracks bigger than Celesyria's own.

"No idea," she heard Aelrie reply.

Briefly, she considered rushing down to try and knock them aside with her own powerful claws, but she couldn't risk it, not with such precious passengers on her back.

Fortunately, the human soldiers noticed the beasts, leaping out of the way before entire rows of men could be bowled over by them. King Ursa's men were impressive, their swords flashing as they slashed at the creatures, the elves on their backs trying to shoot the soldiers with arrows as they fought.

Before Celesyria could see more, she felt several arrows hitting her tail ridge, stinging for a moment before they plinked off of her scales and fell harmlessly to the ground. She flapped her wings and flew upward.

"We can't stay here much longer," she said to Wes. *"I want to get another look at something."*

He didn't argue. She turned again, letting her unfurled wings glide upon a gust of wind as fresh snow continued to fall on the scene below. She reached the first row of elves, who were trying to push through the Red Army line with little success, and continued over their heads.

There.

In the middle of the elves, she finally caught sight of the Blackmasks. There were hundreds of them, more than she'd imagined, and both dwarves and men made up their number. She shook her head. In the end, the elves would have no use for them, or for any other traitors that they had managed to pull over to their side. They had sold themselves out to evil, and the cost would be heavy, but it was too late to help them now. They had chosen.

As she circled back toward their own men, she saw two Guardian dragons soaring toward the elves, their claws raised as they dove for the ground.

The larger of the two was struck by arrows as they approached, but fortunately, they missed the membranes of his wings, the arrows falling aside uselessly as they struck at his armored flank. His companion rushed forward, and Celesyria couldn't help but to look away as the offending elf archer was crushed between the dragon's powerful jaws.

She could feel Wes on her back, shifting his weight, no doubt trying to shield Aelrie from witnessing the terrible sight below. She swung around once again, watching as the dragons attacked the front lines with claws and teeth.

She longed to join them, to fill her lungs with air and to breathe out in a rush, sending a plume of fire into the black crowd below. If they used their fire, they would be able to take them out ten at a time. But she didn't dare, and neither did the Guardians. The fear of exile was strong, even when she hadn't taken their oath.

She let out a roar of frustration instead, flying as low as she dared over the men and dwarf bandits who swelled the ranks of Nox. A couple of the men tried to flee, only to be shoved forward by the next line of sword-wielding elves.

"We need to go to our men," Wes called out to her. *"Moorn isn't going to be able to stumble his way through this."*

He was right.

With a final glance at the two Guardians, she turned back, pumping her wings as she sought a higher altitude. Her scales deflected a few final arrows as she passed, but fortunately, Wes and Aelrie seemed to have gotten through the situation unscathed. The snow was still coming down strong, obscuring her view of the battlefield below.

She moved as quickly as she dared, eating up the shrinking distance as the elves and Blackmasks continued to press forward. She spotted their own men at last, their expressions unreadable through the heavy veil of white, but she could imagine the fear that would fill their eyes. They were running, swords and spears raised, and within what seemed like only seconds they had nearly reached the rear of the Red Army lines.

"Our army looks so small," Wes said, his voice hollow.

Knowing how many of their enemies lay ahead, she had to admit that what he said was true. Combined with the Red Army, they had a lot of men fighting for Kaveryth, but the elves and Blackmasks were as thick as a swarm of flies.

"The wolves!" Aelrie shouted, shattering her thoughts. She shook her head as she flew lower, watching in horror as a group of elves cut through a line of Ursa's pikemen and raced through the snow.

Two elf-women on wolfback came out ahead, their raised swords dull against the gray sky as they rode. Before Celesyria could even attempt to stop them, they reached two young Auranthian soldiers. The men raised their swords, but it was of little use. The elves sat with amused expressions as their mounts tore at the men with their teeth.

She continued to fly toward the ground, watching in horror as more and more elves broke through the Red Army lines, clashing with Ursa's men and their own alike. She didn't know where to begin, or what to do. Everywhere she looked she could see only death, the red stains of blood blooming on the snow in all directions.

She tried to listen for the orders of the Aridmoorian commanders, but their voices were lost on the wind. She could see arrows doused with Galeharborian liquid fire being shot from Red Army bows, but most of them were extinguished by the falling snow before they could hit their marks. She knew that Ursa's men must have other explosives, but perhaps they too would fail in such bad weather.

Even if they worked, it's not enough. None of it is enough.

Not knowing what else to do, she circled back behind their men, trying to look away from the blood, trying to quell the panicked hammering of her heart.

Think, think, think.

As she circled back around, she spotted a strong line of Red Army men holding back a horde of Blackmasks, but they could do nothing to stop a fresh wave of elves from rushing past them. If they couldn't hold these lines, they would be surrounded.

Aelrie and Wes had gone silent as well, no doubt sharing in her overwhelm.

All of their study, all of their preparations, all of their experiences, none of it seemed to mean anything now. She continued to fly, scared to look at the ground, and scared to look away.

Celesyria tried to think, desperately trying to unearth some buried idea from her childhood training, some strategy that would make sense, but her mind felt numb.

She forced herself to breathe, taking in huge gulps of freezing air.

I'll get Wes and Aelrie back to the camp, and I'll–

Before she could finish even a single thought, she felt weight shifting on her back.

"Wes!" Aelrie cried out, her scream loud enough to be heard even over the howling wind. "Wes! Hold on!"

She tried to slow her body down, tried to sense where her new center of gravity should be, but it was already too late. Celesyria felt something sliding from her back, and a moment later, she could see Wes beneath her, his body tumbling through the air as he plummeted toward the ground below.

***

How stupid.

After all of the things that haven't managed to kill me.

The thought was there and then gone in an instant. Wes could feel the stinging of snowflakes as they pelted at his eyes, could feel the rushing of the wind as it hissed past his ears.

He was falling.

The faces of his mother, father, and brother filled his vision. For once, the images were clear, the haze of memory lifted away. All three of them were smiling, and Wes could almost feel the warm glow emanating from behind their bodies like an impossible sun. All he wanted was to go to them, to collapse into his mother's arms, to be free of this world and all of its pain.

He looked down and saw the elves below, their ferocious swords slashing at soldiers who rose up again and again, trying to push them back.

All at once, he was aware of the pounding in his head, so strong that he was certain his skull would crack open even before he hit the hard ground beneath. He felt his jaw clenching against the pain, willing the seconds to move faster, anything, anything to make the ache stop.

High One, please. Please, let me go home.

I've had enough.

Another face.

The pain remained, but he could just barely see through it now. Blackness pressed at the edges of his vision as his heart continued to thunder, but he could see.

He could think of her.

Her pale blue eyes, cutting through him like the sharpest knife. The gentle curve of her smile. The softness of her cheek as he planted a kiss, hoping for a future where he could give her a love that was so much bigger and more complete.

He could hear her screaming, all at once, the sound flooding his ears. He did not care about the wind, the snow, the hard-packed ice he was racing toward.

No. I am not dying today.

"Take hold!"

He heard Celesyria's thunderous yell, vibrating through his ribcage as he continued to tumble through the air, trying to get his bearings. "Wes, grab onto me! Come on!"

He stuck his arms out, grasping nothing but air.

There was a jolting pain against his chest, and then he could see the orange scales beneath him. He took hold of a section of Celesyria's neck ridge, realizing that he had to be near her head.

"You're okay," Aelrie was saying, her voice husky and desperate over the wind. "Just hold on. Don't let go."

Celesyria lurched slightly. Wes could see the elf crawling toward him, her arm extended gently until she was able to take hold of his own.

The ground was approaching faster now, and he could hear the harsh sound of clashing swords ringing in his ears. The ache in his head coursed through him at full force the nearer they got to the elves, and once more, he felt his vision beginning to fade. Aelrie was saying something, her fingertips pressed hard into his skin as she gripped him, but he could hardly feel it.

He felt he would do anything, anything to make the pain stop.

If you can't do it for Me, do it for her.

The voice that was not a voice was in his head again, clear

and bright over the haze that surrounded him. Celesyria was moving faster now, trying desperately to get to a safe landing place. He could feel Aelrie moving again, trying to get closer.

He could hear words emanating from her, but the pain in his head would not allow him to hear them.

All that he could acknowledge, all that he could comprehend, were the same words, repeating over and over with the beating of his heart.

Do it for her. Do it for her.

Every pump of the dragon's wings was enough to nearly shake him loose, but he dug his fingertips in between her scales, using every ounce of his strength to keep his grip.

Everything was fading now, the edges of his vision blurring, a dark fog washing in over him until he closed his eyes, too tired to do anything else but surrender to the pain.

But he didn't let go.

20

Chapter 19

KING ERROL MANTA

King Manta stared at his hand.

It was an ugly thing, with missing fingers and more scars than could be counted, but tonight, he felt nothing but gratitude for the pains he had borne for the sake of those whom he loved.

He held his daughter's hand within his own, waiting for her to break the silence.

She was breathing loud enough that he could hear it, staring down at her own feet or the wall or anything but her father's face.

"Don't be afraid," he said at last.

He stroked her soft thumb beneath his scratchy one, remembering so many nights just like this, when Kessara was only an infant, asleep on his lap.

The Princess glanced up at him for a moment before looking away again.

"I never expected this to be frightening. It's all I've ever wanted."

King Manta raised an eyebrow. "All you ever wanted was a wedding attended solely by your parents, hosted in your bedchamber?"

The Princess chuckled. "Point taken."

He allowed the silence to fall again, but it was comfortable now.

He looked over at his daughter again, wanting to shake his head at the impossibility of time, of growing, of fate. Moonlight was pouring in through the window, illuminating her fierce blue eyes that had always reminded him so much of his own.

To his surprise, he recognized the dress that she was wearing, though he couldn't say from where. It was a darker blue than she usually wore, with long delicate sleeves and a glimmering skirt, a small fur wrap tucked over her shoulders.

She looks like Jinna. She looks like a queen.

Before he could look away, Kessara was staring at him, her eyes searching his own.

"What?" she said, smoothing an invisible wrinkle out of the front of her dress.

He felt a tear rolling down his cheek before he could brush it away.

"I'm glad to have the Princess of Galeharbor back," he said at last.

She smiled at him.

There was so much more he wanted to tell her. So many more words that threatened to spill out of his mouth. Apologies for all of the ways that he had hurt her, and especially for pushing her away. But he couldn't bring himself to say them. He wasn't sorry, not really. He had done the best he could, with the limited options that he'd had.

"I love you, Papa," Kessara said, reaching up and wiping his remaining tears away with her thumb. "You're a great king. If Alder can do even half as well as you have done, our people will be blessed."

He let out a long breath. He supposed there was no point in holding back now.

"Despite my better judgment, I think that Alder has a chance to do well," he admitted, stroking his graying beard. "We will help you all that we can before that time comes."

If you survive.

He swallowed back the words, not wanting even to consider the thought, but to ignore it, he knew, was folly.

All he wanted was to follow his daughter to the battlefield, to take up his once proud sword and to stand fast against the enemies of Kaveryth, but he couldn't bring himself to do it. His people needed him here. If the Red Army failed to repel the elves, none of it would matter, but at least the men and women of Galeharbor would die behind the slain body of their king.

A glow seemed to spread over Kessara's face as she smiled at him.

He allowed himself to stand there like that for just a moment, hand in hand with his only child, lost in memory.

He and Jinna had dreamed of more children. When they didn't come, month after month and year after year, it had been painful. But eventually, peace came, and he knew that they couldn't have been more blessed by the daughter they had been given by the High One or whoever else.

He heard footsteps sounding in the hall, and Kessara nearly jumped back in surprise, no doubt lost in her own quiet thoughts.

She looked up at him again, holding his gaze as he tucked a stray strand of blonde hair behind her ear.

"I'm proud of you, you know," he said, swallowing the tears that threatened to spill over.

"I will try my best to honor you and Mother, and our great House," she said, her voice barely above a whisper. "I promise."

"Come."

He took her hand and led her behind her dressing screen, shielding her from view of the doorway. It would hardly be the most traditional entrance to a wedding, but then again, were they following the usual traditions, Jinna would be standing with their daughter now. As it was, he'd insisted that he be the one to wait with Kessara in her final moments as a single woman, and Jinna had agreed.

After all that had passed between them, all of the hurt and politics, he had felt that it was necessary.

He was a man of tradition, to be sure. His own wedding had followed the customs of the House of Manta with impressive precision—a temple, hundreds of well-dressed guests, a dinner of many courses—but in the end, it was the marriage that had counted. It was the marriage that lived and breathed, the marriage that had to be nurtured even once the gifts and the well-wishing faded away.

There were three short knocks at the door, followed by Jinna's lilting voice.

"Are you ready?"

King Manta felt Kessara's hand stiffen within his own, and he gave it a quick squeeze. His eyes met hers as her mother's question hung in the air. He would not answer for her.

"Yes, Mother," the Princess called out, her voice clear and unwavering. "Bring him in."

The King drew a breath as the door drew open, daring to steal a glance from around the edge of the screen.

It was not Jinna waiting there, but Alder, still dressed in his worn traveling clothes.

The boy nearly jumped out of his skin as the King caught his eye, but he settled himself just in time, giving a composed nod.

King Manta returned it, searching his handsome young face. There was something new about him, something he had not noticed straight away. His head was held as high as ever, his green eyes so full of strength and youth.

But there was something else, the King was sure of it. A voice, or almost a voice, calling out to him.

He will be a noble and worthy king. Fear not for your Kingdom, nor for your precious one.

The moment passed in an instant as Jinna strode toward him in two quick strides, half shoving a simple silver circlet into her husband's hands.

He felt the weight of the metal against his palms, strange and familiar at once.

Kessara had not made a sound, nor had she moved. He could picture her there in the shadows of the room, her palms sweating as she tried to perfect her hair one last time, as though the man she was about to marry didn't already think she was the most beautiful thing he'd ever seen.

King Manta cleared his throat, banishing the latest threatened tears. "This is for you, Cadogen."

Alder nodded, no doubt having already been briefed on the procedures by Queen Manta. He got to his knees before them, his back straight, his chin held aloft, and closed his eyes.

Jinna laid a hand on one of his shoulders, and Errol did the same.

For the second time in as many days, he began to speak, the words not quite practiced enough to feel natural, but they felt right all the same.

"By my House, I proclaim. By my duty to kin and Kingdom, I declare. By my blood, I command," the King said, placing the circlet of silver upon Alder's red curls.

Alder waited, lowering his face toward the ground, his eyes pressed firmly shut. Kessara appeared from behind the dressing screen and moved to kneel beside her beloved. Queen Manta knelt beside her, and at last, King Manta followed.

For a long moment, he closed his eyes, hearing nothing but the gentle rushing of the wind outside.

At last, Alder cleared his throat. King Manta couldn't help but to grin as the spell was broken, opening his eyes and helping Jinna to her feet. He supposed there was still a rather important part of the ceremony left.

Kessara and Alder clasped their hands together and strode toward the balcony, and King Manta followed closely behind. Jinna was crying now, her eyes wet and red, but she pulled her own cloak around her shoulders and headed out into the night to join them.

The King could hear the pounding of the North Sea in the distance, though he could not see it through the blowing snow. He shivered, but Kessara and Alder seemed not even to notice the cold. Their eyes were locked on one another as they waited for the perfect moment, a soft smile tugging at the corner of Kessara's mouth.

A part of King Manta wanted to take his daughter's hand and pull her away, dragging her back into their old plans for her old life.

This marriage was going to bring her pain, no matter how virtuous Alder tried to be. Kessara had already lost one love, and here she was, ready to throw her heart forever into the hands of another.

But he knew that it was too late, and if pain was inevitable, he was thankful that his daughter would experience, at least, this moment of sheer joy.

He felt Jinna placing her small hand within his own as she rested her head upon his shoulder, passing him a spare handkerchief. He took it, realizing that his cheeks were already wet with tears.

"Thank you," Kessara said, her eyes glistening with tears as she smiled. "Thank you both."

Alder nodded in agreement, his hands shaking ever so slightly as he leaned forward and planted a soft kiss upon her lips.

It was done.

King Manta glanced out into the night as the wind continued to howl, surrounding the lonely palace in every direction.

The servants were gone, the soldiers were quiet, but the House of Manta would hold on, as solid as a fortress against the waves.

21

Chapter 20

KESSARA

"I can't believe I used to travel without the aid of a dragon," Alder grumbled from atop his stag, trying to hold on with one hand and untangle his waterskin from the saddle with the other.

Kessara laughed, watching the growing line of hoof-prints as his animal continued to pick its way across the plain. The sun was shining, the snow had stopped falling, and they had made particularly good time for the last couple of days. Still, she couldn't blame Alder for feeling impatient. After traveling on dragon's back, everything else felt excruciatingly slow.

Without the aid of Nazzan's speed, it was clear just how enormous the Kingdoms of Galeharbor and Aridmoor were. They had been traveling for well over a week, and still they had not yet reached the site of the battlefield where, hopefully, their friends would be awaiting them.

"It really does feel like it's taking forever," she admitted, reaching down to give her own stag a well-deserved pat on the shoulder. It was a gelding from her parents' stables, and though she had not ridden him before, she had quickly grown fond of the large black creature. "On the other hand, the elves have never felt further away."

"As far as we know," Alder said darkly.

She rolled her eyes and kicked at her stag with her heels, urging him to move faster until they were riding side-by-side. Not bothering to slow down, she leaned over and planted a kiss on Alder's smirking mouth.

"My dear husband," she said, enjoying the unfamiliar word on her tongue. "You worry too much."

He said nothing, staring off at the small group of Galeharbor palace guards who were riding ahead of them. Kessara followed his gaze, noticing only the unruly lines of stag footprints that now marred the perfect white snow.

She glanced over her shoulder, where a small cluster of Protectorate men—Captain Drohma was not among them—as well as several hundred freshly conscripted Red Army soldiers made up the bulk of their procession.

These were all of the soldiers that she and her parents had been able to bring in to fight in their new alliance. Many of the Galeharborian men had joined the Red Army already, so she supposed she should be thankful that they'd been able to draw a little more blood from Windshear's surrounding stones. Still, the numbers made her nervous. She hoped that King Ursa's existing force was still standing strong on the battlefield.

"I hope my parents are all right," she said, turning back to Alder. "They have no one left."

He smiled, but it didn't reach his eyes.

"They're brave to stay with their people. The High One will watch over them."

She nodded. He was right, of course, but the fact brought only a little comfort.

At least we had the chance to reconcile.

"He's watching over us, too," Alder continued, gesturing to the soldiers that surrounded them. "There's danger, and I wish you were far away from it. But at least we're not alone."

She desperately wanted for him to be right. After the agony of believing that loving Alder was forbidden, the stakes now felt higher than ever, just as her mother had warned her they would. They were husband and wife now. They were one. They had to make it, to build a life together, to have a future. She couldn't fathom the alternative.

The sound of pounding hooves shook her from her reverie. King Kylan Ursa rode up beside them on his surefooted horse, pulling back on the reins until the creature slowed to a brisk walk at her side.

She could see Alder's fists tightening ever so slightly on the reins, but a second later, he relaxed. There was no love between the two men, to be sure, but they both seemed willing to work together when the good of Kaveryth demanded it. She could only hope that Alder could keep his temper in check.

"We were right," the King said, his expression grave beneath his messy red curls. "One of our scouts has just returned. We've reached the battlefield at last."

He paused.

"The Auranthians are here."

Kessara felt her heart beginning to beat faster. "I knew it. I knew they would come."

"Kessara," Kylan said, his brow furrowing.

She paused, glancing over at Alder, but he said nothing. Kylan let out a plume of breath.

"Kessara," he started again. "There are so many elves. We don't have enough men, even with the Envoy's army."

Her chest felt as though it had been clamped in a vice, and she had to force herself to loosen the sudden tight grip she had taken on the poor stag's reins.

"What of the Guardians?" Alder cut in. "Surely, there must be a good number of them by now. Their oath would have drawn them to the battlefield."

"There are some, yes, but still, the elves are pushing forward. Our men have lost ground. Soon enough their camp will be overrun. I suspect that many of the Guardians stayed in Umrym, trying to keep hold of their own lands."

Kylan let the words hang in the air for a moment, and Kessara couldn't help but to think about how incongruous the message of doom seemed against the backdrop of a beautiful winter-blue sky.

"If that's the case, most of them are probably dead," Alder said, spitting into the snow. "High One, save us."

Kessara said nothing. If he was right, Jaconial probably wouldn't have survived, either. She could only hope that Nazzan still had a chance. She tightened her fingers around the reins again and kicked at her mount's side, urging the stag forward as they came to a particularly deep patch of snow.

"There has to be something we can do," she said at last, waiting for a moment as Kylan's horse fought through the deep powder. Alder followed without comment, seemingly lost in thought. "We need to find Wes. He has to be here somewhere with his men. Perhaps he has a plan."

Kylan quirked an eyebrow, but to his credit, he made no comment.

They all knew that Wes Cervos was hardly a brilliant military mind, but that wouldn't decide a war. The High One's plan would be fulfilled, one way or another.

"I'm open to ideas," Kylan said finally. "I hope your friends have been able to hold out this long."

"Thank you," Alder said, though Kessara thought he sounded rather pained to admit any sort of gratitude toward the Aridmoorian king. "I think it's best if Kessara and I ride ahead to the Auranthian camp. We can find Wes, at least, and tell him that we are now allied with the Red Army. I'm sure we'd all prefer a peaceful transition of leadership."

King Ursa gave a curt nod of approval.

"It's settled, then." Alder agreed. Kessara couldn't help but to feel a rush of pride at the man who was now her husband. Humility didn't always come easily to him, and it pleased her to see how much he had grown since the day they had met.

"What do you plan to do, my King?" she asked, turning to Kylan as the three of them pulled their animals to a stop. She supposed that the Red Army men coming up behind would be slowed by the thick snow, and she was thankful for a moment to catch her breath. Though the weather was pleasant as far as a winter on the plains went, she had still been in the saddle since sunrise, and she was exhausted.

"My men and I will fight to the last," the King said, giving her a blank stare, as though it was an insult even to be asked. "However poor the odds, we stand our ground. It is our duty. That is all that can be done."

She looked at him, trying to find some weakness in the steely set of his green eyes, but there was none. For all of his faults, it was clear that he meant every word.

High One, help his soul. Bring him to You before his end is come.

CELESYRIA

Landing on the frozen ground had felt like crashing into the side of a fortress, but so far as Celesyria could tell, they were all in one piece.

"Apologies," she choked out, still trying to force the air back into her lungs, as several men tried desperately to get their belongings out of her way. Fortunately, she had missed a row of barrack tents, but only barely.

She felt Aelrie jump off of her back, landing on the snow and leaving scarcely a bootprint as she rushed to pull Wes off of the saddle. Several more of the Auranthian soldiers rushed over to assist her, but before they could make it to Celesyria's back, the elf had already managed to get Wes onto the ground.

"He's breathing," Aelrie said, pressing her ear to his chest. As she pulled back, Celesyria could see it rising and falling ever so slightly.

His eyes were closed, but he looked almost peaceful. She watched as Aelrie pressed against his neck, feeling for the strength of pulse with shaking fingertips. The elf gave the slightest smile of relief.

Celesyria let out a held breath, but her heart continued to pound. It had been so close. Too close. It was only by a miracle of the High One that the Envoy lived, of that she was certain.

"We need a medic!" Aelrie was shouting at the men who had quickly gathered to watch the strange scene playing out in the center of their camp.

The elf looked breathless as well, her face grim as one of the younger soldiers shooed the rest of the onlookers away, giving Wes space to breathe.

A moment later, Aelrie was resting against Celesyria's side, a delicate silvery hand pressed against the dragon's flank. They said nothing, listening as the news of what had happened spread through the camp.

Somehow, Wes had lived, and for the moment, that was enough.

22

Chapter 21

ALDER

Up ahead, Alder could see the edge of what he hoped was the Auranthian camp.

Since they had left King Ursa and his men behind, the snow had begun to fall steadily once again, the warm sun obscured by a blanket of gray clouds.

"Let's go," he called over to Kessara, pulling his cloak over his head and neck as his wife did the same. She kicked at her stag with her heels, and the animal responded immediately, jumping into a spirited run despite the snow. His own stag was far more stubborn, but fortunately, Kessara had not allowed herself to get very far ahead.

Alder kept waiting to be ambushed, looking over his shoulder every few steps, but no guard ever emerged from the blinding snow.

As they finally reached the first row of tents, they realized that the back of the camp did not seem to be guarded at all.

A ripple of apprehension filled him, and he gestured to

Kessara to wait. He slowed his stag to a walk, searching for hidden threats around every corner, but all was quiet.

"We come as allies of Auranth!" he shouted as loud as he could. Though some of the people knew them, it was likely that many did not, and he was not willing to take any unnecessary risk. Especially with Kessara at his side.

Finally, as they rounded the corner of the row of tents, they came upon a small clearing filled with men hiding out under makeshift canopies. Some were eating or cleaning weapons, but several of the younger ones looked almost lost, as though they were waiting to be pelted with shouted orders at any moment.

Alder had expected for the soldiers to straighten up and to inquire as to who they were, but most of the men ignored them completely.

"An elf could bring a bomb in here and do half this camp in," he muttered under his breath to Kessara.

"I know that you're not thrilled to be offering control to King Ursa," she said, "but it seems to be the only choice. We need to make sure this camp is under control."

He nodded. She was right. Bargren and the others had done all they could, but it was difficult to train a volunteer army so quickly. Still, from Alder's time in what had once been the Aridmoorian army, he knew that such a lack of discipline should have been met with serious reprimands.

Kessara urged her stag forward once more, sitting up to her full height in the saddle as she caught the eyes of the men.

"Who is in charge here?" she called out, pulling her stag to a stop in the center of the space as the snow continued to fall. For a moment, no one answered. In the distance, Alder could hear something that sounded very much like a scream of pain, and he wondered just how far the elves had been able to push toward their camp.

"Our stags require care, and we have other matters to attend to," she continued. Alder could see the annoyance flashing in her eyes, though she did her best to conceal it from the soldiers.

Before anyone in the clearing could reply, a young boy came running from the opposite side of the camp, breathless as he came to a stop in front of the two of them.

Alder recognized the teenager—one of the youngest volunteers that he had helped to train back in Auranth—but he could not recall his name.

"Lady Kessara," the boy said, getting to his knees at once in the snow and looking very much like he might faint on the spot. "Thank the Dracodei you're here. Oh, by Providence that you are! We need a healer."

Alder wished to correct them in the use of her proper, reinstated title, but at the moment, a few missed niceties hardly seemed important.

Kessara gave Alder a quick glance, and he nodded, her question clear even without words.

Even though he trusted her judgment, he couldn't help but to feel a warm glow within his chest whenever she sought his approval or his advice.

"Soldiers," Kessara said, offering them a nod. "I need to speak to those in charge of this camp, immediately. There must be another healer who can—"

The young boy cleared his throat, glancing up at Kessara.

"For-forgive me," he stammered. "We've been trying to find one of our own, but they're all closer to the battlefield."

Alder noticed Kessara's face softening. He doubted that

she'd be able to say no again, not if someone was in immediate need of help.

"How serious is it?" the Princess asked. "Can it wait?"

The other soldiers were talking amongst themselves now, and Alder could scarcely hear the younger soldier's reply, but he could make out enough of the words to send a cold chill to his bones.

"It's the Envoy. Wes Cervos. He's hurt."

Within seconds, Kessara had leapt out of her saddle, thrusting the reins of the exhausted stag into the hands of the man who happened to be standing the closest. Alder did the same, albeit a little less gracefully.

"Show me," she said to the teenager, who took off at once toward the western end of the camp. Alder and Kessara followed at a run, trying to keep their footing as the snow continued to fall.

WES

Wes could see nothing but white.

His eyes were stinging, and he blinked once, and then twice, but the feeling did not go away. He tried to raise a hand to shield his eyes, but he couldn't seem to make his muscles obey.

The pain in his skull was still hammering away. It was enough to make him feel dazed and lightheaded, but at least–so far as he could tell–he was able to remain conscious.

With all of the effort that he could muster, he turned his head a little to the side, realizing at once that he was laying on his back on the ground with icy snowflakes landing on his face.

Celesyria. Aelrie.

He tried to look for them, but lifting his head was enough to send a ripple of nausea coursing through him, so he stayed where he was.

"Aelrie," he choked out, the single word enough to bite at his raw throat. He wanted water, but he feared that it would come back up if he was offered any.

All at once, he was surrounded by a flurry of activity. Memories flooded his mind as the soldiers rushed to his side. He had passed out on Celesyria's back, she had managed to catch him in mid-air, and they must have landed somewhere in their army's camp.

"Wes! Wes, hold on. Don't move, okay?"

It was a familiar female voice, but it didn't belong to Celesyria, nor Aelrie. Wes closed his eyes again, trying to think.

It couldn't be her. It couldn't be.

Before he could ponder the mystery further, he felt a jolt of pain shooting up his spine as several people pressed their hands against him.

"It's only going to hurt for a second, but I need to make sure you don't get sick on your back like this," the woman's voice said.

He said nothing, focusing all of his energy on rolling onto his side with the help of the soldiers. Someone stuck a rolled up cloak beneath his head to use as a pillow, and immediately the pain in his head and neck began to lessen.

"Mmm," he muttered, his eyes still closed. The sudden relief was enough to make him want to take a nap, but he knew that probably wasn't the wisest idea.

"Better?"

Wes forced his eyes open, finding himself face to face with Kessara Manta.

He felt a cold tear sliding onto his cheek as he looked at her, and then at Alder, who stood only a couple of feet away. It had been her voice. They were alive.

Alder reached over and rested a hand carefully on his shoulder. "Thank the High One. I've missed you, brother."

Kessara shooed the Aridmoorian away, and Wes watched as Alder strode over to stand with Aelrie and Celesyria, who were waiting nearby. He tried to catch Aelrie's eye, but she looked down at her feet. He could imagine the tears pooling in her eyes as she tried to fight them back.

It's not your fault, my beloved.

He wanted to reassure her, to kiss her a hundred times until she believed him, but for the moment he could only wait. Kessara was prodding at his body now with the usual shamelessness of one accustomed to providing medical care, muttering to herself as she worked.

"I know it'll be exhausting to talk, so don't try, but thank the High One you're all right," Celesyria was saying in his mind. *"I was afraid I'd lost you."*

"Take care of Aelrie," he said, the few words enough to send a fresh wave of pain pulsing behind his eyes.

Kessara lifted up both of his eyelids in turn, watching as he squinted against the bright white snow. "Good," she said, running her fingers lightly along the edge of his hairline, probably searching for lacerations.

"Sit still," she scolded as he tried to shift his leg to a more comfortable position. "We'll get you into a tent just as—"

He ignored her and moved it anyway, relieved to find that it seemed to be in working order, as was his other leg. He swallowed the rising nausea as he planted his hands against the ground, pushing himself up.

"Wesley Cervos," Kessara said, crossing her arms across her chest as he managed to get himself into a sitting position. "I'd shove you back down if I didn't think it would injure you even more."

"You couldn't shove me," he said, swallowing the dryness in his throat. "I've gotten too strong these days. Maybe stronger than Alder."

His other three friends were at his side in moments, Alder chuckling as Kessara glared at him. "He needs water, straight away," Kessara called out to one of the nearby soldiers, who raced off toward the tents.

"Thank you," Wes said, reaching out to give her hand a quick squeeze. Kessara glared at him, but she couldn't conceal the smile that had risen to her lips.

Aelrie sat down next to him in the snow, careful not to put her weight on him as she leaned over to kiss his cheek. He turned to look at her beautiful face, but she said nothing.

He could see the guilt on her face, and in that moment, he knew that it was time.

"Kessara," he said as she continued to poke at his spine and the base of his neck. "Can this wait?"

"Wes, I need to check for any additional injuries," she said, sounding exasperated. "You fell from—"

"Kessara," he snapped, his tone harsh enough that she stepped back at once.

He shook his head. "Sorry. I need to talk to you. All of you."

Aelrie reached out her hand, and he took it, cradling it gently within his own. Finally, the snow had slowed once again, and though the inside of a tent would have been more comfortable, at least they weren't getting pelted with ice every few seconds. He had to speak now, before he lost his nerve. He'd put off the truth for long enough.

Celesyria got as close as she could, partially unfurling a wing so that she could shield the others from the wind.

Soldiers walked past them, carrying weapons and pretending not to listen in. Wes sighed. There was no way that this secret would stay within his circle of close friends. Soon enough, all of Kaveryth would know. Somehow, the thought brought only relief. He didn't need to hide his weakness any longer. The High One's strength was what had always mattered, not his own. He only wished that he could have realized it without nearly falling to his death.

"I should have told you before," he started, casting a quick glance up at Alder and Kessara, who were glancing between one another with worried expressions. "But I was afraid."

He could feel Aelrie's thumb tracing softly against the back of his knuckles. He pressed on.

"I fell off of Celesyria's back because I fainted."

Wes allowed the words to sink in for a moment, glancing between the confused faces of his friends. He could have told them long ago, sparing them uncertainty and himself embarrassment, but there was nothing to be done about it now. At least, at last, the secret he had been carrying for so long would no longer be quite so heavy to bear.

"I fainted because I'm ill, and I have been for quite some time now. It began as occasional headaches, but they got worse and worse, especially whenever I am close to the elves, or to evil in general," he said.

Alder's eyes went wide.

"Back in Kingsvier Landing, after Aelrie defeated the

Gorok..."

The elf, Alder, and Kessara nodded in unison.

"Yes," he said. "That was when it all began to make sense. Aelrie had channeled darkness, and it was enough to weaken me badly as soon as I went near her."

Aelrie said nothing, but Wes could see her glancing down at her feet, not wanting to bear the stares of her friends, even though he knew they would not blame her. Not any more.

"The sickness began long ago, not long after I'd met Celesyria," he continued, glancing up at the dull sky. It had warmed significantly, and he knew that they wouldn't have much more time to stand around talking. Part of him wanted to leave the explanation as it was, leave them with their questions, but he couldn't bring himself to stop now. It felt good to tell his secret, to lift such a heavy weight off of his shoulders. He would no longer have to carry it alone.

"The water!" Kessara said, sounding almost triumphant. "This is why I've been telling all of you to use that tincture that herbwoman gave us—"

"It was the water," Wes said quickly. "But it was before any of that. I was with Holga, Gohr, and Celesyria, in the Dread Ruins of Boneshire. It was there that we drank."

Wes caught Alder and Kessara glancing between one another, unspoken words passing between them.

"There is more to that story, as far as the little ones go," Kessara cut in quickly. "But there is no time for that now."

Wes nodded. In the distance, the sounds of war continued to thunder.

"And the symptoms are even worse here due to the evil that is nearby?" Alder asked.

Wes turned to Aelrie, who brushed a few strands of her

black hair away from her face. She quickly explained to the others how the ancient elven curse had worked, and told them that so far, she had been able to avoid hurting Wes herself, at least since the incident at Kingsvier Landing.

Kessara and Alder went quiet, no doubt pondering the implications of what they had just heard. So many of them had drank the water, their soldiers included, but at least they had been at a much greater distance from the source.

"I wish you had told us before now," Kessara said at last. "*Long* before now."

"I should have," Wes agreed. "As I said, I was a coward. There was so much going on, so many ways that our people needed me. I didn't want you to know that I was weak."

Alder shook his head. "You've more than proven your strength, Wes. Sickness can't change that."

It was only then that Wes noticed that Celesyria had yet to utter a single word.

The dragon was staring at the ground, and though she had kept her wing up to buffer them from the wind, she had pulled back a little from the others.

"Celesyria?"

"I'm glad you're all right now," she said stiffly. "You terrified me up there."

"I know," he said, guilt coursing through him. "I'm sorry. I should have–"

"Yes, you should have told me!" the dragon snapped, her yellow eyes narrowing, her usually soft voice thick with fury. "You know I'd do anything for you, Wes. I always will. Yet, you kept this from me?"

The others were giving each other uneasy glances, their mouths clamped firmly shut. He and Celesyria rarely argued and never fought. He couldn't blame them for being surprised, but he knew that he certainly deserved the dragon's ire.

"I'm sorry, Celesyria," he said again, stepping forward and resting a hand on her flank. She did not pull away, and for many long seconds, he did not move. Slowly, her racing heartbeat began to slow, and he waited until her chest rose and fell with gentle breaths before continuing.

"You're right," he said. "You've never hidden anything from me. I should have shown you the same trust, without hesitation."

The words were not flattery. He did trust the dragon. As much as Aelrie was the love of his life, Celesyria was his best friend, and the one who, in so many ways, had saved his life. Without her, he would be someone else entirely.

"I know," the dragon said at last, glancing between him and their other friends. "I'm sorry for being so harsh."

"It's okay. I deserved it."

"I won't argue," she said, offering him a small smile. Celesyria still looked rather melancholy, but in time, he hoped that her hurt would fade. Unfortunately, they did not have much more time to talk things over.

"So," Alder said, crossing his arms over his thick chest. "This changes things."

Wes couldn't argue, so he chose to say nothing.

"You can't fight," the Aridmoorian continued. "You can't be here at all. If you get any closer to the front, you're going to die."

"We need to stop the elves, Alder," Wes argued. "If we don't, there's not going to be anywhere to hide from them anyway. They're going to keep pushing until we stop them.

There's no other way that this ends."

"*We* need to stop them. We. *You* can't stop them. Not if you're dead."

"It's not so simple. There's a lot that we can try. We know at a minimum that the sickness can be resisted. Besides, I've fought them before and managed to remain upright."

"Not like this. Not so many," Alder said, taking several steps closer until their faces were inches away.

His chest felt tight. It was exactly as he'd feared. He'd told them the truth, and now he would be cast aside, a meddling invalid who must be pushed out of the way.

"Alder, you're letting our friendship cloud your judgment," he said, ignoring Aelrie and Kessara, who were begging them to calm down. "We've come this far. The High One has strengthened me all the while."

Alder was shaking his head, his green eyes flashing with anger. "Strength is not what's driving you. Not now. All I'm hearing is pride."

Wes felt his cheeks go hot.

"How would you know?" he spat. "You've never had to prove yourself. You've always been Alder Cadogen, protector and war hero, while I was still a pathetic teenager carting gold coins across the continent and wishing I was dead."

For a moment, Alder's rage seemed to subside, but Wes couldn't bring himself to stop, not without a final barb. It felt good to lash out, to let the anger that so often turned inward hurt someone else for a change.

"I had to fight to get here in the first place, and now you're telling me I have to step aside like a cripple and leave this war for you to win?"

"Wes, that's not what we're saying," Kessara pleaded. "We

love you. We want you to fulfill what the High One has asked of you, and you can't do that if you're laying dead somewhere."

"Why is the only option that I stand down, or die?"

Wes tried to shout, but the words came out as more of a pathetic-sounding cry.

He glanced around the camp, noticing the teenage soldiers staring at him as they passed, and all of a sudden the whole argument felt completely ridiculous.

Silence fell at last.

"We don't have time for this," Celesyria said firmly. "We have huge problems, right here and now, and we need you and Alder both to stand up and lead. We will figure out the rest."

Aelrie nodded. "May the High One guide us all," she said quietly.

"I'm sorry," Wes said for the second time in just a few short minutes, reaching out to clap Alder on the shoulder.

"Don't worry about it, brother," he said, returning his embrace.

Kessara shook her head, no doubt thinking of some witty comment about the strange habits of males, but before she could say anything, something else caught their attention.

All at once, the soldiers had stopped what they were doing, glancing off between the tents. Shouts erupted, and for a terrible moment, Wes was certain that they had fallen prey to an ambush.

Alder and Aelrie were on their feet in what seemed like only an instant, racing off toward the commotion, and Celesyria tried her best to follow them down the narrow path between two long rows of canvas tents.

Kessara waited for a long moment, staring off after her husband as he rushed away.

Wes's eyes met hers, and she shook her head.

"You should wait here. We don't know what's happening."

"Kessara, please. I'm fine, okay?"

At last, she relented, likely not wanting to set off another round of arguing. Wes leaned on her shoulder, but was pleased to find that for the most part his legs seemed to be working properly.

It only took them a few minutes to reach another clearing, now filled with a small crowd of onlookers. Kessara ordered them out of her way, and to Wes's surprise, they complied at once. Up ahead, they could see Alder and Aelrie, standing off to the side and shouting something at the crowd.

Laying there on a patch of well-trodden snow was King Ursa, the end of Moorn's sword pressed directly against his neck.

23

Chapter 22

KESSARA

"Get off of him! Now!" Kessara shouted, scarcely able to contain her fury as her mind registered the scene playing out before her. Alder and Aelrie were both attempting to urge the other soldiers to return to their business, but so far, they were being largely ignored.

Moorn paid the Princess no attention either, but Kylan caught her gaze, and she did not doubt the fear that was reflected in his deep green eyes.

"Moorn!" she shouted again, ignoring Wes's protests as she pushed him back and headed toward the two men. Celesyria arrived just then, knocking a huge plume of snow into a row of tents that only barely managed to stay standing. She let out a roar loud enough to draw Moorn's eyes away from his helpless opponent, her sharp teeth bared.

"Drop the sword," Kessara commanded, giving Celesyria a grateful nod as Wes strode over to stand beside her on unsteady legs. "Do it now."

Moorn hesitated for a long moment as a few stray snowflakes fell, dotting his brown hair with bits of white. Kessara could see his fingers shaking as he held the sword aloft. The slightest movement would bring Kylan's end.

At last, he let the sword fall to the side, the sharp blade landing quietly on the blanket of snow. Kylan leapt to his feet at once, scrambling to free his own sword from its hilt. Before he could do so, however, Aelrie was on him, yanking his belt free with a single fluid motion. She tossed his belt, sword, and dagger to Alder, who caught the items easily.

"How dare you," the King said, closing the space between him and Moorn in an instant. The Silverfell soldier pulled back, nearly tripping over his own feet as Kylan shoved a finger in his face.

Kessara raised a hand and forced herself between them.

"You're both acting like barbarians," she hissed, refusing to move out of the way even as Kylan tried to push past her.

"You touch her, Ursa, and—" Alder started, but Kessara cut him off before he could say more.

"Enough!" she shouted as loud as she could, wishing that she had Celesyria's voice for times such as these. Even so, she was not the type to yell often, and when she did, people almost always listened. Kylan and Moorn were no exception. The two men did not take their eyes off of one another, but both took a step or two back and made no further comment.

"This chaos ends today," she said firmly. "The armies of darkness have already breached our borders, and you fight with one another? Our people need you. All of you. It's time to stop acting like children and start acting like men."

She let the final few words linger, knowing that for both Moorn and Kylan, the accusation would sting.

"This is my fault," she continued, shaking her head. "I should have—"

"No," Alder interrupted, striding closer until he was at Kessara's side.

"This is the Auranthian army, Moorn, and despite recent events—" he shot Kessara a warning glance, though she had no plans to share news of Wes's illness with the King "—Kylan Ursa is now in charge of it."

He met Kylan's eyes as he spoke, tightening his fingers around the hilt of his own sword.

"There's been a change of plans," Kessara said quickly, watching as Wes's eyes went wide. "We didn't have time to explain."

She paused to glance over at Celesyria and Aelrie, who both wore confused expressions.

"We don't have time now, either," Alder said. "You'll have to trust us."

Moorn, who had finally found the good sense to step out of the center of the clearing, crossed his arms and bore a wary expression. Wes stayed where he was, fiddling with the sheath of his sword.

"A deal was struck," Kessara said, giving Alder a warning glance. She couldn't explain much, it was true, but she had to make them understand, all the same. If they didn't, the camp would fall apart just as soon as they turned their backs. "King Manta is in agreement, as well. We have offered the Auranthian army to fight under the command of the Red Army."

As soon as the words escaped her lips, she wanted to close her eyes, or perhaps to duck for cover behind the nearest snowbank, but she wouldn't allow her nerves to show on her face. They'd had no other choice.

Wes was stubborn, but he was not stupid. She trusted that he would go along with it, but she couldn't let her own resolve waver even for a moment.

"You did *what*?" Wes asked, his voice dangerously low. Moorn looked even more murderous, but fortunately his fallen sword remained on the ground, now half-buried by the falling snow.

"I—*we*—did as I said," Kessara answered firmly. "And in return, King Kylan Ursa has agreed to step down as Steward of Silverfell, permitting the coronation of a new monarch."

Aelrie looked as though she was about to faint, and Kessara couldn't help but to let a half-smile fall across her lips.

"New monarch?" Moorn said at last, his brows pulled low over his dark eyes as he glanced between Wes and Kessara. "Are you two finally getting married?"

"Well, if by 'you two', you mean Kessara and I, the answer is yes," Alder said easily, holding up his hand, which now bore a silver ring. "With the blessing of King and Queen Manta, back in Windshear."

Kessara looked between the faces of each of her friends, blushing a little at the surprise on their faces. This was hardly how she had planned to tell them—really, she had hoped they would have been present at the ceremony—but at least they knew.

Moorn, of course, still looked horrified, and Kessara had no doubt many of the other soldiers would feel the same. Eventually, they'd have to explain why this marriage did not in fact spell disaster for the peace of their Kingdoms, but for the time being, they had bigger concerns.

"Yes, congratulations to the lovely newlyweds," Kylan said

dryly, turning to Wes and giving him a quick nod. "Exciting as it is, there will be time for your celebrations later. For now, I must know that our deal remains on the table."

There was a pause, and for a terrible moment, Kessara feared that Wes would disagree after all.

"Fine," the Envoy said after a pause, standing at his full height and taking a few steps closer to the center of the clearing. Kessara felt relief sweeping through her body. When it counted, he trusted her, and she was thankful.

"Moorn," Wes continued, "Go to Bargren and the other leaders at once. Tell them that we are fighting under the command of the Red Army now, and this includes the Protectorate. Do as King Ursa's captains tell you. That's an order."

Kessara wondered if Drohma was lurking somewhere around the camp, or perhaps on the battlefield himself, though Kylan had not mentioned him. She couldn't imagine him standing aside as the greatest battle for the fate of Kaveryth was waged. However much she disliked the Captain, he had helped to fight the Gorok and the elves in Kingsvier Landing, and she did not doubt his ability to lead their men. Assuming that they listened in the first place.

Moorn was staring at Wes as though he'd suddenly grown a tail, but he did as he was told. The soldiers who had continued to meander past the clearing stared at him as he strode off between the tents in search of Bargren, a few of them close at his heels, demanding answers.

"It's settled, then," Kylan said at last, heading over to Alder to retrieve his sword. The two men locked eyes, but to Kessara's relief, Alder was quick to lower his gaze as he handed over the King's belt and weapons.

There would be no more fighting. They were brothers in

arms once more, whether they were pleased about it or not.

CELESYRIA

Celesyria shoved her head inside the flap of the tent, feeling rather foolish, as the rest of her body was still sticking out into the camp.

Not only did she envision some foolish young soldier tripping over her tail with an armful of weapons, but if elves decided to ambush them, she'd be a nice large target for their arrows.

Oh well. Dragon-sized, private places to talk are in short supply in a war camp.

She glanced over at Wes, who was pacing along the far wall of the small room, seemingly deep in thought. She wondered if there were yet more secrets that he was keeping from her, and the thought sent a fresh pang through her heart.

I know you have Aelrie now, and you do not need me as you once did, but I just want you to know I'm here for you all the same.

There's nothing you could ever say that would make me love you any less.

She let the words remain unsaid as Alder cleared his throat, calling the small assembly to some sort of order. Kessara and Aelrie stood near him, their backs pressed against the large sticks that were serving as tent poles.

"Well," Kessara started, drawing her cloak more tightly around her shoulders. "I hope this is our final meeting."

"I'm fairly sick of them myself," Alder added, smiling for only a moment before his expression fell serious once more. "But we need to figure out our next move. Every moment that passes, our men are dying out there. Kylan's men, as well."

As if to prove his point, they heard a terrible yell from somewhere in the distance, loud enough that it seemed to seep in through the gaps in the tent's walls, sending a chill through the space.

"Currently, we're doomed," he added, earning him an elbow to the ribcage from Kessara.

There was another pause, and Celesyria wanted to break the silence immediately, but she had nothing she could say. After so much time apart, their once tight-knit group felt strange, as though the air that surrounded them had become just a little more difficult to breathe.

So much had happened, on all sides, and all she wanted was a leisurely dinner or a night by a cheerful fire, talking and laughing until everything made sense again. But that was a luxury there was no time for, and she knew it.

"There are more elves and Blackmasks than any of us expected," Kessara said. "Even King Ursa has his doubts that this combined army is going to be big enough to stop them."

"For him to admit that..." Aelrie started, her pale blue eyes growing wide before she went quiet again.

Kessara nodded. "It's bad, and we cannot allow ourselves to be deluded into thinking otherwise. Kylan told me that their army would fight to the last man, because there is no other choice. Our men will have to do the same."

Celesyria felt a shiver sliding down her tail that did not seem to be caused entirely by the snow that was falling upon it.

Kessara's voice had gone cold as she spoke of the deaths of their men. It was the voice of a greater House noble, of someone who had watched her parents make decisions that lead to life and death for their subjects. As much as the dragon knew that such decisions were sometimes necessary, they still made her feel sick. It was one thing to demand bravery from yourself. It was another thing to demand bravery from those who were most likely to die because of it.

"Does Ursa think there's even a small chance we'll win?" Wes asked, rubbing at his temples.

"Headache?" Celesyria asked in his mind, unable to help herself from wondering.

"No. Just good old human stress," Wes replied, sounding almost amused. She let out a breath. She was glad that he wasn't in pain, and even more glad that she had been able to reach out to him just like she always had, able to ignore the hurt that still lingered in her heart.

Alder reached out to take Kessara's hand, and the familiar pang of jealousy followed by guilt shot through her. She wanted someone to be strong for her, but it wasn't an option, especially not with her father gone and her mother injured. She'd just have to do her best to be strong for her friends, instead.

"It doesn't seem like there's much of a chance, no," Alder said, looking down at Kessara's hand in his.

"The High One may yet intercede," Celesyria chimed in.

"Wise men believe in miracles," Alder agreed. "But they don't wait for them."

She couldn't argue.

"We have done that already, more than once," Wes pointed out. "But Alder's right. We still need to make a decision."

The room fell silent again, save for the occasional gust of wind blowing against the tent outside. Even Alder had no comments to offer.

It had to be well past noon by now, another day of fighting and death passing by as they waited for a solution that refused to present itself.

A part of Celesyria wanted to go back to the front, free of humans to worry about, and take down as many elves and bandits as she could, but she knew it wasn't so simple. Each one of them had to be part of a greater plan, or all would be lost.

At last, words came to her.

Not an idea, not exactly, but perhaps the start of one.

She cleared her throat, gazing up at the dull canvas ceiling overhead, hoping that the High One was guiding her like she thought He was.

"Not so long ago, all I wanted to do was to go to Nox. I wanted to free my father, but the timing was never right," she said carefully, glancing between the worried faces of each of her friends. "Now, I think I feel something different."

She paused, waiting for an argument, but there was none.

"I know I haven't been myself lately," she continued. "Well, Kessara and Alder have missed it, but it's true. When my father died–"

Kessara gave a small gasp, but Celesyria pressed on, wanting to get all of her thoughts out at once.

"–I was devastated. For the first time since coming to know the High One, I truly doubted Him."

Kessara and Alder both looked shocked at this admission, but she ignored them.

"I still miss my father. I'm still wounded. But I know the High One is still there, *making* me see Him, even in the dark. He isn't hiding from me," she said, her words pouring out in a rush. "He's looking for me. For all of us. And I think... I think I hear His voice, despite everything."

It was true.

Ever since Wes had fallen from her back, during the chaos that had ensued, she had heard the soft voice that wasn't quite a sound.

"I hear Him, too," Wes said after a moment, looking at each of his friends in turn, his gaze finally settling on Celesyria.

Alder let out a breath.

Not so long ago, it had been the Aridmoorian who had received prophetic dreams, who knew the very tone of their Creator's voice, but now, it seemed, the High One had chosen only to whisper.

"So what is He saying?" Alder prompted, reaching out to pull Kessara nearer to him. Celesyria tried not to let herself be distracted by the couple's recent news.

There would be time later to think about the implications of what they had done, but for now the long-term problems of Kaveryth seemed to pale in importance compared to the hostile army that was standing well within their borders.

"The real fight is not in Kaveryth," Wes said, glancing over at Celesyria for a moment as though for approval before carrying on. "Here in Kaveryth, it's already too late."

The dragon nodded. "We have to go to the source, in Nox. We can't fight the edge of the darkness. We have to go for the heart."

"No," Aelrie said at once, her eyes going wide. "We can't. You'll be killed. All of you. They are too strong. I know the power of the darkness that awaits you there."

Wes reached over and tucked a few strands of black hair under the hood of the elf's cloak.

"Celesyria is right," he said, shaking his head. "We have to defeat the Elf-queens. If we don't, the threat will never go away. Even if we somehow manage to push their armies back, they will return."

Aelrie opened her mouth to protest, but Wes continued.

"It's just like you told me, Aelrie. Elves don't think in years, but centuries. They will keep fighting to smother the light. There will be no peace for our peoples, not until the prophecy of the thousand years is brought to an end."

"What if this is the end?" Alder argued, gesturing vaguely toward the canvas flap of the tent. "This battle, right here, right now? Perhaps he will intervene after all, fulfilling his promise."

Celesyria wanted to believe he could be right, but the chill in her heart told her otherwise.

"No," Wes said. "I wish that was how it was going to end, but it's not. I know that sounds strange, but I'm sure of it. For whatever reason, the High One has chosen to work through us to fulfill His promises. It is we who must act."

For a few breaths, the dragon waited in silence, unsure whose eyes she should meet. At last, she watched as Alder's white-knuckled fists went slack, his arms resting at his sides.

"If you're certain, and Celesyria is certain, I'm ready to listen," he said, his voice an uncharacteristic whisper.

"I am," the dragon added, touching Wes gently with her snout. "He's right. We are not to wait any longer."

"What of the sickness?" Aelrie asked. "What of the curse? Wes, if you're sick just being near the battlefield, how exactly are you going to go straight into the elven lands?"

"If he stays, and the elves overtake Kaveryth, he'll die here, too," Kessara said, her fingertips toying with the ends of her hair. "There is nowhere he can go that will be safe. Not for long."

Celesyria felt numb.

"You think you're going to die either way, don't you?" she said at last, not quite able to meet Wes's eyes. His silence made sense now. He was not hiding secrets. He was trying to spare her yet more pain.

"I don't know," Wes said. "All I know is that the High One is the only protection I have from the curse. He has kept me alive so far, and I believe He will bring me through to the end. Perhaps if we can stop the Elf-queens, it will weaken the power of the darkness enough to free me from the curse, or perhaps it will be too late, and I'll die. Either way, it must be done. Kaveryth cannot survive like this for much longer."

Everyone was quiet for a moment, and they could hear yet another faraway cry mingling with the sound of blowing snow. Celesyria felt as though she was inside a giant hourglass, watching the final grains of sand beginning to slip away.

"Destroying them will change things," Aelrie said at last. Her eyes were wet with tears, but she blinked them away, pressing her hand into Wes's own. "The elves are barely elves anymore. They are not as the High One created them to be. My race relies on the power of the four Elf-queens. Without them..."

She let her words trail away. Celesyria glanced at Wes, noticing his mouth was set in a firm line.

Would Aelrie survive if the Elf-queens were destroyed?

She wanted to ask, but none of them really knew the answer. All of their lives would be at risk, whatever option they chose. That much was a given.

"But even so," Kessara cut in, "if Wes goes to Nox, he's not going to get a chance to even try to bring them down. If what we saw today is any indication, it would be suicide."

"Unless the High One has a different plan," Wes said, giving his shoulders a shrug. "We don't know what will happen to me."

Celesyria watched him as he spoke. He looked defeated, like the matter of his very life or death had grown almost tiresome to talk about.

It was wrong, all of it. The High One's voice was quiet now, competing with the opinions of her friends, but she was sure of that much.

She thought of the Codex, the prophecies, the feasts, the bread of hope, her mind struggling to put the pieces together. Was it even possible to know the ending of the story, or would they have to live through it first?

The others were bickering now, their voices raised, annoyance on their tongues.

Outside, the wind began to howl louder, lending its voice to the tumult within.

"Quiet!" Celesyria cried out at last, her rumbling voice loud enough that she was certain she'd made the flimsy canvas walls shake.

Four mouths closed at once as the others fell silent and stared up at her.

Wes walked closer to her, placing a hand gently upon her flank.

"I'm listening. I'm sorry," he said, his words covering her mind like a warm, comforting blanket.

She let out a breath.

"The winter Feast of Offering is in two days," she said,

pausing for a moment to consider her calculations. The pieces were falling together now, one by one, and she was certain that, finally, she had gotten it right. She knew what the High One wanted.

Wes nodded. "I know. I can feel it. Even if the treasures are no longer being brought, there's always a slight change in the way of things. The Dracodei, the darkness, whatever—it's angry. It does not like to be denied. "

Celesyria nodded.

"So far, Kaveryth has begun to forget," she said carefully. "But the High One has not forgotten. The Feasts of Offering were His, once."

"What are you saying?" Alder said.

"We need to go to Nox and defeat the Elf-Queens. It's the only way. But Wes cannot be a part of it."

Alder crossed his arms over his chest, his brows furrowed in confusion, but he did not speak.

"Wes," Celesyria said, leaning gently against her friend. She wanted to laugh, somehow, despite everything, but she managed to hide her escaping smile.

"Wes, you do not need to go to Nox. That's not how this ends. You need to go to Whitespire. It's time for you to fulfill the true task of the Envoy."

24

Chapter 23

WES

Wes stood still, trying to focus his thoughts on only the inhale and exhale of his breath. Outside, he could hear the wind screaming through the Auranthian camp. The afternoon light was wasting away, hour by hour, and even through the tent walls he could feel that the air had grown colder. Aridmoorian winters were rarely predictable, and he knew a sudden blizzard could come through at any second, making the battle even more difficult for his men.

No matter what he did, no matter what he chose, it wouldn't be only him who would suffer. Thousands of others, maybe hundreds of thousands, would bear the consequences of his decision.

He looked over at Celesyria, wanting to speak with her in his mind, but failing to find the right words.

"It makes sense," Alder said at last. "Remember the elf that we helped back in Windshear, all those months ago? We gave him the bread of hope. Maybe it really is as simple as that. Maybe it really is just what the prophecy says. No riddles."

Celesyria looked at him expectantly.

He sighed, glancing down at his feet as he began to recite the words, still half-expecting to forget the passage partway through, needing the dragon to jump in and rescue him after all.

"He will bring the bread of hope to all Kaveryth, even to a Kingdom long thought dead. The usurpers will be cast out, the mighty will be brought to lowliness, and the High One will rule forever."

Kessara tucked her cloak in at her sides even more tightly, blowing out a cloud of white breath.

"Those words usually warm me," she said with a half smile. "Today, I just feel scared of what they mean for you."

"If the High One is with us, we don't need to be afraid," Aelrie said quietly.

"As I said before," Celesyria added, "I know it sounds crazy, but I want you to trust me. This is what He is asking of you. Of us."

Wes laughed without mirth.

"Even if you're right, how exactly am I supposed to do what the High One asks?" he snapped, the brewing frustration finally bubbling over. "How am I going to do any of this? In case you've all forgotten, we're in the middle of a war."

"Wes–" Alder began.

"I have no Deermaster, and no deer even if I did manage to scrounge one up," Wes said, ignoring Alder as he tallied off the problems on each of his fingers. "More importantly, I have no Witness, and no way to procure one without a Septemvirate. Oh, and to top it off, where exactly do you all think that I'm going to get bread for a few hundred thousand people?"

He paused for breath, trying not to meet Aelrie's concerned blue eyes. He knew he was not being fair to his friends, but he couldn't help it. The High One wasn't around to yell at, and at the moment, they felt like the next best thing.

They would choose to march to Nox, and even if he made it somehow, even if he got to Whitespire alive and performed the Offering, he knew better than to trust that fate would be so kind to all of them. He'd lose someone he loved, maybe everyone he loved. Everyone that was left after his parents and his brother were taken away.

And worst of all? It's not even the possibility of their deaths that scares me the most.

I'm afraid that they will go to be with the High One, and I will remain here, alone, with nothing.

"Wes, you need to take a breath," Kessara said, after a few seconds had passed. He wanted to inform her that trying to breathe had done little good, but he clamped his mouth shut, trying to push the evil thoughts deeper inside where they couldn't so easily escape.

"I know it's not the same," Alder ventured, "But when we helped that elf, we didn't let the imperfect circumstances stop us. We used what we had."

Celesyria was nodding emphatically, her body shaking the rickety tent frame.

"We have to remember that the role of the Envoy today is not precisely as it was in the beginning, and I don't just mean the fact that the sacrifices were being offered to false gods. The Feast was never just about what the people offered. It was about what the High One gave back."

Wes opened his mouth to argue, but Celesyria continued before he could speak.

"I'm not saying you don't have to sacrifice. You have to offer everything. You have to give yourself entirely to this task. And if you do, the High One will provide the rest. I know it, Wes. I'm certain."

I know I have to sacrifice. That's never been in doubt. What I wonder is if what I have to give will be enough.

"We don't have time to sit around here arguing," Alder added. "I think Celesyria's right. Wes goes to Umrym, and the rest of us can go to Nox and put an end to this war."

Kessara's face looked pale as she took Alder's hand more firmly in hers, but she did not argue.

"But Umrym is still going to be dangerous," Aelrie protested. "It's crawling with elves and their darkness. We don't even know if..."

She let the words trail away, and Wes glanced up at Celesyria. No one had to ask Aelrie what she'd meant. Jaconial and Nazzan were there, and the possibility that they were still alive felt more unlikely with each passing hour.

Still, if that was their fate, his presence would not change it.

"I've always believed that the elves cannot enter the spire itself," Wes mused aloud. "Maybe it's nonsense, like the Dracodei and all the rest of the lies, but–"

"But it would make sense," Celesyria cut in, sounding almost excited. "It's like Luna said. The great spire was the High One's true temple. He would protect it. He *will* protect it. No. If Wes can get to the base of the spire, he'll make it the rest of the way."

"There's another problem," Aelrie argued. "As you said,

the Feast is in two days. That's not enough time to make it on foot, or even by horse."

Alder glanced up at Celesyria.

"No," Wes said, shaking his head. "She has to go to Nox. We need her to help fight the elf-queens."

He knew that the excuse was flimsy.

The truth was, he couldn't bear the thought of Celesyria flying him over Whitespire, taking in the sight of her ruined home once again, or finding the bodies of their friends. Evil followed him like a black cloud. Even if it meant facing a horde of elves, she would be safer if she was far, far away from him.

"Don't be stupid," Alder said, shaking his head. "There are other dragons here who can help us to fight."

Aelrie lifted a hand. "They're right, Wes. Like I said, the headaches are going to come when you go to Umrym. Even if you had the time, you wouldn't make it to the tower on the ground. You'd die before you reach it. You need to get there from the sky, and you need to do it fast."

Kessara said something else, but it was drowned out by the sound of voices outside. Men were rushing past their tent, shouting something about readying more explosives and liquid fire, but the words barely registered.

He had no arguments left to give.

"You don't need to do this alone," the dragon said, poking gently at his shoulder with the end of her snout. "And even if Jaconial or Nazzan was here, I would still want to be the one to do this with you. From the very beginning, the High One brought us together. This is how it's meant to be. Whatever happens."

Wes closed his eyes, the headache beginning to crest behind

his eyes once more. There would be little rest. At dawn, they would begin their flight through the wind and the snow, and he would hold on, as long as he had to.

"I think you're right," he admitted at last. "This is what He wants. This is how it's meant to end."

25

Chapter 24

AELRIE

"Wait!" Aelrie cried out, her small voice loud within the confines of the small tent.

Alder and Kessara stared at her, but obeyed, stopping short where they stood. Celesyria pushed her head back through the flap of the tent, shaking off the snow that had already accumulated across her neck ridge.

"The snow is growing heavy," the dragon said. "The wind, too."

"Just what we need," Alder grumbled, staring past Celesyria at the white haze that lay beyond the door. "We don't have time for this. We need to eat, and sleep, and hope that this latest blizzard blows over before we leave."

"I know," Aelrie said quickly. "I'm sorry."

"What's wrong?" Wes asked, resting a hand on her shoulder. She leaned into him as she drew a breath.

The others looked about ready to bolt, and she knew that time was short, but if she was right...

"We need to give consideration to the other part of the prophecy," she said at last. Wes wore a puzzled expression, but Celesyria's yellow eyes immediately went wide with understanding. The dragon said something under her breath that might have been a curse.

"Of course," she said, shaking her huge head and sending a few stubborn flakes of snow flying into the others. "The part before the offering and the bread of hope. *'He will bestow a crown, he will reverse the oath.'*"

Kessara frowned. "That's hardly news."

"No," Alder said, his fingertips tapping on the pommel of his sword. "Aelrie's right. We need to do this in order. If Wes offers the bread but Aelrie falls in battle, the prophecy is not going to be fulfilled."

He paused for a moment, letting the others consider this before continuing. Aelrie waited for him to say more, glad that for the moment, the others would likely do all of the arguing on both sides without need for her to speak.

"On the other hand," Alder continued, "If Aelrie puts an end to the oath, will the Guardians still be able to help us? Will any of the dragons?"

Kessara rested a hand on her hip. "That's exactly the fear that Luna warned us not to fall into. Kaveryth has relied too much on human understanding, rather than on trust in the High One. The fate of the Guardians is not in our hands."

Aelrie cleared her throat. "I still don't know how to free the dragons from their oath, anyway."

"As you said, we must follow the prophecy in order," Celesyria said gently. "You and Wes need to marry before we let ourselves worry about the rest. The words to nullify the oath will come to you when the time is right, not before."

Aelrie looked up at Wes, feeling a ripple of excitement and nerves pouring through her as his eyes met hers. For so long, she had believed that her love for him was forbidden, even evil. She still couldn't quite fathom that not only were her feelings for him acceptable to the High One, but necessary to His plan. And that somehow, he loved her in return.

Wes rested a hand against the small of her back. "Well, there's another small problem. Who is going to marry us in the middle of a war camp?"

The tent was silent as they pondered their options.

They were nowhere near any temples, and even if there had been, Aelrie did not want to accidentally offend the High One by a ceremony tainted with false traditions of Dracodei worship. There were no ship captains at hand. An army captain was permitted to marry civilians, but she assumed they'd all be on the battlefield at the moment.

Before Aelrie could point this out, however, Alder spoke, rubbing at his temples as though trying to stave off a headache.

"A King has the authority. If Ursa is still here, he might be the best option," Alder said, grimacing as he spoke.

King Kylan Ursa was hardly Aelrie's ideal choice, but if it meant marrying the man she loved and fulfilling the will of the High One, he would do just fine.

Wes did not object.

"Give me your cloak," Kessara said, stretching out a hand to Alder. He looked like he might demand to go with her, but to Aelrie's surprise, he kept quiet and handed the thick wool garment over to his wife. "I'll be right back."

A moment later, Kessara had ducked out into the snow, the crunching sound of her footsteps on the frozen ground swallowed up by the wind.

"Perhaps we should give Wes and Aelrie a moment to talk before the King arrives," Celesyria suggested, giving Alder a pointed glance.

"Assuming he does," the Aridmoorian said, heading for the door before realizing that he no longer had a cloak. Wes shrugged his own off of his shoulders, and Aelrie watched with some amusement as the much larger man tried to make it fit as best he could.

A moment later, they were alone, the flap of the tent falling back into place as Celesyria backed away with Alder at her side.

Aelrie stood there in silence for a moment, listening to the sound of the growing storm outside as she realized what they were getting into.

"Wes," she said, an unexpected lump rising in her throat. "Are you sure about this? About any of it?"

He watched her for a long moment, his brown eyes searching hers. At last, he pulled her into his arms, pressing her firmly against his chest, his fingers cradling the back of her head.

She rested against him, her questions hanging heavy in the air.

WES

Wes drew in a deep breath, inhaling the smell of Aelrie's hair, wanting to memorize every part of her.

How can I marry her now? How can I promise her that I will love her, that I will take care of her, when the first thing I'm going to do is walk away?

He could hear the gentle whoosh of her breathing. Even though he was certain she had to be at least a little afraid, her elven nature ensured that her body did not reveal her emotions unless she allowed it to. As far as he could tell, she was completely relaxed, just a girl resting in her lover's embrace.

High One, how can I be good enough for this?

How can I be good enough for her?

Aelrie cleared her throat, and he remembered at once that he had left her question unanswered.

"Am I ready?" he repeated, wishing that he had more time to think of a better answer, but he knew that no amount of hours would suffice.

She didn't pull away. He could feel her nodding her head as she drew herself in more closely against his chest.

"No. I'm not ready," he said, forcing the words out before he could hide them away.

She stiffened, pulling back from him, his arms falling away as she glanced up at him with hurt in her eyes.

"Aelrie," he said softly, reaching out a hand that she did not take. Instead, she stepped back, looking down at her feet as she brushed a few strands of dark hair behind an ear. "Aelrie, please, I just want you to understand. I wasn't ready for my parents to die, leaving me alone as the last of my House. I wasn't ready to meet Celesyria or to find the High One, either. And I wasn't ready for anything that has happened since."

He paused, and she looked up for a moment, her ice blue eyes meeting his before she glanced away again.

"Most of all," he said, striding toward her and taking his hand in his own even as she tried to pull away. "I wasn't ready to fall in love with you. But I did. I stepped out in faith, and I don't regret it."

"Despite the pain?" she said, her voice a whisper.

"Yes. I'm not ready, but I am going to do this. Despite the odds. Despite the pain."

Their eyes met again, and this time, neither turned aside.

He wanted to kiss her, and he knew that she wouldn't refuse, but he forced himself to wait. The next time his lips touched hers, he wanted her to be his wife. And if Kylan disagreed, they would just need to find someone else.

Aelrie was correct. They couldn't risk fulfilling only half of the prophecy. They needed an elven queen to reverse the oath when the time was right.

Even if I don't make it. Even if I get to be her husband only for a day or two before I get killed, it will be worth it for the future of Kaveryth.

It will be worth it even for us.

Just then, he heard a rustling at the entrance to the tent. Alder stepped through the door, followed by Kessara, an ornery-looking King Ursa, and finally, Celesyria's head.

"I'm moving out ahead with my men in ten minutes. We want to make progress before full stars. They won't suspect us to bring in reinforcements during a storm," the King said, his voice revealing no emotion. "If you want to do this, it has to be now."

Wes opened his mouth to speak, but no words came. The courage he had felt mere moments ago seemed to have flooded away in an instant, darting off into the night to follow the cold and the wind.

"Marrying Kessara was the best decision I've ever made," Alder was saying, reaching over to plant a kiss on Kessara's forehead. "And I can see by the way that you and Aelrie look at each other that you will feel the same."

"You can do this, Wes," Celesyria chimed in in his mind. *"You're ready."*

Wes caught King Ursa rolling his eyes, but he made no comment as final encouragements were shared. Kessara gave Wes a hug, and then turned to Aelrie and embraced her as well.

"I wish I had a dress," Aelrie said at last, looking down at the black traveling outfit she was wearing.

Wes shook his head. "The fact that you love me, that you're saying yes to giving our lives to one another... You have never looked more beautiful to me than you do right now."

He felt heat rising to his cheeks, unused to offering romantic comments in front of a group, but he meant every word, and he wanted her to hear them.

The King cleared his throat, and a quiet fell at once over the tent. Even the distant battle cries chose that moment to fall silent.

He began to speak, the words of the Aridmoorian ceremony different and familiar all at once, but Wes could scarcely hear them. He was focused only on the beautiful elf standing before him, her small hands clasped in his own, her gaze meeting his without faltering as a smile teased on her lips.

At last, the King raised his own hand and pulled a small ring off of his pinky finger, handing it to Wes. Wes held it aloft for a moment, unsure what to do, until Alder reminded him that he was to put it on Aelrie's finger. He did so, pleased to find that it fit her ring finger perfectly.

"It's legally required to have some kind of ring in our weddings," the King explained quickly. "Consider it a wedding gift."

Wes could see a hint of a smile in Ursa's eyes, and for a moment, he found himself able to believe that perhaps things really were different now, despite everything. Perhaps he would relinquish control in the end, just as he'd promised. Maybe the good that Kessara saw in him really was there, after all.

Kylan said a few more words, and at last, the final moment had come.

"And thus, by my authority, bind thy vows with a kiss," the King recited, his voice solemn, as Wes and Aelrie came together.

He closed his eyes as his lips touched hers, everything else fading from his thoughts.

Somehow, miraculously, forever, she was his.

ALDER

Despite the warmth of Kessara's body next to his own, Alder could not rest.

The sounds outside were too sudden, too loud, interrupting every time sleep began to take hold. The battle had calmed somewhat for the night–even the elves, presumably, had to seek sleep eventually–but it had not ended.

He wondered if King Ursa and his men were still out there, leading the charge as many of their soldiers retreated for their own rest and evening meals.

However he felt about Kylan, he was thankful that Kessara had managed to broker an alliance with him. So far, the Red Army men were fighting bravely, and Alder was reminded of the better times he had shared as a soldier of Aridmoor and a member of King Radagar's Protectorate.

Still, despite the humans' strength, the elves were pushing them back and taking further ground. This camp would not be here for long, but at least he would not have to see it taken down, the land littered with forgotten things as their enemies filled the open space.

As soon as dawn came, he and his friends would be gone.

They would not hear the cries of the dying, nor would they witness the moments of victory, of camaraderie, of courage.

We may never even get to hear the stories.

He stroked absently at Kessara's hair, the blond strands feeling messy beneath his fingers, marveling at the beauty of a monarch who wasn't afraid to get her dresses dirty for the sake of her people. He would be the same in his own role within the House of Manta—he'd never known any other way—but Kessara could have so easily chosen to be something else. She could have been lazy, or spoiled, or looked down on those who bowed to her. But she had chosen goodness, and he believed that no matter what was yet to befall them—violence, torture, death—her choice would remain the same.

She was extraordinary.

For a second, he was certain that he had woken her up as she stirred beneath the weight of his hand, murmuring in her sleep as she tried to get comfortable on the thin bedroll, but she soon went quiet again.

It would hurt to leave Wes and Celesyria again so soon after their reunion, but he was thankful that he was not going to be separated from the other half of his heart. He did not envy Wes's fate.

He couldn't imagine how it would feel to watch as she walked away, knowing that he may never again get to see her laugh or feel the comforting softness of her hand in his own.

He couldn't bear it. It would break him.

"High One," he whispered into the darkness of their tent, waiting a moment as he let his greeting rise toward the hidden sky, as though the Creator might choose to say hello right back. "You have given Kessara and I so many miracles already. We don't deserve another one. We are not owed a happy ending. I have always expected a difficult life, and when it came, I was ready."

He paused, listening to the Princess's steady breathing, wondering how late it was and whether or not the night sky was visible beyond the snow. The High One was out there, somewhere, apart from the world and yet filling every inch of it. He was listening.

"I won't expect another miracle, but I will hope. I will hope for me and Kessara, for Wes and Aelrie, for Jaconial and Nazzan, and for Celesyria. I will hope for our people, that something better is waiting for them, and that your promises of restoration will come to pass."

He drew a breath, waiting.

He wanted to end the prayer there, to think of all of Kaveryth, everything that mattered, not only himself. But as he looked over at Kessara's sleeping face, her eyelashes brushing against her cheeks, he couldn't help but to make one more request, a failsafe for the worst possibility, even if he couldn't bring himself to say it out loud.

I would die a thousand deaths, however painful, however slow, if it meant that I could keep her safe.

If Nox is where everything must end, let it be me who returns to dust.

26

Chapter 25

CELESYRIA

The dawn was bright and clear, the snow a glimmering blanket of white.

Celesyria flew behind the camp, away from the battlefield, her eyes alighting on a group of several deer who were picking through a stand of bushes in search of something to eat.

She swept down toward them, gliding as silently as she could, until she was able to grasp one of them, a large buck, with her sharp claws. She silenced the anguished cries of the animal as quickly as she could, watching wistfully as his companions darted off over the horizon.

The others were in the dining hall eating breakfast, or perhaps they had finished by now, and were gathering together the meager supplies that they would be able to carry to Nox and to Whitespire.

In the distant sky over the battlefield, she could see the flash of dragon scales, gleaming in the bright sun. A flash of guilt mingled with longing coursed through her.

Had she followed the path that her life had been expected to take, she would be there with them, a Guardian, just like her parents and most of her ancestors that had come before them. She would be brave, facing the battle head on, using the natural strength that the High One had given her to do good.

Just like Jaconial and Nazzan.

She shook her head, and took a fresh bite of meat, trying to push any thoughts of her two friends away. She wanted to meet them in Umrym, to find them alive, but she knew that her hope bordered on folly.

She glanced toward the southwestern sky, just able to make out the gray peaks of the Severed Summits. A shiver ran through her. Whatever the truth was, she would know soon enough.

Just as soon as everyone was ready, Wes would climb upon her back. She would fly him past the elven army, past the bandits, past whatever evils still waited within the borders of the dragon homeland, and she would take him to the base of the great spire.

It was an impossible task, but she was resigned to carrying it out. It was what the High One wished, and He would be sure that they made it.

But though she believed it to be true, she couldn't shake the hollow fear that filled her heart.

The sun was stinging her eyes, making her blink, and she found herself unable to stare up at the endless blue, in any direction.

The High One seemed so far away, just then.

It was easy for her to imagine that He was powerless, a delicate whisper that struggled to be heard over a never ending storm.

Would He do anything if I chose to run?

She thought of the east, of the place where the maps all ended, where some of the remnant still remained. Would she be welcomed there? Was there still a way out, even now?

She got to her feet, taking the remains of the deer in her teeth and flinging it off into a stand of sad-looking trees. She was ashamed of her cowardly thoughts. They made her feel sick.

But the urge to run remained.

The Farplace felt so close now, waiting for her, as though it had reappeared somewhere beneath her feet, beneath the light, pulling her under.

She pushed off from the ground, flapping her wings as she rose higher and higher, ignoring the burning of the sun in her eyes.

She looked up, up, up at the blue and the emptiness, wanting to see Him, wanting to see any evidence that He was there, any shred of hope to hold on to.

I believe in You, High One.

Help me to believe.

KESSARA

Kessara raised a hand to her brow, trying to shield her eyes from the harsh morning sunlight. After a rather uncomfortable sleep, she had woken up to a silence so complete that, at first, she had been worried that some terrible slaughter had visited their camp in the night.

Instead, she and Alder had walked out of their tent into the predawn light, the weather more warm and pleasant than it had been in weeks, the wind finally having gone silent.

Now, after a hurried breakfast and a brief stop at the camp's makeshift armory to fit her and Aelrie with additional weapons, they were almost ready to leave.

"Do you think the Guardians are coming?" Alder said from beside her, his own green eyes squinting against the brightness.

"Kylan said he would send them," she said firmly, hoping that she sounded more confident than she felt. The King had kept most of his promises so far, but that was hardly a guarantee of future trustworthiness.

"We can afford to wait a little longer," Alder said, "I suppose we have to, at least until the newlyweds arrive."

He turned around to look at the camp that they were leaving behind instead of searching the horizon for glittering scales. Kessara did the same, trying her best to rub away the spots of light that lingered on the backs of her eyelids.

They had been up as early as they could manage, but already, the morning was racing away from them. While little had been heard from the battlefield when they'd first woken up and left their tent, Kessara could hear more and more commotion with each passing hour. Soon, the screams and cries that had filled the camp the day before would return and, perhaps selfishly, Kessara did not want to be there to hear them.

"Look!" Alder called out, pointing in the vague direction of where the battlefield now lay.

Kessara was alert at once, blinking quickly as she searched the sky. On the horizon, she could see two small, dark dots, growing larger and larger with each passing moment.

"Only two. A male and a female," Alder announced flatly

as the two creatures came into clearer view. A minute or two later, they were landing, their claws cleaving deep furrows in the otherwise immaculate morning snow.

The male stepped forward first, offering as much of a bow as his height would allow, his grayish scales reminding Kessara of cobblestone after a rainstorm.

"I know you needed three, but King Ursa told us to tell you that we were all he could spare," he said, gesturing to his companion.

She offered a bow of her own, her strange dark eyes searching Kessara's face even as she bent her snout toward the snow. Her scales were a paler green than Nazzan's, but even the slight resemblance was enough to make Kessara's heart ache for her friend.

"We will serve you as well as we can, Your Highness," she said, blinking slowly, her eyes kind despite their jarring appearance.

They exchanged introductions, though with so much on her mind, Kessara had forgotten their names almost as quickly as she'd learned them. Still, she tried to be as diplomatic as possible, despite the fact that she did not feel very much like a princess at the moment.

She adjusted the heavy armor that the Auranthian soldiers had fitted her with, trying to remember the precise locations of the four hidden daggers that she wore along with her sword.

Alder gave her a pointed look, but she ignored him, suddenly deeply interested in the ties of her traveling boots. He had tried to convince her to stay behind, but as usual, even though she was thankful for his concern, she had refused.

Now, the time to change her mind had passed, and she

hoped that he would let the matter drop.

If I stay here, I could die anyway. And if I'm going to die, I'd rather die beside him than die alone.

WES

Wes wove between the tents, nearly knocking to the ground a young woman who was carrying a bundle of washing.

"Forgive me," he said quickly, helping to pick up several socks that had fallen into the snow. Her face was kind, and she said something in return, though Wes barely heard it.

"Are you all right?" Aelrie asked at his side as the girl hurried off, the elf's dark eyes filled with concern. He squeezed her hand, not sure whether to confess to the particular horror of this morning's headache. He didn't want her to wonder if it was her fault, or if she had done anything wrong the night before.

Despite the pain, she had made him happier than he'd ever been. He still struggled to believe that she was his, really his, their vow now cemented forever.

All around, the camp was beginning to buzz with activity, and he tried his best to ignore the hammering soreness they caused within his head. They watched as three injured men were carried into what he presumed was a healer's tent, borne on rudimentary stretchers. The morning was young, but already, the war had taken fresh casualties.

As they broke away from the final line of tents, he couldn't help but to notice the beauty of the open plain that lay before him, the unbroken whiteness of the snow. A certain part of him wanted to run through it, leaving dragging boot marks behind, marking his place, but he hesitated as morbid thoughts swirled within his mind.

There's no time for childish things. Perhaps there never will be again.

"There they are, with those dragons," Aelrie said, gesturing toward the horizon. "Alder and Kessara, anyway. I don't see Celesyria yet."

Dragging him by the hand, she took off toward them, racing across the expanse. She reminded him of a beautiful apparition, her raven hair stark against the endless white of the snow and blue of the sky.

Forgetting his thoughts of a mere moment before, he broke into a run beside her, the deep snow filling the tops of his boots and stinging at the skin his woolen socks did not quite cover. He struggled to keep up with her, her elven athleticism far superior to his own, but he refused to let go of her hand.

In only minutes, he would be forced to watch his new wife fly across Kaveryth, leaving him behind.

High One, help me to bear it.

Help us to endure.

Alder and Kessara embraced each of them in turn. "Do you have everything?" Alder asked Aelrie, his eyes roaming over the small leather pack, the bow, and the quiver of arrows she carried. On her belt hung her sword, and Wes suspected she had many more daggers hidden besides.

Aelrie nodded, a cloud of breath escaping her mouth in the slight chill. Wes couldn't read her expression. She didn't look pleased to be leaving him behind, certainly, but there was a fire in her eyes that he was not used to seeing. The gentleness that usually marked her movements had changed just slightly, giving way to a firmer set of her limbs as she moved.

She's strong. Stronger than any of us, save Celesyria. You don't need to worry about her. She'll be all right.

"I forgot to ask, have you both eaten?" Kessara asked the two dragons, who nodded. Wes had hoped that King Ursa would have been able to spare more Guardians, but at least Aelrie and Kessara were light enough to share the larger male's back without being much of a burden.

"Yes, Your Highness," the female said.

"We are ready to leave at your most noble call," the male chimed in, his gravelly voice sounding almost meek as the two of them bowed once more.

Despite the sadness of the situation, Wes couldn't help but to smile at the look on Kessara's face, wondering how Aelrie would fare with all of the attention she'd receive once she became Queen of Silverfell. The thought lifted his spirits a little, as in order to think of her as Queen, he had to imagine a future where she survived this journey to Nox. It was not much, but at that moment, he was thankful for even the smallest glimmer of hope.

"I'll be there in just a moment," Celesyria's voice sounded in his mind.

"Celesyria told me she's on her way now," he announced. The new dragons looked at one another, clearly puzzled as to how he could mindspeak, but they asked no questions.

A few moments later, he spotted Celesyria's orange wings as she flew low over the camp, casting a huge, dragon-shaped shadow over the rows of tents.

Wes felt Aelrie's hand stiffening within his own, and the dread that he had almost managed to forget for the last few minutes came flooding back in an instant.

There was nothing else to wait for. The time had come.

He swallowed back the bile that was rising in his throat, only half-listening as Celesyria introduced herself to the other dragons and began to say her goodbyes.

Finally, Alder cleared his throat loudly, resting a hand on the sword that hung from his belt.

"Noon will come quickly, and not long after will come night. I want to cover as much distance as we can," he said firmly. "We could linger for hours and our goodbyes would never suffice. It's time to leave."

Wes felt a flicker of anger rising within his gut.

"You say it like it's so easy. Perhaps it is, when you're not the one leaving your wife behind," he said, knowing that the words were unfair, but unable to stop them from pouring out.

Alder stared at him with piercing eyes, his hands balled into fists.

He took a few steps toward Wes, closing the distance between them in an instant, close enough that Wes could feel his hot breath against his face.

Aelrie's hand slipped from his, and he flinched, certain that he was about to endure one of his lectures, but instead, Alder embraced him, pulling him so tight against his chest that Wes could scarcely breathe.

They stayed like that for a long moment, until finally, Alder released him.

"It's going to be okay, brother," he said, the words catching a little in his throat. "I will do whatever it takes to protect her. I can promise you that much."

His green eyes were so fierce that, somehow, Wes believed him.

He nodded firmly, trying with little success to blink away his own tears.

Kessara gave him a hug as well, leaning into his chest, and assuring him that it was going to be all right. They would see each other again soon. They would all make it.

He wanted to believe her, too.

As Kessara pulled away, he couldn't help but to notice the two dragons, who had taken a few steps back, trying not to intrude on the intimate goodbyes. He was thankful for them. He doubted that Kylan had gotten many volunteers to go to Nox from among the Guardians.

At last, he turned back to Aelrie, taking her into his arms for what he hoped would not be the last time.

They stayed like that for a while, Aelrie fiddling with the ring that had once been Kylan's as she pressed her hand against his chest. She looked up at him, her blue eyes even more clear and beautiful than the perfect sky, and kissed him for a long, long time.

"I love you, Wes," she said at last as she pulled away.

"I love you, Aelrie," he replied, cradling her cheek within his hand, no longer caring who else was around to hear his sentimental declaration. "No matter what happens, the High One is with you. He will give you the strength you need to overcome the darkness. Don't forget. Don't doubt."

The next few moments passed in an instant, until suddenly, she was on the unfamiliar male dragon's back, sitting in front of Kessara. Alder was riding the female, his sword and armor clinking against her green scales.

Now that she was finally leaving, he noticed that his eyes held no more tears. Perhaps they were waiting, waiting until he himself was in the sky on Celesyria's back, heading off into his own oblivion.

"Let's finish this. I'm ready for us all to go home," Alder

said, taking the leather saddle straps between his fingers.

Wes wanted to race forward, to pull himself up to Aelrie, to kiss her one last time, but he knew it would only prolong the pain.

There was the sound of flapping wings, and then they were gone, leaving Wes and Celesyria alone in the sea of snow.

She was at his side in an instant, and he collapsed against her, tearless sobs choking his throat.

At that moment, shameful as it was, he knew the true danger that love could bring.

He would take any bargain, pay any price, forsake his very soul if it meant that he could protect her from harm.

All he could do was hope that the High One would be gracious enough never to tempt him with such a choice.

27

Chapter 26

FALLOREN

"You're not going to tell her?" Jishon asked, staring off after the two soldiers as they retreated back toward their tents.

General Falloren gave him a dismissive wave, having already grown exhausted with his subordinate's constant questions and needless commentary.

"But two dragons were spotted heading for the West Strait," the younger elf protested, his eyes gleaming with what Falloren could only describe as excitement. "And they had humans on their backs! Don't you think Meira will want to know?"

Falloren drew a slow breath, waiting for the urge to wring the man's neck to pass. When he finally felt his heart rate beginning to slow, he spoke, deciding that perhaps exercising patience would be the wisest course of action. After all, the other elves around him were, by and large, more foolish than Jishon. And anyway, he didn't particularly love killing idiots. He considered himself somewhat more civilized than that.

"Jishon," he said indulgently, "they aren't going to get anywhere. There are too many troops still in Nox. Our borders are secure."

Jishon paused for a moment, perhaps wondering how far he could push the General's patience.

"It could be a delegation. Or perhaps another message," he suggested meekly.

Falloren clenched his fists, remembering the foul trick that King Ursa had pulled before he had left Nox.

"The humans wouldn't dare," he said. "In any case, they could much more easily speak to one of our commanders on their own land. There are plenty of elven captains in Kaveryth already."

He felt a ripple of pleasure at the thought. Their men were taking the continent, inch by inch. Soon enough there would be entire elven cities in every one of the Four Kingdoms.

For a long while, Jishon did not speak.

Falloren let his hands rest at his back as he surveyed the war camp, wondering if he would have the time to tour the actual battlefield before nightfall. The army had long since caught up with him and his scouts, and now they were able to enjoy much better accommodations. He'd actually slept properly the night before, and the rest of the afternoon stretched out before him, brimming with possibilities.

"General?" came Jishon's voice again, interrupting his ponderings.

He said nothing, hoping that his blank expression would convey to the fool that the discussion was now over.

"It's just that I'm surprised you're taking such a risk," Jishon said quickly. "After your recent mistakes, I mean."

Falloren turned to face the man—still a boy, really, by elf

standards – and strode forward until their faces were mere inches apart.

He stared into Jishon's eyes, savoring the look of fear that filled their depths.

When he tired of watching the younger man quiver under his gaze, he pulled back, noticing that Jishon's fingertips were still shaking in terror.

"I suggest that you be quiet, and let me make the decisions, dear Jishon," he said calmly.

No good can come of wasting her time with such trivialities.

Still, as much as he doubted that anything would come of this latest human nonsense, he wanted to be on top of it, just in case.

He glanced toward a group of Blackmasks who were passing a nearby row of tents, with sandwiches and tankards of ale in their hands. He supposed that the day's fighting had to be going quite well, if at least a few of their men could spare the time for a late lunch.

Jishon stared after them, not daring to ask if he could join the meal.

"We will get to Nox as soon as possible, and deal with the intruders when – and if – it becomes necessary," he said to the boy, almost kindly. "Go and eat. We will leave tonight."

With any luck, Meira would never have to know.

KESSARA

The battle was raging below, a savage scene that looked out of place in the winter sunshine. Kessara and Aelrie both leaned over the gray dragon's side as far as they dared, not wanting to look, but unable to turn away.

The Princess wished that she was with Alder, feeling his warmth against her back, but she understood why it was wise not to needlessly tire the dragons. She glanced over to where the green female dragon flew nearby. Alder, too, was leaning over in his saddle, squinting down at the distant clash below.

They were too high for arrows to reach. They couldn't hear much, but they were low enough that even the humans with their inferior eyesight could pick out certain details. Kessara watched with rapt attention as yet another war in miniature broke out, tiny figures stabbing and fighting and bleeding without a sound.

Somewhere down there are Galeharbor soldiers I grew up with. Acquaintances from Silverfell. New friends from Auranth.

She gripped the leather saddle straps tightly between her hands, settling back into her seat and forcing her eyes to focus straight ahead along the dragon's spiny neck.

Not so long ago, they had been in Auranth, sharing meals over a crackling fire, preparing for a day such as this to come. Even then, their merriment had always been tainted with the taste of coming war, but it was nothing compared to now.

It felt dark here, even as the sun gleamed, like they would never laugh again.

She shook aside the feeling as they finally crossed over the far end of the field, flying higher as they got nearer to the elven camps. It got colder the higher they went, and most of the day passed in a lonely, chilled silence.

Finally, after dusk had long since fallen, she thought that she noticed the ground beginning to change beneath them. She asked the dragon who carried them to fly a little lower, and the creature did so, seemingly unconcerned about elves that could be hiding out so far from both Umrym and the battlefields of Aridmoor.

"Look," she called out, glad that despite the cold, the wind was minimal. "We're over the foothills of the Severed Summits."

"We should be well into the outer range by midnight," the dragon said, the exhaustion clear in his voice. Kessara felt a flash of pity for the creature. After all, unlike her and Aelrie, the dragon couldn't exactly take a sip of water or eat a piece of bread as he flew. It had been a long day, with two passengers on his back no less, and the Severed Summits were unlikely to offer much by way of substantial meat for him to eat.

"You have carried us fast and far," she said, peering down again as the little hills below them began to take on more sharp edges. "We are in your debt."

"Yes," Aelrie agreed, speaking for the first time in a long while, her voice reminding Kessara of a chiming temple-bell in the stillness. "Thank you for agreeing to help us. This journey would have taken us ages on the ground, having to cut so far to get around the bandits and the elves."

For a moment, the dragon did not reply. Kessara glanced over at Alder. His dragon had gone ahead, and she could not seem to catch her husband's eye. No matter. She would be able to embrace him soon enough.

"I am not sure if we were clear about this arrangement," the dragon said at last.

Kessara waited for him to say more, twisting her wedding ring around and around on her finger.

"As soon as we make it to the shores of Nox, you're going to be on your own. The King was adamant that he will need every last Guardian back in Aridmoor to end this fight."

Aelrie turned back to face Kessara, her blue eyes filled with worry, but Kessara shook her head, offering the best attempt at a smile she could manage.

"I understand," she said. "You are taking a risk, even now, and it remains appreciated. We will find a way on her own."

The dragon thanked her, relief written clearly in his voice, and Aelrie offered a small smile of her own before turning back around.

Kessara had meant what she said—really, she should have expected as much—but she couldn't help but to feel a twinge of annoyance when she thought of all of the other non-Guardian dragons who had long since fled east. She wondered if they had sought the remnant, or if they were hiding out somewhere in the wilderlands of Galeharbor, hoping that the war would never reach them. In the end, war would find them, and she wished that at least some of them would come back to stand firm and fight.

The final hints of pink sunlight had faded away on the western horizon, leaving the mountains below bathed in inky shadows, awaiting the blue light of the rising moon. Kessara wondered if Jaconial and Nazzan were somewhere within the caverns that lay beneath the peaks, still alive, still fighting.

"I hope Wes is all right," Aelrie said after another long silence, still facing forward to watch the dark sky. "If he falls off of Celesyria again..."

She let the words fall away, but Kessara shared her fears.

Celesyria and Wes would be somewhere above the mountains, too, but they would have gone more toward the southeast, where the great spire and the ruined city of Whitespire that surrounded it awaited them.

She, Aelrie, and Alder would have no idea if their friends had succeeded until after they returned from Nox. Even by the quickest dragonflight, the land of Kaveryth was vast, and however fast news tended to spread, it never felt fast enough when someone they loved was in danger.

"We can't let ourselves get lost in these worries," she said to Aelrie, resting a hand on the shoulder of her armor. "I know it's difficult, but keep turning to the High One. Keep trusting that this is where your husband, and my friend, is meant to be."

She believed what she said, but she couldn't deny that the same doubts had been swirling in her mind, especially since finding out Wes's secret. Before, she'd been afraid of the Envoy dying in battle, but now, she feared the cursed water that was poisoning his body every moment of every day.

"You're right," Aelrie said, leaning back a little until the back of her head rested on Kessara's shoulder, an uncharacteristically cozy gesture for the shy elf. The Princess stroked her dark hair, no longer hidden by her cloak, and Aelrie did not pull away from her touch. "The High One is more powerful than the evil he has drunk. He's kept Wes alive so far. I don't believe he's going to let him fall now, not so close to the end."

The elf closed her eyes, looking almost relaxed as Kessara continued to embrace her, letting her rest. The Princess felt rather soothed herself, thankful that Aelrie had decided to let her in, and to truly accept her as a friend.

Neither of them would speak of what came after the end.

The will of the High One would be fulfilled.

Anything more would have to rest upon hope.

ALDER

The first arrow was a surprise.

It flew out of the darkness, seeming to come from nowhere at all before plinking off of the dragon's pale green scales and falling uselessly into the West Strait.

"Well, we're here," the dragon joked, her voice echoing through the quiet night air. "I'll mindspeak and warn the others."

Alder looked over at Kessara and Aelrie, who were flying a few dragon-lengths behind them. He was glad that they had both agreed to wear armor, despite the uncomfortable weight.

They had all hoped that the port of Nox would be quiet, but he had prepared himself for the possibility that it would still be full of elven guards. So far, he feared that he was going to be proven correct.

After a few more minutes had passed without arrow fire, he dared a glance over the dragon's side, clinging tightly to the straps as he leaned out over the black water. Far below, he could see several boats leaving the port, small and open affairs bearing enough elves each that it seemed certain they would capsize.

Probably headed for the Black Beach, and carried by magic.

He remembered seeing similar boats back in Kingsvier Landing, in the North Sea, but these looked much plainer, and some of them were downright ugly. The whole port looked to have been built without any sort of aesthetic impulse at all. Or perhaps the elves just enjoyed parading around in their glamors, with nothing in the background to distract from their own beauty.

"Some look like they're headed south," the dragon said, letting herself glide on the air current for a moment as she stretched out her neck to look at the water below. "A more direct route to Umrym, I suppose. I wonder how they're bypassing the cliffs and the mountains."

Alder saw those boats, too, heading along the current of the Strait, toward the once well-protected dragon lands.

"Perhaps it's a little easier to access now, with Helmm and who knows what else blown to pieces," he said, realizing a few seconds later how insensitive the remark was, but the dragon only chuckled.

"I hear you're going to be King of Galeharbor one day," his companion said, flapping her wings a few times as they caught an updraft. "Might need to work on your communication skills. You men are rarely very good at it."

"*You're not wrong there,*" Alder mindspoke, no doubt surprising the dragon with his ability. "*Kessara has told me the same, more than once. Ideally, I'll let her do most of the talking.*"

Another growling chuckle rose in the dragon's chest, making the saddle shake.

"*On second thought, you're not doing as bad as I thought, my Lord.*"

The two of them fell silent then, waiting for the other dragon, Aelrie, and Kessara to catch up to them before moving forward. This would be the difficult part.

Alder eyed the port city that lay ahead, and the docks that were now directly below them. Several more arrows had soared up from the boats, but none had managed more than a glancing blow off of the dragon's firm scales.

He knew that the attacks would only become more dangerous now that they had actually made it to Nox, but there was nothing they could do but trust in the High One's protection. The elves were still pouring directly into Umrym. Despite his lingering hope that Jaconial and Nazzan were somehow still alive, he had his doubts. So far as he could tell, Umrym was finished, and the rest of Kaveryth was not far behind.

If they wanted to put a stop to it, they had to succeed here and defeat the Elf-queens. There was no other way.

"Pull up until we're over the bowmen near the docks," he said.

"Of course, my Lord," the dragon said, signaling to his male companion as she pumped her wings, taking them high over the docks and away from the arrow fire. "But we will need to land soon, and return to the battlefield. We have orders from the King."

Alder rubbed at his temples, pushing his overgrown curls away from his forehead. *Perhaps if more of us on this continent defied stupid orders, we wouldn't be in this position in the first place.*

He shook his head, scolding himself. He couldn't blame the dragons, or even Ursa. As far as the Red Army was concerned, their missions to Nox and to Whitespire were nothing but foolishness. He was thankful to have received any help at all, however temporary.

Finally, they cleared the docks and the main port area, and the two dragons began to circle lower. He glanced over at Kessara as they flew, but she did not return his gaze, her eyes focused firmly on the strange, quiet streets below.

Alder sat back in his saddle, stretching his tired limbs as best as he could before they landed. There was no going back.

Once they landed, he would have to give every ounce of strength he had to destroy the Elf-queens, protect the woman he loved, and protect the woman Wes loved.

Even if they ended up having to go home without him.

28

Chapter 27

CELESYRIA

The moonlight had grown cold as Celesyria and Wes flew over the jagged peaks of the Severed Summits, and the wind had slowed to only the slightest whisper. It was a perfect darkness for stars, and tonight the dragon did not need to worry about using them for navigation.

She knew these mountains, every crag and valley. They brought her home. At least, they had, back when her home still existed.

But still, she loved to be able to see the endless expanse of twinkling light, like messages from another world that most people never bothered to notice.

Her father loved the stars so much that he longed for winter nights like this, even though the cold blood of dragons made the chill especially unpleasant. He'd always said that the stars were brightest at the time of the winter Feast, and now, Celesyria knew that he was right.

Perhaps he was somewhere better now. Perhaps he could

see these same stars, could communicate in this rare language that he had taught his only daughter to understand so very well. Perhaps, with the permission of the High One, he was telling her that, despite the war, everything would come together for the good in the end.

I want to believe you, Papa. So very much.

She banked to the left, allowing herself to fly a little lower than she had previously dared as they approached a long ridge. The elves were here, she knew, though she suspected that many would be hidden away in their own settlements by now, their enchanted lanterns extinguished for the night. She would keep a close watch for them, but it was so much warmer and easier to fly in the thicker air that clung to the peaks of the mountains.

As she turned, she felt Wes shifting on her back, his weight unbalanced for a moment before he righted himself. He had not bothered to deny that the headaches were becoming more unbearable the closer they got to the elves in Umrym, but so far, he had managed to hold on.

"*I'm fine,*" he said quickly in her mind.

"*I wasn't going to ask, because I don't want you to talk. Conserve your strength,*" she said gently, wishing that there was any real comfort that she could offer. All she could do was to carry him toward the great spire, and to protect him until they got there.

There was a pause for a few moments as the wind whispered, but then, Wes spoke aloud.

"It's only bad when I mindspeak," he admitted. Celesyria should have figured as much—though mindspeaking came naturally to dragons, the rare human with the ability to do it usually found it exhausting.

"Okay, no more of that, then," she said, giving a little laugh. It wasn't awkward, not quite, but she couldn't help but to feel that a strange gulf had opened up between them, a barrier between her and the Envoy that she could no longer overcome.

Even though he had borne the moonscar since birth, his role as the chosen one felt different now. It had become real tonight, beneath the watching stars. He was important to the future of all Kaveryth in a way that she could never fully understand.

"It's too quiet," Wes said at last, sounding a bit more alert as he shifted on her back.

"It's strange, but I don't mind it," she replied. "I feel like I can hear the night."

"I like it better than the sounds of the battlefield."

She let his words hang in the air for a moment, unsure if she could think of anything adequate to say. The cries of war were not easily forgotten, even though she and her friends had been fortunate enough not to be on the front lines themselves.

"I hate this," Wes continued after a few moments. "I hate what my Kingdom has become, what this continent has become, I hate all of it."

There was a sudden edge of anger to his voice, so she waited, wanting him to let out whatever was trapped within him. She was thankful that despite the walls that existed between them—Envoy and nobody, ensouled and soulless—he still turned to her. She was still his best friend, and even here, the thought filled her heart with warmth.

"After I met you, once I finally began to believe that the High One was real, and that our history was mostly lies, I thought things would be different. I thought that bringing truth to the world would change it. Maybe that was foolish."

Celesyria waited a moment to answer, focused for a moment on avoiding a large stone outcropping.

"It's not foolish. I've had the same thoughts. It's what the Codex, the parts I've read, seemed to imply–that if we followed Him, he would aid us. I still believe that to be true, but I guess it's not so easy for me to accept that I'll never quite see this life through the eyes of the Eternal Lands. We can only see a little bit of the plan."

Wes's expression had softened slightly, his flinty gaze looking more like that of the man she knew.

Perhaps she wasn't quite a nobody. Perhaps even now, the High One was giving Wes the right words through her.

"Separating from Aelrie is the hardest thing I've ever done, save perhaps losing my family," Wes said. "But seeing what is happening to our men, and even to the Red Army...I am finding strength in it. It's something to hold on to."

"What do you mean?"

"So many people in Kaveryth have never had a chance to choose like we have. They were born into a corrupt world, and they took it for what it was. No matter what else you, me, and the others have been through, we have been given the choice to fight back. And even though it hurts like the Wrathlands, and all I want to do half the time is to run away, I'm not going to spit on that chance to do good. It's a gift, and I won't waste it."

Celesyria flapped her wings, drawing them both into a sweeping circle as she gazed once more at the stars. Too soon, daylight would come. Perhaps even before then, this momentary peace would be torn from them, but for the moment, the Envoy's wise words seemed to hang heavy in the air.

She couldn't seem to shake the bitterness combined with guilt that rose in her chest, suffocating her from the inside out. Wes was so much braver than she was. So much more noble, so much more willing to suffer for the sake of what was right. How could she still be jealous of him? How could her pride have taken such deep roots in her heart?

She remembered the little prayer, waiting, right when she needed it most.

I believe in You, High One.

Help me to believe.

"Are you all right?" Wes asked, shifting his weight in the saddle. "Did I say something wrong?"

"No," she said quickly, straightening out her back as best she could so that he would be comfortable. "It's you I'm worried about. We're close now."

"It's so quiet. The elves must be underground, and we haven't seen a single dragon or dwarf, either," Wes mused.

Celesyria's chest felt tight. "And no sign of Jaconial or Nazzan."

Wes didn't say anything for a long time as Celesyria continued forward, following the path between the peaks, their craggy faces as familiar as any marker on a map. She could see the higher mountains before them, the final ridge that marked the edge of the valley where Whitespire rested.

"You're going to need to hold on," she said softly, circling a final time to be sure Wes was ready before she threw herself higher into the air, flying fast so that she would reach the needed height.

"The pain is bad," Wes said, his words escaping in a gasp of air. "But I'm still breathing."

"Just try and stay tight against my back," Celesyria said as they crossed over the top of the ridge, marveling at the size and strength of the natural barrier. "You'll make it."

"The Feast begins at midnight. It can't be far off," Wes said, the words coming out one at a time, punctuated by wheezing breaths. "If we're right, it's all going to be over soon. One way or another."

Celesyria swallowed a lump that had risen in her throat, not trusting herself to answer, not trusting any of the words that she could find.

KESSARA

There was a sound in the air that Kessara almost recognized.

Before she could figure out what it was, Aelrie had turned around and pushed her back, nearly sending her off of the saddle entirely.

"Arrows," Aelrie hissed. "Stay down."

Kessara did as she was told, pressing herself as close as she could against the dragon's back. She felt his rumbling voice beneath her before she heard it.

"There's a line of archers, but I see some weird trees. Some small forest, I hope. We'll make it."

She had no choice but to trust his word. From her position near his tail, she felt suddenly disoriented, unsure where the port was, or in which direction the West Strait lay.

"I can see Alder," Aelrie called to her. Kessara felt some of the tension leaving her limbs. He was all right.

Shouts erupted from below, the savage words reminding her of the way the Blackmasks had screamed and chanted back in Galeharbor so very long ago. The elves usually sounded as beautiful as they looked, but not now. Now, their darkness and hate was plain to her ears, no longer hidden away, and it filled her stomach with a cold terror.

After what felt like a very long time, she managed to turn carefully back around in the saddle. She could see a huge outcropping of rock, and she watched as Alder and his dragon rushed ahead of them, diving beneath it, and disappearing out of sight.

"Hold on. This will be fast," the male dragon said in a rumble. She held tightly to the leather saddle straps and to Aelrie. As they flew faster and closer, she was certain that the sheer rock face was too close.

"We're okay," Aelrie said, sounding almost breathless. Some logical part of Kessara's brain knew that she could trust the elf's senses above her own. She closed her eyes, pressing her face against Aelrie's armored back until she was sure the metal would leave a mark.

She felt her stomach lurch as the dragon dived, and for three full seconds, she couldn't make her lungs take in air.

A moment later, she felt the dragon's claws scraping rock below. They were on the ground.

She clambered off of the saddle on shaking legs, and collapsed into Alder's waiting arms. Even here, as close to the Wrathlands as she could get while remaining alive, she still felt a hum of joy as he held her close against his chest. He smelled like he always did, and his lips felt familiar and comforting as they pressed against her own.

She pulled back with some reluctance, giving Aelrie an apologetic glance. She could see the elf touching the ring on her finger, the silver metal nearly disappearing against her skin. She wanted to offer comfort, to promise that they'd get her back to Wes, that they'd make it, but she couldn't bring herself to offer any more hope.

Aelrie knew the stakes, and still, she had selflessly chosen to separate from the man she loved in order to serve the High One. How the elf could have ever doubted her worthiness was beyond Kessara.

For a moment, the dragons and the humans looked at one another, none wanting to be the first to speak. The Princess knotted her fingers within her skirts, wishing that she could say anything to make them stay, but knowing how badly they were needed elsewhere.

At last, the male dragon cleared his throat. "We ask for the protection of your High One for our return journey," he said, glancing over at his female companion, who nodded. Kessara's mouth nearly fell open in surprise. Talk of the High One was spreading among the Guardians, but a confession of any sort of belief in Him was still controversial even for humans, let alone the traditional servants of the Dracodei. She composed herself in time, however, and held her chin aloft, offering a few words of prayer as Princess of Galeharbor and asking for the High One's blessing upon these noble strangers.

"Thank you for bringing us here," Aelrie said softly, extending a hand and resting it gently upon the gray scales lining the male dragon's shoulder.

"Fight well," Alder added, giving the dragons a quick bow.

For the next few moments, Kessara and her friends watched as the dragons took off and headed back out from beneath the outcropping, flying off toward the Strait once more.

"Do you think the elves will be able to see that we're not on their backs?" Kessara asked, directing her question toward

Aelrie, who shook her head.

"I don't think so. They'll likely be flying at an even higher altitude than we did on the way here, since they already know where they're going. I suspect the elves will assume they only came inland to gather intel. Believe me, they would never suspect that three humans would dare to walk into Nox."

Aelrie smiled a little at this, as though the thought of defying her past life was rather pleasing.

Alder nodded. "I think she's right. That's been my hope, anyway. In any case, even if we have the advantage of stealth for now, it's not going to last long. We can't waste any more time than we need to. Aelrie, where do the Elf-queens reside?"

The hint of a smile fell from Aelrie's face at once, worry clouding her pretty blue eyes.

"They're with Meira," she said at last, her voice barely above a whisper.

"What do you mean?" Kessara asked.

"It's as Luna said," Aelrie answered. "They don't have bodies like we do. As far as the rumors go, they usually stay in the old palace, but I assume that during a war they won't take the risk. They will feel more secure with their Regent."

Kessara furrowed her brow. "What do you mean *with* her?"

"Like in a mysterious necklace or something?" Alder asked. Kessara felt the side of her mouth curling up into a smile, but Aelrie shook her head. She looked almost pale, if such a thing were possible for someone with silver skin.

"As far as I know, it's nothing so simple. They are more deeply with her. Somewhere within."

Alder fiddled with the hilt of his sword, his eyes lighting up with excitement. "Perfect. So all we have to do is kill Meira

Daeleth, and the Elf-queens will die right along with her."

Kessara felt hope rising in her chest at the thought. Sure, the Regent would be strong, but at least there was only one of her. Between the three of them—

"No," Aelrie said quickly, shaking her head. "You don't understand. We can't."

"Yes we can," Alder argued. "If anyone deserves death, she does."

"Alder," Kessara said, shaking her head. "Let her explain."

Alder crossed his arms against his chest and went quiet. She waited, watching as Aelrie paced around the small forest clearing where they had landed, her quick elven eyes seeming to search every tree in a matter of mere seconds. Seemingly satisfied, she turned back to face them.

"Killing Meira Daeleth won't destroy the Elf-queens. It will let them out."

WES

Wes leaned over onto Celesyria's neck, his fingers gripping the ridges along her spine as tightly as he could. They had already tried their best to secure his legs to the saddle, but he knew that there was only so much that a few spare leather straps could do if he lost his balance entirely.

He sat in silence for what felt like a very long time, listening to the gentle flapping of Celesyria's wings against the still night air. He had been cold before, but now, he had nearly forgotten his discomfort.

It was the pain in his head that now demanded all of his attention, the piercing agony that seemed to radiate from his eyeballs and straight through the back of his skull. The rest of his body felt like it had been partially severed from his brain, his limbs refusing to obey most of his orders. He forced his fingertips to flex more tightly around Celesyria's thick scale plates. His hands, at least, were still functioning well enough. His legs, however, had gone almost completely numb.

He felt Celesyria shift a little to the right.

With all of his strength, he forced his torso to move with her, trying to reorient his center of gravity. She was flying as gently as she could, but still, every slight motion drove a fierce spike of pain into his forehead.

Still, despite the torment, he felt his eyes falling shut. Sleep was the only demand that his body could make to try and push away the pain, but it could bring him no healing now.

Somewhere below, somewhere he could not see, there were hundreds of elves, perhaps thousands, roaming within the mountains. Even Celesyria's draconic eyesight could not see them, but he knew that they were close. The darkness was thick here, perhaps even thicker than it had been back on the battlefield in Aridmoor. He could almost imagine it, black and smoking and stinking of filth as it clouded out the moon and the stars.

A few seconds later, he forced his eyes open, though perhaps more time had passed than he'd realized. The ground below looked different here, but he was too exhausted to try and orient himself.

His palms were stinging from holding on to Celesyria's neck, but at least he had not let go.

With every bit of strength he had left, he lifted his head a little to the side.

He could see the stars now.

He forced himself to take them in, to search for the constellations that Celesyria had attempted to teach him so many times, to let those pinpricks of light remind him that even the darkness of the night was not impenetrable. A glowing moon, a single star, even a single candle was enough to vanquish it.

He prayed without words.

The High One understood.

Just keep looking at the stars.

Hold on, my child.

It won't be long now.

29

Chapter 28

ALDER

Alder stared at Aelrie, unable to find words.

He felt the chill of the night air on his skin, but all thoughts of the fire that he wanted to light had been forgotten in an instant.

At last, Kessara spoke. "If killing Meira won't kill the Elf-queens within her, what can we do?"

Aelrie bit her lip, her usual elven grace faltering for a moment. "I don't know. The Elf-queens draw their power from the darkness, and that darkness will remain even if Meira falls. They will be enraged, of course, but I don't know what they will look like. I'd always figured that they would have no physical form, not after all these years and all of their corruption, but I can't know for sure."

"As usual, no one knows anything," Kessara said, a hint of bitterness in her voice. "As usual we're going in blind."

Aelrie looked at her feet. A breeze had risen amid the trees, sending a curtain of dark hair in front of her face. "Forgive me. I should have warned you. I should have said something earlier."

Kessara let out a slow breath, reaching over and placing her hand in Alder's own.

The three of them stood in silence for a moment, all of them pretending to search the trees for potential threats.

"You're already forgiven," Kessara said finally, giving Aelrie a half-smile.

To his surprise, Alder found himself agreeing with her.

"I'm not angry," he said, bowing his head ever so slightly in her direction. How differently he felt about her now, after how much they had all been through together. Whatever her mistakes were, he knew beyond a doubt that she was a true servant of the High One, as well as a true friend. "It changes nothing. Knowing us, we would have come here anyway. We all knew it was going to be a long shot."

Aelrie's smile seemed to light up her face.

Kessara stared up at the stars overhead, and Alder did the same. The silence between them no longer felt so heavy.

We all knew this was insane. We all knew that even if we succeeded, it might not be so easy to get home, not without the dragons.

He thought of Celesyria, somewhere far away, her orange wings carrying her and the Envoy over the heights of the Severed Summits. He knew what she would say. She would remind them that the High One had brought them this far, and that they would have to keep trusting that He would lead them on the right path, even if it was clouded in fog too thick to see through.

"First of all, we need to find the Regent," Kessara said, glancing off into the depths of the strange forest once again.

"Dare I hope that you at least know where she is, Aelrie?" Alder asked, giving her a quick smile.

"That would be lovely, but no," the elf said, returning his smile.

Alder rubbed at his temples, pondering.

"Well, it's not like we can throw a cloak over Aelrie and have her ask a random soldier for directions," he said at last.

The two women said nothing, each lost in her own thoughts. Alder reached into the small leather pack he carried, taking out one of his waterskins and taking a long drink. Though he doubted the elves would curse their own drinking water, he wasn't going to take any chances unless he was forced to.

Everything about this land felt strange and hostile. The ground where they stood was a deep brown, but somehow, it didn't look like the rich soil of a garden. It seemed to give off a slight smell, unpleasant, but impossible to name.

Alder noticed the gnarled shapes of the trees, wondering if they would look any more welcoming when they were covered in spring leaves, or if they even got leaves at all. Eventually, he hoped to get the chance to learn more about Nox from Aelrie, but for the moment, he had more pressing concerns.

All of a sudden, Aelrie stood up straight, her eyes widening. "Wait."

"What is it?" Kessara asked, letting go of the end of her braid, which she had been playing with between her fingers.

"We can throw a cloak over you after all?" Alder joked.

Aelrie shook her head. "No, they would know me immediately. We can recognize our own. It's like a scent, but not one you can smell."

Alder made a face. That didn't even sound possible, but the thought was eerie nonetheless.

"Okay, so how does that help us?"

"I can't disguise myself," Aelrie said, her voice shaking a little as she spoke. "But Kessara can."

Alder nearly dropped the waterskin he was holding.

"Absolutely not," he said quickly, staring between Aelrie and his wife. "I wasn't serious! We aren't going to be able to just–"

"Alder!" Aelrie said, almost shouting at him.

Without quite meaning to, Alder closed his mouth, stunned into silence.

"Alder, I know, it sounds absurd–"

"It's dangerous. I won't put her at risk," Alder said, clearing his throat.

"I get a say about the risks I take, my love," Kessara chimed in, not taking her eyes off of Aelrie.

"We're married," Alder argued back. "Your life is entwined with mine now, forever. It's not just a matter of your independence–"

Aelrie took two steps until she was standing between the two of them, her hands on her hips.

"Can you both please listen, just for a second?" the elf pleaded, looking altogether uncomfortable with the confrontation.

Alder met the elf's eyes.

All at once, realization dawned.

"Kessara speaks fluent elvish," he said, shaking his head and staring at his feet. "If I disguised myself, I would be given away at once as soon as they heard the common tongue."

The Princess looked surprised, as though she'd forgotten all of the years she'd spent as a child and a teenager studying the complex language of their enemies.

"Yes," Aelrie said, letting out a slow breath. "It has to be you, Kessara."

Alder could feel his heart hammering in his chest like a war-drum.

Perhaps if they had more time to think, they would have been able to come up with a better navigation plan, but every moment they stood here, Wes Cervos was drawing nearer to the great spire. Dawn would be here in a matter of hours, and the winter Feast of Offering would be upon them.

Everything was coming together now. Alder could feel it. The ancient prophecies of the Codex, the myths, the rituals...

Aelrie was right.

It was time for them all to take their place in history, and whether he liked it or not, that included the woman he loved.

CELESYRIA

She could see the top of the spire, peering out over the top of the mountain ridge.

Celesyria called to Wes out loud, certain that the echo her voice would wake every elf in Whitespire, but he did not answer. Terror clawed at her chest. Was he dead, hanging onto the saddle only by the straps on his legs?

She dismissed the idea at once. He was still holding his own balance. She would have noticed if she had suddenly started carrying dead weight.

She drew in a breath. She didn't want to worsen his headache, but she had to wake him.

"Wes, we're flying down into the valley. Wake up. Please wake up," she called out in his mind, letting her words pour into his pounding head with their full intensity.

For a moment, she heard nothing inside of her skull or outside of it. She flapped her wings, using a final burst of energy to carry them over the lip of the valley's edge.

She could see the valley below them now, and the destroyed stone building-tops and sunken caves that had once been Whitespire.

"Close," came a voice from her back. "So close now."

She wanted to cry tears of joy. He was holding on. He was conscious. They were going to make it.

She didn't dare to say anything in reply, not wanting to add any more torture to his pain. She focused instead on gliding down into the valley, watching every shadow for movement as they flew lower and lower.

The whole valley was beautiful still, despite the destruction. The moon and stars bathed the surrounding mountains in a blue glow, gleaming in a circle around them like a great halo. She could almost forget where they were, and imagine that she was at the entrance to the Eternal Lands, pondering the wonders that lay beyond her in every direction.

An arrow bounced off of one of her neck plates. Before she could react, she felt another one strike between two scales somewhere along her tail, the sharp tip biting at her flesh for a moment before falling away to the stone floor below.

"Stay down, Wes," she called aloud. For a moment, he didn't react, and she flapped her wings, bringing them a little higher. She pulled them into a tight circle, still unable to see where they were being attacked from.

To her relief, she felt Wes changing his position, leaning forward and taking hold of her neck scales, just as he had done after he fainted back in Aridmoor.

He would be all right for now, but her belly was exposed,

and elves were very good shots. Sooner or later, they would strike in the wrong place, and she would be hurt, perhaps badly enough to fall from the sky.

She began to descend, flinching in expectation of the next round of arrow fire, which came a few seconds later.

There was nowhere else to go.

She had to get him to the base of the spire.

KESSARA

Kessara shivered, pulling Aelrie's black cloak more tightly around her body as she walked.

Any remaining warmth from the day's sunshine had long since seeped away, and the air seemed to be growing colder each passing minute. Fortunately, there was still no snow, and she found it easy enough to navigate back in the way they had come, even though it looked very different on the ground than it had from the air.

Alder had worried that the elves in the port city might be on high alert after their intrusion, but at last Aelrie had convinced him that it was their only option. There weren't any other settlements nearby, and besides, as they'd established, the elves probably thought that they had ridden out on dragonback just as quickly as they'd flown in.

Kessara glanced behind her, searching the forest for movement, but still, there was not even the sound of a squirrel snapping a twig. She had seen nothing alive here at all, and she wondered if Nox was free of animals entirely, or if they happened to be in a geographical area where all of the species hibernated during the winter.

For all of her years studying elven culture, language, and

geography, there was so much she didn't know.

At last, she spotted something elf-made poking out from behind the trees ahead. She had only been walking for a half-hour or so. It frightened her to think how close Alder and Aelrie still were to the city, but at least there did not seem to be any natural path or road heading in the direction of their hideaway. In fact, the terrain had been rather difficult, and she suspected the elves would prefer a more convenient route.

She continued forward, brushing past several scrubby, smaller trees as the building came gradually into view. It was nondescript, painted in a plain white or gray, with no indication as to its function. It sat at what appeared to be the end of a dead-end street. She could see no one, but still, she felt her heart beginning to race as she stepped out from the safety of the trees and onto the road. She had promised herself that whatever happened to her here, she would not scream, though she knew that if she was gone long enough, Alder would surely come looking for her anyway.

Their last kiss had lasted for a long while, gentle yet hungry, and she couldn't help but to think about how unfair it felt. They were young newlyweds, and yet every kiss they shared felt like it might be their last.

She pulled the hood of the cloak more tightly around her face, and adjusted the black gaiter that she was wearing over the lower half of her face. Aelrie had assured her that such fashion was acceptable in Nox, particularly during the cold months, and she was glad of it. Though she was the right height and build—elves tended to be highly uniform in their weight compared to humans and dwarves—her tanned skin tone would be an instant giveaway. She was thankful that she still had several hours of night shadow left.

She made her way slowly down the street, marveling at how tidy it looked. It reminded her of an unfriendly version of the palace courtyard back home, swept perfectly, without even a single weed poking up through the neat square stones. She kept her hands resting at her sides, trying to act as natural as possible, which was not so easy. Aside from Aelrie, she didn't exactly spend much time hanging around elves and picking up on their typical mannerisms.

Kessara's breath caught in her chest as she turned the corner. Coming toward her were a group of five female elves, walking in a neat line. The one at the front had harsh features, and something about her dark eyes looked especially cruel.

Well, I'm not asking them anything.

She gave the slightest dip of her head as she let them pass, and to her great relief, they barely seemed to notice her.

She passed by several more buildings. They were still square and plain, but much smaller, with tidy windows on two floors. She would have guessed that they were homes, but so far as she knew, elves didn't like to set up their residential areas so close to the Strait. Perhaps they had been temporary dwellings for the port workers that had now been taken over by the army for the duration of the war, or perhaps they served some elven purpose that had no human equivalent.

She crossed the street, feeling exposed as she walked under the bright light of the moon. On the other side of the road, there were two towering stone blocks, with similarly dark windows. Two more elves passed her, two males this time, who were dressed very lightly for the cold weather. They seemed deep in conversation, and though they looked much less threatening than the other group had been, she decided that she wasn't quite ready to ask for directions just yet.

Glancing down the next few side streets as she passed them, she at last found what she was looking for. Most of them were narrow, lined with more houselike buildings, but one was larger and headed rather steeply uphill. She turned and stepped into the side street, glancing over her shoulder and finding no one.

While she was here, she figured that she may as well try and gather as much intelligence as she could. Alder wouldn't be pleased that she was deviating from the plan, but she knew that they might not have a better chance later.

She continued up the hill, feeling her legs tiring quickly on the steep climb. She was cold and exhausted already, and she could see the moon slowly making its way toward the horizon. She forced herself to keep moving. She couldn't waste time, but the hill was much larger than it had first appeared, and she was fighting the urge to turn back.

She thought of Wes, flying off to Whitespire, even as the pain of his headaches crippled him. He had looked so pale and weak and lost when they had left him. It had reminded her so much of the boy she had known for so many years, and the realization worried her. Still, there were changes in him that even suffering could not take away. She believed in him, and the thought drove her forward.

I have no right to complain about a little hill. I'm almost there.

After several more exhausting minutes, she felt the ground beginning to even out a little. A few moments after that, it became nearly flat. She paused, leaning against one of the sparse trees that were growing on the hill, and tried to catch her breath.

The city was much less dense up here, but still, despite the empty look that the buildings had, there were still people on the streets. She watched another group of males in soldier's garb pass by in front of her, crossing a side road, talking amongst themselves. They looked normal, almost. Aside from the fact that every face was chiseled and perfect, and every hair was in place.

She suppressed the urge to laugh. Elves had amazing senses, vastly superior to any human, and yet here she was sneaking around their city in the middle of a war while they ignored her.

They're so proud. They don't believe that they need to be careful. They don't think that we have a chance against them, let alone that anyone would dare venture into their lands.

A few steps ahead, she saw a tall building that was resting toward the downward crest of the hill, with a steep staircase on the side that was nearly hidden in the shadows.

Perfect.

She hurried toward it and, with a final glance behind her, she darted up the stairs, taking them two at a time until she reached a small balcony. She was completely hidden here, and she allowed herself a few moments to take off her gaiter and lower her hood. Her body had warmed with the exertion of the climb, and it felt good to breathe freely for a few minutes and to sip from her waterskin.

She could see that the moon's position had changed once more, however, and she would take no chance of being stuck amid the elves when dawn arrived.

Leaning over the short balcony railing, she took a long look at the vista that spread before her at the base of the hill. If she turned toward the east, she could just see the waves of the West Strait, laying beyond row after row of tightly-built stone boxes. The city was larger than she had realized, having been more than a little distracted as they'd flown over it the first time.

Her real interest, however, lay in another direction.

She could see the outskirts of the city from here, though the huge rock outcropping was just out of sight. The buildings grew more and more sparse until they met the edge of the thick forest, but now she could see that the trees did not go as deep into the interior of Nox as she'd assumed.

Beyond their strange dark shapes was a great plain.

It looked flatter and more empty than even the wilderlands of Aridmoor, and without any of the lush green grass of summer or the blanketed snow of winter. Instead, it looked dry in the blue cast of moonlight, covered with the same dark soil that they had seen before, almost like the deserts of Boneshire but without any of the odd plants or red rock formations.

The strangest thing about the place was not the ground, but the buildings that jutted out from it like great stone teeth. There was an obelisk every hundred feet or so, and the top of each seemed to be lit, emitting a cast of green light, though she could see nothing that looked like a torch or a beacon. Toward the horizon, nearly as far as her vantage point would allow her to see, there was one obelisk that was different from the others.

This one was huge, towering above the others at a dizzying height. She squinted at it, trying to figure out a sense of scale, but it was difficult. There was nothing around it that even came close to its size.

It looked like a nightmare vision of the great spire. There was no beauty in it. The whole thing, from the shape to the smooth stone that it seemed to be built from, evoked only dread and terror.

It's a mockery of the High One and our worship of Him.

She felt a shudder coursing through her body, making the hairs on her arms stand on their ends.

She knew exactly where Meira Daeleth would be.

30

Chapter 29

WES

Wes clung to Celesyria's neck as another arrow flew past, the sound of it reminding him of his mother tuning a stringed instrument that she used to play. He forced himself to take several breaths as Celesyria took a wide loop, and when no more arrows came, he lifted his head a little.

Something seemed off. He had been expecting a much more unfriendly welcome, but there was no hail of arrows, and despite the usual elven skill with a bow, none of the arrows that had come had managed to strike the exposed flesh along Celesyria's belly.

There must be only a few bowmen to contend with. Perhaps just one.

He wanted to mention his thoughts to Celesyria, but he was too tired. His mouth felt thick, like his jaws weren't working properly, and the inside of his skull was throbbing.

He slid back a little, trying to settle his balance on the saddle as Celesyria glided back down toward the ruins that covered the ground. He heard another couple of arrows hitting her flank, one after another, but they pinged off of her scales without causing her even to flinch. He ducked down again, trying to balance while simultaneously avoiding taking arrow fire to any exposed parts of his body.

He was thankful that the Auranthian soldiers had fit him with armor before they left, even though the weight of it made him feel even worse than he had before. He was tired, and despite the chaos surrounding him, he felt his eyelids drooping once again.

He glanced at the ruins of Whitespire below, trying to find a memory to cling to, anything at all to help him remain conscious. His thoughts wandered to Gramnok Beastbane, to Elder Dorold and his gruesome death, to all of the events that had led to the destruction of this once great city.

He let his eyes fall closed for a moment. It would be so pleasant to sleep. It was the one place where the pain went away.

Celesyria's voice met his ears. "Wes, we're so close. Hold on."

He felt her take another banking turn to the right, and he woke up a little, enough to grasp the leather straps of the saddle a little more tightly. They had to be near the base of the spire by now. They had been so close, and yet, the flight never seemed to end, like they were crossing the distance from Aridmoor once and over again.

Her words sounded like they were far away, or perhaps like they didn't quite exist. It was her voice, but there was another voice there, too.

Hold on.

He let his hood fall back, allowing the chill of the night air to touch the back of his neck and to sting at his ears. *Memories. Focus.*

He thought of that past spring, not even a year gone. The last normal Feast. Before his Witness and his Deermaster were killed in front of him, before he met Celesyria, before everything fell apart.

His head protested again, the pain like the light of a bright warning beacon searing into his eye sockets from mere inches away. He heard a sound escape his mouth that scared him. It was not even a cry. It was too weak to be heard over the wind, but he had heard it. He could barely believe it had come from him at all.

He felt anger then, his heart pounding, his muscles tensing. He looked down at his knuckles, and they had gone white around the leather straps.

My life was not normal. My family was already years dead, and even before that...

He reached his fingertips to his cheek, feeling the burn mark that had replaced his scar, the mark of his fate given twice.

"I was never going to have a normal life," he choked out, his words a whisper. Celesyria could not hear. His throat stung, but he couldn't stop. He had to say it. He had to hear it in his own ears, from a voice that was his voice, but not only his. "My life was always going to be greater than a normal life. The High One has always had a bigger plan for me, from the moment He placed me in the womb of my mother."

An arrow struck his arm, the metal making a clinking sound as it hit his armor. He leaned down over Celesyria's neck again, trying to get a better view. They were near the ground now, Celesyria's wings flapping every few minutes as she raced over the destroyed city.

Usually, looking down made him feel like throwing up, but for once, he didn't care.

The feeling of unease was there again, stronger than before. His eyes searched ahead, trying to peer through the thick shadows of the uneven land, and then, he saw it.

No.

Celesyria pulled up a little, and he strained to look closer, to make out the figure that waited there near the spire, his bow raised. He wanted to believe it was a hallucination, that it was impossible, but another arrow struck mere inches from his head.

"It's just one! Celesyria, get out, it's just one," he screamed, as loud as he could, ignoring the way that his own yell seemed to echo again and again in his ears. He didn't know if she could see into the shadows, if she knew. He drew a breath again, feeling weightless as Celesyria pumped her wings again. It was too slow. He cried out, using every bit of energy he had left.

"Captain Drohma. Get out! You have to get out!"

ALDER

Before Kessara had fully broken through the darkness of the trees, Alder was rushing to her, ignoring the branches that scratched at their faces as he took her into his arms.

He pulled her against his chest, feeling her breath rushing in and out, and all at once the tears that he had tried to ignore were spilling onto his cheeks.

He wanted to brush them away, but he wanted to keep holding her even more.

He had sat there for hours now, trying to hold it together as Aelrie attempted to comfort him, reminding him that Kessara was capable and that she would be fine. He believed her. It wasn't Kessara's strength he doubted. It was the opposing strength of the evil that surrounded her that chilled his heart.

"You're okay, my darling," he said, stroking at her blonde braids with his dirt-streaked hands, trying to reassure himself more than her. "You're all right."

Kessara pulled away, and he could see the remains of her own tears, but there was a determined expression on her face that worried him.

"What happened?" he asked gently, reaching up to stroke her cheek with his thumb.

Kessara was quiet for a moment, not quite meeting his eyes.

"Kessara," Aelrie prompted, "did you find anything out?"

"I didn't speak to anyone about Meira," she said quickly. "No one noticed me at all, actually. I'm fine, I promise."

"What do you mean?" Alder asked, running a hand across his hair. She was almost too calm. He didn't like the sound of where this was going.

"I—I found my way to high ground," Kessara added. Despite the darkness, Alder was sure he could see a slight blush rising to her cheeks.

Alder swallowed, trying to keep himself from losing his temper.

"So you chose to act suspicious."

"Wouldn't it have been more suspicious had I stopped to ask after the Regent?" she argued, crossing her hands over her chest. He could see the silver band on her finger. She was his wife now, and he had to trust her. But at the same time, he wished that she had not always insisted on taking such risks without discussing them with him first.

He forced himself to take several slow breaths.

"Either option would have necessitated taking a risk," he conceded. Aelrie looked over at him, and he couldn't help but to be amused at her stunned expression. Perhaps he was usually more disagreeable than he'd thought.

Or perhaps Kessara just makes it impossible to avoid arguing.

"I'm sorry I didn't say anything," the Princess said, finally meeting his gaze. "I wasn't exactly planning on changing tactics. But I saw an opportunity, and I took it. Be angry with me later."

Alder shook his head. "I'm not angry," he said through gritted teeth.

"Sure you're not," she said, giving him an exaggerated eye roll.

He took her face between both of his hands and kissed her, perhaps enjoying it a little more than he should have in Aelrie's company.

He pulled away, satisfied by the silly smile on his wife's face.

"I'm not angry. I'm glad I married a woman who knows how to think on her feet, even if I hope that once in a while, you'll listen to my judgment."

Kessara brushed his forearm with her fingertips. "It's a deal."

"Sorry to, er, interrupt," Aelrie said, clearing her throat. "But I'd like to know what you saw in the port city."

Kessara let her hand fall to her side, raising her chin and assuming her usual regal posture.

"Right. Beyond the outskirts and the trees, there's an open plain, filled with obelisks. There must be a hundred of them."

Aelrie shook her head. "I could have told you as much, but–"

"The huge obelisk in the center," Kessara said, her blue eyes shining with what might have been excitement or fear, Alder couldn't quite tell. "I couldn't take my eyes off of it. It was like it was calling to me, staring out at all of Nox, a warped version of the great spire. Meira Daeleth is there. I can feel it."

"But she could be anywhere, Kessara," he said, struggling to push away the earlier frustration that had once again risen to the surface, though he very nearly reminded her that this was precisely why they had agreed to ask after Meira. "Nox is vast. We can't be sure–"

It was Aelrie who spoke.

"No," she said, shaking her head. "I should have thought of it before now. The great obelisk is the most powerful magical object in Nox, used to draw from the darkness. Kessara's instincts are right. I'm sure of it. She will be there, enjoying the taste of power."

Kessara shuddered. "I didn't realize such a place existed. In all that I have studied, I've never come across it."

Alder had never heard of it, either.

"We do not allow our legends about the great obelisk to travel beyond our shores," Aelrie said, gazing off into the distance, as though the obelisk may be watching her from beyond the trees. Perhaps it was. "It is akin to a holy site. There, the stories say, elves are given power to see, to hear, to know all things."

"And if the stories are even half true, Meira would want to be there," Alder said. It made sense, but still, the thought of chasing after the Regent into the heart of elven darkness made him nervous. They could still be wrong, and if they were, he doubted they would be able to live long enough for a second chance.

He looked over at his wife. The steely look had returned to her eyes, and he knew that he was going to trust her, no matter the risk.

She and Aelrie had both turned to him, as though waiting for his final word.

He let out a breath.

"We're going to stop her," he said, smiling grimly. "And while we're at it, if we can, we're going to take all of the elven illusions and glamors down with her. It's time to bring the fight to the darkness."

CELESYRIA

Celesyria could hear Wes shouting at her, his words tumbling over one another as they echoed beneath the stars. His throat sounded hoarse, but she could make out one word, the only word that mattered.

Drohma.

She didn't understand.

Drohma was with King Ursa, surely, somewhere on the battlefield back in Aridmoor. What did he have to do with—

There was no time to finish her thought.

Pain seared through her, so intense and sudden that she almost forgot to breathe. It felt like fire spreading over dry tinder, hungry, devouring. She howled without realizing she was doing it, her cry so loud that she was sure she would wake the mountains.

Drohma was here, somehow. She was flying low, he was a good shot, and his hatred for her had drawn him to her one last time.

And he had punctured her skin in the one place where there were insufficient scales to protect it.

She could see Alder's face in her mind, scolding her, demanding that she wear armor if she was going to fly into Whitespire, but she had not listened. Like the humans, she found the armor cumbersome. She hadn't wanted to risk not being able to fly quickly if Wes needed her to.

That's not the only reason. I knew. I knew that armor would not change anything.

Her vision was blurring now. The edges of the sky grew darker and darker, as though the sun's opposite was rising behind the mountain ridge, bringing shadow to the coming dawn.

I can still see the stars.

She found a constellation, and she trained her eyes on it, ignoring the way that the pinpricks of light seemed to warp and to move, ignoring the shadows that pressed in on all sides.

Wes was saying something, but she couldn't hear him now.

She realized that she had turned, flying in a tight spiral, but now she could see it again.

The great spire was there, watching her, watching everything.

KESSARA

Twigs snapped under Kessara's boot, each little sound seeming to echo through the quiet darkness of the forest. She continued forward, her heart taking a couple of minutes to slow as she followed Aelrie, with Alder close at her heels. The elf seemed to be taking no logical path, instead leading them through narrow gaps between thick trunks and over deadfall. Aelrie insisted that she knew the way, now that she was sure of where they were headed, and Kessara and Alder had no choice but to follow, not unless they wanted to double back to the city.

She felt her husband's comforting hand on the small of her back as she knelt under a low branch, narrowly avoiding catching her hair in the gnarled fingers of the tree. He followed, giving a final glance behind them. There was still nothing, not a bird, not a squirrel or even a beetle. Only silence.

The light was changing, however. Kessara could see that the sky to the east was beginning to fade into light blues and pinks along the horizon. She was glad to see that, so far, sunrises in Nox looked much the same as they did in Kaveryth, but the familiar sight brought little comfort. They made several more tight turns, and were it not for the telltale light of the coming sun, Kessara would have lost her sense of direction a while ago.

At last, Aelrie stood still. Kessara and Alder stepped over a few more cracking twigs until coming to a stop behind her. Alder glanced around, a puzzled expression on his handsome face. This bit of forest looked exactly like the rest of it had.

"We will have to try and keep to the shadows as best we can, which won't be easy, but at least we will have the sharp angles of sunrise shadows on our side."

Alder nodded. "Seems sensible."

Kessara suppressed a bitter laugh. She had seen the plains

that, apparently, they were now near. There was scarcely a bush to hide behind, let alone proper trees or buildings or anything else useful. They'd be completely exposed, save for the long shadows of the smaller stone towers themselves.

"Let's go," she said at last, following Aelrie as she stepped forward into the dark trees.

A few moments later, without warning, the forest fell away.

The barren plains stretched out beneath their feet, and for a moment, Kessara found it difficult to believe that they were still in the same world. In the light, she could see just how strange the dark dirt really was. The color seemed, somehow, to be both dark brown and gray at the same time, peppered with tiny pebbles with a yellowish tint.

She brushed a few of them aside with her toe, a sick feeling rising in her stomach as they tumbled away along the dirt. They reminded her of broken teeth.

"Well, I guess we should keep moving," Alder said, staring off toward the great obelisk that lay in the distance. "I doubt we'll beat the sun, but we have to try."

Kessara felt a flash of guilt. Sure, she'd spotted the obelisk and given them the idea that Meira was located there, but she'd also wasted time. Perhaps if she had returned to the forest earlier, they would have made it here before dawn, but she supposed that there was no use dwelling on it now.

She felt Alder's hand on her shoulder as he leaned over, giving her a quick kiss on the cheek.

"He will see us through," he said.

The elf waited for a long moment, staring out at the expanse, likely trying to figure out which of their suicidal route options was the safest.

"I'm afraid," she said with a sad-looking smile. "But I

guess I always knew it would come to this. I always knew that I'd end up back here, facing them. Facing *us*."

Kessara shook her head and stepped forward, embracing her friend in a tight hug. Aelrie carried so much history with her, so many secrets, so much darkness. She had seen so many years pass, but still, she had not rejected the High One when He called her to new life.

"Don't say that," the Princess said firmly, stepping back and taking Aelrie's hand in her own. "There is no 'us'. You share a race, not a heart, and not a soul. Your soul belongs to Him, and He has no intention of sharing it with the darkness."

Alder stepped forward then, taking the elf's other silvery hand and giving it a squeeze.

For a long while, they stood there together hand in hand, staring out at the elven lands.

It was three against thousands, but Kessara was ready.

He was on their side, and they would not fall.

Not until all was finished.

31

Chapter 30

WES

"Celesyria!"

Wes heard Celesyria snarling in pain, his scream of fury mingling with her cries. He was wide awake now, hate and rage pouring through his blood as he stared down at Drohma. He was smiling up at them, his eyes trained on Celesyria as the arrow stuck into the narrow unprotected area along her belly did its work.

Wes watched as he sent another arrow after it. The dragon was too wounded already to get out of the way. It was all Wes could do to hold on as Celesyria dipped into a spiraling turn, her wings contorting strangely, her muscles shaking beneath the saddle.

As they circled once more, he saw only Drohma's back as he raced away, shouldering his bow and racing off amid the broken stones.

He thinks she will fall. He thinks we're both as good as dead.

"Celesyria!" he shouted again, listening to the rasp in his

voice as his throat protested.

Once more, Celesyria did not respond. They remained in the air, somehow, and she gave a half-hearted flap of her wings every few seconds, but they were still headed firmly downward.

His head was pounding, and for a split second, he realized that Drohma had become so consumed with darkness that his presence was as excruciating as that of an elf.

Part of him wanted to pity the poor soul, but he couldn't afford pity. Not with the ground rushing to meet them. For the moment, he allowed himself to be angry, the fury within him helping him to focus.

Celesyria circled again, still without a word, and Wes bent down to undo the straps that held him to the saddle. She was flying faster now, her turns tighter, and Wes felt his stomach lurch as he sat back down, his knuckles white as he gripped her neck crest.

He glanced up, trying to get his bearings, but even the stars, the mountains, and the spire itself seemed to be moving now. He pressed his eyes shut for a moment as he balanced on Celesyria's back, swallowing the sickness bubbling up in his stomach.

If he had to get out of the way as she crash landed, he would have only seconds to react.

He stared as the rocks grew close, close enough that he could see the cracks in the stone and notice pebbles resting in the shadows.

He opened his mouth to utter a prayer, but the words did not come in time.

He closed his eyes just as they slammed into the frozen, jagged ground.

ALDER

Alder raced across the open space, not allowing himself to quite catch up with Kessara or Aelrie. He glanced over his shoulder every few seconds, watching as the dark forest receded, but seeing no one. There were no roads here that he could see, no sign of civilization at all, aside from the huge blight of obelisk-stones that dotted the expanse.

He missed Aridmoor. He missed galloping on a war horse across the open fields, listening to hoofbeats thudding against the soft green grass and moist brown dirt.

Our children will run there, one day.

He glanced forward again and picked up his pace, watching as Kessara reached the obelisk a few seconds behind Aelrie, her slender form almost disappearing beneath its dark shadow.

We will have a future. We will have a life, a life with flowers and grass. And even the smell of the sea, for you, my darling.

He reached the shadow himself, and he found he was too out of breath to talk. He was wasting energy with his daydreams, he knew, but as the sun continued to creep over the edge of these strange horizons, he knew that he had to do something, anything to keep himself alert and moving despite his exhaustion.

After only a few seconds, Aelrie gestured for them to move forward, stepping out into the light for a moment before they did. When she was not accosted with arrows, Kessara and Alder followed, and once again the three of them took off for the next shadow at a run.

They carried on like that for a long while, Alder's legs burning as they raced across the landscape. He was used to exercise, but running here felt especially terrible. The ground was not only flat, but hard, and more than once he'd had to bite back curses as he slammed his ankle into a flat stone or twisted it as he stumbled over the strange yellow rocks.

At last, they reached what he hoped was the final shadow.

Aelrie and Kessara sank to the ground, breathing hard, and Alder did the same, reaching to drink from his waterskin.

"Make sure to conserve it," Kessara said, giving him a pointed look as she reached for her own. Alder nodded. After seeing what was happening to Wes, Kessara's caution about their water seemed wise.

Aelrie said nothing, instead staring off the way they had come, seeming lost in her own thoughts.

"Is everything all right?" Alder asked after a while. The sun had broken the horizon now, and every minute that passed shortened the shadow that hid them from view. He did not feel comforted by the emptiness of this place. In fact, the easier they found it to reach the great obelisk, the more that he began to fear a trap was waiting.

The elf nodded. "I think so," she said. "It's just... the darkness is thick here. It's heavy. I can feel it."

Her eyes looked haunted, and Alder felt a chill slithering down his back as he remembered her defeat of the Gorok. He couldn't imagine the temptation she must be feeling to draw power from the dark places once again.

"You can get through this, Aelrie," Kessara chimed in, resting a hand on the elf's shoulder. "We're so close now. It's all going to be over soon."

Alder nodded in agreement. Aelrie had overcome the temptation time and time again. It had taken him a while to get there, but he trusted her.

"The High One is with you, and He is stronger than any darkness. You just need to keep fighting."

Aelrie gave them both a small smile and got to her feet, dusting the clinging gray-brown soil from her trousers and tunic. "If we're going to do this, we should do it now."

Alder did not argue. He waited as Aelrie darted out into the open plain and gave Kessara a few seconds to catch up with her before heading out himself, with a final glance over his shoulder. He could just see the forest that lay behind them, nothing more than a dark smudge at the edge of the horizon.

The tower seemed to pierce the sky, growing larger and more menacing the closer they ran. The magical green light it exuded seemed to hang in the air like mist.

Alder looked up at it every so often, but if he gazed too long, he began to feel dizzy. From a distance, it had seemed too small for a Regent to reside in it comfortably, but now he realized it had only been a trick of perspective. Up close, it looked nearly as big as King Ursa's fortress back in High Keep.

Beyond it, he could see more shadows, reminding him of the forest.

"Aelrie, what lays beyond this plain?" he asked between labored breaths as the three of them fell in beside one another. "A forest?"

The elf shook her head, eyes narrowed as she tried to make sense of it.

All of a sudden, Kessara stopped short, a hand flying to her mouth.

"No," she gasped, staring wide-eyed at the shadow that was not a shadow at all.

Alder nearly stumbled to the ground, pulling Kessara and Aelrie back toward where they had come, rushing for the nearest small obelisk, which projected only a sliver of shadow.

He half-shoved the two women down, throwing himself into the cover of darkness after them as the sound of pounding boots filled the air.

There was no chanting. There were no songs.

He leaned forward, peering around the stone.

There were thousands of men, perhaps tens of thousands, walking in neat regiments across the plains. They poured past the tower in droves, a sea of black clothes and perfect faces as they headed toward the port city.

"High One, save us," Kessara was saying under her breath, over and over, staring at the impossible scene that lay before her. Alder reached for her hand and held it tight, though he had no comfort to offer the woman he loved.

Aelrie opened her mouth and closed it again, saying nothing as she stared.

There was an army between them and Meira Daeleth.

32

Chapter 31

ELDER JATE
BEFORE

Elder Jate leaned upon the stone sill of his window, watching the gray sky that lay outside.

The window was a nice one, all leaded glass in neat diamond panes. The room itself was nice, too, far nicer than anything he should have been offered. It was plain, of course, and nearly as gray as the walls of the city or the sky that lay above it, but the bed was done up in deep red velvet blankets and the fireplace was kept burning.

Most people thought that Graveheim was a depressing place. The Elder supposed it was a reasonable enough assumption–anywhere known as the 'city of the dead' was probably not going to be lively–but he had long known it to be wrong.

It was a happy place, really, once you got used to its gentle comings and goings, and the chiming of the daily bells. He had long appreciated the work of the Cenobites in their care for the dead, but it wasn't until now, spending time with them, that he saw their love and care for the stranger as well. And, even more astonishing, their love and care for him, despite all that he was.

He shook his head, trying to amend the thoughts of guilt and self-condemnation that so often rose within him. He had once been lost, it was true. And in some ways, he still was. But even so, he had begun the work of reaching out to be found, and that gave him comfort.

Even long ago, when he could properly use the title of Elder, what little good he had done could be seen here.

He had fought for years for the Septemvirate to expand the resources given to Graveheim, not to mention demanding that the Cenobites be allowed to increase their membership. Elder Dorold and most of the others had resisted this use of funds at every turn, but in the end, as he often did, he had found a way.

It was apparent now as he looked down at the courtyard below that his efforts had borne fruit. The women walked about to and fro, their long robes brushing the neatly swept cobblestone streets and passages. There were not only older women serving here, but teenaged novices as well, girls who had chosen to sacrifice their liberty to serve something greater than themselves.

Still, he found the sight to be rather melancholy. It was a lovely thing to see that their order had grown, and yet it pained him to know how much their services would be needed in light of the war.

Already, there were others here just like him, civilians who had made their way across Kaveryth seeking refuge for one reason or another. He had gotten to know one such family quite well. They were from High Keep, in Aridmoor, but as to their other family connections or what trades they had been involved in, they were oddly tight-lipped. He did not press them. The quiet city of the dead was a place where some secrets remained unspoken.

He could hear his stomach rumbling beneath his borrowed tunic, but he did not make his way to the dining hall. Not yet.

He waited there a while longer, trying to track the obscured sun as the minutes blended together into what he was sure was at least an hour, perhaps two. He stepped back from the window once or twice in order to check on his nephew, who was still sleeping peacefully, but he always returned as soon as he could, not wanting to miss the sight that he had been waiting for.

At long last, he saw it, and his heart filled with the joy of a small child on his birthday.

He could see a yellow dragon passing over the city, followed by another with scales of deep red. He stood, barely daring to move, his wrinkled fingers gripping the stone sill as though he might drop to the ground at the sight of their beauty.

More came, most too young or too old, but war did not respect the realities of age.

At least I know I did a few things right in my life.

He couldn't believe that so many of them had listened when he begged them to join their Guardian brothers and to fight. He was a persuasive man within the halls of Stronghollow palace, debating policy with the other Elders, but he had not expected to have much success here, with the proud, stubborn dragons.

As a point of fact, he hadn't expected to meet them at all. He was becoming more and more sure that this High One that the child Holga had spoken of had to be real.

How else could he explain that he had made his way to Graveheim just as the non-Guardian dragons had sought respite within its walls? It was impossible, and yet, it had happened.

He had thought that his purpose in life had been reduced to caring for his nephew, that he was too old and powerless now to be of use in this war, but clearly, he had been wrong. He had been able to do one more thing right, one more thing that he hoped would matter a great deal to the fate of Kaveryth.

"Uncle?"

He turned at once, his fingers falling away from the sill at the sound of his nephew's voice.

"I'm all right," the boy said quickly as he began to stride across the room. "I just want a better look, if you can help me."

Elder Jate considered denying the child's request. It was winter, though a mild enough day, and the open window was already letting a draft into the room.

Instead, he allowed the boy to place his arms around his neck, helping him from the bed and onto the wheeled chair that the Cenobites had provided. He grasped a few of the blankets from the boy's bed—heavy and red, just like his own—and tucked them in around him.

"There's a balcony at the end of the hall," he said, watching with joy in his heart as a huge smile lit up the child's face. He pushed the chair out of the room and down a long passage, pausing at the end to heave open the huge wooden door that kept out the winter cold.

"There must be a hundred of them," the boy said in awe as they made their way out into the gloomy day. A few flakes of snow had begun to fall, swirling merrily through the air as the rainbow of dragons continued past Graveheim, their scales bright against the clouds.

Elder Jate nodded, not wanting to quash the boy's joy by reminding him that not so long ago, there had been many thousands. Still, even a hundred dragons made his heart swell with joy. Their noble race was declining, but as long as there remained a good few, there was always hope.

"I can't believe they're helping us," his nephew continued, his pale face seeming to light up from within as he continued to watch them. "The Guardians have their oath, of course, but these dragons could have said no."

Elder Jate smiled, ruffling his nephew's hair gently. He wanted to tell the boy that it was his story, really, that had made the difference, but he couldn't figure out how to explain it in a way that the young child would understand. It was his nephew who would pay the greatest price of choosing good over evil, but his illness, and the events that it had set in motion, would leave behind a legacy greater than anything Elder Jate or the dragons themselves could have hoped to give to their descendents otherwise.

At first, as he'd expected, the dragons had resisted.

As far as they were concerned, the Septemvirate no longer existed, and considering the loss of the sacrifices, they saw no reason to accept any authority of the last remaining Elder over them. So, Elder Jate had chosen not to invoke any idea of authority at all. Instead, he tried to speak to them as the Cenobites spoke to everyone, trying to show humility and to listen to their side of things.

The dragons were angry, and despite his initial annoyance at their cowardice, as he listened he began to understand how they had ended up in Graveheim.

They had watched as their dwarven allies were corrupted, as their resources began to dwindle, and as their population faded away. And now, at last, they had watched as the elves finally took hold of Umrym, killing their Guardian relatives in the process.

No oath bound them to fight, or even to remain in Kaveryth, and so they had chosen to seek after the remnant, to hope that the stories of the High One were true and that there was a way out of the nightmare, even for them.

It had taken Elder Jate weeks to build up a rapport with them, weeks that they had not intended to stay in the first place. But eventually, conversation by conversation, he saw that he was having an impact on them. Sometimes, he brought his nephew with him to their meetings, usually held in the Cenobites' temple, which was the only place in the city where they could fit and keep out of the cold. The dragons all seemed to like the child a great deal, and he was fascinated by the creatures, their customs, and their stories.

Finally, during one such meeting, the first bodies from the war had made their way to the gates of Graveheim.

Elder Jate had not wanted to look, not at first. But when Priya, the head of the Cenobites, had asked for his aid, he found that he could not deny her, not after all of the kindness that her order had shown to him and his nephew. Two of the dragons had gone with them to the gate, helping to ferry several of the bodies into the city where their bodies could be anointed and wrapped for burial.

They had learned that the victims comprised almost an entire village on the border of Boneshire and Aridmoor. A few of their bravest men had sought to disrupt the elven armies, sabotaging their camps and stealing supplies, and the elves and bandits had retaliated harshly. The armies of Nox had no qualms about burning an entire village to the ground, man, woman, and child.

And finally, when that terrible task had come to an end and the last body was carried in out of the cold, the dragons relented.

They could no longer stand aside, leaving only the remaining Guardians to stand up to the evil that was coming for dragon and dwarf and human alike. They could no longer deny that they had a duty to use the power they had to fight, even if the victory may never come in the way that they wanted it to.

"I think that's the last of them," his nephew was saying, barely getting the words out before a deep yawn bellowed out of him. "I'm getting a little cold. I'm not very hungry, but I know it would be good for me to try to eat something."

Elder Jate put aside his thoughts for the moment and turned to the child, the one person that he had left in this dark and unfamiliar new world. He did look very thin, certainly too thin to be out here in the winter air, watching as the last of the dragons made their way west.

He knelt down at his side and took his hand within his own, clasping it tightly as he tried to will away the tears. Even now, his nephew was so strong, so brave, so determined to keep trying to live even as his body rebelled against him from the inside out.

"I know that the women in the kitchen will make me something lovely," the boy said, closing his eyes as he let out a breath, relaxed despite the chill breeze that rustled through his hair. "I feel bad when I can't eat it all. I see how hard they try to make things I will like. They are very kind."

Elder Jate leaned against the side of the boy's chair, pressing his face into the red velvet of the blanket, certain that there was no way he would be able to hide his tears without a moment to compose himself.

Somewhere within him, words came. And in that moment, it seemed the most natural thing in the world that they would.

It will be all right in the end, Elder.

You and your nephew will be strong enough for whatever comes.

Life or death.

Elder Jate breathed slowly, listening, turning over the thought in his mind again and again.

Overhead, a few bands of sunlight pierced the gray clouds.

For the moment, at least, he believed.

33

Chapter 32

CELESYRIA

Celesyria watched as her front legs connected with the ground. An ugly sound of breaking bone and screeching metal filled her ears, but she couldn't seem to feel it.

She could hear Wes crying out to her, but she struggled to focus on his words. All she knew was that she had gotten him to the ground safely, and she was thankful.

There was a warmth spreading through her now, filling her veins, gentle and happy. It was nice not to be in the sky anymore, no longer carrying the weight of the Envoy and the manacles that clung to her ankles.

Snow had begun to fall, the tiny flakes mingling with the stars overhead, and she wished that she had the strength to lift her head and get a better look at them.

She could feel Wes clambering off of her back, still calling out to her, his voice filled with fear. She opened her mouth to answer, but she couldn't make the words come, not yet. She closed her eyes for a long moment, trying to fight off the sleepy feeling that seemed to pull her downward.

When she forced her eyes open again, Wes was in front of her, urging her to roll onto her side.

It was the last thing that she wanted to do, but she knew that if she didn't let him at least try to help, he wouldn't be able to let her go.

Trying to rest her weight on her wing and her back leg, she managed to lean to one side, revealing her belly. She could see the look of horror on Wes's face as he stared, and a moment later, she felt the cool trickle of blood as it dripped from her wound. Judging by the pain, Drohma's arrow had likely struck some important organ, though at the moment, she couldn't bring herself to care very much about which it was.

"I'll get help, Celesyria," Wes was saying, his voice filled with panic. He had leaned in closer now, pressing his cloak against the wound, though he couldn't do much about the arrow that still jutted out of her belly. "Just hold on. I'll find someone."

She swallowed, trying to make her jaws work.

"Wes," she rasped as loud as she could, blinking slowly as he rushed over to her head, his eyes meeting hers.

"Celesyria, please," he said, tears falling freely now. "It doesn't look that bad, really. You'll be fine. I can take the arrow out, I can–"

"I don't have the energy to say much," she said within his mind, her tone firm. *"You need to calm yourself."*

Wes ran a hand through his hair, searching the sky overhead with wide eyes. *"I'm fine. You need help, Celesyria. You need to let me get help. We can fix this."*

"No."

"You can't just give up—"

"Wes, I'm not giving up," she said, each word sending a fresh wave of pain radiating through her head, and probably his as well. *"We're here. I got you here, just like I set out to do, and you can finish this... Do what He asked."*

Wes was sobbing now, his head resting against her neck, his body curled up beside her like a hatchling.

"You can't die," he said between sobs, wrapping his arms around her neck as well as he could. The pain in his voice nearly shattered her heart.

She sent up a silent prayer for strength. There were a few words left to say, no matter how much it hurt her to speak them.

"The fire-breathers have come to us out of the Farplace..." she started aloud. Her voice sounded strange to her own ears as it echoed through the valley, speaking truth to the shattered city and the spire above it. Wes was crying harder now. She could feel the sobs rattling through his body, but she knew they were words he had to hear, too.

"...and to the Farplace again they must return."

"Don't say that—"

"Wes, please. Shh," she continued, mindspeaking once more.

She said nothing else for a few moments, continuing to shush him as he curled up against her. He was so very young to carry the world.

"It's not a sad thing," she added, realizing as she said it that it was true.

She wasn't sad. Not anymore.

Despite the pain in her head and in her torso, she still felt warm. Comfortable, almost, laying there as the snow piled up around her. It would blanket her soon enough, drawing away any heat that remained in her blood, but the thought did not bother her.

This was where she was meant to be.

This was where her story was always meant to end.

"Wes, please listen," she said, her voice feeling small amid the vast future that was calling to her.

"I'm listening," he said after a while, stroking her neck gently with his warm fingertips. *"I'm scared for you, Celesyria. After all you've done..."*

His voice broke as fresh sobs coursed through him, but she knew what he was going to say. His fears had long been her own, but now, beneath the snow and the last of the stars, she was not afraid any more.

"The High One knows what He's doing, Wes," she said, the words coming slow and soft. *"I know that now."*

"But He has denied you a soul," he said, swallowing back more tears. *"You have served Him, and He has promised you only oblivion."*

Without knowing exactly why, she felt a smile settling onto her face.

"Either the Farplace will be beautiful, or He will allow me to join Him in the eternal lands. Whether or not I am allowed to have a soul, He loves everything that He has made. Even me."

KESSARA

Kessara could only watch as the elven army continued to swell across the barren plain, the sound of their boots thunderous in the oppressive silence. Alder held her arm firmly, and she realized then that she was swerving where she stood, her legs no longer wanting to uphold her.

After everything, after making it so far, an army now blocked their way.

She wanted to scream with rage, but instead, she allowed her husband to pull her back into the safety of the diminishing shadows. Aelrie stepped back as well, walking closer to the stone wall of the obelisk, seeming to vanish altogether thanks to her black clothes. Alder stood in front of them, though he did not dare to move, nor to speak.

Kessara waited, trying to focus only on the inhale and exhale of her breath, but she couldn't quell the fury that threatened to overtake her. The High One had led them this far, only to permit this obstacle to fall before them. Worse still, it was not just their own lives at risk, but the lives of Wes and Celesyria, as well, not to mention the rest of the people of Kaveryth.

The Princess took the end of her braid in her hand, undoing the strands and rebraiding them as she wracked her brain for something else that they could do. They had not come all the way to Nox only to give up when things got difficult. This mission had always been impossible, and perhaps it had only been luck and chance that had gotten them through it thus far.

Perhaps You never wanted us to come here at all, High One. Maybe we didn't understand You like we thought we did.

She stared up at the sky. The stars were gone now, replaced with thin, hazy clouds that looked pale and strange in the dawning sunlight. Their color reminded her of the tooth-rocks that dotted the ground, and all at once, she realized just how much they had acted on faith, and just how wrong they had been.

Maybe You never cared about us at all.

She let the ends of her hair fall loose, trying to contain the snarl of frustration that was rising in her throat. She didn't want to give up. She didn't want to be so weak, just when courage was most needed, but she had no hope left to hold on to.

It was easy for her to say that she would stand for the truth, but what happened when the truth ceased making sense?

"I don't see how we can possibly get past them," Aelrie was whispering under her breath, her head cocked as she listened to the continuing footfalls. "There's more coming. I can't see those at the front, but by the sound of their footsteps, their march is slowing. Perhaps they will remain here in this field."

Aelrie looked puzzled, but Kessara didn't have the heart to share her own theory. It made sense to her that the army would stop here, at least for a while.

The Regent and the Elf-queens were here, she was even more certain of that now. Here at the great obelisk, they would be able to feed on the darkness, gorging on their hatred before they marched off to Kaveryth to spill the blood of dragons, dwarves, and men. When they reached the plains of Aridmoor, the war would end, in the most terrible violence yet.

"Well, we need to do something," Alder said after a long pause, closing his eyes and rubbing at his temples. "Perhaps we can go around from behind."

"Even if we did, it's useless unless we can reach the obelisk," Aelrie argued, gesturing vaguely in the direction of the imposing stone structure.

"I'd hardly call our own survival useless," Alder said, his

face grim, "but I see your point."

Alder turned to Kessara and held out his hand for her to take. She took it, allowing him to pull her in toward his chest, but even the warm embrace of the man she loved could do little to ease her despair.

Alder must have seen the grief in her eyes, because he took her cheeks in his hands and looked at her, their faces inches apart. "It's all right, my darling. Whatever happens here, I promise, I am going to protect you."

She accepted his kiss before leaning into his chest, hiding her face against his tunic. She couldn't bear to tell him the truth: if even the promises of the High One did not come to pass, she had little hope in the promises of mortal men, even the man she adored most in all the world.

All of a sudden, she felt Alder's arms stiffen around her as he stood still. She felt the air rushing out of his chest all at once.

She didn't move an inch, fear pooling in her gut as new and horrible imaginings filled her mind. She could see nothing but darkness, and hear nothing but the sound of her own breath moving against the fabric of Alder's tunic. She didn't dare to say a word.

She waited, the seconds expanding in the silence, until at last, she could hear Aelrie speaking.

"Wait," the elf was saying, sounding very far away. "Look. Alder, Kessara, look!"

Kessara shrugged out of Alder's arms, blinking in the sudden light as she crept toward the final edge of the shadow where Aelrie now stood.

"By the Dracodei," Alder said, coming up beside her, his mouth hanging half open as he stared.

Kessara recognized the sound before her vision had quite cleared.

It was familiar and wondrous, all at the same time.

It was the sound of beating wings.

"This is... this is impossible," she said, squinting against the sun as she stared at the eastern horizon.

She could make them out now, dozens of dragons, in every color.

"No," Alder said, clasping her fingers within his own. She looked up at him, and his green eyes were shining as he smiled. "No, my darling. Look."

She turned to face the eastern sky once more.

On the ground, the elves were beginning to realize what was happening.

Kessara watched, unable to breathe, as the elves stopped marching, standing firm where they were in their neat lines. She watched in horror as a few attempted to flee, only to be cut down by their fellows, their bodies left to be trampled upon.

There were a lot of dragons–several dozen, at least–but it was clear now as they approached that many of them were small, barely bigger than hatchlings. The elves were organized, with bows slung across their backs and pikes in their hands.

Kessara wanted to close her eyes as a battle cry began to rise, the dark sound of furious voices filling the sky as they chanted something in elvish that she couldn't quite understand.

All at once, the first of the dragons met with the first line of elf warriors.

She gripped Alder's hand, staring as dragons flew low, their claws tearing at elven armor and flinging aside bodies like they were weightless. Other dragons rushed up behind those that had gone first, picking off stragglers that had managed to slip through the lines.

And then the first volley of arrows came.

Somewhere deeper in the ranks, a signal had been given, and dozens of arrows were sent flying at once. The dragons pulled back, trying to flap their wings fast enough to gain sufficient altitude, but it wasn't enough. Most of the arrows struck. Kessara could hear the plinking sound of the ones that hit only scales, but there were also roars of pain as wing membranes were pierced.

The other dragons who had been coming up behind the initial offensive slowed their approach, taking wide circles overhead, waiting for some kind of opening.

The elves could see their reluctance, and it drove them forward, their eyes dark with hate as they began to press forward with their pikes, another round of arrows soaring over their heads and striking most of the dragons who had escaped the first shots unscathed.

Alder swore, and she leaned against him, the hope that had so filled her only moments before beginning to trickle away.

The pikemen were fast, their elven steps sure as they covered the distance between their army and the wounded dragons. Their war cries rose to a fevered pitch, thousands of voices making the air feel thick in Kessara's ears.

The dragons were trying to pull back, stumbling as they tried to lift tattered wings and pierced bellies, but the elves were too fast. They reached their helpless prey, their silver pikes gleaming in the morning sun, their teeth bared in mirthless smiles as they stabbed at the majestic creatures.

"How can they watch this and do nothing!" Aelrie shouted

at no one in particular, her eyes scanning the sky, where the other dragons continued to circle. "Fight! Fight for your race, and for Kaveryth!"

Kessara thought perhaps that she should tell her to be quiet, but what would it matter? If the dragons fell so easily, what chance would they have, anyway?

Kessara felt Alder's hand slipping from her own. She glanced over at him, watching in horror as he drew his sword from his belt. Aelrie nodded to him, lifted her bow from her back, and began to nock an arrow.

"We can't allow this, Kessara," Alder was saying, tying the strings on his shoulder armor more tightly across his chest. "We can't let them be slaughtered like this. We have to stand with them."

She nodded, reaching for her own sword with shaking hands. She was not used to fighting with the weight of armor. Even without it, her sword was heavy.

"You need to stay," her husband said firmly, resting his hand over her own on the pommel of her blade. "I promised you I would protect you. You can still walk away from all of this. Don't be rash."

She looked up at him, and shook her head.

"I agree with him, my Princess," Aelrie added, giving her a soft smile. "You have more to offer back in Kaveryth. You will find a way."

"I can fight," she protested weakly, making no attempt to remove Alder's hand from atop her own. "I slayed one of them by myself, if you've forgotten."

Alder's green eyes flashed with anger. "Whether or not you can fight is irrelevant. What matters is that you're my wife, and the future Queen of Galeharbor. It is not your duty to die here today. Know your place. It is greater than ours."

He paused for a moment as her eyes met his, her jaw set firm.

"But I would do it. I'd do it in an instant."

His hard gaze softened just a little. "I know you would. Which is why I cannot let you."

He touched a hand to her cheek, and moved toward Aelrie, the two of them falling in step as they strode out from behind the obelisk, breaking into a run as they reached the open space.

For a long moment, the Princess paused, waiting, the decision not yet fully made.

Her husband was right, she knew, but it made no difference.

Kessara slid her sword into its sheath and followed at a run.

The sounds of the battlefield were louder now, and she wanted to cover her ears, but she couldn't. She stared at the ground, trying to watch only the terrain below as she ran, her feet skittering on the yellowed stones as her lungs burned.

Something else was mingling with the sound of the elven war chants.

Her head was pounding, each step on the hard ground sending a jolt through her skull, but the high-pitched noise in her ears was worse.

Magic, perhaps? Emanating from the great obelisk, coursing through the air and into my head?

She stumbled, unable to catch herself as she slid to the ground, pressing her eyes shut tight. She expected to be pierced with an arrow at any second, but no pain came. Chest heaving, she lifted her hands to her ears and looked up, searching for any sign of Aelrie or Alder in the mass of black bodies.

By the Dracodei.

She could still hear the horrible sound, and now, she understood where it was coming from.

The elves were screeching in agony, their bodies consumed by flame, leaving only a smudge of dark ashes behind as they fell one by one to the ground. Dozens of them, perhaps hundreds, melting away before her eyes.

The dragons had not fled.

They had come back.

And they were breathing fire.

34

Chapter 33

WES

The pain that clenched at Wes's heart was all-consuming.

The sun had risen a while ago, but it was obscured by heavy clouds, and in any case, he no longer had any concern for how much time had passed. The seconds were marked with his struggling breaths and the shaking of his body as the growing cold coursed through him, his headache pounding away all the while.

Celesyria had begged him to go to the spire and finish what they had come here to do, but he couldn't bring himself to leave her.

She was barely breathing now.

He watched the unsteady rising and falling of her chest, glad that she had finally given up on trying to speak to him in his mind or with her voice. She had no energy left to waste on an argument that she wasn't going to win.

He would stay here with her until the final breaths left her body.

What came after that, well, that was up to the High One to choose.

He had nothing left to offer. His body was now giving its final warning cries, and the morning cold and wind had only grown fiercer.

The snow was falling harder now, the huge white flakes blanketing the dragon's huge body with astonishing speed. At first, he had tried to wipe it all away, his hands freezing through his thin leather gloves as he worked, but eventually he realized it was impossible to keep up. Now, he contented himself with doing his best to keep her head uncovered, making sure that she was able to breathe as comfortably as possible, even as his own lungs ached from the frozen air.

He had considered lighting a fire beside her, but there was no way he'd be able to make something big enough to make a difference, and furthermore, he wondered if the cold was, in a way, a blessing. Celesyria's body did not regulate its own heat, and if she was cold enough, many of her organs would slow their functioning. She would not be in so much pain as she would be if her body was trying more forcefully to stave off her death.

Despite his protests, he knew that she was right.

Even if help were to appear out of the clouds at that very moment, it was too late. There was nothing that he could do for her but to wait, and to stroke her neck, reminding her that even in this life, she was loved.

He glanced around him, seeing no sign of Captain Drohma or anyone else. The coward had done his terrible deed and fled away into the mountains. For all Wes knew, he was returning to his elven friends. He found it difficult to care. What did it matter now? There would be no good end for a man who had given his life over so completely to darkness. Despite the tragedy of his own situation, now that his fury had abated, he found himself pitying Drohma even more.

Wes laid quietly against Celesyria's neck, curling up beside her as close as he could. Though her scaly body offered no warmth, and her mouth offered no more words, he felt better here. Even if all he could do was to wait.

His headache was intolerable, and his legs felt so weak that he doubted he could walk any longer, even if he did try to leave. He knew that his fingertips had to be frozen from brushing away the snow, and he was afraid of what he might see if he removed his gloves to assess the damage.

Now that he had stopped moving, the cold was becoming easier to ignore with each passing minute.

He was no longer shivering despite the thinness of his tunic, trousers, and cloak, and the thought of trying to root through the snow in search of rare branches to make a fire even large enough for himself seemed an impossible amount of work.

He wondered absently if he should pray now, should ask the High One what to do, but that, too, seemed exhausting.

In any case, what could the High One tell him to change his mind?

Celesyria had chosen to pursue the greater good instead of trying to save her father, and Wes could see the pain that her choice had caused her, the bitterness she had carried for so long. It was a brave choice, a choice he had deeply respected, but now, watching the dying breaths of his best friend, he knew that he did not have the strength to do the same.

The High One remained stubbornly silent, but he could hear a humming sound coming from Celesyria.

He forced himself to inch forward, brushing away newly

built-up snow as he leaned in near her mouth, straining to hear.

"Wes," she was saying, her words as quiet as landing snowflakes. "Wes, it's right there…"

"Please don't talk," he said, pressing a hand gently against her neck. "Just focus on breathing."

"The tower is right there…" the dragon continued.

"Talk in your mind, at least," he said, his own head screaming with the effort.

"No… it hurts… you," she said, each word coming out slow, with long rasping breaths in between. "You can't wait… for me. Do this now… you still have the strength."

He couldn't bring himself to tell her that his strength was fading nearly as fast as hers was, that nothing save a miracle would get him up that staircase now.

"Do it now," the dragon was muttering again, the words barely audible over the sound of her labored breathing.

Wes tried to get a grasp on what Celesyria was saying, but he couldn't seem to focus. The pain in his head had lessened now, and his body had already long since begun to ignore the cold. He felt like he was floating. The truth was somewhere close by, just out of reach, but he couldn't get ahold of it.

He closed his eyes, feeling the soft touch of snowflakes against his cheeks, as warm as summer rain in the forests of Silverfell. He smiled to himself, imagining childhood days spent rushing between the trees, playing games with Roven as his mother called out to them that it was time to come in for tea.

I want to come and see you. Both of you. I miss you so, so much. Dad, too.

He could feel his mouth moving, but he knew that he

was not making a sound, the longing whispers left behind somewhere deep in his heart.

The snow was deeper now.

He could feel it curling up along the sides of his neck, and slithering down his back.

Without warning, he felt a sting, and he somehow managed to roll onto his side, swatting at the snow that had made its way into the top of his tunic.

He heard someone calling his name, the voice echoing through the valley before reaching his ears.

He stopped where he was, staring at Celesyria, who was quickly being buried. She was breathing, but only just. She had said nothing.

But the voice was loud, it was female, and it was familiar.

No. She's dead.

He leaned down and dusted more of the snow away from Celesyria's mouth and nose, ignoring the burning in his hands. The pain was immediate and brutal now, ice-fire spreading through every vein in his body, his exhaustion replaced at once with agony.

"Wes. I'm coming, just hold on," the voice said again, louder this time, unmistakable.

He turned and searched the sky, seeing nothing but blowing snow for several long seconds.

He squinted into the haze, trying to ignore the pounding of his skull and the jolts of frozen lightning racing through his fingertips.

"Go. Go to the spire," Celesyria was choking out once again, her breath no longer warm enough to stop the ice crystals that were forming on her nostrils and stifling her breathing.

Wes leaned in closer, trying to listen to both her and to the voice of the ghost on the wind.

Her eyes were closed, and he could see by the set of her jaw that she had few words left. He felt like he was frozen where he stood, rooted to the stone floor of the valley, unable to take a step forward or back.

All at once, there was a rush of wings.

Orange scales appeared, and Wes pulled his legs out of the way just in time to avoid Jaconial's massive claws as she slid to a landing.

"Thank the High One," she was saying, shaking the snow from her neck as she leaned in toward Celesyria, prodding her shoulder gently with her snout.

For a long second, he could only stare at her, unable to form words.

He reached out and touched a scale that had been dislodged at the side of her right leg. She was real. She was alive.

"Wes, please. What happened?" Jaconial said, listening for the sound of Celesyria's breaths.

Before he could think of how he might begin to explain why he was here and what they were attempting to do, Celesyria raised a claw weakly. It shook as she held it aloft in the swirling snow, but as she began to speak, her words were clear.

"The High One has answered our prayers. I am not alone. Leave me, Wes," she said, her ravaged voice sounding as sweet and full of love as it ever had. "Do not waste my sacrifice."

His tears were gone now, their final remnants frozen fast against his cheeks.

Taking hold of one of Jaconial's neck spines for support, he got to his feet, struggling to keep himself upright. The world seemed to be spinning all around him. The snow and the mountains, the sky, the solid stone, none of it could be trusted.

But he could see the great spire.

He was so close. Celesyria was right.

She had given everything for him, everything for the High One.

He had to try.

If he didn't make it, so be it, but he wouldn't give up.

Not as long as his heart continued to beat in his chest, however uneven and slow.

"I can't explain," he said aloud, too terrified to mindspeak with the terrible headache screaming in between his ears. "I have to go to the top of the tower. It is the Feast of Offering today. I need to bring the bread of hope."

The dragon stared at him through slitted eyes, searching his face, as though she might find more information written there than he was able to speak aloud.

After a moment, she nodded, her expression solemn.

"It would be an honor to stay with Celesyria until the end, my lord Envoy," she said, offering him a quick bow along with her unusually formal words. "Your duty to her is now upon my shoulders. Please go. Do what you came here to do."

Wes swallowed the sob that rose in his throat and leaned down, planting a kiss on Celesyria's half-frozen cheek. He couldn't wait. If he was going to have the strength to do this, it had to be now.

"I love you, Celesyria," he said, longing for the release of tears that could no longer come. She opened her mouth, muttering as she attempted to speak, to tell him to hurry, to tell him she loved him just as dearly.

"Shh," he said, stroking the scales along her neck. "Save your words. I already know."

Wes walked away into the haze of blowing snow.

He looked over his shoulder, but already, the two dragons had faded from sight. He could no longer see the footprints marking the path he had trod.

He looked up at the great spire ahead, praying that it would guide him the rest of the way through the blinding whiteness of the storm.

ALDER

Alder and Aelrie stopped short at the edge of the army's ranks, staring at the scene unfolding before them. The black-clad elves were only a few feet away, but none so much as turned around to meet them. They were instead pushing forward toward the eastern horizon, pikes and swords raised, howling their hateful cries.

The dragons had met the front of their lines now, sending endless plumes of flame into the mass of black soldiers. The air was flooding with acrid smoke that obscured the morning sunlight to the east, but every few seconds, a fresh streak of bright orange flame lit the sky anew.

Alder couldn't figure out how to process what he was seeing. Such a thing had not happened before, so far as he knew. Not in a thousand years, perhaps not since the beginning of the world.

Not to mention the fact that these dragons were clearly not Guardians. Alder could tell by the way that they assembled themselves, leaving obvious vulnerabilities and often narrowly missing crashing into one another whenever they circled back around, that they had not been trained in combat.

So where had they come from? And where had they found the courage to use their forbidden weapon?

Before he could come up with any intelligent theory on the matter, however, he felt something bumping into him from behind. He turned, sword gripped in his fingers, only to find Kessara.

Her dress was torn, and the palms of her hands were bloodied. He swore and shook his head before drawing her closer, trying to shield her from view of the elves that continued to pour past them, replacing those in the front ranks who continued to fall to the dragon-flames.

He opened his mouth to order her to go back to the obelisk before closing it again. She was stubborn to a fault. It drove him mad, but it was too late to send her back now. The concealing shadow would be long gone, anyway.

The smoke had caught on the breeze, and within a matter of mere minutes, it had shrouded them and the army in every direction. The only hint to the locations of the obelisks was the strange green torchlight that surrounded their peaks. Before he could think of any other way to keep his wife out of harm's way, Aelrie spoke.

"Argue later," the elf said, gesturing toward the tail end of the ranks. "Look. They're pushing forward. We can get behind them if we hurry."

Alder heard Kessara coughing as he squinted in the general direction of the great obelisk's torches, trying to see where the tail ranks of the elven army stood. The more that he tried to focus on the scene before him, the more terribly his eyes stung. He swiped away the tears with filthy hands, but still saw nothing.

Kessara gave another choking cough.

"I vote we take her word for it," the Princess said, reaching out and placing her hand in Alder's own. He turned to Aelrie and offered her his other hand, which she took. Running side by side would slow them down, but he didn't want to risk losing sight of the elf if she led the way from up ahead.

A moment later they were moving, not quite running, trying to keep their footing on the unforgiving divots and the endless yellow stones that made it so easy to slip. More than once, Kessara nearly went down, and Alder did the same himself. He was glad that Aelrie was able to uphold his weight so easily.

The sounds of the angry battle cry changed, little by little. He could hear the rage still, but it was now mingled with sounds of agony. Some of the elven cries sounded downright pitiable, but he found he had little pity to spare them. The elves had chosen to seek evil again and again. The High One would decide the fate of their souls, taking all things into His perfect account, but here in this life, as Alder saw it, justice was finally being paid.

He could hear the cries of dragons, and that sound was much worse. Even with their fire, they were hardly invincible, and wherever they had come from, they were not trained Guardians. Many more of them would fall this day. Alder wondered if their great skeletons would remain here, as they had in Boneshire, a macabre memorial of the fights lost by those who won the battle.

"It's just ahead!" Aelrie called out to his right.

The smoke was so thick now that he could hardly breathe, and he had not been able to look up from the ground as he tried desperately to lean as close as he could to the lower, cleaner air. He could feel the elf's hand and Kessara's hand firmly within his own, their mingled sweat slick against their joined palms. He could keep holding on, and keep moving, no matter how little he could see.

All of a sudden, he felt a jolt of pain in his nose as he hit stone face-first. He wanted badly to swear, but refrained, thinking that he would need every ounce of favor from the High One if they were going to survive the next phase of their ill-conceived plan.

"Thanks for the warning, Aelrie," he muttered, reaching up to feel his nose, which seemed unbroken.

"Sorry," the elf muttered as her hand slipped from his. Kessara did the same, and within a few moments, all three of them were feeling the stone face of the obelisk, searching for any indication of a door.

Kessara felt it first, calling out to them from what felt like very far away. Alder did not dare take his fingertips from the wall as he made his way toward her, glancing over his shoulder to get his bearing and seeing only the thick gray fog. He could still hear the cries of the elves and the occasional roar of the dragons, and it was enough to figure out the direction he was facing, but the whole thing was uncomfortably disorienting.

He was relieved when he reached his wife at last, nearly falling through the door that she had opened up in the stone face, with Aelrie stepping in softly behind him into the dark interior. Kessara closed the wooden panel behind them, sealing off the inside of the obelisk from the smoke. An immediate hush fell over the three of them.

"There," she said quietly, her voice seeming to echo in the

empty space.

Alder closed his eyes for a long time, trying to allow them to adjust from the burning smoke to the oppressive darkness. By feel, he managed to unhook a watersack from his belt, the cool water glorious against his smoke-ravaged throat.

When he opened his eyes at last, he realized it was not fully dark, only dim, with several gleaming lights emanating along the walls at either side of the wide hallway where they stood.

He moved to examine one, wanting to understand how it worked, but there was nothing to make sense of. Each torch was nothing more than a large metal goblet, empty save for the greenish light that hovered a few inches over the bowl of the cup.

"We need to move," Aelrie said, already hurrying up ahead along the passage. "This place is quiet, but who knows for how long."

Alder hoped that the elves would be sufficiently occupied outside for a good long while, but he could understand her caution. He was exhausted, and longed to rest here, where there was at least the appearance of safety, but he knew that there would be no true relief until Meira Daeleth was dead and the Elf-Queens were vanquished.

"I am not staying here, Alder, so do not ask me to," Kessara announced, sauntering up beside him, her own now-empty watersack clutched between her bloody fingers. "Like Aelrie said, we don't know who will walk in, and had I listened to you and stayed behind by the small obelisk, you might have not been able to find me again."

She was right on that point, and the thought caused a chill to pour through him. He had not anticipated the extent that the smoke would obscure their navigation. Still, he hated the idea of her walking into what could very well be nothing but a trap.

"Fine," he said, clenching his jaw. Aelrie was right. The time for further discussion about their roles within this marriage would have to wait until a more opportune time. For now, keeping her close may be the best that he could do to protect her.

Outside, he could hear the sounds of the battle, but they were muffled by the thick stone of the walls. He gave Aelrie a moment to take the lead before ushering Kessara along after her, following at last with his sword drawn.

The hall went on for a long time, and they hurried along in silence, the only sound the echoes of their footfalls. At last, they reached the end of it, and found themselves met with a blocky stone staircase that spiraled up and down.

Aelrie stared at it for a few long seconds, pondering. "She'll be at the top," she said at last. "I'm sure of it."

Kessara was already following the elf onto the steps, and Alder had no reason to argue. He sheathed his sword and followed. At this point, they were operating mostly by instinct, and indeed, something did feel right about the idea of the Regent lurking somewhere over their heads.

Alder's knees began to ache as they rushed up the seemingly endless flight of stairs. They were steep, and there were no real landings to speak of, only the occasional door that didn't quite meet the edge of the steps. The battle below could no longer be heard, and Alder tried to reason out how close to the top they must be by now, but there was nothing to orient himself with. There were no windows to speak of, only more of the goblet-lights set into alcoves every several feet.

At last, he heard Aelrie coming to a stop up ahead.

As he turned the corner, he saw her and Kessara balanced on the final step. Aelrie's ear was pressed to a plain wooden door, and his wife was examining a deep alcove that rested beside it.

"It doesn't look like this leads to a throne room," he said in a whisper, ascending a few more steps until he could reach out and finger the old, worn wood. "I have no interest in heading back down, though. Even if we did, we might not find another way up."

Aelrie stepped back from the door.

"I can't hear anything," the elf said, shaking her head. "But that doesn't mean much. They could be using magic to conceal their voices."

"Nevermind. This is the place," Kessara said, stepping back with a satisfied nod. She pointed to the alcove. "Look. There's a rope here, and a pulley."

"A dumbwaiter," Alder said, a smile spreading across his face. Of course. This was probably some kind of back stairwell for the servants, which included a way for them to bring food or other items without having to carry them.

"Brilliant, Kessara," Aelrie said, beaming as she turned to give the door a final listen.

"Palace life has prepared me for the outside world more than I might have thought," Kessara joked, though her face revealed no emotion. Alder reached over and gave her a kiss on the cheek. He knew how she felt.

Whatever was behind that door, it was likely that they would lose the advantage of stealth, and the thought made his palm sweat against the pommel of his sword.

Aelrie paused with her hand grasping the handle, glancing back at her friends.

Alder nodded, stepping in front of Kessara and drawing his sword, the blade gleaming in the greenish light.

Alder braced himself as the door opened, expecting some sort of immediate ambush, but what he saw was much more frightening.

They had indeed found what was unmistakably the throne room, and sitting there at the end of it was a beautiful blonde elf in a black dress, looking out a small window with raised eyebrows.

"Falloren!" she said briskly, not taking her eyes off of the battle scene below. A male elf scurried over to her from where he had been standing along the wall, his spine as stiff and straight as the back of the stone chair that Meira Daeleth sat in.

Alder clasped his sword more tightly, his heart thundering in his chest. Even with the help of Aelrie and Kessara, taking down even a single elf would be difficult, and it was likely she had more guards waiting nearby.

Without warning, the Regent stood up from her chair, her own sword moving so quickly through the air that Alder could not see the flash of the blade.

He stared as the elf called Falloren made a choking sound, blood rising in his throat and mouth. For a few seconds, the guard wobbled on straight legs before crumpling to the stone floor with a sickening thud.

The Regent ignored him, examining the bright red that now marred the edge of her sword, a teasing smile tugging at the edges of her perfect red lips.

"Allowing our enemies to march right into Nox. Fool."

CELESYRIA

The dragon opened her eyes, trying to ignore the cold barbs of falling snowflakes as she peered up at the sky. There were clouds, but through them, she could just make out the comforting glow of the morning sun. The mountains surrounded the Whitespire valley on all sides, and instead of feeling trapped, she felt protected, as though the High One had put up a wall just to keep her safe.

Jaconial was beside her now, trying to brush the cold snow off of her scales with the tip of a wing. With a great effort, Celesyriaturned her head to face her friend. Looking at the beauty of the sky and of the mountains was well and good, but even the most perfect landscape was nothing compared to the face of someone she loved.

"I'm here," Jaconial said softly, pausing for a moment, ignoring the snow.

Celesyria wanted to ask after Nazzan, wanted to know all that had happened, but she knew that her remaining words were limited. She had to make them count.

"Make sure my mother is safe," she said firmly, closing her eyes for a long moment, trying to muster up fresh strength before she said anything else. She was not in pain anymore, not really, but she was tired, more tired than she had ever been. It was the kind of exhaustion sleep could never cure.

"I promise," Jaconial said fiercely, pressing her head gently against Celesyria's shoulder, offering what little warmth her own body still held.

"Jaconial, please, I..."

Celesyria knew the words that she was trying to say, but her mind refused to obey her. She moved her jaw, wondering if she could speak aloud, but her tongue felt like it was stuck in place.

"I will make sure those manacles are removed before your burial," Jaconial said. *"Bargren will find a way, I'm sure of it."*

For so many months, the metal around her ankles had burdened her, a permanent reminder of pain and captivity. Now, at the end, she realized how foolish she had been. Despite her pleas, the High One had refused to free her of her bonds.

He wanted her to have them. He wanted her to have no choice but to turn to him, every time the metal bit at her ankles or weighed her down. He wanted a permanent reason to give her His strength instead of relying on her own.

"No," she said simply, the word hanging in the air for a long moment as she sucked in a new breath, *"Don't. They are a gift. A reminder."*

"I don't understand."

Celesyria wanted to smile, but the muscles in her face would not obey.

For a long while, she said nothing, listening to the comforting sound of Jaconial breathing in and out. She stared at the mountains, marveling at their crags and peaks, and the snow that never left their crests and summits.

"One day you will," she said.

The clouds remained stubborn and heavy, but she focused on everything else, her eyes drinking in every bit of the beauty that she could, wanting to hold all of it close, wanting to remember the smell of mountain air and the taste of fresh snow.

She could feel her heart beating, and her lungs filling with air, but both were working slowly now, her body struggling to hold its pieces together. The pain was returning now, blooming through her chest and her legs, making her cough as she tried to breathe.

She could feel Jaconial's head pressed against her own, and she could imagine herself as a hatchling, her mother close, everything warm and safe and good.

"You'll be free, Celesyria," Jaconial was saying after the silence had stretched on for a long while, her voice distant now, as though she was calling to her from across a great expanse that continued to grow with every passing second.

"It won't hurt anymore. Don't be afraid. Go to Him."

Her chest felt tight now, and the edges of her vision were going blurry.

She focused on Jaconial's words.

Her own strength was gone now. The last of it had brought Wes here, and now, it was her turn to draw courage from another.

Don't be afraid.

She drew another shuddering breath.

Don't be afraid. Go to Him.

Celesyria closed her eyes, content with her memories of the sun and the stars, trusting that beauty could not end here, not even in death, not so long as the High One lived.

35

Chapter 34

KESSARA

Before Kessara realized what was happening, Meira was moving, her sword slicing the air as she dove for Aelrie.

"Alder!" she screamed, her cry mingling with the sound of clashing swords.

Aelrie jumped out of the way just in time to avoid being slashed across the gut, her own sword flying, but the Regent pressed forward, her blade moving so quickly that Kessara could hear its hum.

Kessara fumbled for her own weapon, dragging it out of its sheath and holding it aloft, feeling foolish. The others had been right from the start. She was a diplomat, not a warrior. The blade felt unwieldy in her shaking hands.

Giving up on the heavy sword, she let it fall to the ground, yanking a dagger free from her boot and lunging in Meira's direction. To her astonishment, the edge of her blade caught the hem of the Regent's black silk skirt, tearing through it like it was no more substantial than wet paper.

Aelrie and Alder took advantage of the elf's momentary surprise and leapt forward. Kessara was amazed at how in sync the two of them were, despite the fact that they'd had no time to formulate a plan.

Meira raised her own sword and parried their repeated blows, the clash of metal echoing through the sparse stone room and smarting in Kessara's ears. Alder's face was red and slick with effort, and though Aelrie looked as perfect as ever, Kessara knew her well enough to read the worry in her eyes as she continued to spar with the Regent.

Kessara stepped back, her knuckles white against her dagger as she waited for another opening, unsure if she wanted to risk getting in the way.

Alder slashed low, and to Kessara's surprise, Meira let out a snarl of pain as his sword slid across the side of her thigh, leaving a streak of bright red blood against her silvery skin. She struck out in Aelrie's direction, but she parried the blow easily, and the Regent stepped back, half stumbling as she collapsed onto her throne.

Kessara glanced at Alder, who looked over at Aelrie, clearly waiting for some indication as to whether or not he should press forward.

The whole scene felt surreal. It felt wrong.

Why hasn't she killed us yet?

Kessara took a few tentative steps forward, standing beside Alder, her dagger still grasped firmly in her fingers. The elf did not appear to be harmed. In fact, she looked almost relaxed now, sitting and staring out the window like she had when they had first arrived. Kessara could see a few dragons in the distance as they flew by, their bright wings just barely visible through the lingering smoke.

The Regent beckoned them forward, as though inviting them to huddle around her throne for a more intimate chat, but they stayed put. Meira gave a long sigh, leaning her head back, her pale blonde hair falling over her shoulders in perfect order.

"I have seen history unfold for so many hundreds of years," she said, her fingertips tracing up and down the edge of her chair. "I have seen great men rise, and I have watched them die. You cannot fathom the depths of what I have witnessed."

Alder scoffed. "You're old and putrid beneath the glamor," he said, daring to take a single step closer to the throne. "We get it."

Meira laughed then, and for a second, she sounded exactly like Aelrie. Kessara glanced over at her friend, who looked equally horrified at the note of resemblance.

"Your elf-pet could have told you right after walking in here that I am weaker than I should be."

Aelrie nodded, but said nothing. She didn't need to. Even without the benefit of elven senses, Kessara had known that something was off about the Regent, and she was sure that Alder knew as well. Despite the healthy size of his ego, even he knew that he should have had a much more difficult time striking a successful blow against her.

"This foolishness about the High One has consequences, it seems, even for me," the Regent said, pausing to let her words sink in. Kessara glanced at Alder, but his face revealed nothing.

"Oh, don't misunderstand me, Princess Kessara," Meira said with another tinkling laugh. Kessara had not made any conscious expression of surprise, hope, or anything else, and for a terrible moment, she wondered if Meira Daeleth could read her mind. "The darkness will win eventually. Whether the victory comes now or in a thousand years makes little difference to us."

Kessara noticed Alder's fist tightening around his sword, but he did not attempt to argue.

"Your good, brave men will become cowards. Your rising Houses will fall once again. So long as the High One allows choice, the created ones will choose darkness, in time."

She paused again and let out another long sigh, a few tendrils of hair falling out of place as she cocked her head.

"Even some of you will choose darkness. Isn't that right?"

Without warning, Meira's sword was in her hand, her body flying through the air as she overtook the back of the throne. She landed mere inches from Aelrie, her blade closing the distance between them. Before Kessara had time even to scream, Aelrie was shrinking back, her hand pressed against her pierced shoulder, her ice-blue eyes filled with fear.

Alder responded within an immeasurable fraction of a second, his own sword cutting through the air. Kessara felt her own dagger slip from her hand, clattering onto the stone floor at her feet.

Before she could make sense of the scuffle, it was over.

Meira Daeleth lay on the ground, blood pouring from a gaping hole in her torso and dribbling out across the stone. She was laughing again, but it was different now, a deep and ugly sound, a sound from another world even more terrible than the plains of Nox.

"I am weak," she spat, staring up at Alder with eyes full of hate. "But *they* are not. *They* are eternity."

Kessara wanted to step back, but she couldn't seem to get her feet to move. A haze of green light began to fill the room, rollicking and tumbling like smoke. She felt Alder's hand encircling her wrist, trying to pull her back, just as Meira Daeleth's body vanished from the floor.

The Princess screamed, stumbling back as the strange glow became even thicker, obscuring her vision. Alder and Aelrie stepped ahead of her as four distinct beings began to take shape, their hideous faces forming out of the rushing mist, with mouths open in rictus grins.

A scream filled the room, four voices at once crying out, impossibly loud. She pressed her hands to the sides of her head, desperate to keep the dark sound out of her ears, but it was no use. Her head felt like it was going to burst as the pitch of the scream began to rise to an impossible note, like a strung wire about to snap.

She felt fingertips grasping at her from behind, but it was too late. She could see herself falling toward the stone floor, the Elf-queens continuing to scream, the green haze clouding everything.

She felt no impact. She saw only blackness.

WES

The staircase had never felt so tall as it did that day.

Wes forced each of his feet to move one step at a time, hauling his weakened body higher and higher, and trying to restore body heat after he escaped the freezing wind of the storm outside.

His head still ached, and his limbs felt like they were burning, his muscles stretched and battered far beyond its limit. He took another three steps, each footfall sending pain radiating through his leg and into his spine.

He was in agony, but at least he was moving. That was more than he could ask for.

His best friend was dead, had died to get him here, to give him this chance. He had to keep fighting.

High One, please, have mercy. Have mercy.

He was too tired even to whisper the prayer aloud, so he repeated it within his mind every few moments, ignoring the pain that any sort of focused thought always sent searing through his skull when his headaches got bad.

He couldn't do this alone. Every step upward was possible solely due to the strength of the High One. Of that much, he was certain. His own body had run out of strength a while ago now, resting there against Celesyria's neck, desiring nothing more noble than the oblivion of sleep.

He leaned against the wall as the staircase began to curve more tightly, trying to keep his balance on the broken and uneven stones. This was good. It meant he was making progress, that he was near to the final stretch, but it also made the trek all the more treacherous. One misstep would cause him to slip, and he doubted he'd be able to arrest downward motion once it began.

He gritted his teeth and leaned into the damp stone of the wall, forcing himself to take three more steps, noticing that the front of his boot had finally given way, revealing the gray wool of his sock.

He could imagine himself as a little boy then, bringing yet another bit of mending to his mother as she scolded him gently for being so careless with his things. Roven would always be there, too, withering under the harsher gaze she reserved for the elder brother, who really should have known that getting on the yearling stags without riding tack was a foolish thing to permit Wes to do.

His mother would usually bring up her sons' infractions at the dinner table, but by then they had already become nothing more than funny stories, and his father would always laugh right along with the rest of them.

Wes took another step, his fingertips slipping a little against a patch of moss, mere inches from the safe grip of a small windowsill. It was enough to send him reeling backward, but fortunately, he was able to jam his foot down hard against the edge of the wall, steadying himself, though his ankle now ached almost as terribly as his head.

He swore without being able to stop himself, listening to the echo of the unpleasant word in the empty silence, the pain behind his eyes giving him a firm reprimand for daring to speak aloud.

The memories were gone now, the faces of his parents and his brother disappearing into the depths of his mind like dissipating mist.

He took three more agonizing steps, reaching a small landing and sitting down against the wall, breathing hard.

Memories are a distraction, High One. Must You torment me with all that I have lost?

There was no response, and now that he was sitting down, he found very much that he wanted to stay sitting for a long while, perhaps forever.

He looked up at the staircase stretching above him, where he could count at least four more rotations before the top disappeared out of his view. Perhaps he wasn't even as close as he'd hoped. He'd tried to look out the windows and to see how far he was from the ground, but the white mask of blowing snow made any accurate calculation impossible.

Even when he wasn't ill, the staircase had always been a grueling climb, the stags that he brought with him always tired and foul-mannered by the end of it. The once grand tower had been left in disrepair for far too many years, and now with even the dwarf-women ceasing to care for it, the decay seemed to have accelerated even within the last few months.

Wes closed his eyes for a long moment, drawing slow breaths in and out as his head and ankle continued to simmer with pain, never giving him even a moment's peace. His body could not continue on like this forever, he knew. Not while he remained so close to the elves and their darkness. Even if he left, he doubted that the headaches would recede.

No. This curse was going to kill him. What did it matter if he died right here, right now?

He could close his eyes. Eventually, sleep would come, and he would not wake up again. He was sure of that. Not here, not in the damp and the cold, where no one else would dare to come and seek after him...

Do not waste my sacrifice.

He could almost hear Celesyria's words in his mind, kind and gentle, even at the end.

The tears that had been frozen fell freely now as he swallowed back his sobs. She had done what was right, and it had cost her everything she had to give.

He felt a surge of rage coursing through him; rage at the darkness and the elves, rage at himself and his weakness, and rage at the High One for choosing him in spite of it.

He forced himself to his feet once again, taking a few long breaths before continuing onward, leaning against the wall as his feet carried him up the steps. He was making progress now. Three steps, eight steps, ten steps, his chest heaving with the effort, his legs stiffening every time his half-shod feet struck the hard, worn marble.

More memories filled his mind, appearing and disappearing without order or sense. He could see them all there, Alder, Kessara, Nazzan, Jaconial, their faces flashing before him, calling to him to keep going. He could see others, too, others who were so easily forgotten when the pain got bad enough—Odrigh, Holga, Gohr, Lev, Oria, Elder Bram, Luna, their friends in Auranth...

He heard a cry of pain escaping him as he reached another small landing, fingertips gripping the edge of the window as he allowed himself three breaths worth of rest. That was all he could risk taking. He pushed on once again, his feet taking the steps as quickly as he could, his body disoriented as he circled around and around, the staircase growing even tighter.

He saw Aelrie then, as clear as a portrait.

He could see her eyes of ice, her sleek black hair, the gentle smile that made his heart seem to tighten in his chest, too beautiful to look at. He could see her silvery fingertips, twisting her little borrowed silver wedding ring around and around.

Do not waste her sacrifice, either, Wesley Cervos.

Whether she was calling to him from this life, or the next, or from his own imagination, Celesyria was right.

All of the times that Aelrie had doubted, all of the times that she had been certain that she couldn't escape what she'd seen, what she'd done. All of the times that she had thought that the High One couldn't possibly want her.

Like Celesyria, she had chosen Him anyway.

She had chosen to face her deepest fears, her most danger-ous temptations, to walk into Nox and to believe that she had indeed been made new.

Maybe he wasn't as strong as they were.

Maybe he wasn't strong enough to sacrifice everything for the truest love, for the pure desire to do good for the sake of the High One. Maybe that was true.

But he could do it for his family. He could do it for his friends. He could do it for the dragon who had changed his life.

And, perhaps most of all, he could do it for the woman who loved him, even when he least deserved it.

36

Chapter 35

AELRIE

Aelrie tried to yell at Alder and Kessara to get out of the way, but it was too late, her voice swallowed up in the hissing and screaming of the Elf-Queens as her two friends fell to the floor.

Their eyes were closed, but she could see that they were breathing. All she could do was hope that the darkness would only affect them temporarily, and keep the demons focused on her.

There was no time for anything more.

She stood where she was, sword raised, watching as the terrifying figures twisted and danced in the air around her, their faces appearing and disappearing into the fine green mist.

It was up to her now.

They were ugly in the warped, visceral way that made her want to look away, but she forced herself to face them. She lifted her chin high, as Kessara might have done were she still standing, setting her jaw and staring at them even as her knees shook.

They howled at her in words that she could not understand, the sort of words she knew should never be uttered, the language of foul darkness filling her ears.

And though she could not translate the speech into the common tongue, she knew exactly what they were saying.

You can't resist the dark, Aelrie.

Let go of this pain, this life.

Your husband is going to die anyway, what future do you have in Kaveryth?

Do you think the people of Silverfell will accept you, an elf, as their queen?

Come home.

Be with us!

Become who you were born to be!

The High One has no use for you, not after all that you've done.

It's too late for you.

Not so long ago, the words would have struck at her heart, tempting her, making her long for the life that she had cast aside. Not so long ago, she would have believed them, would have believed that the Creator of all the world had better people to serve Him than someone like her.

And yet, here she was.

By her own strength, she should be on the floor like her friends, blacked out against the stone, but she wasn't.

She was still standing, and the words could not touch her. No matter what she encountered, so long as the High One resided within the depths of her heart, she was invincible, even in death.

She took a few short steps over to Meira Daeleth's throne,

climbing onto the hard stone surface as she held her sword aloft.

"Manta, Cervos, Ursa, and Noctua!" she shouted over their twisting words, ignoring their snarls of protest. Aelrie stole a quick glance at Alder and Kessara as the Elf-Queens moved through the room, surrounding the throne where she stood.

"We have not forgotten your names. We have not forgotten what you have done!" she cried out as loud as she could, her throat burning from the effort.

She felt her body becoming weightless as they rushed in beneath her, suspending her above the throne, still gripping her sword. A part of her knew that she should feel terrified, but instead, she could feel something else as she spoke, a warmth that poured through her, strengthening her. She could barely hear herself over their hisses and screams, but she knew that it did not matter. Not anymore.

"By the power of the High One," she shouted at them, "I command you!"

Their protests rose to a fever pitch, their cries filling her ears, threatening to drown out all thought. She tried to grip her sword, wanting to hold onto something, anything that was solid, but they began to shake her in mid-air, and she felt it slipping from her fingers before clattering against the throne below.

"By the power of the High One," she said again, pressing her eyes closed, every shred of energy focused on getting the words free, "I command you. Leave us! Go to the Wrathlands where you belong."

She paused then, forced to draw breath as the shrieks continued, but before she could finish, she felt a sudden release.

She fell at once, with no time to adjust her body or to attempt to break her fall. She heard the sound of crunching bone as her ankle struck the edge of the stone armrest, shattering it instantly. The warmth and strength she had felt seemed to slip away in an instant, replaced with an all consuming pain, louder even than the screeching of the demons. They continued to undulate around her, shouting, laughing, speaking.

She remembered the first time she had met Wes Cervos, when she had turned her ankle between two stones. He had helped her, not realizing how fast elves could heal. Even then, she had seen something special about him, a hidden quality that no one else around her possessed, but she had never dared to imagine that they would one day fall in love.

She thought of him now, far more physically broken than she was, forging his way into Whitespire and climbing the great spire.

He was fighting alongside her, half a world away.

She forced herself into a sitting position, clutching at the sides of the chair as the Elf-Queens drew closer, their misty faces pressed inches from her own.

She drew a breath, searching for the warmth that was still within her, calling upon the grace that was waiting for her when she needed it most.

"I command you," she said again as the green haze obscured her sight completely, encasing her in the darkness, trying to draw her away.

She smiled, letting her voice fall to something just above a whisper.

Loud or soft, it did not matter.

The power—*His* power—was in her words, and they could

not stop it.

"Go to the Wrathlands, and never come back."

For a moment, there was no sound.

And then, all at once, the air seemed to rush from the room, roaring against her ears as she slipped from the edge of the throne, her head meeting the floor as she went.

She pressed her eyes shut, forcing down sudden nausea, listening as her ears continued to ring for what felt like a very long time.

The room was perfectly silent once more, and aside from the slight ache in her skull and the lingering pain of her not yet healed broken ankle, she felt well enough. She opened her eyes, tilting her neck to examine the sword-mark on her shoulder, but it had already faded away. It seemed that her elven healing abilities had remained.

She got to her feet, surprised by the unsteadiness of her legs, and made her way toward Alder and Kessara. They looked almost peaceful now, their chests rising and falling, their eyes closed softly. She would almost hate to disturb them, were it not for the triumphant joy demanding to be shared.

"Wake up," she said, taking Alder's shoulders and shaking him gently until his eyes opened. "We did it. We won. The Elf-Queens are gone," she said in a rush as he blinked up at her. The news seemed to register in an instant, and he got to his feet, looking around the now-empty throne room.

"At least, I hope they are," she added, a shudder running through her. The reality was, she had no way to tell what had really happened.

The Elf-Queens channeled the power of darkness, to be sure, but it still existed without them.

For all she knew, it could have been nothing more than a demonic disappearing trick. She could still feel the telltale power of the evil that always filled Nox, humming in the air, just below the surface of the world that the humans could sense.

Only Wes was different.

He would know for sure by the pounding in his head.

She closed her eyes for several long seconds, trying to swallow the lump that was rising in her throat as she touched the silver ring on her finger.

Separating had been the right thing to do, she had no doubt. He wouldn't have survived this tower, let alone their encounter with Meira and the four Elf-Queens. Still, she worried for him. As much as her heart longed for him to be near to her once again, another part of her wished that he was so much further away, beyond Kaveryth's borders to the east, where the darkness could not quite reach.

Aelrie opened her eyes again.

She was here now, he was not, and there was still more to be done before this was truly over.

Alder knelt down at Kessara's side, his hands placed gently against her cheeks.

"Darling, you're safe now," he crooned, leaning in close and listening to the rush of her breathing. "Open your eyes."

Aelrie strode over to her fallen sword and picked it up, hanging it against her belt once more. Even if she had succeeded in banishing the Elf-Queens to the Wrathlands, she wasn't sure what effect it had. So far, everything seemed to be just the same as it was. She doubted that they would remain alone up here for much longer.

She listened to Alder as he continued to try and wake

Kessara, striding across the floor until she reached the single window. She was just tall enough to peer out of it, but the view told her nothing. She still could not see the ground below. No dragons were passing by, either, and for a terrible second, she worried that perhaps her command of exile had been too broad.

She knew that soon enough she would be called upon to reverse that oath, as well. The dragon Guardians would no longer be compelled to protect Kaveryth. As far as she knew, once their burden in this world was lifted, the High One would call them home to the Farplace, where they would protect the gates of the Eternal Lands as they had always been created to do.

But today was not that day.

At the moment, she feared that the elven army was out there and back in Aridmoor, just as strong as ever, with or without their rulers. And if that was the case, they needed the dragons more than ever.

"What happened?"

The sound of Kessara's voice jolted her out of her thoughts. She spun around, only to find that the Princess was on her feet, resting her weight against Alder's shoulder. She was blinking slowly, staring around the unfamiliar room as though she'd never seen it before, but at least she was awake.

"Thank the High One," Alder muttered, pulling her in close and planting a kiss on her forehead. He glanced up at Aelrie, their eyes meeting for a long moment. Neither of them knew what to say. Aelrie had done what felt right, but had she succeeded? Had anything changed?

She cleared her throat.

"We can't stay here," she said, gesturing toward the door

where they had entered from. "We're too exposed to attack, and until the smoke clears, I won't be able to see anything useful from the window. We need to get back to the ground."

Alder gave a nod.

"Can you walk?" he asked Kessara.

The Princess nodded and began to stumble forward, though her mouth was set in a firm line and her face was pale. "I'll be fine."

Aelrie stepped out ahead of her, but before she could reach for the handle of the door that led to the narrow back stairwell, she heard a fantastic crash coming from somewhere outside.

Screams filled the air once more, but this time, they were loud enough to hear even through the thick stone walls of the great obelisk.

Aelrie turned, glancing up at the window that lay beyond the throne, searching the greenish, hazy sky. There was nothing.

Another crash, this one even louder, closer than the first.

More screams.

Alder swore.

"Head for the main stairs!" Kessara ordered, trying to turn around, dragging Alder with her. "I'll be too slow if we go down the servant's route. We have to get out—"

Before Aelrie had time to react, there was a third crash.

This time, it was coming from somewhere beneath their feet.

37

Chapter 36

WES

Wes forced himself up the last of the stairs, his mind planted firmly on memories of Aelrie and his friends. He did not feel so alone as he had before. His friends were with him, cheering him on, and he would not let them down. Not after everything that they had sacrificed.

At last, he ascended the final step, and all he wanted was to lay down on the old marble for another long rest. His entire body ached, but he was so close now, too close to waste any more time arguing with himself.

He continued on, listening to the hollow sounds of his footfalls echoing through the room. It was not a grand place, nor was it very large, but without the usual cavalcade of deer, it felt huge and menacing. The walls up here were rough-hewn stone, likely the oldest part of the structure, built up hundreds of years before the talented marble workers got hold of the staircase.

He could see the dark hole that led into the sacred cavern

up ahead, just a few paces away. It looked just as it had last time, unassuming, never drawing much attention to itself, but Wes knew better. It was there where the treasures were brought. It was there in the darkness that the whole warped business of the Dracodei came together.

He stared at it for a few long seconds, lost in memory despite the protests of pain hammering in his head.

He had spent so much time here, for as long as he could remember, and much more time on the road between Stronghollow and Whitespire. Even as a child, he had not been spared the task of the Envoy. All for this. All for lies.

But it was not the cavern that he sought.

He turned to the side. The little stone fountain was waiting there. It had always been even more unassuming than the cave, coated with thick dust, forgotten. Now, it had changed.There was clear water within the large bowl, and it was bubbling just a little, suggesting that it was being fed from some hidden source.

The outside had changed, too. Both of the bowls—the small one resting neatly inside its larger twin, though it held no water—had been cleaned to gleaming. Wes could see the careful details that had been crafted, little scenes of sculpted stone fauna and vines with twisting, meandering lines that seemed to be attempting to escape into the floor. His mother would have liked it very much. She would have shown him the detailed strokes of a chiseler's pick, explained that it would take hours and hours for each tiny detail to look just right.

But she had never been able to see it. Wes had walked past it every season since he was a child, and had never had anyone tried to show him the significance of it. Not that they were allowed to come anywhere near it, save for the dwarf women who cared for the tower, but it saddened him just the same.

What else had he missed on his journeys? What else had he spent so long failing to see?

He took a couple of steps closer, fingering the piece of dry bread in his pocket for a moment before pulling it free and examining it. It had been crushed nearly flat, with crumbs tumbling off in all directions across the worn floor, but it would have to do.

He drew in a shaking breath. His headache was worsening once again, pulling his mind in twenty directions at once, desperate for any thought to cling to that was not pain.

His condition was deteriorating, he knew, noticeable in terms of minutes let alone hours, and if the illness carried on this way, he would not live for very long.

All that remained for him was his duty, and he would not fail to see it through to the very end.

He lifted the bread between two fingers, uttering what he hoped was the right sort of prayer, and dropped it into the smaller upper bowl of the fountain, the water tinkling merrily just below.

He closed his eyes and waited, not daring even to lean against the wall, lest he fall asleep and never wake up again.

He let his thoughts drift to pleasant memories, heading off every new flash of pain, every new pang of loss that took hold of his heart. There was so much to leave behind, so much goodness in his life, so many blessings he had been given despite the losses that he had endured.

He felt a smile rising on his lips. How funny it was that to truly appreciate his life, he had to accept the coming of his death.

He opened his eyes at last, expecting things to look different, but they remained as they were.

There was no voice in his head, no fresh light pouring in through the last window at the top of the stairs. There was only the quiet of the stone room, interrupted every few seconds by the sound of gurgling water and his own struggling breaths.

And yet, he knew that he had done what he must.

He could feel it.

Something had changed, something imperceptible to human sense, something that lay beyond.

Something that lay above.

He plucked the bread from the little bowl, examining it, and as he suspected, it remained completely unremarkable.

He took off a tiny piece and ate it, chewing carefully. He found that he was hungry, and the taste was pleasant, gone just as soon as it had come.

He placed the rest in his pocket, trying to stop as many crumbs as he could from being lost, and headed toward the stairs.

ALDER

Alder stared at the floor of the hall below as they hurried down the final stretch of staircase, watching as huge pieces of stone came hurtling down from the ceiling, shattering against the slick-looking floor as they struck it. Dust filled the air, making him cough, but there was no time to catch his breath.

Kessara was leaning against his arm, trying to keep up with him. Though these stairs were much larger, twisting down in a square from landing to landing, they were steep, and they had almost lost their balance more than once.

"Come on!" Aelrie was shouting from a few steps down, her words lost as yet another stone clattered down from the direction they had just come, thumping along down the staircase before reaching another landing somewhere above their heads. "There's no more time."

"Sorry, darling," Alder said, hauling Kessara into his arms in one fluid motion before she could offer up any protest. He gritted his teeth, ignoring the ache in his arms as he continued carefully down the steps, precious cargo in tow.

"Alder–"

"Do you trust me?"

"You'll fall, I–"

"Kessara, do you trust me?" he asked more fiercely, pausing just long enough to look down at her, allowing her eyes to meet his own. He breathed hard, his heart pounding, until finally she nodded.

"With my life."

"Good."

Without another word, he took off again, faster now. Falling wasn't an option, but he didn't dare take the time to hesitate.

"Here! To the right!" Aelrie shouted, disappearing down into the hall below, which was now almost completely obscured by dust. He could hear more rocks falling behind him now, more thunderous smashes of stone hitting stone, and they sounded like they were getting close.

"I can run the last bit," Kessara was saying, gesturing toward the end of the staircase. "Hurry."

At last, he nearly leapt off of the final step, putting Kessara down as soon as they reached flat ground. He took her hand firmly within his own and they broke into a run, choking and coughing as they chased after Aelrie, able to see only the swishing of her black cloak through the thick dust.

At last, they reached a huge wooden door, and to Alder's surprise, it was already partially open, hanging halfway off of its massive iron hinges. Beyond it, they could see nothing. The smoke still hung in the air, heavy and yellow, and since they had entered the great obelisk it had begun to snow.

"Shall we?" Alder said, gesturing out into the thick mist, just as another crash came from somewhere behind them. Aelrie nodded, and the three of them pushed against the heavy wood of the door, shoving it outward until they were able to pass through.

He dared a glance at Kessara beside him. She looked better than she had a few moments ago, perhaps, but still weak. Whatever Aelrie had done—there'd hardly been time to ask—the darkness of Nox had clearly harmed his wife. He wasn't going to allow her to remain here a single second longer than he had to.

There were more sounds from behind them, much louder now, and he had no choice but to chase after Aelrie as close as he could, trusting that she had some destination in mind. He stole a final glance over his shoulder as they passed deeper into the smoke and falling snow, watching as the huge tower began to topple to the ground, huge chunks of stone and a few bits of broken wood flying in all directions.

"By the Dracodei," Kessara was muttering under her breath as they rushed across the plains, trying to avoid stumbling on the stones that were now slick with snow.

Somewhere off to their right, Alder heard more crashing and shattering as one of the smaller obelisks began to disintegrate.

"The green lights have gone out," he pointed out between labored breaths, gesturing through the snow toward another tower that still looked to be mostly intact.

Kessara's eyes caught his own, but she said nothing. Despite her exhaustion and the hollow look of her cheeks, he could see the hope that lit up her eyes. Whatever Aelrie had done, it seemed to be working.

Without warning, he saw the elf stop in her tracks up ahead, her back stiffening as she stared at something he could not see.

"Come on," he said to Kessara, gripping her hand more tightly as they hurried over a patch of particularly uneven ground, the pits and hollows only partially visible beneath the snow. Of course, Aelrie had been able to clear the rough terrain without slowing, and now they had to move quickly to catch up with her.

She waited for them, unmoving, a cold black shadow against the dull sky.

"Prepare yourselves," she said stiffly as they came up behind her. Alder felt Kessara moving a few inches closer to him, but she did not inquire as to what the elf meant.

It only took a moment for her warning to become clear.

Lying on the ground a little ahead of her were three elves, their lifeless eyes staring up at the hidden sun. Were it not for their long hair and their armor, however, Alder would have struggled to identify them as elves at all.

Kessara let out a retching noise beside him, her hand slipping out of his as she stepped aside, turning her back on the terrible scene.

The elves were completely disfigured.

Is this what Celesyria saw at the council so long ago? No wonder she claimed not to be able to truly describe it.

Their skin reminded Alder of melting wax, and even their bones seemed out of place, the shape of their faces not quite making sense. Their limbs were thin and strange, reduced to bone and sinew, resting at odd angles against the ground. Only their eyes looked the same as they always had. Even in death, they were filled with hate.

Mercifully, the snow was falling faster now. Soon enough, they would be hidden away on their battlefield, buried beneath the soft white crystals.

Kessara turned back to the others, averting her eyes so as not to glance at the bodies.

"Does this mean that the glamors have been broken?"

"Yes, Aelrie said, twirling her ring around her finger. "To think…This is the consequence of choosing the darkness. This is how we really look."

Alder reached out and rested a hand on Aelrie's shoulder, his eyes meeting hers.

"This is how *they* really look," he said firmly. "You do not belong to them."

Kessara nodded, reaching out and squeezing Aelrie's hand.

"You fought on the side of the High One. He worked through you. Do you forget that so quickly?"

Before the elf could reply, however, they heard several more crashes, and though Alder could not presently see any of the other obelisks through the mist and snow, they sounded close.

He pulled Kessara nearer to him as the sounds grew louder. Fresh dust was rising in the air now, great plumes of it rollicking over the plain despite the snow, irritating his lungs all the worse. The light of the midday sun grew even more dim, and he struggled to get a bearing on what direction they were facing.

Aelrie glanced down at the bodies of the elves and pointed past them. "We have to move. Go."

Her eyes were wide, her mouth hanging just slightly open, as though the sight of the elves had been enough to shake something loose inside of her.

A moment later, Alder understood.

He heard the stomping of hundreds of feet, punctuated with hollow shouts, the sound dampened by the snow.

He looked over his shoulder, his chest going tight.

The elves were there on the field once more, their black-clad bodies emerging from the haze as they ran, thin limbs jerking back and forth as they skittered over the stones that looked like teeth. There were still thousands of them, and they were running in all directions, trying to escape a fate that they could not outrun.

Kessara screamed, but her legs were steadier now, and Alder was able to run without having to assist her. The two of them took off after Aelrie, covering ground as quickly as they could, but it was impossible to tell how much further they had to go, or if the edge of the forest and the city remained as they had been before the towers fell.

To Alder's surprise, it was Aelrie who looked shaky now, her pace slowing until he and Kessara were able to easily catch up to her.

"Are you all right?" he called out over the din, not daring to slow down.

"The darkness," she said, gasping as she tried to keep running, her legs slipping on the stones below. "The rage.

The rage of the Elf-queens. I can still feel it, I–"

Before she could say more, her foot got caught up beneath her, and she pitched forward.

Her arms flew out to protect her face, but she didn't quite make it. Alder listened in horror as her cheek connected with the ground with a sickening crunch.

Alder stood frozen for a long moment, the screams of elven rage thundering in his ears, the lingering smoke and dust stinging at his eyes. He felt trapped where he stood, rooted in place as the whole world burned, unable to change anything, unable to escape.

Kessara rushed forward, kneeling at Aelrie's side and turning her over until she rested on her back. Her cheek had been fractured, and blood poured from her face, dripping onto the dark soil. Without a word, his wife tore off the edge of her dress, using the hem fabric to press against the wound.

Blood had never bothered him before, but now, he felt bile rising in his throat. His head was aching, and he felt for a terrible second that he was going to pass out just as the elf had.

"Alder, I need you to help me to keep her neck steady, at least until her body starts healing itself, assuming it still can," Kessara said calmly, barely seeming to notice as a group of four elves raced past her, only a few feet away. "Just take a deep breath."

Her voice steadied him.

He was not in the Wrathlands. He was not dead. He was here, alive, and he could keep fighting.

"I'm sorry," he said, dropping to the bloody ground and lifting Aelrie's head onto his lap as Kessara directed him.

"Don't be," she said, not looking up from her work as she

examined the shattered cheekbone.

"She's breathing well, her pupils are responsive," she said without emotion, placing a hand on the elf's chest, feeling it rise and fall. She moved until she could reach Aelrie's shoulders and neck, her fingers carefully tracing her bones and muscles. "Thank the High One, her neck doesn't–"

A roar split the sky as a large dragon flew overhead, its outstretched wings casting a shadow over them.

"Help us," Alder cried out in his mind, hoping desperately that his mindspeaking would be sufficient to reach the creature from the ground.

"Please, help us. We need to get back to Kaveryth. Please!"

Kessara leaned against his shoulder, tears filling her eyes as the dragon disappeared into the haze.

"Please, I'm begging you!"

There was no answer.

Despite the continued screams of the elves, it felt somehow quiet, as though lightning had struck, tearing all of the other sounds from the sky.

Alder closed his eyes, stroking Aelrie's hair as she breathed slowly, her head still resting on his knees. He turned to kiss Kessara's forehead, saying nothing.

Leaving Aelrie behind was not an option.

They would do all they could for her, and then they would carry her out of Nox, one way or another. He closed his eyes, biting back a snarl of anger that threatened to burst from his throat.

He had promised Wes that he would protect the woman he loved.

And he had failed.

At that moment, he felt Kessara stiffening beside him, her

hand falling away from his own.

"Look," she said pointing at the sky. Her eyes were shining once again.

To his amazement, the dragon had returned.

He made no sound, either out loud or in Alder's head, but there was no mistaking his intentions.

He was flying low, taking slow circles over their heads as he made his way toward the ground.

It was a male, and his scales were bright white, sparkling despite the dimness of the sun.

As he landed before them, Alder could see by the length of his gnarled claws and the way his fangs protruded from his jaw that he was very old, and very large.

He was big enough to carry all three of them home.

It was finally over.

38

Chapter 37

WES

The stairs passed beneath his feet in a blur as the edges of his vision dimmed.

By the time Wes reached the bottom landing, stumbling toward the huge door that led outside, he could scarcely remember how he'd gotten there at all.

The burst of energy that had driven him up the final ascent was long gone now, and he could feel his body giving out a little more with each step he took. He could feel the piece of bread in his pocket, and he fingered it every few moments, trying to focus on what he had done rather than on the pain that filled his every nerve.

He had offered bread, and now, he had to believe that what he held was something much greater, something that could feed an entire continent of people, if only they would accept the One who truly offered it.

He pushed against the door, half expecting his muscles to falter and his legs to give out, but to his relief, he pushed the wood outward without difficulty.

He paused for just a moment before stepping out into the blinding white of the storm.

He was miles from anyone, save hostile elves who would be all too pleased to kill him on sight.

There would be no one here to meet him. No one here to guide his way back.

If the High One wanted this bread to be given to the people, He would have to intervene.

Wes forced his legs to bring him forward, the heavy snow growing thick against his leather boots. It was even colder than it had been when he went in, and the wind was stronger, biting at his neck and making the end of his nose burn, but he pressed on.

His best friend's body would be just where he'd left it, and his only hope was that Jaconial would still be at her side. Celesyria had guided him to the path of the High One once, and she was his best shot at finding the hidden road, just one last time.

He coughed as a fresh gust of wind assailed him, blowing snowflakes into his face. Nothing looked familiar, but he knew that she couldn't be far.

He struck out into the blowing whiteness, and before long, he could not even see the tower that lay just behind him.

It was impossible to know exactly how much time had passed while he was hidden within the gloom of the tower, but for whatever reason, he assumed it had to be around noon.

A small part of him had expected something different when he walked through that door, out into the snow-masked light.

He had held on to hope that there would be a blue sky, sunshine, a welcome party—anything at all that would assure him that his quest had succeeded.

But there was another part of him, grown up and wise, that knew such dreams were naive.

The world was still dark. It was still cold. It was still full of hate, and rage, and loneliness. It had borne darkness for centuries, and even now, Wes knew, the evils of dragons, elves, dwarves, and men remained.

Restoration would not happen in an instant. That was a pleasant story to comfort little children.

He had struck a match, but the fire of the High One still needed to be kindled, and he would not live long enough to see the pillar of flame that would eventually burn away the darkness.

He had succeeded, but the reward for victory was yet more sacrifice.

Nothing more.

His hands were shaking along with his legs now, the leather gloves he wore insufficient to keep away the biting of the wind. His eyes were pressed into slits, trying desperately to make out the tower, the mountains, the sun, anything that could help him get his bearings, but all he could see was snow.

"Celesyria," he called out, his throat burning, realizing the moment he said it that she could no longer call back to him, and never would again.

He fought through more snow, and it seemed to be growing deeper now, deadening his legs with cold and concealing the treacherous stone below.

It was not long until he misjudged one of his intended steps, his leg jutting into a deep patch of snow and sending him reeling backward. His arms flew out at his sides, catching only air, and a moment later, he was on his back, peering up at the pale sky between frozen eyelashes.

His body did not ache quite so much any more, but still, he could not find the strength to get back to his feet. Celesyria was gone, and there was no sign of Jaconial. No one else would come to Whitespire. No one else would notice that he was lost, aside from his friends, and they may as well have been a world away.

He was alone, with only the whispers of the High One for company.

***

"Here! He's over here!"

There was a voice, he was quite sure of it.

What was less clear was whether the voice was real, or if it existed only in a dream. By now, Wes had become quite confident as to which explanation was more likely.

He was waiting now, only waiting, his mind not quite working any longer.

"Hurry!"

He had closed his eyes for a long while, and he had not expected to open them again.

It was not comfortable here, not quite, but it wasn't the worst place he could have chosen to die.

He was confident that Celesyria was nearby, and despite the fact that she was dead already, and buried beneath the snow, she still managed to make him feel safe.

He was tired. Tired to his very core, tired in a way that he could not hope to describe.

And, truth be told, he was feeling a little impatient about the whole affair.

The piece of bread was in his pocket. Someone else could take it easily enough, so why couldn't everyone and everything just let him rest at last?

He wanted to say as much to the sky, but he couldn't bring himself to risk further pain by attempting to speak.

He heard the voice again, more insistent, closer, refusing to go away.

With a weak sigh, he opened his eyes, turning his head in hopes of evading the piercing sunlight.

He could see the mountains now, stretching out into the distance, their peaks shining beneath the blue sky. He could no longer see even a single flake of snow, at least, aside from the ones that had piled up around him in great fluffy white hills.

"Wes. Wes!"

The voice was gravelly and deep, and it was in his head.

"Thank the High One," said another voice, female this time.

He lay there in silence for a long moment, resting his eyes again until he heard the thud of heavy dragon-feet landing in the snow.

He wasn't sure if he should smile, or even if he could.

"He's alive," Jaconial was saying aloud to Nazzan, perhaps for his benefit. She leaned her neck toward him, and he stared at it, knowing that she expected him to take hold of her.

The very thought of dragging his body upright was intolerable, but it was not what kept him lying where he was.

He had to know. He had to know she wasn't lost.

"Where is she?" he asked, his voice rasping, barely loud enough to be heard. "I need to find her. I don't see her. She must be hidden beneath the snow."

Nazzan lowered his own head and peered down at him, his

green scales reflecting the bright sunshine, sending fresh pain through Wes's skull.

"Shh," Jaconial said. "I remember where she is. Don't worry."

"We will come back for her body. I promise," the male dragon said firmly, as Jaconial nodded. "You're safe now, Wes. We're taking you home."

He gave the slightest nod.

He had nothing left to give, not even to preserve his own life.

His strength was gone now, the last of it given away at the top of the great spire, leaving only bread.

His fate was up to them now.

It was up to Him.

KESSARA

Kessara watched in disbelief as the Envoy's eyes fluttered open, terrified to move, or even to breathe.

She glanced over at the door, debating whether or not to run for Alder and Aelrie.

The three of them had taken turns at his bedside, keeping him company. Waiting.

For Alder and even for Aelrie, waiting was all that they could do.

He was as close to home as he could be, surrounded by the living who loved him, and after two weeks had passed without improvement, the two of them had begun to make peace with the fact that this was the end.

Kessara, however, had not given up.

During the day, she spent as much time as she could with

Aelrie, listening to her and drying each fresh wave of her tears, but at night, she was hard at work.

Insisting that Alder and Aelrie rest, she always hurried from the dinner table straight into Wes's room, and did not leave it until well after dawn, when one of the others came and forced her to go and get some sleep.

She would sit beside his bed, pressing cool cloths soaked with herbal tinctures against his head, checking his nerve responses, searching every book in the libraries and personal collections of Auranth for any possible cure for the sickness that ailed him.

Ever since she'd learned what the curse was, everyone including Wes had tried to force her to believe that there was nothing she could do, that the wound of a curse could not be healed by the treatments of a healer. But deep within her heart, she had doubted, and now, when all hope seemed to have faded away, her doubt remained, as stubborn as ever.

It was hope.

The High One held life and death in His hands, no one else, and she would not deny Him any channel, any instrument through which to work. Herbs, dried flowers, dusty old bottles of liquor found at the back of Bargren's drink cabinet, she offered them all.

And now, his eyes were open, staring up at the stone ceiling.

She had to find the others. He might be able to manage only a few minutes of consciousness.

"Aelrie?" he asked in a whisper.

"Shh," she said, placing a gentle hand on his forearm. "It's Kessara here with you, but I'll find her. Just hold on."

She slipped from her hard wooden chair, nearly tripping on the edge of her dress in her haste to get out into the hall.

She rushed past two young soldiers, ignoring their apologies as she bumped against them in the narrow space, and nearly flew out the door that led into the great hall, shouting all the while.

"He's awake!" she called to anyone who would listen, her eyes roving across the huge room, where dozens of people were carrying on as usual, gaping at her.

They knew who she meant, of course, but like Alder and Aelrie, they had not thought such news was a possibility. So far as they were concerned, their Envoy was already dead. They were only awaiting his body so that a funeral could be arranged.

"I need Aelrie, and Alder," she continued, not seeing them anywhere in the crowd. "Does anyone know where–"

The final words fell away as her eyes fell upon Aelrie, coming in from the back courtyard, a bow still slung over her shoulder. Alder was with her, fiddling with the sword at his belt.

"Hi, darling," he said, raising an arm to wave at her. "We were about to join you. "

He gestured to Aelrie. "I thought the practice field would be helpful to... both of us."

"Alder, he's–" Kessara stammered, "He's awake. Wes is awake."

Aelrie's eyes went wide. She dropped her bow on the floor with a loud thump, taking off as fast as she could in the direction of the corridor. Kessara and Alder followed, and though they cleared the distance in barely a minute, the Princess still held her breath as they reached his door.

Even without a curse, it was rare to wake up from the sickness of long sleep. When it did happen, she knew, it rarely lasted for long. A full recovery was more than she dared ask of the High One, but even a few minutes for him to spend with the elf whom he loved was worth every sleepless night. And aside from that, there was other business to attend to, business that they all wanted him to be present for.

Please, just give him a day or two, at least. Please.

Aelrie pushed the wooden door inward, rushing over to his bedside on shaking legs. Kessara pressed her eyes shut, taking a slow breath as she felt Alder grasping for her hand and leading her forward.

He was awake just as she had left him, turning his head just a little to gaze upon the face of his wife.

Aelrie was weeping, tears spilling from her pale blue eyes and onto the bed as she took hold of his hand, her plain silver ring sparkling in the lamplight.

The Princess swallowed her own tears and slipped her hand out of Alder's, all business once more. She held Wes's free hand, testing the strength of his muscles and checking the pulse on his wrist. It was rather slow compared to what she would like, but his grip was better than she'd expected, and his eyes were tracking properly.

She let out a held breath in relief as she stepped back out into the hall with Alder, wanting to give Aelrie and Wes their privacy for as long as she could.

He was far from well, but everything medical indicated that the day or two of awareness that she had begged the High One for would be granted. She hoped he would be lucid even longer than that.

She said as much to Alder in a whisper, thankful for the comforting weight of his palm against the small of her back. The hallway was deserted. The news would have no doubt spread through half the city by now, and Kessara was comforted to imagine the thousands of prayers that would surely be joining with their own.

After a long while, Alder cleared his throat and gestured toward the door.

Kessara nodded, tapping her knuckles against the door-frame before stepping through.

"I hate to interrupt," Alder said. Kessara watched Wes, who was now able to lift his head a little. Good.

"I know what you will ask," Aelrie said, tucking a lock of black hair behind a silvery ear. "Yes. I must complete what the High One has set out, and I would like Wes to be present when I do. His time with us is not guaranteed."

Kessara gave her friend a tight smile, hating that she was unable to deny the precarity of the situation.

"The High One comes first, even now," the elf added.

"Always," Wes agreed, Aelrie's hand still clasped tight within his own.

Kessara watched as Alder brushed away a tear and turned toward the door. It was time.

39

Chapter 38

ALDER

Alder shoved Wes's bed over the uneven stones, his muscles aching with the effort. The bed was small and simple, hardly fit for a greater House noble, but still far too heavy.

Of course, several of the Auranthian soldiers had offered to assist him, and he'd instead chosen to attempt to impress his wife by doing it himself, so he supposed it was his own fault.

"Careful!" Kessara scolded as one of the bed's legs caught against a protruding tile, sending vibration thrumming through his arms and making him wince.

"I'm fine," Wes said, his body rocking slightly as Alder righted the bed once more.

He nodded, though Wes could not see him, and glanced over at Kessara, who was fretting about at one side of the bed, with Aelrie on the other, her hand never letting go of Wes's own.

She waved a hand, urging him to continue forward as a few servants skittered by, opening the doors to the great hall so that they could pass through.

The room was just as they had left it before the war, an old forge halfway transformed into a proper fortress. Now that the Auranthians had returned, Alder was sure that the place would be finished properly, but after that, its future was uncertain.

He leaned forward a little and glanced at Wes. His eyes were closed, his breathing steady, but he looked pale and far too thin. Kessara had assured him that there was a chance he could recover completely, but even she conceded that his odds were very slim. The curse had weakened every system in his body, and with the darkness of the war, it was a miracle he'd survived even this long.

Alder swallowed, his throat thick with threatened tears. Just when he'd begun to get used to the prospect of losing the Envoy, Kessara had managed to revive him from his long sleep. His hope had been renewed, only to be dashed once more, and he struggled to hide the fear that he carried.

But he had no choice.

Just as Aelrie said, they had to put the will of the High One first.

They had to finish what they started.

He looked around the room, giving the bedframe another hard push as he took stock of those present. He could see Jaconial and Nazzan, who both bore bandages for several injuries, but were otherwise in good shape. Sharsi was there along the back wall, her head in a respectful bow that partially hid her severed limb. Bargren and Mella stood near the vast dining table, hand in hand, smiles plastered on their faces that did not quite reach their eyes.

Luna appeared at his side without warning, her black hair

bouncing in its braids.

"Are you ready?" she asked, placing a hand along the bedframe. Alder supposed that she was talking to Wes, but he found himself wanting to answer that, no, he was not ready, not even close.

He said nothing, watching as Luna bounced over to Aelrie, looking altogether too happy on such an occasion, and engulfed her in a tight hug. The elf looked startled, and Alder couldn't help but to feel a smile tugging at the edge of his mouth.

Luna pulled away, whispering something in Aelrie's ear that he could not make out.

He felt Kessara pressing against him now, her hand resting against his chest, and Alder felt his smile faltering as quickly as it had come. The comforting touch of his wife was enough to send fresh tears to the corners of his eyes, which only became more impossible to hide as he watched Aelrie lean down and plant a gentle kiss on Wes's lips.

He isn't going to die in the next ten minutes, you blubbering fool. Relax.

The reassurance gave him little comfort. He glanced across the room at the waiting dragons, and at Bargren and Mella. Every face looked as sick as he felt.

Too much had happened already. Too much had changed. All he wanted was for things to be still, to stay as they were, but it was a futile hope, and he knew it.

"You can do this," Wes was saying to Aelrie, his eyes still pressed firmly shut as the elf stood at her full height.

She took a couple of steps toward Luna, accepting the remnant leader's outstretched hand. "I'm ready."

"Wait," Alder heard himself saying, letting Kessara's hand

fall away from his chest as he rushed forward. His feet had brought him halfway across the hall floor before he quite realized it, and he found himself flinging his arms around Nazzan's neck, his tears breaking free against his friend's sturdy green scales.

Without a word, he turned to Jaconial and did the same, the very sight of her coloring enough to remind him of Celesyria, sending fresh sobs coursing through his tightened chest.

At last, he offered a deep bow to Sharsi, not sure if he knew her well enough to take hold of her neck.

To his surprise, she stretched out toward him, resting the tip of her snout on his broad shoulder, a gentle hum emanating from her chest.

"I have not forgotten your service to me, Alder Cadogen. Nor will I forget the friendship you shared with my daughter," she said gently, pulling back to peer at him with her yellow eyes. "Thank you."

Several fresh tears rolled down his cheeks. It felt like a lifetime ago that he had helped her to escape from captivity in Skanden.

Would she be even more free after today, or was he standing aside as she was sent into the most terrible exile?

"Tell Celesyria how much she meant to me," he said, struggling to get the words out. "How much she meant to all of us. To all Kaveryth. We will remember and honor her always."

When he turned back, Kessara, Aelrie, and Luna's faces all shone with tears. Off to the side, Bargren and Mella were both sobbing.

Only Wes looked the same, his eyes shut, his cheeks hollow, his hand grasping Aelrie's as though she could stop him from floating away.

Luna nodded toward the dragons. They bowed in return, their snouts nearly pressing against the floor.

They were ready.

Alder thought of the hundreds of dragons that remained, Guardian and civilian, unaware of the fate that was about to meet them. For the first several days after the elves had fallen, he had hoped that they could find another way, that somehow the truth could be known to all, but it was nothing more than a wish, in the end.

The heart of the Creator was, at times, a mystery to His creation. But Kaveryth had done things their own way for far too long. Alder had long since promised himself that he would obey the High One as well as he could, even when it meant surrendering what he thought was best.

Today was no different, and he knew that Aelrie—the Elf-queen of Silverfell—believed the very same.

With a final squeeze of Wes's hand, Aelrie strode into the center of the room, her neatly combed black hair cascading down between her shoulder blades.

She was wearing a simple day dress in the green and silver shades common to Silverfell, no doubt borrowed from the wife of some soldier at Kessara's bidding, and upon her head sat a silver circlet. It was a simple twist of metal, a little too thick to look dainty, possibly made that very morning in Bargren's forge.

And yet, to Alder, no one save for his own wife had ever looked so much like a queen.

She cleared her throat, releasing the dragons from their bows. They stood just as a beam of light filtered in from the hole in the ceiling, making their scales gleam in the midday sunshine.

They were magnificent.

"O High One," Aelrie began, her voice ringing out clear and loud throughout the vast room. She paused for a moment, and Luna offered her an encouraging nod. She pressed on.

"The race of dragons was created to serve You, to guard the gates of the Eternal Lands, to protect all that was beauty and goodness. Instead, they chose to make an oath with the four Elf-queens, and to turn away from Your plan. They chose a mortal life, an embodied life, instead of the life You chose for them."

She took a breath. The room was perfectly silent. Alder could not even hear the usual clashing of swords filtering in from the practice fields outside. For a moment, it felt as though all the world had gone still.

"As Elf-queen of Silverfell, given such title by my marriage into the House of Cervos, I ask that you permit us, Your humble created ones, to reverse that oath."

Aelrie paused again, her eyes roving over the faces of Sharsi, Nazzan, and Jaconial. All of them wore peaceful expressions, and they bowed their heads in unison, beckoning the elf to carry on.

Alder felt as though he could hear his heart thumping in his ears, the only sound in the silence of the room as they all waited for the Elf-queen to continue. He gripped Kessara's hand a little more tightly, thankful to have her by his side.

"High One, let the dragons return to Your service, whatever it is that You wish for them to do, and wherever it is that You wish for them to go. Restore order to Your creation. Hold not our sin against us."

She let out the final words in a rush of breath, looking as

though she might stumble as she walked back toward Wes's bedside and took his hand once more.

The dragons stood facing the ground, their eyes pressed shut. Bargren had placed his arm over Mella's shoulder, kissing the top of her head as she cried softly.

For a long moment, everything was just as it always had been, but after what had happened in Nox, Alder knew just how quickly things could transform.

He pulled Kessara tight against his chest just as the room exploded with light.

Though he had pressed his eyes shut, he could still see it, impossibly bright even through the cover of his eyelids. He heard Kessara cry out in pain as she buried herself against him, and he held a protective hand over the back of her head.

He had thought the great hall had been silent before, but it was nothing compared to now.

He could hear nothing, not even the beating of his own heart.

At last he worked up the courage to open his eyes, staring at his feet as he blinked away the burning afterglow.

When he looked up, he saw that it was true.

The dragons were gone.

WES

Wes found it almost impossible to open his eyes.

Never had so many simple things become so difficult, or so painful. He was breathing, but every inhale and exhale seemed to require intentional effort, as though his body would simply forget to keep him alive if he was not vigilant at every moment.

His heart seemed to be beating of its own accord, though, according to Kessara, it was pumping altogether too slowly. After the dragons had gone away, everyone else save Aelrie had returned to their own doings, no doubt needing time to think about what had just happened, but Kessara had pestered him for several hours.

After she'd forced him to drink several vile-tasting plant concoctions, Aelrie had finally managed to get her out of his room. The two of them were alone at last as the sun sank over Auranth, newlyweds who were barely able to kiss, let alone anything more.

He didn't mind, not really.

Just being near her, feeling her hand in his, was the second-greatest gift he had ever been given. He had already said goodbye to her long ago, lying there in the snow back in Whitespire, and every extra second he had with her was worth treasuring.

They had talked a little, though mostly he'd been able only to listen, but now he could tell that she was growing tired beside him, too stubborn to get any real sleep.

He had been awake for several hours now, and with every passing moment, he felt his mind getting a little more hazy, his body a little more determined to do what it wished rather than obeying his commands.

There was so much he wanted to say to the woman he loved, so many things he still had to share with her, big and small, important and foolish.

But there was no time for that now.

If sleep was coming to snatch him away from her, he had to find words for the most important things. He had to share that with her, the fears, the faith, everything that was hidden in the depths of his heart. It wasn't much, but it was all he had to give her now.

"Aelrie," he whispered to into the dim room, half expecting her to already be asleep.

"Can I get you something, my love?" she asked, sitting up straight at once, her hand never leaving his.

He wanted to shake his head no, but the pain was immense, so he stayed as he was, looking up at the ceiling. She'd understand just the same.

"I thought it would... be different," he said slowly, remembering to force the uncooperative air in and out of his lungs between words. "I thought the snow would melt away. I thought the sun would always shine. I thought everything would change... but it didn't."

He heard her beginning to speak, but he pressed on, unsure how much longer his mouth and throat would be willing to form words at all.

"You destroyed the Elf-queens. You exiled the dragons. But when I did what the High One asked... nothing changed. Even the bread still looks the same."

He paused.

What was left of the offered bread of hope was sitting there on the nightstand in a little box Mella had brought for it, drying out in the winter air. So far as the others had told him, it remained unremarkable.

"Did I do something wrong?"

He found himself choking a little on the words, a lump rising in his throat.

"No," Aelrie said fiercely, standing up and leaning toward him so that he could get a better look at her expression as she spoke, without having to turn his head. "It is not so simple.

We've brought new order in some ways, yes, but think of what has been left behind."

She was probably thinking of the chaos and confusion that had gripped Kaveryth anew, but instead, he found his thoughts wandering to Celesyria. Nazzan and Jaconial had been able to recover her body, and bury it, but he supposed that mattered little now. She, like them, was gone in the most complete way. He did not even have her bones to mourn.

"The dwarves have been left with a shattered Umrym. The elves have been destroyed, yes, but the evil they have caused will take decades to repair, if not longer. Without the dragons, their fate is unclear," Aelrie continued, her cheeks flushing just a little beneath her silvery skin.

"Alder will have to learn to become a proper noble, and to become King of Galeharbor one day. King Ursa is an ally for the moment, but it remains to be seen whether he will constrain his control only as far as the borders of Aridmoor as promised. Power will tempt him now, more than ever. And let us not forget that I have to learn to rule Silverfell mere weeks after an elven army nearly destroyed Kaveryth," she said, her words tumbling out all in a rush.

Wes felt his chest tightening. She was right, of course, as she so often was.

"None of this is easy. If you've done anything wrong, you're not alone. I think we all have a lot of screwups ahead of us. Except Kessara, probably. She'd be ready to be crowned queen tomorrow."

She paused for a moment, chuckling a little, the sound like tinkling wind chimes.

"Keep talking," he whispered. "Hearing your voice makes me happy."

"Okay," Aelrie said, reaching over and touching his cheek with gentle silver fingertips as she leaned down to kiss him. He kissed her back as best as he could, surprised at the desire that still arose in his body, despite the pain.

"We don't need to be afraid," she said, pulling away at last. "The High One made us a promise, and He will fulfill it. We need only to be patient. He will restore all things."

Wes turned his head with great effort, his hand gripping hers and pulling her closer again until their eyes met. He searched her face, not knowing what it was he was trying to find, not wanting to look away until he had every perfect detail of the woman he loved memorized.

She hadn't mentioned the obvious, and neither would he.

They were finally married, and he was dying.

After a few more moments and a final, tender kiss, he leaned back again, closing his eyes, as Aelrie settled in at the chair beside his bed.

Somewhere outside, the sun had set, leaving their old forge lit only by candlelight. Auranth and the rest of Kaveryth would sleep, safe from the war, awaiting the fresh uncertainties that the morning would bring. An old world had returned, and so long as the people turned to the High One, everything would be all right, in the end.

Wes lifted his free hand from the edge of the bed, ignoring the trembling feeling that coursed down his arm as he moved.

He pressed his fingertips to the scars that rested on his cheek.

One was old, the Moonscar, the mark of a chosen one whose very purpose had been subverted by the Dracodei and the Septemvirate since the day he was born.

But the other was new.

It was a sign of journeys begun, of friendships treasured, of truths fought for.

He could have continued on the path that had been laid out for him, but by the grace of the High One, he had done something different.

He had done something good.

He had chosen.

He opened his eyes at last, watching the candlelight flickering against the stone walls of his room, and listening to the sounds of crickets singing their nightsong somewhere beyond the castle walls. Aelrie had fallen asleep at last, her head resting against his bed, her fingers still entangled with his own.

His victory had indeed brought sacrifice, but the High One had not forgotten him.

He had not left his hands empty.

Wes could see that now.

And no matter how much longer he got to hold on to those blessings here in this life, he was no longer worried about losing them.

For even when everything else faded, when the sun refused to rise in the morning, when the stars ceased to give their light, the greatest gifts did not wither away.

The love that burned deep in his heart was his to keep.

Always.

40

Epilogue

ELDER JATE

Elder Jate set down his quill with a satisfied sigh, brushing away the stray droplets of ink that had landed on his large oak desk. It was strange to be sitting in an office that had once belonged to the late Elder Dorold, but as head of the renewed Septemvirate, it was now his by right.

Like most of Stronghollow palace, the administrative wing had been badly damaged in the elven attacks, but the craftsmen and laborers of Silverfell were doing an incredible job of restoring it, as well as the surrounding city.

After nearly five years had passed, the stains of war were at last beginning to fade away.

He could almost smell the freshly planted trees that were growing outside, their leaves finally budding in the late spring warmth. Soon, the forest would be thick and green and beautiful again, with birds singing and bugs humming amid the trees.

Elder Jate had felt guilty for a while, hiding out in Graveheim as the war raged and a good while after it ended. But now, having taken up the hard work of restoring a loyal Septemvirate, he could see the reasonableness, if not necessarily the courage, of his choice.

He pushed himself up out of the old desk chair and padded over to the window, peering down at one of the small courtyards nearby. He could see his nephew playing some sort of ball game, kicking it at a wall again and again.

Elder Jate wished that there were more children for the teenager to play with, but that would be a gift for the next generation. Babies were being born, filling the cities and villages of Silverfell with the joy of new life, but it would be a good while before they grew up.

For the moment, however, his nephew seemed happy just to be alive.

He was very short for his age, and the weakness that remained in his body was evident, but still, Elder Jate felt they had gotten away with paying a very small price for the curse the young child had borne.

Even then, it was possible that, with time, the remnants of his illness would fade away completely. He seemed to be healing along with Kaveryth itself, as the darkness was slowly pushed aside, day by day and year by year.

The continent was still damaged—such deep brokenness was never fixed in a hurry—but it was getting brighter, even if Elder Jate knew he would die long before he got to see Kaveryth at its best.

There was a knock at the door, and the Elder turned, his long gray robe swishing against the floor.

It was Oria, peering through the edge of the door.

"You have messages, Elder," she said, "and they're urgent.

At least, the shoemaker's union says they are, and the temple restoration guild. And the women's cheesemaking club wanted to know if you'd give a speech, even though I told them you've never made cheese in your life. Oh, and the Aridmoorian committee for the education of street urchins–"

"I will see to all of it, thank you, Oria," he said, cutting her off with a smile. She ducked out of the room with a nod, her shoes clicking on the smooth tile as she returned to her own desk.

The demands on their time never ended, it seemed, and with the summer Feast approaching, it would only increase. There was a Witness from Stronghollow this season, which would have been convenient, were it not for his stubborn rejection of the High One. Still, he looked forward to it. With each passing Feast, they had managed to bring the bread of hope to more and more people throughout Kaveryth.

Elder Jate smiled to himself as he returned to his desk, taking up his quill once again. He supposed he'd start with the street urchin committee, or whatever it was. His nephew was well, Elder Bram's beloved granddaughter Oria was now his secretary, and the world was growing brighter all the time.

He would do the work laid before him with a smile on his face.

HOLGA

Holga walked down the streets of Rill, trying to use the hood of her cloak to shield herself from view as the midday sun beat down upon her. The air felt sticky and horrible, but she thought that the desert itself looked beautiful, the red sand blowing softly in the wind, the hum of insects emanating from hidden corners.

She had insisted that her royal guard stay behind.

Even after several years under the rule of the restored House of Noctua, many of the citizens who lived in this part of the village were not particularly fond of the new authority that had been imposed upon them. For the most part, they still tolerated Holga herself, but she didn't feel like getting into any arguments today.

She had more important business to attend to.

The summer Feast had come at last, and she could hear the excited cries of little children in the streets, announcing the arrival of the bread-bearers. She stepped into a side street just as their caravan passed by, with smartly-dressed soldiers from all four kingdoms and at least a dozen stags with bells ringing pleasantly on their head harnesses.

She smiled to herself as they passed, not looking up from the dust at her feet. Gohr was hosting a feast to celebrate their arrival, back at the huge house she had still not gotten used to referring to as her palace. In any case, she hoped to catch the men once more as they meandered through the winding streets of Rill, knocking on doors and waiting at gates.

At last, she was alone again, with only the clucking of wandering chickens and the barking of a distant dog to interrupt her thoughts as she strode along the familiar street.

With the help of her advisors, she had been able to provide aid to many of those who lived here, hiring men to replace the old canvas roofs with shingles, to fit new windows, and to shore up leaning walls. Many of the village children volunteered as well, cleaning up the garbage and even planting some hardy flowers along the paths that led between houses. Despite the obvious poverty that remained, the place had been transformed, just as the rest of Kaveryth was being transformed all around it.

Malka's house, however, had remained untouched, save for the roof. She'd been able to convince the herbwoman to replace that, but the strange decorations and the uneven front porch were just as they'd always been.

Before she had even gotten the chance to rap at the door, Malka pulled it open, a strained expression on her face.

"I know what you will ask," she said, before Holga could utter a word. The young queen nodded. Malka knew her better than anyone, save Gohr, and had become quite talented at heading off her ramblings before they began.

The herbwoman sighed, stepping outside and joining Holga on the narrow slats of old wood. "I've been ready for a while, in a way," she said softly, "but then I get to thinking about the little ones..."

Her voice trailed off as Holga gestured toward the street, Malka falling in beside her, her own cloak pulled over her head to stave off any potential gossip. Few of the members of Boneshire's burgeoning upper class understood their queen's relationship with the strange midwife, and Holga could do without their lecturing, whenever it could be avoided.

"You have to ask for forgiveness, Malka," Holga said gently, tucking her long braid back under the hood of her cloak. "There will be no time better than today."

Malka would not meet her eyes. For a few seconds, they walked in silence, dust sticking to the hems of their dresses as they trudged along the sandy road.

"The asking bit makes sense," she said at last, chuckling to herself. "It's accepting the High One's answer that I struggle with."

"What do you mean?"

"How will I ever be able to believe that He accepts me? How will His forgiveness ever feel real, after all of the evil I have done?"

Holga paused as they reached the end of the road, touching Malka's forearm gently and glancing up at her. She looked so much older than she had only a few years ago. The weight of her past had to have been unbearable to carry without the grace of the High One.

"The caravan will pass by here again soon, as they head toward the southeast corner," she said carefully. "Your questions make sense, but no answer I can give will. Not when you have yet to taste the bread."

Malka was quiet for a long moment, patting at her pockets and reaching into several small leather pouches that hung at her waist. "I have nothing to offer," she said, shaking her head. "Not even a pretty piece of glass."

Holga let out a breath. Even after all this time, the communal memory of life under the Dracodei was difficult to shake. For so many years, they had grown accustomed to gods that demanded their pound of flesh. They had been denied the truth, and fed a religion of blackmail, a divine protection racket.

She wanted to tell Malka as much, to rant at length about the injustices that their people had suffered for so long, but she restrained herself. None of that was important now. One person stood beside her now, and it was she who had to understand.

"You have everything to offer," she said firmly. "The High One does not need our treasures. We honor Him by calling upon Him, and by recognizing that He is the Creator, and we are the created. We honor him by accepting the gifts He gives, even when we feel we don't deserve them. Perhaps especially then."

For a long moment, Malka did not respond, her expression hidden from view as she turned to watch for the coming caravan.

The sun had lowered a little in the sky, sending lengthening shadows across the red desert.

It would be a beautiful night, cool and clear, with stars so bright that Holga could imagine what it would be like to reach out and touch them. After the feast, she hoped to get a chance to see them somewhere away from town, preferably with Gohr at her side.

For the moment, however, she felt only frustration. She had tried to make her dear friend understand, and she had failed. Perhaps she had spoken too much, as usual, or perhaps the words had not been right.

"My Queen?" Malka said, interrupting her thoughts.

Holga was so stunned by her use of her title that she couldn't quite open her mouth to answer. She could only watch stupidly as Malka pulled the hood of her cloak back, revealing her half-combed hair and prematurely wrinkled face to everyone who stood along the street.

"If I am going to seek a new life, a forgiven life, I wish to do it without hiding away," she explained, her usually confident voice shaking a little. "So long as being seen with me won't burden you too much among all of the important people."

Holga felt tears springing to her eyes as she engulfed Malka in a hug, throwing her own cloak back and sending her brown braids bouncing. "*You* are an important person. I don't care what anyone else thinks."

Without another word, the two women knelt side by side at the edge of the street, their knees sinking into the dirt. Out of the corner of her eye, Holga could see people pointing and staring at them, the various rumors already beginning to spread like a sandstorm through the village.

She reached out and grasped Malka's hand, giving it a squeeze as the lead stag came into view over the top of the hill.

And there, as their people looked on, a queen and a sinner received the bread of hope.

AELRIE

Queen Aelrie Cervos pushed the gate of the little yard open, listening to it creaking as it swung on old, rusty hinges.

Like many other old things in Stronghollow, the Cervos family plot had been neglected for years, the local laborers putting most of their energy toward more pressing rebuilding projects. The wooden fence was gray and rotting in places, the branches of gnarled trees had begun to hang low over the shrines, and the grass looked positively wild.

The elf smiled as her two children dashed through the gate, bundles of wildflowers grasped in their fingers. They liked it here, despite the decay and the mess. They said it reminded them of their own little wilderland, right outside the palace walls.

"Bram, let your sister go first," she scolded gently as her older child rushed forward, flowers outstretched eagerly toward the nearest shrine.

"Celesyria always goes first, Mama," he grumbled, not turning to face her. She could almost see his little half-silver ears drooping. She ruffled his hair. "Perhaps next time, Celesyria would like to play at being the oldest and having to wait," she suggested, directing her daughter toward the shrine of her grandparents. She dropped the bundle neatly on the stone before turning around and beaming at Aelrie.

"Aunt Kessara told me I'm going to be the oldest already," she said, mispronouncing several of her words in the sweet way that little ones did. Aelrie smiled at her, extending a hand and taking a few of the remaining lilies that her daughter had not yet placed.

"You won't be the *oldest*, Celesyria," Bram insisted, rolling his eyes. "That's not how it works. I'll always be the oldest."

"Right," Aelrie said, letting out a slow breath. It never ceased to amaze her how easily her children could begin an argument about any topic, however pointless. "You won't be the oldest, my love, but you'll be older than your cousin when he arrives. You'll be right in the middle, the best of each."

Her daughter furrowed her brows, and for a moment, Aelrie was certain that some sort of drama was imminent. Not for the first time, she wished that she had a mother of her own, or even a mother-in-law, to help guide her through these difficult young years. Kessara visited as often as she could get away from Galeharbor, and though the kids adored their not-quite aunt, the Princess was not exactly an expert when it came to parenting.

To Aelrie's relief, Celesyria let the topic go, instead wandering over on chubby legs to where Bram was now sitting. He had plopped himself into the tall grass right in front of the far shrines, no doubt covering his trousers in fresh grass stains, and his little sister followed suit.

Aelrie lifted the hem of her green gown and followed them,

forcing her breaths to slow.

This was always the difficult part.

Laying flowers was easy enough, especially on a summer evening like this, when the birds were singing and the breeze was cool.

Talking to her children about the reality of death was quite another thing, and even after all of this time, she'd never quite figured out how to get the words right.

The three of them sat in silence then, looking up at the stone shrines. Bram traced the letters with his fingertips, attempting to read them in a whisper, not quite able to pronounce all of the names. Even Celesyria looked somber, her black hair trailing halfway down her back as she glanced up at the patch of blue sky that was visible through the thick trees.

"It's sad here, Mama," the little girl said at last, turning to face her mother with tears pooling in her dark brown eyes. Aelrie swallowed the rising lump in her throat and drew Celesyria into a hug. She could handle death well enough on her own, she thought, but when her precious little ones cried, she could rarely stop herself from joining in.

"Remember what we've always been taught," Bram said matter of factly, though Aelrie could tell by his downcast face that he was sad, as well. "Death is a sad thing, but so long as we turn to the High One, this world is not the end for us. It's not our home. It's only a journey. We will see them all again when we meet in the Eternal Lands."

Celesyria sniffled, and Aelrie stroked her hair. Her youngest was too little to understand such a complex topic, but she was glad that Bram could elucidate the truth so well. His explanations made even her feel better.

Just then, the gate creaked loudly from behind them, and Celesyria let out a little shriek of surprise.

"Goodness," Aelrie said, her heart pounding in her chest, glad that she had at least managed to avoid letting a bad word escape. Both of her children had quite the knack for picking up swears.

"Sorry, my love," Wes called over to her, raising his hand in a wave as he began plodding through the unruly grass. His cane slowed him down a great deal, but it was so much better than the wheelchair he'd used for the past several years that Aelrie found no reason to complain, even if she was usually the one racing ahead after their energetic little ones while he got to walk in peace.

"Papa, Aunt Kessara told me today that I'll get to be the *oldest*," Celesyria said excitedly, her hair bouncing as she leapt into her father's free arm, nearly knocking his cane to the ground.

"Well, darling," Wes started, leaning down to kiss his daughter's forehead. "You won't be the *oldest*, but—"

He paused, catching sight of Aelrie's warning glare, but it was too late.

Bram had heard the exchange, and was now hand in hand with his sister, dragging her off under one of the large trees. The two of them were already deep in their bickering as they navigated their way through the wild grass.

"You've done it now," Aelrie said, taking Wes by the arm and pulling him to the ground beside her. She laughed at the surprised look on his face, glad that he was no longer quite so delicate as he once had been. He certainly deserved the grass stains on his clothes after setting off a fight she'd tried so hard to avoid.

"On the contrary, my love," he said, pausing to plant a slow kiss on her lips. "*You've* done it."

Aelrie glanced up at their children, already hidden somewhere against the far side of the fence, their argument carrying on the wind. Soon they–or most likely, she, if they did not stop running off–would need to intervene.

For the moment, however, she was content to rest against her husband's shoulder as he cradled the back of her neck, stealing a few hungry kisses that made the thought of getting the kids to bed early quite appealing.

Across the grass, several generations of Cervos family shrines looked on, colorful flowers piled messily on their bases.

"All right," she said, laughing as she pulled away. "A little respect for the dead."

"Sorry, Mother," Wes said, nodding in the direction of the Queen's shrine, and then the King's, giving them each a wink. "Father."

"Roven would approve, then, I take it?" she asked, grinning at him.

"They'd all approve," he said, running a hand through his brown curls, his expression suddenly serious. "I love you, Aelrie. I never dreamed in a thousand years that I'd be building a family with someone like you. I hope you always remember how precious you are."

He took her hand in his own, the warmth of him sending a shiver up her spine, even after all of these years.

She wanted to say something equally romantic back, but before she could think of any words, Celesyria and Bram burst out of the grass near the shrines, shouting that they had just found the biggest frog in all Kaveryth.

Wes smiled, pulling Aelrie to her feet, and the two of them strode off toward the setting sun, their children running up ahead.

***

I hope that you enjoyed the final book in the Storm & Spire series. If you enjoyed this book, I humbly ask you to consider leaving an honest review. It can be just a sentence or two if you like.

Thank you from the bottom of my heart for your support & encouragement.

Dear Reader

Thank you so much for reading *Manifest*, the fifth and final (!!!) book in the Storm & Spire series.

If you want to stay up to date with my future writing projects, please consider signing up for my newsletter.

You can sign up at https://authorstefanielozinski.com/newsletter

In Christ,

Stefanie Lozinski

Behind The Scenes

Writing this series has taught me so much.

Sure, there's the stuff I expected, you know, the writer stuff. I feel (hope?) my skill as a storyteller has come a long way since writing *Magnify*, and I'm so thankful for that.

I have also gained the confidence that comes with knowing I can finish not only a book, but a whole series. A *fantasy* series, no less! Fantasy is not an easy genre, considering the prevalence of big word counts, complex worlds, and of course the typical one-long-story-over-multiple-books structure.

There's something really powerful about having taken on that challenge and survived! It feels good, even if I'm totally 100% certain that it was only by the grace of God that I've made it through alive, lol.

If you read the "behind the scenes" note for *Maker*, you may recall me saying that it was the hardest book in the series to write.

HA!

Well, I was wrong about that (though it was hard). *Manifest* was difficult in a different way. A way that wasn't just about having to wrangle together a bunch of complex story threads, go back and forth on structure, etc, though there was as always some of that, too.

Manifest was my biggest challenge so far because it brought back an old, terrifying foe that I was pretty sure I'd conquered.

I started actively drafting this story (I had the outline done earlier in the winter) back on February 24, 2023. It's a date that sticks out, because it's also the day we found out I was pregnant with baby #3!

My husband and I were — and are — absolutely thrilled. We had been actively trying for over a year, and I was starting to get worried, stressed, and generally turning into a wreck because I wanted to grow our family so badly and it just was not happening.

So this little one felt like a joyous miracle, especially since I had suffered a miscarriage a couple of months prior.

But I've also been pregnant a couple of times before, and I knew that with the joy would come difficulty. Namely, the fact that morning sickness was coming to knock me on my back.

I wanted to outrun it. That was my strategy. "Ok, wow, I'm

pregnant. Time to throw everything I have into drafting this novel and distracting myself from miscarriage fear at the same time! Woo!"

I'm a reasonably fast writer, but not "100,000+ words in three weeks" fast, which was about how much time I had before I started feeling bone-tired and nauseous every day. LOL.

So yes, my plan was dumb and didn't work, and I kind of ended up in my nightmare scenario – I was 55,000 words into a book, and I had to take a break. A long break. A good month, month and a half.

I fought it. I hate losing my momentum. I already suspected that I was someone who relies heavily on "the streak", the routine, whatever you want to call it. But I had no choice.

Once the haze of sickness began to subside, I had the best of intentions that I would jump right back in. Finish this thing! Tell this story! Get this book out into the world!

But I couldn't do it. I felt paralyzed. Imposter syndrome had wormed its way into my writing life and taken a firm hold on me.

The break I genuinely needed became a long lull, a ditch I could not pull myself out of. I was too scared to simply begin, too convinced that I had lost my focus, that it was all ruined, that I'd Never Finish Another Book and I Was A Terrible Writer… it wasn't logical, but the fear was real.

I really turned to God in those final few weeks of sluggishness and doubt. How could I have come so far, only to end up so afraid? Afraid of something so silly?

I wish I could say there was an epiphany like I had while writing *Maker*, where God's peace rushed into my heart and I was *sure* I could do it.

This time, that didn't happen. This time, I felt a lot more like Wes at the end of this story (ha, maybe subconsciously my own struggle made it into the book), where he's waiting for the High One to speak, and sort of realizing that he already has what he needs, that he just has to get on those stairs and climb that tower.

So climb I did. And you know what? Once I got going, it wasn't so bad. Actually, I started having fun again. I started feeling the joy again.

I had kind of worried that I wouldn't feel any sense of relief from the fear or the imposter syndrome until I wrote "The End", but mercifully, it wasn't like that.

Once I found my footing, I could move, and that was enough for me to know I was going to reach the top of that great spire. I was going to finish what God set out before me to do, because He was pulling for me, even when His voice was only a whisper.

Next time, of course, I hope I'll remember the answer to fear is always the same - God's love. It's that easy, and that hard.

The Stats

I've been rambling for far too long, so I'll keep this bit quick.

Outlining this book took a decent chunk of time — about 21 hours total. Drafting FELT like forever, being split up like it was, but it was only about 89 hours. Not bad, for a book that was 2x the length of the first book in this series, lol. Editing went weirdly well this time around, ending up at just 7 hours or so (on my end, of course).

About the Author

Stefanie Lozinski lives in Ontario, Canada, with her husband, soon to be three young children, two cats, and a whole lot of books. When she isn't homeschooling her little ones, you'll find her on a long walk, drinking coffee, praying a Rosary, or working on her next novel.

You can connect with me on:
🌐 https://www.authorstefanielozinski.com
🔗 https://www.instagram.com/lozinskistefanie

Subscribe to my newsletter:
✉ https://authorstefanielozinski.com/newsletter